FISTS of IRON
~ROUND ONE~
ROBERT E. HOWARD

Introduction by Christopher Gruber

Edited by Patrice Louinet, Christopher Gruber,
Mark Finn and Paul Herman

THE
Robert E. Howard
FOUNDATION PRESS

For Glenn Lord (1931-2011), preserver of Howard's typescripts and manuscripts, godfather of Howard studies, and the greatest fan that ever lived.

ISBN 978-1-955446-57-0 (Paperback)
ISBN 978-1-955446-56-3 (Hardcover)
ISBN 978-1-955446-58-7 (eBook)

Published by the REH Foundation Press, LLC by arrangement with Robert E. Howard Properties Inc.

https://rehfoundation.org
https://rehfpress.com

Cover illustration copyright © 2025, Mark Wheatley.

https://markwheatleygallery.com

Book prepared for publication by Ståle Gismervik, Savage Studios.

Version 2.01 - Ultimate Edition.

Acknowledgments

All of the Howard stories, poems and portions thereof contained in *Fists of Iron Volume 1* come from Howard's original typescripts, manuscripts, and carbons, when possible. Virtually all of the type-scripts were scanned from the Glenn Lord collection, now at the University of Texas, Austin; the Robert E. Howard collection at Texas A&M University; or the typescript collection at Cross Plains Library.

The exceptions are: "Kid Lavigne is Dead," from The Ring; "Fables for Little Folks," from the Daniel Baker Collegian; "In the Ring," a mix of original typescript and *REH Fight Magazine #4*; "A Man of Peace," a mix of original typescript and Glenn retype; "Cupid v. Pollux," from *The Yellow Jacket*; "The Spirit of Tom Molyneaux, alternate version", from Ghost Stories; "Night Encounter", from a mix of original typescript and Glenn retype; "Dula Due to be Champion," from the *Brownwood Bulletin*; "Tunney Can't Win," from the *Fort Worth Star Telegram*; and, "The Funniest Bout," from a mix of original typescript and Glenn retype.

CHANGES FROM THE FIRST EDITION: Source for the text of "The Weeping Willow" changed from Glenn retype to original REH typescript.

"Tunney Can't Win" is NEW in this edition.

Poetry titles have been updated to correspond with titles in *Collected Poetry, Volumes 1-3.*

CHANGES in V2.01: Crowd Horror corrected to Crowd-Horror.

Contents

Fists of Iron

Poems

Appendix 1: Early tales, variants and fragments

The Brute Eternal

The Boxing Tales of Robert E. Howard by Christopher Gruber

Boxing—the use of fists in combat or sport—predates written history. Surely some unknown combatants in the dawn of prehistory measured themselves in a contest of physical prowess and willpower that served as the progenitor of all human conflict. But, speculation aside, there is evidence that boxing has always been a part of the fabric of civilization or, at least, a reminder to that part of our human nature that craves order and development that we are never far from our beastly origins no matter how high we ascend the evolutionary ladder. Like the ancient civilizations that rose and fell, whose purple ambitions left a legacy of intrigue, power and glory that embroiled the whole of the world, boxing has danced on the stage of history in many guises and played muse to more than a few literary giants.

As a sport, or bloodsport as the case may be, boxing's lineage can be traced back to the cradle of our species, the North African delta region wherein archaeological discoveries have shed light on the ancient combat methods of the past. Steeped in antiquity and preserved with care, these artifacts speak to the regard boxing was held by our most celebrated and ancient cultures. Consider the blood-stained canvas that was the Bronze Age world where mankind's evolution toward the taming influence of civilization began; Sumerian relief carvings and the famous Akrotiri frescos depict youths engaged in the sport of boxing while ancient pottery images proclaim the significance boxing held to emerging civilizations that sprang from the fertile Mediterranean region.

These historical testimonials only reinforce the esteem that Greek and Roman societies would later exhibit toward boxing as both a pastime and a martial necessity that prepared youth for the rigors of combat—the lifeblood of the conqueror. From the bloody spectacles of Theseus to the first Olympic Games and later in the split personality of Rome (which initially nurtured, then condemned, the sport), boxing has held a unique position in the *gestalt* of the emerging civilized man, one that seems at once incongruous and wholly natural to the essential state of mankind. It was a most striking observation Oliver Wendell Holmes Sr. made when calculating the benefits of boxing upon the civilized man: "It is a fine sight, that of a gentleman resolving himself into the primitive constituents of his humanity." For boxing is, if nothing else, a window from which modern man can gaze inward upon the brute eternal with admiration rather than loathing and not feel as if he has betrayed his "higher calling."

It is not only within the realm of the physical that boxing has stirred the dormant passions of civilized man, but also in his written testimonies, for we find ample cause to celebrate the impact boxing has had upon the crown jewel of human advancement, that litmus test of intellectual expression— literature. Consider these authors: the father of Western epic literature, Homer, felt compelled to include the brief boxing match between Epeios and Euryalos in *The Iliad* as an event of unique social significance. The great Sir Arthur Conan Doyle wrote several memorable boxing stories—such as "Rodney Stone" and "The Croxley Master"—that feature bare-knuckle boxing protagonists. The inimitable Jack London, arguably America's premier author in the early 20th century, is known to much of the world as much for his boxing reports and short stories as for his novels and political leanings. His brilliant entrants into the boxing genre are the standard by which all modern authors of boxing fiction should be measured. Such masterpieces as "The Game," "A Piece of Steak" and "The Mexican" stretched the thematic possibilities of the boxing short and helped to herald in an era of wary respectability for a sport that would eventually lay claim to some of the most enduring and iconic American figures of the Jazz Age. London also reported on the epic contests between James J. Jeffries, Tommy Burns and Jack Johnson (known more for their racial significance than the actual battles) in a serialized collection of news articles that captured perfectly, and sadly, a nation's contentious mood and helped fuel interest in a sport that had, until then, enjoyed only a niche existence in the back alleys and barrooms of the less "civilized" social classes of America.

London was also known to a young, aspiring author from Cross Plains, Texas, named Robert E. Howard, who would come to master the boxing short and stretch the genre's limits in a most unexpected way—with humor. His rollicking, slap-stick tales of Sailor Steve Costigan rank among the most inventive and enjoyable boxing stories of the past century while his gritty, realistic, tales of the ring practically ooze dramatic violence, setting them on par with London's best work. Whether Howard stumbled upon age-yellowed copies of London's news reports that brought the "Battle of the Century" to life for millions of Americans, or had come to the author through his Klondike novels, it is clear that London inspired the young author in profound ways that helped to encourage a desire to write fiction and to develop a lifelong affinity for the sport of boxing.

Modern boxing is in many ways the purest form of entertainment, sport and culture known to civilized man. It provides vicarious thrills to the would-be athlete who appreciates real athleticism when he sees it; an outlet for the socially marooned to channel their impotent aggression through the boxers toward an unfair and disinterested world; and a socially acceptable excuse for individuals to seek out one of their own "kind" and cheer on "their boy" in an almost biological urge to return to a kind of primitive tribalism—if only for the duration of the bout. It also remains one of the better understood spectacles to grace the modern human stage, an event that speaks directly to the human condition in simple, ritualistic language that is recognized immediately anywhere on the planet.

In many ways, boxing is also elemental; two men fight on equal terms—one man wins while the other loses. This is the essence of conflict, distilled to its rawest form; a reliable measure of one's worth not tainted by the perceived corruptness of the modern condition. It is by its very nature the epitome of human struggle and it is in this contest of wills and primal power that we find a core element that drives Robert E. Howard's fiction: the conflict and the struggle against the corruptness of civilization through reversion. Howard reveled in the reformation of modern societies through the cleansing agent of the primitive warrior and his "red" ambitions. It is in this mood of destructive regeneration, deliberately worked out within the early boxing tales, that we find the true essence of all Howard's work—the touchstone concept of human atavism. Howard uses the concept of atavism as a recurring theme throughout his boxing tales. This idea of genetic reversion to an ancient ancestral physical archetype was an especially popular, if controversial, scientific subject during Howard's time. One of Howard's favorite fighters, a boxer known as "Battling Nelson," had been examined by scientists in order to explain his propensity to absorb punishment without apparent harm. His skull was reportedly three times as thick as an average human's and he would come to occupy, as Bert Sugar once wrote, "the same position in boxing as the Piltdown Man in anthropology, a genetic link joining two boxing worlds: the world of roughand-tumble and the world of civilized rules."

It has been noted by Mark Finn and other Howard scholars that Howard "favored fighters who were known as iron men," and he is correct, but as I revealed in my essay, "Atavists All?," Howard's concept of atavism would provide the central theme for his boxing heroes "where human reversion to an earlier type, the degeneration of the species to a model out of our dismal past, finds its modern home in this most violent of pastimes: boxing." Howard paints his boxers in deliberate contrast to their modern peers in an effort to promote the theme of atavism, and his boxing yarns are littered with men who are viewed by society as ungainly monsters, backward in their thinking and dangerous in their quick tempered mannerisms. They feel ill at ease in the normal, mundane placidity of modern life, a placidity for which civilized man has fought and died for from the very beginning, to secure the world for his descendants. As often as not, the atavistic nature of Howard's boxers is neutered by the societal boundaries of polite society—except when unleashed within the crucible of the boxing ring or war.

Witness the early tale "The Atavist," page 236. It starts with a chance encounter between two soldiers, the story's narrator Jimmy Kelliher and Devlin, during the "frenzied days following the Armistice." Devlin agrees to fill in for a no-show on a boxing card and, upon donning the fighter's trunks, is transformed into "a fierce-eyed, snarling savage. There was some latent primitive ferocity in Devlin's soul that came to the fore only in battle." In Devlin, Howard created "the greatest welterweight since the days of Joe Walcott," a lonely man whose only tangible tie to the civilized world around him is the boxing ring—the one place wherein he is allowed to be what he is, a "reversion to the primitive man of the Stone Age!"

Nowhere is this concept more evident than in the masterpiece "Iron Men," companion to Howard's unfinished but revealing essay "Men of Iron" (pg. 405). In this essay the reader is introduced to a roll call of legendary tough-men that defy the normal limits of the human body. Howard asks the reader: "What freak of nature makes an iron man?" In "Iron Men" he answers the question by introducing readers to Iron Mike Brennon, the acknowledged king of Howard's iron men. Brennon is a physical wonder, an iron man of the highest order, who stalks the pages of this fistic epic enduring punishment on a scale that is almost too much for the reader to endure. Brennon is the fictionalized cousin to the real life "King of the Iron Men," Joe Grim, the focal point of "Men of Iron."

In this exposé of brutality, Brennon is driven to risk his life by capitalizing on his toughness in a desperate quest for money. Called by his opponents "the toughest piece of human architecture that ever lived," Brennon is the beneficiary of a genetic constitution that owes everything to those primitive ancestors that tamed the world in mankind's dim past but, once in the ring, he is afflicted with what his trainer calls a "kink"— "somethin' that breaks down his co-ordination and keeps his mind from workin' with his muscle." This kink is Brennon's failure to subdue that part of his nature that houses the animal instinct—it is the brute that lies dormant within most of us.

Until recently, this story of love, sacrifice and violent hubris was virtually unknown outside of Howard fandom but now, thanks to the work of Howard scholars, this story (and its many incarnations and unlikely origins) is on display once again. It is one of three "dramatic" boxing tales, along with "They Always Come Back" and "Fists of the Desert," that ascend to the highest peaks of drama that the genre has ever offered.

Speaking of drama and Howard's boxing tales in the same sentence might seem outlandish, but consider this: Western literature rose to prominence in ancient Greece, and though it may at first seem strange that Howard, with his well documented love of all things Gael, would look to the classical Greek dramas to fuel his boxing stories, it is in this grand tradition that Howard appears to have wed two seemingly antagonistic principles: boxing and classic melodrama. Here, too, Howard reveals his innate understanding of history, literature and sport for, after all, his boxing tales explore almost exclusively the three genres of drama: tragedy, comedy, and the burlesque in all its varied forms. Moreover, the Greeks' fascination with sporting specialization lends itself well to Howard's idea of the throwback—they gird themselves in loincloths, essentially stripping down their civilized facade (clothing) to wrap their knuckles in hardened strips of leather—the whole event is more than just spectacle; it is a ceremony dedicated to the past when men fought tooth and nail one against the other for prize, pride or prejudice.

This ceremony is essentially played out in the same manner today and it is a highly ritualized and potent ingredient in Howard's fiction. It is a poignant reminder of our innate savagery, the hidden animal angst that dwells within our breast, in our psyche, clawing and scratching to get out of the chains of civilization. Howard's boxing heroes are men who constantly look back in time to find virtue and worth in nearly all things. For Howard, his heroes are atavistic in this sense—they are men meant for a different era, alien in their own time, and possessed of a clearness of thought and action that are viewed as simple by "civilized" observers. Howard works in this arena physically as well as socially. His fighters are often described as "hairy," "savage" and possessed of physical attributes and social traits that are intentionally uncivilized. This descriptive formula has been observed by Howard scholars for decades but until now no one has adequately investigated just why Howard chose to do this.

Further fueling the intentional brutishness of his heroes, Howard has his boxing characters subscribe completely to what Michael T. Isenberg describes as a kind of Irish-American "cult of masculinity" which preoccupies itself with rough and tumble friendships, the telling of tall tales, the use of violence as a predictor of "right" and a penchant for alcoholic indulgence— just read about a dozen Sailor Steve Costigan stories and you will begin to see that Howard, and his boxing creations, were cut from the same cultural cloth that birthed the great John L. Sullivan. These attributes were common in the real life inspirations that Howard drew from, legendary figures like Sailor Tom Sharkey, Sullivan, Bob Fitzsimmons, and Kid McCoy. This is what makes the boxing stories so interesting; Howard has created a literary construct that is pulled directly from his personal experiences and perceptions. Howard's literary vision is razor sharp, but what is not quite so common is for an author's early writing attempts to so completely capture the essence and drive of his greatest works; and yet, as can be seen in this brief paragraph from one of Robert E. Howard's earliest boxing tales ("A Man of Peace," pg. 221), the essential elements are already on display:

> Vaguely he sensed some of the quality of the man. Sloan was a giant among men, a superman; but Slade was not a man. He was a wolf, the materialized substance of elemental Nature. His was the essence of the blizzard, the shrieking river rapids, the barbaric, sombre mountains, the yell of the wolf pack, the screech of the panther. Sloan was unconquerable by man; it was as though the wild herself, with her Great Silences, her mighty conflicts, her primal, elemental struggles, had formed and shaped and molded one of her own children for the sole purpose of defeating him. It was not alone Slade that Sloan fought. He fought the land of the big timber, the Great Barrens; he battled the very essence of Primal Power.

It is this kind of blind, passionate insistence that allows Howard to whisk the unsuspecting reader into an imaginary world of absolutes where nature and man are constantly at war with no middle ground in sight, elevating the most brutish of his tales to a place of constant evolutionary confrontation. Whether with gods, nature, or civilization Howard and his protagonists are in a state of constant conflict. The discerning reader can see that there is more at stake than a mere boxing match though Howard clearly revels in the violent details and realistic descriptions of the fight. As in the paragraph above, Howard forces us to stare beyond the fight, to focus instead upon the more significant clash that is etched in sparse, yet symbolically compelling language— the struggle of primordial man against the indefatigable advance of changing times.

Recognizing these thematic layers is the key to understanding his true aim as an author. It is not the blow by blow fight scenes that are meant to capture our imagination so much as it is the way the boxing match frames the very foundation of his evolutionary and historical interests and beliefs. The clash of archetypes, seen so clearly in the above excerpt, is an important tool in Howard's arsenal of ideas and it is a touchstone in much of his best work outside the narrow confines of the boxing genre. But it should be noted that it is within these boxing stories that Howard tests his evolutionary theories and exercises his wistful visions of a romanticized past against the backdrop of the modern, real world.

In these early boxing stories, many of which were unpublished during his lifetime and make up the bulk of this first volume, the discerning reader will find ample evidence that Howard was experimenting with boxing as theme on contemporary issues. Along with "Night Encounter" (pg. 301), "The Atavist" is one of the few Howard stories in which Howard speaks directly to the malaise and sense of displacement that afflicted many American soldiers after they had returned home from the first Great War. Howard has always been considered a prophet of the past, a man Harold Preece claimed "doesn't belong in this sordid age when descendants of Vikings sell ribbon for fifteen dollars a week. Bob is a welcome throwback to the gentlemen adventurers of old." And yet, he was keenly aware of and interested in his own time.

In a letter written to Wilfred Blanch Talman, 1931, Howard describes his interests: "My tastes are simple; prizefights, football games, horse races, and beer." With this remarkably sparse description we get a sense of the kind of man Robert E. Howard wanted others to perceive him as; a simple man with simple tastes and, simply, a man of his time. That prize-fights top his list should come as no surprise as boxing had claimed the throne of interest for a nation still reeling from the effects of The Great War. The Roaring Twenties had ushered in a kind of cultural dynamism that reveled in excess and discovery, eschewing the principles of the past and relying instead upon technical innovations of the future. Boxing became the unlikely benefactor of this national movement toward modernity as it shed vestiges of the past like so much brittle snakeskin.

The higher arts, once the exclusive home of the social aristocrat, found a willing audience for new, less privileged voices to tell their stories and sing their songs. It was against this social backdrop of contrasts, new versus old, barbarism versus civilization, that Robert E. Howard emerged from adolescence to develop his social identity—and to begin writing his boxing fiction. But why boxing? What is it about the sport that lends itself so well to Howard's thematic universal truisms of hate, pride, and struggle? Perhaps the answer lies within the human condition and its reaction to itself as much as anything else. While Howard seems to disagree, it is generally considered that civilization marched out of the brutish past to rescue man from his primal nature, to lift him from the morass of anarchy toward a world where anything is possible and things other than "might" should make "right." But throughout his fiction and personal correspondence Howard espouses the idea that civilization is merely a way in which mankind tries to forget what he truly is. Howard and his boxers are perfect examples of what Camus described in his *Myth of Sisyphus* as those "Absurd Men" who live life fully, refuse to acknowledge defeat or even death, and ultimately find an absurd kind of renewal in the cleansing agent of the past as it cycles back to the future over and over again.

Consider then Howard's continual use of women as biblical Eves in his boxing fiction and you are liable to get a case of déjà vu. His early boxing tales are rife with morality lessons that loudly proclaim the evil influence of wine and women. Females are usually, but not universally, treated as sly antagonists, willing participants in underhanded schemes to wrest from the unwary and naive warrior his hard won spoils. They are portrayed by the author as suspicious temptresses or angelic know-nothings that exist on the very periphery of emotional sanity, riding waves of intense, almost comic sensitivity. In stories such as "The Folly of Conceit" (pg. 315), "The Mark of a Bloody Hand," the fragment "I had just hung…" (pg. 279) and most Sailor Steve and Kid Allison tales, the hero is duped time and time again by less than honest women, or women whose every action proceeds from an emotional reaction. His boxers serve as a kind of allegorical symbol of those "Absurd Men" who know that the only bounty their lust and love will get them is an empty pocket and a broken heart. Having learned their lesson, Howard's boxers nearly fall over themselves in a mad dash to do it all over again—a course of action that Howard is all too happy to oblige. Howard's portrayal of women would become increasingly complex and forward thinking as he aged but these early efforts show his he-men as incapable of recognizing the wicked guile of civilized women. Again, it is worth noting that Howard seems to suggest that these literary iron men are products of a cleaner, more honest origin rooted in mankind's barbaric beginnings.

Boxing has long been viewed by the more adventurous literati as a kind of renewal toward the basic elements of the human experience—especially for one who believes his soul has grown fat upon civilized excess. Consider again Ernest Hemingway, Jack London, and even that cavalier of civilized refinement, Sir Arthur Conan Doyle—they all felt the lure of boxing with a thoroughness that was out of character with their scholarly inclinations. They each spent a great deal of time actually sparring with others, studying the science of the sport, and refining their own skills—often for the simple thrill of it, but always to immerse themselves into "the primitive constituents of humanity."

For years, Howard, too, lived and breathed boxing, and had at an early age become an expert on the sport and its history. His surviving personal correspondence reveals a man who framed his entire worldview as often through the lens of the ring and its bloody adherents as through history's sword wielding red reavers. In a letter written to H. P. Lovecraft, Howard's social antithesis and philosophical foil in the well known "Barbarism vs. Civilization" epistolary debate, Howard states simply but emphatically: "When I say that I'd rather watch a football game, a prize-fight, a horse race or a really able dancing girl, than to delve into the mysteries of the universe, however magnificent and awesome, I'm simply being honest."

But, what is it, exactly, that captured Howard's interest so thoroughly that he would hitchhike significant distances just to catch a fight card? What thing or part of a boxing match could induce in him the desire to "leap into the ring, and challenge Tramel, himself" as Harold Preece recalls when they witnessed the Dula-Tramel fight together? As a literary subject, how can the spectacle of boxing satisfy the emotional requirements of theme, plot, and character and yet splash adequate color upon the canvas of human expression for literary giants the likes of London, Hemingway, Doyle and Howard who use words the way Bach or Mozart give voice and meaning to music?

To understand the primacy of boxing as a vehicle for Howard's most notable themes one must look to the source of his exposure. It seems quite obvious that, like Hemingway, who battered critics and pestered notable scribes like Ezra Pound and Dos Passos into sparring matches and impromptu boxing lessons, Howard was not content to merely learn about the sport of boxing—he was determined to experience it firsthand. Howard is known to have engaged as early as 1926 in bare-knuckled and gloved sparring matches at the local ice-house with a motley collection of farmers, oil-field bullies and itinerant workers. He sparred with friends often and entered into demanding physical fitness regimens tailored to increase his strength, speed and, most importantly—his toughness. He endeavored to learn the science of the sport and to that end Howard would, according to his good friend, Tevis Clyde Smith, read: "everything connected with boxing, from *The Police Gazette* to *The Ring*." Not generally acknowledged as noteworthy, this was a critical period in Howard's development as a writer.

Immensely popular during Howard's lifetime, these two publications are remembered for coloring the sport in garish, racy Technicolor that laced their sports editorials in a kind of hazy caricature of sports journalism. But, while *The Ring* gave the young Howard his historical appreciation for the lore and pageantry of the sport, it was *The National Police Gazette* that infused Howard with its burlesque humanity. More than any single publication, and likely more than all other publications combined, *The National Police Gazette* elevated boxing from the barges and bar rooms of its bare knuckled past to the showcased darling of the emerging technical revolution. Equal parts avantgarde and yellow journalism, the *Gazette* made national heroes of pugs and did so with such pomp and flair that a young Howard could not help being influenced by the fantastic reports of the modern day gladiators they covered. The writers of the *Gazette* were notorious embellishers who were paid to distort and twist the facts with an energetic style that is echoed in Howard's own prose. To what extent the *Gazette* schooled young Robert on the use of dynamic hyperbole can be argued—especially when compared with his Costigan and Allison tales. But what cannot is the fact that, for Howard, boxing represented something more than simple sport, it was for him an endeavor that was worth contemplation and consideration in the same way he sought to digest ancient history or discuss philosophy with friends. Writing to one of those good friends, Harold Preece, in 1928, Howard reveals the diversity of his thoughts and the importance of boxing as an object of social interest: "Our usual procedure is to drive or walk some miles out on the highway or some country road late at night and there sit and converse, varying this with strolls up and down in the vicinity, while our conversation ranges from Metozoan to dinosaurs, and from prize fights to ancient religions."

Perhaps the most impressive feature of the boxing stories in particular can be found in Howard's meticulous attention to detail. Howard's fight scenes are realistic and accurate, and are told with a humming vibrancy that effortlessly carries the reader through pages of boxing action that reads like a Hype Igoe or Damon Runyon blow by blow account. Many writers skim over the science behind a blow but Howard revels in it. Just read the unfinished "The Ghost Behind the Gloves" to get a sense of the ease with which Howard describes, in just a few paragraphs, the tactical ebb and flow of a boxing match that is reminiscent of London's evocative "A Piece of Steak."

Of special interest is Howard's boxing universe; it is very similar to his more famous creation, the Hyborian Age, in that there is a concentrated effort to create a cohesive, believable world that co-exists with the real one we live in. To that end Howard peppers his stories liberally with comparisons and references to real boxers. Howard's own creations may star in one story and then be referenced in others, *à la* Jack Maloney who faces Iron Mike Brennon in a bit part in "Iron Men" but whose life is the subject of "They Always Come Back." In "The Atavist", modern readers may be forgiven if they think of that "other" Joe Walcott (he of Jersey fame) when Howard references the original welterweight named Walcott.

But more interesting still are the subtle nods of respect that Howard pays these real boxers throughout these stories. A typical example of Howard's astute boxing acumen is the subject of his poem "Kid Lavigne is Dead." Not only was Kid Lavigne a real, legendary, boxer, but he was the one who fought the very same Walcott that Howard compares Steve Devlin to. I do not believe Howard chose the name by mere chance—no, "Devil" Devlin owes his moniker to the very real Barbados Demon—the cognomen of none other than the real welterweight, Joe Walcott. Read closely Brennon's anguished recollection of poverty: it captures perfectly the very spirit of Jack Dempsey's "Kid Blackie" days. Howard squeezes this kind of ring lore into many of the stories showcased in this volume and it provides the scholar with an opportunity to investigate the real life origins behind many of his creations. It is a veritable window into Howard's personal interests. Howard's conception of a unified boxing universe is so complete that the reader does not bat an eye when Brennon recounts the list of real life iron men who have come before him—and anoints himself their king!

Howard wasn't afraid to mix it up now and then, as evidenced by his interesting tale "The Right Hook." What makes this story unique is its point of view, which gives the reader an idea of what it is like to go toe-to-toe with one of Howard's vaunted, mythological iron men. This feel-good story features Steve Harmer, a powerful puncher with a glass jaw who comes out of retirement to help his "best girl's" brother: The man stole ten thousand dollars to bet on a long shot fighter who, unbeknownst to the brother, has been instructed to take a dive. This story is very similar to the somber tones found in "Fists of the Desert," "They Always Come Back," and "Iron Men." These stories share a realistic and gritty, almost noir feel that provides a believable, cynical behind the scenes commentary of boxing. They are ripe with mob infiltration, sinister plots, and astute observations of the game that seem penned by a professional boxer rather than a small town writer.

But it's not all brooding darkness as evidenced by stories such as "The Weepin' Willow," "The Funniest Bout," "Misto Dempsey" and "Cupid vs. Pollux." These humorous yarns display the chameleon-like way in which Howard was able to stretch the thematic limits of the boxing genre. These stories appear, for the most part, very early in Howard's writing career and while they do not possess the burlesque perfection of his later Costigan and Elkins stories they are clearly noteworthy for the scholar interested in learning more about this aspect of Howard's writing. While Howard often revealed a near obsession with death he was hardly, as Mark Finn points out in the introduction to *Sentiment*, the "brooding misfit" that some critics posthumously imposed upon his personality. While Howard's work has been in the past categorized by phases, divided by defining terms like Historicals, Westerns, Boxing, Fantasy, etc., the one constant from beginning to end was his use of humor—sometimes subtle and at other times burlesque. It is this complexity of outlook and experiences that help provide a recognizably human balance to the more heralded of his creative works like Conan, Kull or Solomon Kane.

It has been argued that boxing itself is mere diversion, not worthy of serious literary criticism, and devoid of value to the scholar. I would argue that this perspective owes its myopic outlook to the same thinking that once suggested in earnest that Howard "may be fun to read and may stay in print for centuries, and has certainly influenced many writers in style and subject matter, but he scarcely carries any weight as a thinker." The same critic also pointed out the dearth of international or academic conferences devoted to Howard. Much has changed since the 1970s. With this collection of boxing stories Howard joins an elite fraternity of successful, if not legendary, authors who have gone beyond simply telling a tale and have instead placed themselves directly into their stories. Like Hemingway, London, Lamb and Arthur O. Friel, much of Howard's fiction and poetry reveals significant clues about the author but it is in his boxing tales and characters that we see Howard's full reflection laid bare.

Aside from the obvious example of Howard's fictionalized autobiography, *Post Oaks and Sand Roughs*, the author infused his fiction, most especially his boxing fiction, with familiar elements from his own life's experiences. These, ranging from his extensive historical exploration of the vast and forbidding Southwest to the sometimes savage pugilistic bouts he waged in the Cross Plains ice-house remain somehow refreshingly familiar to us even over eighty years later. This ability to communicate a message to audiences separated by decades remains one of Howard's greatest achievements.

Howard remains the quintessential American writer— unavoidably a product of his time, imbued with a literary voice at once melodramatic and beautiful, humorous and spartan, and undeniably talented. The pageantry of boxing is very similar to the writer's life; bright moments, albeit brief, wherein all eyes focus on the ring and thrill to the blast of leather on flesh or a truly well written story.

However, the same facade hides from the audience the grueling and lonely existence both disciples must endure. It seems only natural then that Howard would be enamored of the one sport that most adequately mirrored both his temperament and his sense of man vs. the world.

Joyce Carol Oates once mused: "Perhaps boxing has always been in crisis, a sport of crisis. . . our most dramatically self destructive sport." Just as boxing's popularity has waxed and waned over the years, ever in crisis or facing one, so too Howard's legacy and biography over the years since his death. Or, maybe, like Howard's only published boxing champion, Ace Jessel, his legacy just won't quit; perhaps in its "numbed brain there was room only for one thought—to fight and fight, and keep on fighting—the old primal instinct that is stronger than all things except death."

Fists of Iron

The Spirit of Tom Molyneaux

Many fights are won and lost by the living, but this is a tale of one which was won by a man dead over a hundred years. John Taverel, manager of ring champions, sitting in the old East Side A.C. one cold wintry day, told me this story of the ghost that won the fight and the man who worshipped the ghost. Let John Taverel tell the tale in his own words, as he told it to me:

You remember Ace Jessel, the great negro boxer whom I managed. An ebony giant he was, four inches over six feet in height, his fighting weight two hundred and thirty pounds. He moved with the smooth ease of a gigantic leopard and his pliant steel muscles rippled under his shiny skin. A clever boxer for so large a man, he carried the smashing jolt of a triphammer in each huge black fist.

Yet for all that, the road over which I, as his manager, steered him, was far from smooth and at times I despaired, for Ace seemed to lack a fighting heart. Courage he had plenty, courage to stand up to a vicious beating and to keep on going after his face had been pounded and battered to a bloody mass, as he proved in that terrible battle with Maul Finnegan, which became almost mythical in boxing annals. Courage he had, but not the aggressiveness which drives the perfect fighter ever to the attack, nor the killer instinct which sends him plunging after the reeling, bloody and beaten foe. And a boxer who lacks these qualities is likely to fail when put to the supreme test.

Ace was content to box mostly, outpointing his opponents and piling up just enough lead to keep from losing. And the public was never fond of these tactics. Therefore they jeered and booed him every so often, but though their taunts angered me, they only broadened Ace's good-natured grin. And his fights still drew great crowds because on the rare occasions when he was stung out of his defensive role, or when he was matched with a clever man whom he had to knockout in order to win, the fans saw a real battle that thrilled their blood. And even so, time and again he stepped away from a sagging foe, giving the beaten man time to recover and return to the attack, instead of finishing him—while the crowd raved and I tore my hair.

Now Ace Jessel, indifferent drifter, happy-go-lucky wastrel though he seemed, had one deep and abiding emotion, and that was a fanatical worship for one Tom Molyneaux, first champion of America and sturdy fighting man of color—according to some authorities, the greatest black ringman that ever lived.

Tom Molyneaux died in Ireland a hundred years ago but the memory of his valiant deeds in America and Europe was Ace Jessel's direct incentive to action. Reading an account of Tom's life and battles was what started Ace on the fistic trail which led from the wharves where he toiled as a young boy, to—but listen to the story.

Ace's most highly prized possession was a painted portrait of the old battler. He had discovered this—a rare find indeed, since even woodcuts of Molyneaux are rare—among the collections of a London sportsman, and had prevailed on the owner to sell it. Paying for it had taken every cent that Ace made in four fights but he counted it cheap at the price. He removed the original frame and replaced it with a frame of solid silver, a slim elegant work of art which, considering that the portrait was full length and life size, was rather more than extravagant. But no honor was too expensive for "Misto Tom" and Ace simply tripled the number of his bouts to meet the cost.

So finally my brains and Ace's mallet fists had cleared us a road to the top of the game. Ace loomed up as a heavyweight menace and the champion's manager was ready to sign with us when an interruption came.

A form hove into view on the fistic horizon which dwarfed and overshadowed all other contenders, including my man. This was

Mankiller Gomez. He was all which his name implies. Gomez was his ring name, given him by the Spaniard who discovered him and brought him to America. His real name was Balanga Guma and he was a full-blooded Senegalese from the West Coast of Africa.

Once in a century ring fans see a man like Gomez in action. Once in a hundred years there rises a fighter like the Senegalese—a born killer who crashes through the general ruck of fighters as a buffalo crashes through a thicket of dead wood. He was a savage, a tiger. What he lacked in actual skill, he made up by ferocity of attack, by ruggedness of body and smashing power of arm. From the time he landed in New York, with a long list of European victories behind him, it was inevitable that he should batter down all opposition, and at last the white champion looked to see the black savage looming above the broken forms of his victims. The champion saw the writing on the wall, but the public was clamoring for a match and whatever else his faults, the title holder was a fighting champion.

Ace Jessel, who alone of all the foremost challengers had not met Gomez, was shoved into discard, and as early summer dawned on New York, a title was lost and won, and Mankiller Gomez, son of the black jungle, rose up king of all fighting men.

The sporting world and the public at large hated and feared the new champion. Boxing fans like savagery in the ring, but Gomez did not confine his ferocity to the ring. His soul was abysmal. He was apelike, primordial—the very spirit of that morass of barbarism from which mankind has so tortuously climbed, and toward which men look with so much suspicion.

There went forth a search for a White Hope, but the result was always the same. Challenger after challenger went down before the terrible onslaught of the Mankiller and at last only one man remained who had not crossed gloves with Gomez— Ace Jessel.

I hesitated in throwing my man in with a battler like Gomez, for my fondness for the great good-natured negro was more than the friendship of manager for fighter. Ace was something more than a meal ticket to me for I knew the real nobility underlying Ace's black skin, and I hated to see him battered into a senseless ruin by a man

I knew in my heart to be more than Jessel's match. I wanted to wait awhile, to let Gomez wear himself out with his terrific battles and the dissipations that were sure to follow the savage's success. These super-sluggers never last long, any more than a jungle native can withstand the temptations of civilization.

But the slump that follows a really great title holder's gaining the belt was on, and matches were scarce. The public was clamoring for a title fight, sportswriters were raising Cain and accusing Ace of cowardice, promoters were offering alluring purses, and at last I signed for a fifteen round go between Mankiller Gomez and Ace Jessel.

At the training quarters I turned to Ace. "Ace, do you think you can whip him?"

"Misto John," Ace answered, meeting my eye with a straight gaze, "Ah'll do mah best, but Ah's mighty afeard Ah cain't do it. Dat man ain't human."

I knew this was bad; a man is more than half-whipped when he goes into the ring in that frame of mind.

Later I came into Ace's room for something and halted in the doorway in amazement. I had heard the battler talking in a low voice as I came up, but had supposed one of the handlers or sparring partners was in the room with him. Now I saw that he was alone. He was standing before his idol—the portrait of Tom Molyneaux.

"Misto Tom," he was saying humbly, "Ah ain't nevah met no man yet what could even knock me off mah feet, but Ah reckon dat nigguh can. Ah's gwine to need help mighty bad, Misto Tom."

I felt almost as if I had interrupted a religious rite. It was uncanny—had it not been for Ace's evident deep sincerity, I would have felt it to be unholy. But to Ace, Tom Molyneaux was something more than a saint. I stood in the doorway in silence, watching the strange tableau. The artist who painted the picture so long ago had wrought with remarkable skill. The short black figure seemed to stand out boldly from the faded canvas. A breath of bygone days, it seemed, clad in the long tights of that other day, the powerful legs braced far apart, the knotted arms held stiffly and high, just as

Molyneaux had appeared when he fought Tom Cribb of England so long ago.

Ace Jessel stood before the painted figure, head sunk upon his mighty chest as if listening to some dim whisper inside his own soul. And as I watched, a curious and fantastic thought came into my brain—the memory of an age-old superstition. You know it has been said by delvers into the occult that the carving of statues or the painting of pictures has power to draw back from the void of Eternity souls long flown, and to recreate them in shadowy semblance. I wondered if Ace had ever heard of this superstition and thought by doing obeisance to Molyneaux's portrait to conjure the dead man's spirit out of the realms of the dead for advice and aid. I shrugged my shoulders at this ridiculous idea and turned away. As I did, I glanced again at the picture before which Ace still stood like a great image of black basalt, and was aware of a peculiar illusion; the canvas seemed to ripple slightly, like the surface of a lake across which a faint breeze is blowing.

However I forgot all this as the day of the fight drew near.

The great crowd cheered Ace to the echo as he climbed in the ring; cheered again, not so heartily, as Gomez appeared. They afforded a strange contrast, those two negroes, alike in color but how different in all other aspects!

Ace was tall, clean-limbed and rangy, long and smooth of muscle, clear of eye and broad of forehead.

Gomez seemed stocky by comparison, though he stood a good six feet two. Where Jessel's sinews were long and smooth like great cables, his were knotty and bulging. His calves, thighs, arms and shoulders stood out in great bunches of muscles. His small bullet head was set squarely between gigantic shoulders, and his forehead was so low that his kinky wool seemed to lower over his small bestial and bloodshot eyes. On his chest was a thick grizzle of matted black hair.

He grinned cavernously, thumped his breast and flexed his mighty arms with the insolent assurance of the savage. Ace, in his corner, grinned at the crowd, but an ashy tint was on his dusky face and his knees trembled.

The usual remarks were made, instructions given by the referee, weights announced—230 for Ace, 248 for Gomez— then over the great stadium the lights went off save for those over the ring where two black giants faced each other like men alone on the ridge of the world.

At the gong Gomez whirled in his corner and came out with a breathtaking roar of pure ferocity. Ace, frightened though he must have been, rushed to meet him with the courage of a cave man charging a gorilla, and they met headlong in the center of the ring.

The first blow was the Mankiller's, a left swing that glanced Ace's ribs. Jessel came back with a long left to the face and a straight right to the body that stung. Gomez bulled in, swinging both hands and Ace, after one futile attempt to mix it with him, gave back. The champion drove him across the ring, sending in a savage left to the body as Ace clinched. As they broke Gomez shot a terrible right to the chin and Ace reeled into the ropes. A great "Ahhh!" went up from the crowd as the champion plunged after him like a famished wolf, but Ace managed to dive between the lashing arms and clinch, shaking his head to clear it. Gomez sent in a left, largely smothered by Ace's clutching arms, and the referee warned the Senegalese.

At the break Ace stepped back, jabbing swift and cleverly with his left, and the round ended with the champion, bellowing like a buffalo, trying to get past that rapier-like arm.

Between rounds I cautioned Ace to keep away from infighting as much as possible, where Gomez's superior strength would count heavily, and to use his footwork to avoid punishment as much as he could.

The second round started much like the first, Gomez rushing and Ace using all his skill to stave him off and avoid those terrible smashes. It's hard to get a shifty boxer like Ace in a corner, when he is fresh and unweakened and at long range had the advantage of his superior science over Gomez, whose one idea was to get in close and batter down his foes by sheer strength and ferocity. Still, in spite of Ace's speed and skill, just before the gong sounded Gomez got the range and sank a vicious left to the wrist in Ace's midriff and the tall negro weaved slightly as he walked to his corner. I could see the beginning of the end. The vitality and power of Gomez seemed endless; there was no wearing him down and it would not take many of his blows, landed, to rob Ace of his speed of foot and accuracy of eye. Then, forced to stand and trade punches, he was done.

Gomez, seeing he had stung his man, came plunging out for the third round with murder in his eye. He ducked a straight left, took a hard right uppercut square in the face and hooked both hands to the body, then straightened with a terrific right to the chin, which Ace robbed of most of its force by swaying with the blow. And while the champion was still off-balance, Ace measured him coolly and shot in a fierce right hook flush on the chin. Gomez's head flew back as if hinged to his shoulders and he was stopped in his tracks, but even as the crowd rose, hands clenching, lips parted, in hopes he would go down, the champion shook his bullet head and came in roaring. The round ended with both men locked in a clinch in the center of the ring.

At the beginning of the fourth round Gomez attacked and drove Ace about the ring before a shower of blows which he could not seem to wholly avoid. Stung and desperate, Ace made a stand in a neutral corner and sent Gomez back on his heels with a left and right to the body, but took a savage left to the face in return. Then suddenly the champion crashed through with a deadly left to the solar plexus and as Ace staggered, shot a killing right to the chin. Ace fell back into the ropes, instinctively raising his hands and sinking his chin on his chest. Gomez's short fierce smashes were partly blocked by his shielding gloves and suddenly, pinned on the ropes as he was, and still dazed from the Mankiller's attack, Ace went into terrific action and, slugging toe to toe with the champion, beat him off and drove him back across the ring!

The crowd went insane but, crouching behind Ace's corner, I saw the writing on the wall. Ace was fighting as he had never fought before, but no man on earth could stand the pace the champion was setting.

Battling along the ropes, Ace sent a savage left to the body and a right and left to the face but was repaid by a right-hand smash to the ribs that made him wince in spite of himself, and just at the gong Gomez landed another of those deadly left-handers to the body.

Ace's handlers worked over him swiftly, for I saw that the tall black was weakening. A few more rounds of this would spell the end.

"Ace, can't you keep away from those body smashes?"

"Misto John, suh, Ah'll try," he answered.

The gong! Ace came in with a rush, his magnificent body vibrating with dynamic energy. Gomez met him, his iron muscles bunching into a compact fighting unit. *Crash—crash—* and again, *crash!* A clinch. And as they broke, Gomez drew back his great right arm and launched a terrible blow to Ace's mouth. The tall negro reeled—he went down! Then, without stopping for the count which I was screaming for him to take, he gathered his long steely legs under him and was up with a bound, blood gushing down his black chest. Gomez leaped in and Ace, with the fury of desperation, met him with a terrific right, square to the jaw. And Gomez crashed to the canvas on his shoulder blades! The crowd rose screaming! In the space of ten seconds both men had been floored for the first time in the life of each!

"One! Two! Three! Four!" the referee's arm rose and fell.

Gomez was up, unhurt, wild with fury. Roaring like a wild beast, he plunged in, brushed aside Ace's hammering arms and crashed his right hand with the full weight of his mighty shoulder behind it, full into Ace's midriff. Jessel went an ashy color—he swayed like a tall tree, and Gomez beat him to his knees with rights and lefts which sounded like the blows of caulking mallets.

"One! Two! Three! Four!—"

Ace was writhing on the canvas, striving to get his legs beneath him. The roar of the fans was a torrent of sound, an ocean of noise which drowned out all thought.

"Five! Six! Seven!—"

Ace was up! Gomez came charging across the stained canvas, gibbering his pagan fury. His blows beat upon the staggering challenger like a hail of sledges. A left—a right—another left which Ace had not strength to duck.

"One! Two! Three! Four! Five! Six! Seven! Eight!—"

Again Ace was up, weaving, staring blankly, helpless. A swinging left hurled him back into the ropes and rebounding from them he went to his knees—the gong!

As his handlers and I sprang into the ring Ace groped blindly for his corner and dropped limply upon the stool.

"Ace, he's too much for you."

A grin bent Jessel's bloody lips and an indomitable spirit looked out of his bloodshot eyes.

"Misto John, please suh, don't t'row in de sponge. Must Ah take it, Ah takes it standin'. Dat boy cain't last at dis pace all night, suh."

No, but neither could Ace Jessel, in spite of his remarkable vitality and his marvelous recuperative powers which sent him back up for the next round, with a show of renewed strength and freshness, at least. The sixth and seventh were comparatively tame. Perhaps Gomez really was fatigued from the terrific pace he had been setting. At any rate, Ace managed to make it more or less of a sparring match at long range and the crowd was treated to an exhibition showing how long a man, out on his feet, can stand off and keep away from a slugger bent solely on his destruction. Even I marveled at the brand of boxing which Ace was showing, even though I knew that Gomez was fighting cautiously, for him. He had sampled the power of Ace's right hand in that frenzied fifth round and perhaps he was wary of a trick. For the first time in his life he had sprawled on the canvas. He knew he was winning, and I think he was content to rest a couple of rounds, take his time for a space and gather his energies for a final onslaught.

This began as the gong sounded for the eighth round.

Gomez launched his usual sledgehammer attack, drove Ace about the ring and floored him in a neutral corner. His style of fighting was such that when he was determined on a foe's destruction, skill, speed and science could not avert but only postpone the eventual outcome. Ace took the count of nine and rose, backpedaling.

But Gomez was after him; the champion missed twice with his left and then sank a right under the heart that turned Ace ashy. A left to the jaw made his knees buckle and he clinched desperately. On the breakaway Ace sent a straight left to the face and right hook to the chin, but the blows lacked their old force and Gomez shook them off and sank his left wrist deep in Ace's midsection. Ace again clinched but the champion shoved him away and drove him across the ring with savage hooks to the body. At the gong they were slugging along the ropes.

Ace reeled to the wrong corner, and when his handlers led him to his own, he sank down on the stool, his legs trembling and his great dusky chest heaving from his superhuman exertions. I glanced across at the champion who sat glowering at his foe. He too was showing signs of the fray, but he was much fresher than Ace. The referee walked over, looked at Jessel hesitantly and then spoke to me.

Through the mists which veiled his bruised brain, Ace realized the import of his words and struggled to rise, a kind of fear flaming in his eyes.

"Misto John, don' let him stop it, suh! Don' let him do it! Ah ain't hu't nuthin' like dat 'ud hu't me!"

The referee shrugged his shoulders and walked back to the center of the ring, and I turned to one of the trainers and bade him bring me the flat bundle I had brought with me into the stadium.

There was little use giving advice to Ace. He was too battered to understand—in his numbed brain there was room only for one thought—to fight and fight, and keep on fighting—the old primal instinct that is stronger than all things save death.

At the sound of the gong he reeled out to meet his doom with an indomitable courage that brought the crowd to its feet yelling. He struck, a wild aimless left, and the champion plunged in hitting with both hands until Ace went down. At "nine" he was up and backpedaled instinctively until Gomez reached him with a long straight right and sent him down again. Again he took "nine" before he reeled up and now the crowd was silent. Not one voice was raised in an urge for the kill. This was butchery, primitive slaughter, and the courage of Ace Jessel took their breath as it gripped my heart.

Ace fell blindly into a clinch, and another and another, till the Mankiller, furious, shook him off and sank his right to the body. Ace's ribs gave way like rotten wood, with a dry crack heard distinctly all over the stadium—a strangled cry went up from the crowd and Jessel gasped thickly and fell to his knees.

"—Seven! Eight!—" and the great black form was writhing on the canvas.

"—Nine!" and the miracle had happened and Ace was on his feet, swaying, jaw sagging, arms hanging limply.

Gomez glared at him, not in pity, but as if unable to understand how his foe could have risen again, then came plunging in to finish him. Ace was in dire straits. Blood blinded him and his feet slipped in great smears of it on the canvas— his blood. Both eyes were nearly closed, and when he breathed gustily through his smashed nose, a red haze surrounded him. Deep cuts gashed cheek and cheek bones and his left side was a mass of battered red flesh. He was going on fighting instinct alone now, and never again would any man doubt that Ace Jessel had a fighting heart.

Yet a fighting heart alone is not enough when the body that holds it is broken and battered and mists of unconsciousness veil the brain. Ace sank down before Gomez's panting onslaught and this time the crowd knew that it was final.

When a man has taken the beating that Ace had taken, something more than body and heart must come into the game to carry him through. Something to inspire and stimulate the dazed brain, to fire it to heights of superhuman achievement. I had planned to furnish this inspiration, if the worst came to the worst, in the only way which I knew would touch Ace.

Before leaving the training quarters, I had, unknown to Ace, removed the picture of Tom Molyneaux from its frame, and brought it to the stadium with me, carefully wrapped. I now took this, and as Ace's eyes, instinctively and without his own volition, sought his corner, I held the portrait up, just outside the glare of the ring lights, so while illumined by them, it appeared illusive and dim. It may be thought that I acted wrongly and selfishly, to thus seek to bring to his feet for more punishment a man almost dead from the beating, but the outsider cannot fathom the souls of the children of the fight game, to whom winning is greater than life, and losing, worse than death.

All eyes were glued on the prostrate form in the center of the ring, on the wind-blown champion sagging against the ropes, on the arm of the referee, which rose and fell with the regularity of doom. I doubt if four men in the audience saw my action, but Ace Jessel saw. I caught the gleam that came into his bloodshot and dazed eyes. I saw him shake his head violently. I saw him begin sluggishly to gather his long legs under him. It seemed a long time; the drone of the referee rose as it neared its climax—then, by all the gods, Ace Jessel was up! The crowd went insane and screaming.

I saw his eyes blaze with a strange wild light. And as I live today, *the picture in my hands shook suddenly and violently.*

A cold wind passed like death across me and I heard the man next to me shiver involuntarily as he drew his coat closer about him. But it was no cold wind that gripped my soul as I looked, wide eyed and staring, into the ring where the greatest drama the boxing world has ever known was being enacted. There was Ace Jessel, bloody, terrible, throbbing and pulsing with new dynamic life, fired by a superhuman power—there was Mankiller Gomez, speechless with amazement at his foe's new burst of fury—there was the immobile-faced referee—*and to my horror I saw that there were four men in that ring!*

And the fourth—a short, massive black man, barrel-chested and mighty-limbed, clad in the long tights of another day. And as I looked I saw that this man was not as other men for beyond him I saw the ropes of the ring and dimly, the ring lights, as if I were looking through a dark mist—as if I were looking through him.

His mighty arm was about Ace Jessel's waist as my fighter crashed upon the weary and disheartened Gomez; his bare hard fists fell with Ace's on the head and body of the desperate Mankiller.

Whether Gomez saw or realized he saw this Stranger, I do not know. Dazed by the unnaturalness of Ace's sudden comeback, by the uncanny strength of Ace who should have been fainting on the canvas, Gomez staggered, weakening; bewildered and mazed he was unable to decide upon a stand to make, and before he could rally was beaten down, crashed and battered down and out by long straight smashes sent in with the speed and power of a piledriver. And the last blow, a straight right that would have felled an ox, and did fell Mankiller Gomez, was driven not alone by the power of Ace's mighty shoulder, but by the aid of a shadowy black hand on Jessel's wrist. As I live today, that Fourth Man guided Ace's hand to Gomez's chin and backed the blow with the power of his own tremendous shoulders.

A moment the strange tableau burned itself into my brain. The astounded referee counting over the prostrate champion, and Ace Jessel, standing, head lowered and arms dangling, supported by a short, mighty figure in long ring tights. Then this figure faded before my very gaze and, as the portrait of Tom Molyneaux fell from my nerveless fingers, I felt it shake as if it shuddered.

As I climbed into the ring with the roar of the insane fans thundering in my brain, I wondered dazedly as I wonder today—was I given to see that sight alone of all that throng because I held the picture in my hands?

The crowd saw only a miracle, a man beaten nearly to death coming back with unexplainable strength and vitality to conquer his conqueror. They did not see the Fourth Man. Nor did Mankiller Gomez.

Ace Jessel? A negro never talks on some subjects and I have never asked him any questions on that matter. But as he collapsed in his corner, I bent over him and heard him murmur as he lost consciousness:

"Misto Tom—he done it, suh—his han' was on mah wrist—when—Ah—dropped—Gomez."

That old superstition is justified as far as I am concerned. Hereafter I will not doubt that deep devotion coupled with the possession of a lifelike portrait, can conjure back from the unknown voids of the astral world, the soul or spirit or ghost which inhabited the living body of which the portrait is a likeness. A door perhaps, a portrait is, through which astral beings pass back and forth between this world and the next—whatever that world may be.

But when I said no man save Ace Jessel and I saw the Fourth Man, I am not altogether correct. After the bout the referee, a steely-nerved, cold-eyed son of the old-time school, said to me: "Did you notice in that last round that a cold wind seemed to blow across the ring? Now tell me straight, am I going crazy or did I see a dark shadow hovering about Ace Jessel when he dropped Gomez?"

"You did," I answered. "And unless we are all insane, the ghost of Tom Molyneaux was in that ring tonight."

Double Cross

Ace Jessel, ebony giant and heavyweight champion of the world, after years of absence longed to see his old hometown again, and his manager, John Taverel, though with some misgivings, arranged a sort of triumphal tour for his fighter.

So Ace came back to the little seaboard town far below the Mason-Dixon line where in his youth he had toiled in the fields and, later, on the wharfs, before he started out to blazon his name across the stars. The lazy bayous with their cool, grass-grown and tree-shaded banks, the brooding and mystic swamplands, the long reaches of desolate seashore, dreary with salt-crusted sand—all these called to the primitive in Ace Jessel's soul and greeted him as of old, unchanged by the passing years. But the people had changed.

A prophet is not sure of honor always in his own land. The people in Ace Jessel's hometown, with their hot, fierce Southern pride and class consciousness, looked upon Ace as more or less of an upstart, a black man who had forgotten his place. They resented his victories over white pugilists and felt as if the fact reflected on them, somehow.

This hurt Ace, hurt him cruelly. To meet with cold reserve or open hostility where he had looked for friendliness and understanding, cut him to the quick, and even more so the patronizing, smirking attitude adopted by those who feared public sentiment, yet wished to hob-nob with the foremost fighting man of all the world. And Ace found he had gone beyond his former black friends.

John Taverel, himself a Southerner, was the buffer between Ace and the rest of the world. He knew that underneath that black skin there beat a heart as loyal and honest as any man's, black or white. Through all the long years of their association, Ace had never addressed or referred to Taverel as anything except "Misto John" and had maintained toward him a consistent reserve and respect. Honesty without insolence, respect and courtesy without servility, that was Ace Jessel's attitude toward everyone and no man, in or out of the ring, could say that the great Negro had ever fought a dirty fight or had ever given any man a crooked deal.

But John Taverel alone could not alter the opinion of the townsmen and after a few days' stay, Ace spoke to his manager:

"Misto John, Ah reckon if 'n you-all is ready, we bettuh move on. Ah thought when Ah come back heyuh, dat mah old friends would have a kind w'ud for me. Ah kinda thought dey'd say, 'Ace, boy, you has done us proud and we is proud uh you-all.' But Misto John, all de white persons Ah knowed when Ah wuz uh boy, dey pass right by me on de street and look de yuther way. Or does dey speak its so cold an' far-away dat it kinda freezes me.

"De white people think Ah'm stuck up and proud Ah guess, dat muh success hass puffed me all up and made me think Ah'm better'n dem. But Ah ain't—Ah'm jest de same Ace what used to wu'k on de river plantations, an' sweat on de docks. Ah'm de same—Ah ain't changed none, but dey ain't foun' it out yit. An' Ah guess dey ain't gwine to, 'caze dey won't.

"An' de darkies, dat Ah knowed, dey seems like dey're afeered uh me—an' when dey talk, it's jest like chillern. Ah'm mighty mo'nful 'bout all dis, Misto John, an' if it's de same to you-all, Ah'd like to go back to New Yo'k an' fight somebody an' kinda forgit—Ah think sometimes if a cullud boy wants to keep on bein' happy, de best thing for 'im is stay uh farmhand or uh wharf hand."

Having delivered himself thus, Ace walked out of the hotel where they were staying and strolled moodily along the wharfs where of old he had toiled. As he walked his face suddenly lighted.

Out of a low dive, frequented by daylight skulkers and night-time scum, a man stalked. A young man he was, and while his dirty, ragged garments were in keeping with his surroundings, his face was not, for though lined and marked by dissipation, his features were those of a high-born aristocrat, intelligent and sensitive.

"Misto Clive!" Ace started forward eagerly, his old sunny smile curving his lips—his hand instinctively went forward, then fell back as he remembered.

"Misto Clive, don't you-all remembah me—Ace Jessel?"

The young white man looked at Ace with recognition but without favor.

"Yes, I remember you," he said harshly. "Are you another ghost of the lost years come back to taunt me?"

"Misto Clive, suh," answered Ace, bewildered, "Ah suah ain't no ghost, an' Ah suah ain' gwine ta'nt you-all. Why, Misto Clive, don't you remembah how Ah used to row yo' boat for you down on de riveh, and tote yo' gun when you-all wuz huntin' in de canebrakes an' de swampland? 'Membah dat day you killed dat ole swamp rattler on Spook Island? Golly, he wuz a whopper! Dem wuz de great ole days, w'ant dey, Misto Clive?"

There was a wistful note in the great Negro's voice that seemed to touch some long forgotten chord in the white man's soul. His eyes softened and then hardened again.

"You've not done so bad since then," said he coldly. "Champion of the world, I hear." He laughed sardonically and rubbed a slim hand over his unshaven chin.

"Even the Negro boy who was proud to be my companion in my early youth," he continued evenly, "has surpassed me in the race of life. Destiny. I'll call it that anyway. My friends forged on and I stayed behind."

"Misto Clive," said Ace, "Whiskey wuz always yo' fault— yo' only fault, suh. Back when us wuz kids togedder Ah seed it comin' an' begged you-all den tuh stop drinkin', but you went right on. Ah's mighty mo'nful to see you dis way, but Misto Clive, don't you reckon it 'uz mostly yo' own fault?"

The white man's eyes blazed at this candor and then he shrugged his shoulders and laughed again, a cynical, empty laugh that went to Ace's heart.

"Yes, you're right. I drank myself out of a high position and a fortune and you see me now, a sodden drunkard, penniless and hopeless, existing only on the bounty of friends who are ashamed of me. Better be careful about talking to me—even a black man has a character and it won't be helped by associating with me."

Ace positively writhed. This remark was the most hopeless and despairing that a Southern white man could make. The champion fumbled in his pockets.

"Misto Clive, suh, if some greenbacks could he'p you-all out—"

Clive Damor recoiled as if from a blow in the face.

"Damn you, I haven't sunk low enough to take money from a Negro."

Ace lowered his eyes mutely, most cruelly hurt. Then he raised his head and his clear eyes looked straight at Astor.

"Misto Clive, suh, Ah'm just uh black boy, Ah know. You-all don't have tuh remind me 'bout dat. But Ah wuz yo' friend when we wuz kids an' Ah'm yo' friend now—mah people has stood by yo' family since befo' de wah. Ah wuz bo'n on yo' grandmammy's plantation. You-all is de last uh yo' line, Misto Clive. De Damors wuz always quality, suh, an' 'sides my friendship fo' you, suh, Ah hate to see de name brung down to wheah trash and low-down scum like hang around dat white mule j'int you just come outa, kin make mock uh hit."

As Ace spoke a slow red stole over Damor's face though his eyes never altered. When he ceased, the white man sighed strangely.

"Yes," he replied in a changed and quiet voice, "you're right Ace, and I'm a fool, I reckon. I've realized all of what you've just said but somehow you've brought it home to me more strongly than anyone has done. But it's too late now. This path is too long. Thank you, Ace, but your road is yours and my road is— mine. And they lie far apart. No, not a word; I want to get by myself and think."

Ace Jessel returned to his hotel, thinking sadly of the bygone days, and the vanished glory of the great Damor family and more than all of the downfall of Clive Damor, whom, reckless and good hearted, young Ace had worshipped in boyhood.

At the hotel John Taverel met Ace and with John was a certain shifty-eyed, offensive-mannered individual boasting the name of

Aaron Gold, who was owner of the small stadium and promoted local fight shows.

"Ace," said John Taverel, "Mr. Gold wants you to stage an exhibition bout in his arena."

"What you-all think about dat, Misto John?" asked Ace listlessly.

"I'm against it," said Taverel bluntly.

"So'm Ah," said Ace. "Mah hometown people don' like me no mo'. Dey wouldn't come an' if dey did dey'd wanta see me make uh fool uh mahself."

"Now, now, Mr. Jessel," said Gold, "I'm sure you have it down all wrong. The good people of the town really like you and appreciate you. Numbers of them have come to me requesting that I match you up with some local man, merely so they can get a chance to see you in action. Of course, I realize that as champion of the world, you are too busy a man to have your time taken up needlessly. But merely a little exhibition of, say, four rounds, just to please the home people? Not much money in it, of course, but I am giving the free use of my club, just as a favor for the town and you would draw down eighty-five percent of the gate receipts—the other fifteen go to the other man."

"Has dey suah 'nough come an' ast you-all to match me?" Ace asked eagerly.

"Yes sir, honest! That's the only reason I'm putting it on, for you see it's no money in my pockets."

Ace grinned boyishly.

"Maybe dey does like me after all! Suah, Misto Gold, Ah does it, but Ah don' want no money for it. Ah does it tuh please my town people. Don't charge no more'n you has to and give mah sha'h to de public school fund."

So in spite of John's half-hearted protests, the town blossomed into life and posters announced a four-round exhibition boxing match to be held in Aaron Gold's Arena between Ace Jessel, Heavyweight Champion of the World, and Dmitra Kamanos, local heavyweight of some repute.

"I don't like the looks of it," John Taverel reiterated. "The day is past when a champion is free to put on free exhibitions in hick towns. And this fellow Gold, he looks like a crook to me."

But he put no real obstacles in the way, for Ace Jessel had set his heart on it, and imagined, in his simple way, that by an exhibition of his prowess in the ring, he could win back the trust and friendship of his "people."

But John Taverel's suspicion was heightened when Gold came to them the day upon the evening of which the bout was to be.

"Mr. Jessel," said Gold smoothly, "the bout is billed an exhibition and all, of course, but the people are coming to see a real fight—they really expect a battle and they'll go away disappointed if they have to sit through four rounds of clinching and dancing."

"What do you suggest?" asked John Taverel, his fine eyes beginning to smolder.

"Why, like this. This Kamanos now, he's a good boy and all, but just a second-rater after all—they don't know him outside this state scarcely. I suggest this. Mr. Jessel, being as he couldn't hurt you with a piledriver anyway, we will let him do his best and make as good a showing as possible and you handle him easy until the fourth round and then knock him out."

"I suspected something like this," John Taverel lashed out. "The obstacle is that I happen to be managing a world's champion. He has everything to lose and nothing to win here. Kamanos, who in the ordinary course of events would never get a chance to step into a ring with a champion, has everything to gain and nothing to lose. Suppose my man hurts himself, or a chance swing knocks him out?"

"My goodness!" wailed Gold, gesticulating wildly. "All I'm doing is trying to make it a favor for everybody! If Jessel ain't good enough to keep him from hitting him, then he ought not to be a boxer, much less a champion! I tell you this: Dmitra is a dub that Jessel will k.o. sparring with if he ain't careful!"

Seldom Jessel went against Taverel's will but now he rose, his giant form dominating the scene.

"Misto John, with all due respect, suh, Ah think you-all is need-less wrought up 'bout dis. Misto Gold, you is right 'bout de people not likin' exhibitions. I don' like um mahse'f. Tell Misto Kamanos dat Ah won't hu't him an' for him tuh just smash in wid everything he's got. Ah'll carry him along and us'll give de town people a real boxin' treat, if Ah got it in me tuh."

After Gold had left, exuding effusions of admiration and grat-itude, John looked at his giant battler.

"Ace, you're a fool."

Ace grinned cheerfully.

"Yessuh, Misto John. Ah wouldn't do dis anywheah but in mah hometown, but shucks, Misto John, you-all ain't figurin' dat Kamanos man givin' me uh real fight, is you?"

"Anything can happen in a prizefight," said John cryptically, embodying the hard-learned wisdom of a score of ring-years in that sentence.

Still, things seemed to flow smoothly enough and the moment came when Ace Jessel sat in the dressing room of the dingy stadium, waiting for the preliminary bouts to be concluded. He had not trained especially for this match, any more than was his ordinary wont. Ace had always lived cleanly and sensibly and he kept in fighting trim all the time.

He was chatting with John Taverel when an outer door opened suddenly and a man entered.

"Misto Clive!" Ace sprang up grinning. "Misto John, meet Misto—"

Damor raised his hand for silence.

"Ace," he said calmly, "you've been framed like they framed Napoleon at Waterloo!"

"Huh!" Ace gasped—blinked.

John Taverel sprang up.

"How's that? Talk fast!"

"I'll talk as fast as it suits me," the Damor pride showed for an instant. "Listen, this is straight goods. I was lying in one of those bootleg dives that Aaron Gold hangs around, and he was there. I was just half-asleep but I suppose that he and the fellow he was talking to thought I was dead drunk.

"At any rate, he was telling this man, a cheap sort of tinhorn gambler, to plunge all he had on Kamanos and was explaining why.

"Gold told you to go easy on Kamanos, didn't he? Certainly. But Dmitra's going to be in there trying his hardest to put you away. The referee is bought, the timekeeper's bought. Everybody connected is paid off! Kamanos, his manager, all the officials and Gold are in on it and they figure on cleaning up! They've sunk all their money that Kamanos is going to win. Ace, they've framed you to take the title away from you."

Ace sank back, weak and unnerved, half-dazed and completely bewildered.

"But I don't see—" began John Taverel. "What can they expect to gain? This is billed as an exhibition—if Kamanos knocked Ace out with the first punch, that wouldn't give him the title. Nobody would recognize him as champion."

"No? Gold didn't tell you this—there's an act of the legislature against 'prizefighting' in this state, and every fight that's ever been fought here, has been billed as an 'exhibition.' Decisions can't be officially given, but just the same, two titles have changed hands in the state on knockouts—and they were both billed as 'exhibitions.' Gold was right when he said the people were coming here expecting a real fight. They're used to having fights called 'exhibitions.' If the bout is given to Kamanos on a knockout or a foul, his manager will claim the world title for him and the state papers will boost him to the skies. Of course, the boxing commissions and the newspapermen won't recognize the claim, but most of the general public will and the publicity will give Kamanos and his ring a chance to clean up on some real money and force Ace to meet him again."

"To think Ah'd be given dis double cross right in mah hometown," muttered Ace heart-brokenly. "Misto Clive, suh, does all dem people out dere know Ah'm framed?"

"No, Ace, the crowd thinks everything is on the level. The only men in on the deal are those I've mentioned and a few more lowdown gamblers."

"It doesn't make any difference," said Taverel savagely. "I'm calling the whole thing off right now. You're not going to step into that ring."

"Misto John," said Ace, with the unusual stubbornness which had characterized his actions during the whole affair, "we cain't do dis. De people is already out dere, dey's paid dere money an' we cain't disappoint 'em, suh. Besides, dis is my chance to show mah people what so't of a man Ace is."

He fell silent a moment and his eyes began to burn as if from lurid fires lit in his skull behind them.

"Dat Kamanos and his trash plottin' to shame me 'fore mah people!" he roared suddenly, plunging erect, his gigantic body fairly vibrating with battle lust. "Ah'll smash dat man—"

He subsided suddenly and his unusual rage vanished as soon as it came.

"Suhs, Ah ask yo' pahdon. Misto Clive, thank you, suh, fo' tellin' me. Misto John, Ah'll treat dis Kamanos like he treats me. Does he box, Ah boxes. Does he git rough, Ah gits rough. But mah people is expectin' a treat an' Ah ain' gwine knock him out 'less'n Ah has to."

"All right, suit yourself," answered Damor. "But do you know who you're fighting?"

"Name Dmitra Kamanos, says Misto Gold. A Greek, Ah reckon. Neveh heered uh him myse'f."

"That's his name, alright," returned Damor. "But up to a year ago he didn't fight under it. He fought under the name of Battling Hansen. He was, and is, a rough and tough slugger, a terrific hitter and about the dirtiest fighter that ever climbed through the ropes. He got ruled out of so many states for his foul tactics that he dropped his ring name and has been fighting here for the past year under his own name."

"I remember Hansen," said John, "and that makes it even more foolish for Ace to go in with him under wraps and with the referee bought off. This Hansen is likely to knock out anybody that he hits."

"He won't hit me, not in fo' rounds," retorted Ace imperturbably. "An' if he does, he won't hu't me. Misto John, please not to arguh, suh, 'caze mah mind is done made up, and it won't do no good, suh."

So John Taverel cursed and gave it up. After all, despite all the tricks of the trade, it did not seem likely that this Greek could be very dangerous to the champion, even with the referee behind him.

A loud buzz of conversation ran through the crowd, rather than a cheer, as Ace climbed through the ropes and waved his hands and bowed. A certain cold disapproval was manifest and Ace felt it. It froze his ardor. This was the moment of which he had secretly dreamed, like a small boy "showing off," this showing his wares before his townspeople. But now—Ace sighed. At any rate he would do his best.

He glanced icily at his opponent. Dmitra Kamanos was the brute type of fighter. Shorter and more bunchily made than Ace, his chest was matted with black hair and his arms and legs were iron knots of muscle. His face showed that he had been to the wars, what with the flattened nose, the battered eyebrows, and the various marks of hard blows all over his unsightly features. His forehead was low and sloping and his small eyes gleamed wickedly from under heavy, misshapen brows.

To the novice, the Greek must have looked much more formidable than the smiling Ace but the ring-wise took in the long, smoothly flowing muscles of the Negro, the catlike ease of movement and the magnificent spread of the dusky shoulders.

The weights were announced as approximately 230 pounds for Ace and 219 for Kamanos. Moreover Ace had an advantage of some two inches in height.

From the first gong it was apparent as to who was the master. The Greek rushed in bull-like, swinging his formidable arms but compared to the smooth ease of Ace's motions, he seemed slow and clumsy. Ace did not dance and leap about as many boxers do; he glided, moving about the ring like a great leopard, never making a single wasted motion.

His long arms worked in and out with a piston-like regularity, moving in perfect rhythm with the motions of his shifting legs. The audience, cynical or hostile, was struck with the beauty of a perfect physical animal in action, and not a jeer was heard.

And as Ace boxed, John Taverel thought. He took in the ring, noted Kamanos' handlers and his manager, a rat-faced fellow with a perpetual sneer on his pallid lips. He noted that in this small arena there was no electric bell, but that the timekeeper sounded the gong by jerking the cord.

Throughout the first round, Ace kept Kamanos away by perfect boxing, spearing him with his long straight left and clinching cleverly when the Greek bulled too close. At the gong a faint cheer went up from the crowd.

Between rounds John urged Ace to crash in and finish his man but Ace merely grinned and glided out for the second, sparring lightly.

But now Kamanos began his customary tactics. He covered up and worked in close, then fired away with both hands. He butted in the clinches and drove his heels into Ace's insteps. He backheeled, hit in the clinches and on the breakaway. And never even a warning from the referee. More, the Greek proved he could hit by getting through Ace's guard twice with rights that stung.

He was hooted by the crowd as he walked to his corner at the end of the round and it was easy to see that sympathy was swinging to the giant black who had consistently fought clean, refusing to punish his foul opponent and refraining from retaliating in any unfair manner.

John, furious, ordered Ace to flatten his man in this round and Ace, somewhat irritated by the Greek's tactics, agreed to do so.

At the gong, he whirled in his corner and met Kamanos in the ring. A quick straight left sent the Greek back on his heels and drew the first blood of the fight, and a right uppercut to the body made Kamanos grunt and retreat. Ace, who was really too good-natured to show much of the killer instinct, made no attempt to follow up his advantage and the Greek came back with a heavy right swing to the body, and an instant later landed hard with his left to the face.

Ace grinned with pure enjoyment and shook off these blows as if he scarcely felt them. He feinted Kamanos into position and then, ducking a wild right, doubled the Greek up with a right to the body. Kamanos was staggering about the ring under a fusillade of straight lefts which he could not seem to avoid and just as it seemed he was about to go down, Ace suddenly slowed up and stepped back.

Over in the champion's corner, John Taverel was cursing under his breath. That was always Ace's greatest and only real fault as a fighter. That lack of the killing instinct, that kindheartedness which made him ease up on a beaten man.

Kamanos peered up over his crooked arms, grotesquely like a giant frog, and suddenly plunged forward, hitting with both hands. A shout of anger went up from the crowd as he sent his blows dangerously low. One of these stung Ace and, angered for the first time, he threw in a left hook to the chin with all the power of his mighty shoulder behind it.

Kamanos went down, his feet flying off the canvas from the force of his fall—then while everyone rose shouting, he was up again without a count. Truly Kamanos was a tough one! Not many men could boast of rising after having received one of Ace's smashes squarely.

But even while they yelled at the miracle, Ace stopped the charging Greek in his tracks with a left and instantly crashed his right under the heart. Kamanos gasped and crumpled. From his corner went up a shout of "Foul!"

John Taverel clenched his fists; he had expected something like this! The crowd held their breaths, and the writhing Greek, lowering the hands which had involuntarily pressed his ribs, clutched at his abdomen! He too had heard the shouts and remembered the instructions which Ace's blows had jolted out of him for the moment.

The referee stepped forward and leaned over the Greek. The crowd was shrieking for him to count, but he paid no heed. Then suddenly from ringside heaved up a commanding figure: Joe Cameron, dean of sportswriters and the Grand Old Man of journalism.

Taverel had not seen him, had not known he was there. But Cameron had sensed the unfairness of the bout, knew that here was something underhanded and he rose up to see justice done.

"That punch was fair!" he bellowed. "Call it a foul and I'll see that your license is revoked and that you're run out of the country!"

The referee paled; the weight of Joe Cameron's wrath was something to reckon with, and moreover the crowd was yelling bloody murder. He weakened, glanced hesitantly toward Kamanos' corner where the manager and handlers were going insane, and then began to count over the fallen Greek.

John Taverel, in spite of his rage, laughed rather wildly to himself. Truly the old times seemed to have come back with a vengeance and scenes of bygone battles flitted chaotically through his mind—scenes of the bad old bare-knuckle days. Here was the old time setting and action—a framed fight, an old-fashioned arena, a bribed referee, a crazy, threatening crowd, and an intimidation of fight officials; this referee must be indeed a weak-spined soul. Guns and blackjacks had failed to move the old timers.

But now the referee was counting. Something like twenty seconds had already elapsed between the time the Greek had hit the canvas and the time that the referee had begun to count, and now the count was slow—flagrantly slow, while the fallen fighter struggled to rise.

"Eight————nine—"

Now the Greek was up, having been on the canvas something like thirty seconds and Ace was plunging in to finish him. *Zam!* The gong, with the round still forty seconds to go.

Ace snickered in his corner. The whole affair struck him as being rather humorous. He looked about for Clive Damor and finally located him, on the top row of ringside seats, seated next to the timekeeper. Ace noted with satisfaction that Clive showed undoubted efforts at sprucing up his personal appearance at least.

He was clean shaven, had had a recent haircut and his clothes, while still worn and rather ragged, had been cleaned and pressed. Ace smiled with sincere gladness, hardly heeding John Taverel's instructions to flatten the Greek and use only chin punches to do it.

The gong. Ace came out fast and boxing superbly, forced the Greek across the ring, stinging him with jabs to the head and body and avoiding his vicious returns with ease. Fighting along the ropes, Kamanos landed twice with lefts to the face, but Ace came back with a right-hander to the body which made the Greek grunt.

Kamanos was missing repeatedly, completely at sea, and Ace was making no effort to batter him down, being content to box along lazily, piling up a lead the Greek could never hope to overcome save by a knockout.

Then as the crowd began to complain at these tactics, scarcely appreciating cleverness, Ace elected to slug and, toe to toe in the center of the ring, they traded blows in a mix-up that brought every fan in the house to his feet. This was Kamanos' game, but though he landed a number of hard smashes, he was the first to back away.

Ace jabbed at him tantalizingly, swished a light right to the body, and then suddenly Kamanos plunged desperately into close quarters and swung hard and foul. John Taverel shouted as he saw the Greek's right distinctly sink into Ace's groin.

The great Negro gasped and went down with amazing quickness. A man who has been badly fouled always drops suddenly and without preliminary reeling.

The crowd rose as one man, shouting. They were wild and bewildered. Few had seen the blow, fewer were in position to see where it landed. John Taverel made to leap into the ring and then halted, speechless with pure fury as the referee leaped forward and began to count swiftly, paying no attention this time to the bellowing of Joe Cameron.

"Four—five—six—seven—eight—"

And then while John Taverel, clinching his fists until the nails sank deep into the palms of his hands, saw the title slipping away, every light in the building went out! The referee instinctively stopped short in his count and as he did, the gong sounded clear and loud above the confusion.

Taverel, with a sob of relief, groped his way into the ring and as he did the lights came on again. Chaos reigned as he helped Ace to his corner. The referee, the timekeeper, and the crowd were shouting simultaneously and no one knew or cared what anyone else said. Over in Kamanos' corner, the handlers and especially the manager of the Greek were exhibiting sure signs of violent insanity.

Taverel bent over Ace and made a hasty examination.

"Ah ain't hu't much, Misto John. Lemme go back in dah an' Ah'll clean up de ring wid dat fellow dis time."

"Get your man back in here," screamed the referee. "The round wasn't over!"

"I never sounded that gong!" yelled the timekeeper. "Somebody else did! The round lacked twenty seconds of being over!"

John Taverel paid no attention until the referee came charging over to his corner and then he turned on that worthy with such a sinister gleam in his eye that the referee beat a hurried retreat and gave voice to his sentiments from a safe corner of the ring.

Taverel glanced at Ace, decided that the great Negro had suffered no major harm from the foul and with his immense vitality and quickness of recuperation could go in without injury to himself.

Kamanos' manager was shouting that he claimed the bout for his man on a knockout or else a foul when John Taverel spoke quickly and decisively:

"Sound that gong and send Kamanos in or I'll claim the match on a default. You haven't anything to argue on. The gong sounded before Ace was counted out, and how did you know the round wasn't over? The timekeeper couldn't see his watch. You've got your choice—fight or quit and do it now."

The timekeeper hesitated, glanced weakly at the crowd who by now had realized that the blow must have been foul, and were threatening to lynch all concerned, and then gave in.

At the sound of the gong, Kamanos rushed desperately across the ring, trusting all upon a wild effort. It was evident that Ace still felt the effect of that blow for he moved slowly forward and his face was rather drawn. He halted just outside his corner and waited for Kamanos, dangerous as a wounded tiger.

The Greek charged in wide open, swinging wild and furious. Ace dropped into a half crouch and smashed a left to the midriff that could be heard all over the building. Then as the Greek bobbed forward, mouth open and guard dropped, the champion straightened, catapulting a single terrible right to the chin. Kamanos crashed to the canvas face down, out for the evening.

Later Ace sat in his hotel apartment and watched his handlers pack with a certain wistfulness in his gaze. A warm glow pervaded him as he remembered the ovation "his people" had given him at the end of the bout, but something was missing.

"Misto John, why you reckon Misto Clive ain't been 'roun' to see me? Ah ain't seen him since—"

The door opened and Clive Damor came in. He was smiling, though his right hand showed a set of bruised and skinned knuckles.

"Ace, that was a great fight."

"Misto Clive, Ah'm glad you think so. But Ah spect if Ah hadn't been pow'rful lucky 'bout dem lights—"

Clive laughed.

"Luck don't come often that way, Ace, and you have to fight crookedness with crookedness. I anticipated something like that and I had a colored boy planted in the basement and another on the stairs where he could see the fight and still be seen by the one in the basement. He had instructions that if you were floored to give the signal to the other who would then switch off the lights for several seconds. Then, in the dark, I simply reached over and sounded the gong myself."

"Misto Clive," said Ace fervently, "Misto John and Ah is much obliged to you-all. Ah mighta knowed dem crooks couldn't do nothin' to me while Misto Clive wuz about. Ah cain't begin to tell you how Ah appreciates dis—"

"That's all right," Clive smiled, the genial jaunty self that Ace had known and worshipped. "What are you going to do now, Ace?"

"Ah'm leavin' while mah people is still in good nature at me. Gwine back tuh New Yo'k Ah 'spects. But Misto Clive, what you-all gwine to do? Ah don't want to offend you, but if you needs money Misto John will be glad tuh—"

Clive grinned.

"No, not now. I bet all I could beg and borrow—a considerable sum—and I bet it on you. The gamblers knew they had such a cinch that they plunged. I won enough to start me in business in a small way and a start's all I want. I'm through with the old life once and for all, and that's final."

He surveyed his bruised hand and laughed.

"Gold had an idea I had something to do with breaking up his scheme but he couldn't prove anything and now I doubt if he wants to try. My fist and his face found a remarkable affinity.

"No, Ace, you've done more for me now than you'll ever realize. I didn't know how far I had fallen until you brought it home to me so strongly. Nor did I realize how a man could rise above conditions until I reviewed your own life and saw how you had struggled against and conquered the obstacles confronting you. The old life never really appealed to me with its dirt, squalor and filth; I'd simply gotten in a groove and I needed stimulus. You were that stimulus."

"Misto Clive," said Ace sincerely, his eyes shining, "dat makes me gladder dan winnin' de fight; gladder dan when Ah won de title, an' dat's de truth, suh."

The Weeping Willow

"Get out of them bamboo-ribs and climb into the ten-ounces," I order. "I'm the famous Monk Costigan, manager of seven non-champions in my time. I'll see what you got—if anything."

He removes the striking bag gloves and slides into the regular leather, showing very little enthusiasm, but I seem to see a gleam of interest in his melancholy eye.

We square off and he strikes an attitude which was out of fashion when John L. Sullivan was in his cradle. I feint for his body and he exasperates me by bouncing an awkward left off my chin. I jab him severely on the nose and a strange thing happens. His Adam's apple wiggles, a mournful expression steals over his face, and tears begin to trickle!

This lays me out with surprize! I drop my hands—

"I should of told you," said Joe Harper, massaging the back of my neck, "that this sap is the original human waterworks! The moment he crosses gloves he begins to weep."

"Yes," said I, still dizzy, "but what has that got to do with the earthquake?"

"You dropped your guard when he started crying," says Joe patiently, "and he leans on your chin with a right swing and a couple more of the same as you start to fall."

I rise rather uncertainly and gaze on the weeper, who eyes me even more melancholy than ever.

"I can't help it," says he. "I allers weep when I box, especially if somebody hits me on the nose. The very act of hitting a fellow human—and more especially being hit by him—makes me very sad and mournful."

"Then why does you follow the game?" I ask in wonder.

"I like it," says he simply.

"You can't explain or understand him," says Joe indignantly. "He has had four fights only, two of which he loses on decisions, one is a draw, and one he wins on account of the other atrocity knocking hisself out on a ring post. Each time the canvas is ankle deep in tears before the thing is over."

However, I am deeply impressed. The public always pays out their kale to see freaks, and here was one which would make Joe Grim look like a conventional businessman!

So to make a short story shorter, I sign this bird up.

"And what is your name—not that it matters?" I ask.

"Willow," says he. "Ambrose Willow."

I have already figured that he had no chance in his hometown where everyone knew him, so I take him to New York and set him to work in my modest training camp. I will admit that he is far from promising. He is about as slouchy a boxer as I ever saw. He is clever at blocking and in the clinches, but he does it in such a seemingly haphazard manner and gets into weird positions doing it. When he ducks, he seldom avoids the blow cleanly, but lets it glance off the top of his solid bone skull, and his footwork would make a brass monkey weep. He shuffles around flat-footed and ever and anon gets his feet tangled up and falls flat.

He has a fair straight left on account of his long arms, but his right-hand punch is nothing to write home about. I work and work with him and finally he develops a wild right swing which carries considerable kick—but the catch is, how is he going to land a swat that can be seen coming for half a mile?

I take him to some specialists, but none of them can exactly explain about the weeps. They say, as near as I can figure out their lingo, that his tear ducts are abnormal and a slight jar will set them going. Like an ordinary man will water involuntarily at the eyes when hit hard, this bird weeps profusely at a tap or the expectation of one. I tell them this don't explain his mournful attitude and they reply that it does—weeping makes people sad, so when Willow weeps, he becomes sad naturally; instead of weeping because he is melancholy, he is melancholy because he weeps, if you get it—I don't.

Anyway, I keep his proclivities a secret and match him with a fair second-rater by the name of Leary.

The moment Willow climbs into the ring he begins to reek gloom, and when the referee calls them to the center of the ring for instructions, he gazes at Leary with such a morbid stare that Leary goes back to his corner very bewildered and nervous.

At the gong they move to the middle of the ring and Willow's Adam's apple is beginning to bob up and down. They trade lefts to the face and Willow begins to weep soft and low.

The crowd is struck absolutely speechless, and Leary done just what I done before. His jaw drops and so does his hands. And the Weepin' Willow, tears streaming down his gaunt face, sorrowfully lifts a right from the canvas and Leary is out for fifteen minutes.

From then on publicity is no name for it! Willow becomes a box office attraction overnight, and I could have matched him with mighty near anybody in the country—that is, anybody but the champion. And why? Because the managers saw he was a freak which would pack them in like sardines.

Still, I knew Willow and I knew he wasn't no great fighter. He would never be a champion or anything near it, but he would make both him and me considerable kale if he was handled right. He was a drawing card, but the only reason he would ever win a fight from an ordinarily good man was because of his freakishness. And as the fans care very little for a punching bag fighter as a general rule, the idea was not to let him lose too many bouts.

I match him carefully next with a dub whose name I forget, but the dub is so interested watching Willow's eyes that he forgets to duck and takes the count in the first round.

Then I match him with a fairly good boy named Rourke. The Willow bursts into tears as they touch gloves and between rounds he sobs heartbrokenly in his corner. Rourke plies him with straight lefts for four rounds, ever and anon crossing venomously with the right, and Willow does little but jab occasionally and then clinch, and resting his chin on Rourke's shoulder, let his tears trickle down Rourke's spine. Rourke gets wilder and wilder and in the fifth round he blows up entirely and deliberately takes one on the chin.

Following this bout I am dickering with a promoter out on the West Coast who has a string of matches lined up for some fighter who can deliver the goods. I see a long line of mazuma in front of us if I can sign up with this baby, for most of the men in question were worse dubs than my boxer—if possible.

The promoter tells me that another manager is craving to do business with him—Tom Nelson, manager of Sailor Flynn—and he suggests that we fight it out between ourselves.

I am none too eager to match Willow with the Sailor, for Flynn really looks like a comer and has what my man don't—a punch. Howsomever, Steve Brody took a chance they say, so I approach Nelson and find him in much the same mood.

"Nothin' doin'," he squawks. "That dub of yours would make a fool out of Dempsey. He's all wrong, get me. How can a man fight his best with that Adam's apple of his wigglin' in front of him? The mat gets plumb slippery from his weeps and he soaks up the back of his opponents' trunks by cryin' over their shoulders. His sobs would shake the nerves of a brass monkey and his face would give a nervous man the nightmares. He ain't a fighter, he's a blight."

"That bein' the case," says I, "why are you afraid to toss your curse in with him?"

"Because my man is a boxer and not a case for a padded cell," Nelson scowls. "Your dub couldn't whip nobody if he didn't make nervous wrecks out of 'em by his cruel and unusual tactics. He's a ivory skull if they ever was one. I meet him only once and then I tell him a joke to cheer him up, see, and he merely stares at me in his dumb manner. I walk out on him and as I leave, I hear him bust into shrieks of laughter as the point finally comes home to him. The horse-faced dub."

However, in spite of our mutual distrust, the Coast promoter decides that he wants one of our dubs and only one, and that if we don't hustle up and settle one way or another, he will sign up somebody else. So with this incentive, we get together and shortly The Willow and Sailor Flynn clamber into the same ring and the festivities begin.

Nelson has made desperate efforts to get out an injunction restraining The Willow from weeping and, failing in that, sends Flynn out to finish him as quick as he can, before his eccentricities affect the Sailor's sensitive nervous system.

Following instructions, Flynn rushes from his corner at the tap of the gong and lands a torrid left to the face, followed by a mine-sweeping right to the body. Willow fights back gamely, but Flynn is out for the kill and he crashes a left to The Willow's melancholy face which splatters blood and tears over the ringsiders. Another left puts Willow on the canvas, but he is up without a count and bends Flynn up with a left to the body.

Flynn misses with a roundhouse right, but connects with a left and Willow clinches, sobbing on the Sailor's shoulder. This enrages Flynn so that he puts in two wicked short arm smashes to the ribs for which he is warned by the referee. They break and Flynn stabs two rights to the body; Willow misses a wild left and goes down from the effort. He staggers up and Flynn rushes him to the ropes, battering the midsection with both hands. The gong saves The Willow from a certain knockout.

He is some dizzy and we work over him in his corner. His face is streaked with blood besides tears, and altogether he is the most melancholy-looking critter I ever saw. I just happened to think, as I stopped up a cut on his cheekbone, that I'd never seen him laugh or even grin, and suddenly Tom Nelson's tale about his joke come back. A light like a inspiration hits me!

"Listen," says I hurriedly, while the handlers gape at me like I was suddenly gone Non Compass Mentals. "Once they was two Scotchmen named Moses and Abie—"

For the second round The Willow shuffled out into the ring and the crowd noticed that for once he wasn't sobbing. His low brow was corrugated as with deep thought and an expression of abstraction—of philosophical meditation—was on his face.

Flynn, expecting a trick, came out cautiously and jabbed a careful left to the face. Willow brushed it aside impatiently and mechanically returned the blow, slinging a left which missed by a foot.

He acted as if his mind were elsewhere and Flynn, in response to frenzied exhortations from his corner, measured him with a light tap and at the same time set himself for a right swing which would end it. And at that instant the crowd was struck speechless and twenty men passed out in their seats—for The Weepin' Willow opened his mouth and burst into a shriek of laughter!

If you can imagine the Statue of Liberty suddenly doing a song and dance, you can imagine the effect of this melancholy pessimist's sudden cackling mirth.

Flynn stops short, his eyes take on a wild look, and The Willow, having a slight amount of intelligence after all, swings his right from the canvas. His slam helped Flynn to fall, I guess, but I got an idea that the Sailor was out before Willow hit him. Nelson swears his man fainted.

And likely he did, but the explanation was simple. I merely told The Willow a joke between the rounds and the point didn't come to his slow mind till then.

The Right Hook

There was a note of bloodlust in the yelling of the crowd, now. The pack was calling for the kill.

Two men glided about the bloodstained ring. One, the taller, was reeling, his arms making futile motions of defense. The other, a shorter, heavier-built fighter, was crowding his foe, pushing the fight, yet boxing warily. His left leaped to the taller man's face, again and again. The losing man swung wildly. The other ducked and again started a left jab. The taller man's guard shifted mechanically and, as it did, the shorter boxer crashed his right to the face with terrific force. The taller man went down.

The crowd rose as one man, cheering; the punch had landed high but the most ignorant man in the audience could sense the almost incredible driving power behind it.

"Harmer! Harmer!" the yells rose to the flickering ring lights.

But the fallen man was rising, slowly, with the deliberation of movement which bespeaks an addled brain. Now he was up, as the referee opened his mouth to say, "Nine!"

Harmer was rushing in to finish him. He measured his opponent with a left jab, his right started over again—at that instant the reeling, battered fighter swung wildly and blindly with his left. There was no aim, no timing to the blow—it was scarcely more than a gesture—yet it landed squarely on Harmer's jaw, and the stocky one dropped as if struck by a triphammer.

Silence fell like a sudden curtain over the arena. Fans gaped with open mouths as the referee droned out the count. Then, as he raised the victor's arm, they broke into a volley of yells in which acclaim for the winner and hisses for the loser vied for volume. But the loser did not hear. He was still lying prone and senseless on the canvas, just as he had fallen.

Some hours later Steve Harmer sat in his room, chin propped on fist, and brooded. He was not especially worried over his defeat; his last four fights had ended the same way. But the moral taught by these bouts was soaking in on him, and he made his decision. In a way it was hard—it seemed bitterly ironical that he should so ignominiously quit the game into which he had entered with such high hopes.

Nearly five years before, Steve Harmer, then a sailor on a merchant ship, had been discovered by a certain astute manager of fighters. This manager perceived the makings of a champion in Harmer, and for awhile the sailor seemed in a fair way to justify this opinion. While not a large man for a heavyweight, he was remarkably powerful, without being muscle-bound. And he could hit! His left was fair, but his right carried the numbing smash of a piledriver. His manager worked day and night to develop this right to its fullest accuracy. He had the Sailor batter sandbags weighing over two hundred pounds and pummel light air bags for speed. Straight jolts and uppercuts from a right hand had ruined many a good man, but it was with the hook that Harmer got most of his knockouts. Experts agreed that his right hook was perfection itself.

For months Harmer traveled the road of victory, levelling all opposition. Sluggers or clever boxers, they all succumbed to that man-killing right which slipped over or under their guard, or crashed irresistibly through it.

Harmer had fought nineteen fights and had scored nineteen straight knockouts, when the unexpected happened. He developed a paper jaw. No one knows just how such things come about. Usually a man with a weak jaw is born that way. Occasionally they develop, for no known cause, except perhaps the ceaseless battering to which they are subjected.

Harmer looked as if he could take all the punishment in the world, but a chain is only as strong as its weakest link, and his weakest link was that crockery chin.

He did what he could to protect it; at first he tried to smother and crush his opponents with one rush, seeking to smash them down and out before they had time to land. But this will not always work. Then he began to study the art of defense and became a fairly proficient boxer.

But the fans are not much interested in a boxer who spends most of his time in protecting his chin, especially when they remember this same boxer as a rough and tearing slugger who had never given mercy or asked it. So the Sailor's stock fell considerably and he gradually slumped back into the class of the has-beens and nearly-weres.

He was always dangerous, because of that lethal right hand of his, and from time to time he scored knockouts. But any blow, landing on his chin, finished him for the night, and a man had only to stay away from him, watch his right, and wait for the opportunity to land. His boxing was not of the ring-wizard kind, which allows its owner to flit through round after round unscathed—he was bound to be hit sooner or later, and if it was on the button, he was through.

So his case presented itself: a strong, fairly clever man, with as terrific a punch as any fighter ever boasted, with a chin that the lightest hitter could smash for a knockout.

The public is always quick to look for cowardice, but there was no yellow in Steve Harmer's make-up. He was as courageous as they make them, but no amount of courage can overcome such a handicap as he possessed. During his last few months of fighting, he was knocked out three times, between intervals of winning a few fights, and his last four bouts had been four straight knockouts for him.

Steve decided that seven knockouts were enough for any man with reason, and sitting in his room that night, determined to give up the business and retire from the ring.

He had saved some money, and he decided to return to his old hometown, on the Pacific Coast, and go into business. He had many friends there, and another consideration was a pert, black haired little miss toward whom he had been sentimentally inclined before he left the town to go to sea.

Steve went back to his hometown, really a city of some size, and the first thing he noticed, upon stepping off the train, was a huge poster announcing the coming battle between Battling Rourke and Johnny Varelli, the West Coast Pride. Harmer felt a twinge of envy as he gazed at their features depicted on the poster. Scribes were making the same predictions about them that they had made about him a few years before.

Steve sighed, wishing he had either a ruggedness equal to Rourke's or a brand of speed and skill equal to Varelli's, and then went on his way, brooding with some bitterness over his lot.

This feeling was forgotten though, when he found himself face to face with the girl of whom he had often dreamed. Her name was Gloria Murken and she worked in an office, where he came to meet her. If anyone else had usurped his place in her regard during the years he had been away, it was not evident. From the moment they saw each other again, they dropped back into the easy comradeship of the old days.

Talk drifted around to fistic affairs and Gloria spoke of the coming fight between Rourke and Varelli.

"Steve, Johnny will win, won't he? Everyone on the Coast is betting heavily on him."

Steve laughed. A certain individual known as Solly the Rat had talked to him rather indiscreetly, but a man is loath to divulge trade secrets, even to his best girl.

"Like as not," said he. "Nobody knows just how a bout will come out—as a general thing."

"I wish I knew," she murmured, twining her white fingers nervously. "I—I—wish I knew!"

This show of interest surprized Harmer. He sensed that something deep lay behind this involuntary exhibit of emotion.

"If you really need to know," said he. "Don't let it out—but they're building up Rourke for the next champion. The mob likes a slugger and the Eastern gamblers see a chance to clean up on the side. Between me and you, Varelli could outpoint Rourke and make him look like a dub, but this fight is in the bag, and Rourke's framed to win."

The girl went deathly white and sank back in her chair.

"Gloria!" he was at her side, rubbing her hands and working her arms in fear that she was going to faint. "Gloria! What's the matter?"

"My brother!" she whispered faintly. "He works in a bank, you know; he stole ten thousand dollars from the bank and bet it all on Varelli!"

"Good gosh!" Harmer was struck speechless for a moment. "How do you know this, Gloria?"

"I knew something was on his mind and questioned him till I got it out of him. Oh, what shall we do? If he won, he could return the money before it is missed, but if he loses, he will go to jail!"

"Let me think." Harmer sat down, rested his chin on his fist and ruminated, more to himself than to the girl who sat watching him anxiously.

"I haven't got that much money or I'd give it to him. If Varelli don't show up for the bout, the Rourke men will claim the bout by default. Or they'll find a substitute and frame him too. Or they won't need to frame him—nobody on the Coast could stand up to Rourke except Varelli.

"The stakeholders will be in on the deal and will take the kid's money away from him if there's any possible way. He's betting on Rourke to lose. He loses his money if Varelli forfeits the bout or if some substitute for Johnny loses. Rourke's got to be fought by a man who can beat him—"

Harmer's eyes narrowed to smoldering slits. A grim sardonic shadow crossed his face, then he rose abruptly.

"Write a note for me, saying just what I tell you."

The girl looked surprized, then moved toward her typewriter.

"No, not that; use a pen. I want it to be in a woman's handwriting."

The night of the great fight had come. Already the arena was packed to the guards and frenzied fans were being turned away from the gates.

Varelli and his manager, attended by the usual swarm of handlers and hangers-on, entered the arena through the side door and repaired to the dressing rooms. As they strolled down the passageway, a youth sidled up to Varelli and slipped a note in his hand, unseen by his manager.

The boy faded out of the scene and Varelli unfolded the note and read:

I must see you for a few moments before you step into the ring. Come to the vacant locker room at the end of the hall—alone.

A faint, complacent smile crossed Varelli's dark, handsome face. The writing was that of a woman, and he did not doubt but that some unknown admirer had fallen victim to his manly charms. Saying nothing, he refolded the note and placed it in his pocket, sauntering on into his dressing room with his retinue.

He did not mention the matter to his manager, who was prone to be hard-boiled where women were concerned. He walked across the room, opened the door which led into the next room and stepped through it. The action was so natural that, though all eyes were focused on him, no one even thought of accompanying him. All supposed that there was something in that room which the fighter wanted, and that he would return in a moment.

But once in the other room, Varelli locked the door, crossed that room, and went hurriedly down the passageway between the locker rooms. He did not wish for his manager to follow and perhaps break up an interesting conversation. No apprehension entered his mind. Rourke's gang was not noted for any amount of scruples, but he had nothing to fear since he had already sold out to the Eastern slugger and his followers.

He was wondering who this unknown admirer was as he opened the door to the unused locker room. Doubtless some infatuated girl, or some gold digger who was looking for a supper—he stepped inside. The room was empty.

Varelli stared, bewildered, then started to turn. As he did, the world smashed to darkness and the Pride of the West Coast slumped senseless to the floor.

Sailor Harmer looked down meditatively at the unconscious man. It had been even easier than he had contemplated. Varelli had fallen for the false note more completely than he had hoped for; the door had concealed Harmer as the Italian had opened it, then it had been the work of an instant to step silently out and hook his right to Varelli's chin. That right hook! A tougher man than Varelli would have bowed to it.

He removed the note from the Italian's pocket after a short search, then bound and gagged the fallen fighter securely. After this was accomplished, he stepped out into the passageway, locked the door behind him and strolled in the direction of the Varelli dressing rooms which were already a bedlam.

The semifinal bout was over. It had been a fast and bitterly contested draw, which had sharpened the crowd's ardor for the main event. The ringside shouted and the gallery roared. The bout was being delayed for some reason and the fans were gradually going crazy. At last the gong was sounded for silence, and the announcer stepped to the ropes and held up his arms. Silence fell.

"—So your fellow townsman, Sailor Harmer, has agreed to substitute," he finished, before the dazed crowd could understand what he was saying.

Then pandemonium broke out.

"What's that?" "The old stuff!" "Tear down de joint!" "We want Varelli!" "Give us Varelli!"

The gong sounded faintly over the uproar and the announcer, a hard-boiled product of the old school, yelled himself red in the face.

"Lay off all that racket! I said Varelli has disappeared and neither his manager nor anybody else knows where he is. Steve Harmer just happens to be in town and to come along just after Varelli made his exit. He agreed to fight Rourke at a moment's notice.

"Now friends, I know you're disappointed, but you're going to see a good fight. Harmer was born and mostly raised in this city, so you all know him."

"Yeah, we all know 'im," came a sardonic shout. "De champeen high diver uh de Western Coast!"

A roar of laughter swept the building and a volley of cat-calls and piercing jeers rose mockingly. Those jeers penetrated to the room where Harmer sat as his hands were being taped, and they sank into his heart like a saw-edged sword. Verily a prophet gets little honor in his own country. Harmer laughed bitterly and shrugged his shoulders. Jeers had been his lot of late, and at any rate, his townspeople were going to see him fight whether they liked it or not. He reflected that they had trailed along with him—had boasted of him. But when he began to lose fights, it went the other way. Now they jeered him. He sighed and rose.

But there were neither cheers nor jeers as the fighters entered the ring. The bulk of the audience sat stolid and glum, feeling that they had been cheated. They knew the records of both men, and how could their despised towns-fellow hope to compete against the terrible Rourke, whose specialty was knockouts?

The men presented a contrast. Harmer was dark, black haired and dark browed, with glittering grey eyes. There was a sullen and rather sinister expression on his countenance when he fought.

Rourke was blond, on the other hand; one seldom finds a blond who is extraordinarily rugged, but there are exceptions. He looked rough—caveman-like. His coarse hair, light and almost colorless, fell about his low forehead, adding to his ferocious appearance; his features were practically expressionless.

Both were squarely and solidly built, with heavy limbs and muscles like knots of iron. Both were short for heavyweights— unusually so for this day and time. Harmer stood five feet and nine inches and weighed 185 pounds. Rourke was an inch shorter and seven pounds heavier.

As they squared off, the old-timers commented on the remark-able resemblance Rourke bore to the great Sharkey, the battling sailor of other days, and on the shortness of the men. If any man doubts that fighters of today are taller than those of yesterday, a glance at the relative measurements will prove the point.

If Rourke resembled Sharkey in build, he also resembled him in style, for at the first tap of the gong, he rushed in, swinging savagely with both arms.

He was built for taking punishment. No man had ever knocked him off his feet and he was a wicked puncher with either hand. He was not a one punch mankiller—he was a body puncher, primarily, and beat his men down with savage attacks on the ribs and heart. These smashes were terrific and no set of body muscles could long stand up under his battering.

Harmer was no faster than his foe, but he was cleverer and had an advantage in reach, though this counts for little against an in-fighter. He wished savagely that he could step in and trade punches with this wild swinger. Wished that he dared take a chance; could take a smash to land one. He believed that he could even drop Rourke with that right of his; but it could not be. He was confronted by an enormous task—that of staving the Easterner off, avoiding his blows and at the same time piling up enough points to win. He was glad that the bout was scheduled for only ten rounds. He might possibly keep out of Rourke's way for that long—certainly not for fifteen or twenty rounds.

Rourke rushed. Harmer retreated. He partly crouched, holding his guard high. His right arm was bent about his chin, his left shoulder held high. His left hand almost straight out, found Rourke's face and kept the aggressor off-balance. The Sailor's right would not unwind from about that brittle jaw unless he was sure of landing with it.

Now Rourke had one trick of boxing. When his manager had discovered him in an iron foundry in the East, he foresaw that his man would be subject to tons of punishment because of his wide-open way of fighting, and so, with creditable patience, he finally instilled in Rourke's brain the art of riding with a right hand punch.

That was the slugger's one ace of defense. His jaw was hard to hit with a right arm blow.

He crowded Harmer across the ring, neglecting his usual body beating to swing fiercely at his foe's jaw. He knew the Sailor's weakness and wished to make a quick finish. But Harmer sparred at long range, ducking and sidestepping. Again and again Rourke's fists glanced from his right elbow or his left shoulder which barricaded his chin. He left his body rather open in order to trick Rourke into forgetting his chin.

Fighting along the ropes, Rourke glanced a left from the top of Harmer's ducking head and Harmer suddenly let go his right for the first time. It swished through the air in a wicked arc, with all of Harmer's shoulder weight behind it. But Rourke swayed away, taking it over his shoulder, and at the same time crashed a stinging left under Harmer's heart. The Sailor came back with a left hook to the head and then covered up as Rourke plunged in hitting with both hands. They were fighting out of a clinch when the gong sounded.

Between rounds, while Steve's seconds, selected by chance and at random from the hangers-on of the club, massaged his muscles and hissed unheeded advice at him, the Sailor looked out over the crowd. He met few friendly eyes; many familiar faces were there, but all looked glum and sour. They had come to see a fight and were seeing a dancing match. Steve reflected cynically that had the framed bout gone through, they would have gone away contented, thinking that they had just seen the battle of the age. He was fighting a straight fight and the fans were down on him.

The second round opened with Rourke going back to his usual style and crashing in with a heavy body attack. Harmer sighed with relief. He felt that he could take all the Easterner could hand out in that vicinity and as long as Rourke was hitting him in the body, he would be letting his chin alone. But he underrated both the slugger's craft and his hitting ability.

Harmer retreated, bending at the waist and swaying away to rob the blows of most of their force, occasionally countering with a left to the face. Then suddenly Rourke brought up a terrific right uppercut, deadly and unexpected. The Sailor, caught off guard, just managed to draw his head aside, and so narrow was his escape that the edge of the glove cut his cheek as it swished by. Steve drove in a quick left to the body and then clinched.

As they broke, Rourke missed with a left but landed twice with his right to the body. Again his right found Harmer's body, and again. Steve cut his lips with a straight left and a thin flow of blood started, seeming to enrage the Battler. He leaped in, throwing a hammerlike left at Harmer's face. Steve stepped in, swaying to the left; Rourke's glove went over his right shoulder, and he crashed his right to the Battler's heart. Rourke rocked drunkenly—then, even as the audience rose, bellowing, he plunged forward again, hurling Harmer back into the ropes with a torrent of left and right hooks to the body. The gong sounded.

Sitting in his corner, the Sailor brooded. He had learned that even the famous granite man could be hurt by his blows. If only he dared take a chance! If only his chin were not a traitor which would betray him at the first tap! Steve sighed, and seeing the face he had been seeking in the ring side, he nodded. It was young Murken, Gloria's brother, and his face was white, his eyes wide and staring.

The third round. Battling Rourke rushed in with a right to the heart which staggered Harmer and made him backpedal hurriedly. He had been taking too much punishment and was beginning to feel it. Rourke was after him. *Crash, crash, crash!* His gloves shot back and forth like battering rams. Head down, shoulders hunched, body bunched into a compact unit of destruction, Rourke bored in. A volley of left hooks to the face and head failed to stop him and when in desperation Harmer shot over his right, Rourke swayed away, taking it high on the side of his thick skull, robbing the blow of much of its force. Instantly the Battler changed his tactics and began shooting smashes for Harmer's elusive jaw. His plan seemed to be to force Steve into unlooping that protective right, and then to swing for the unguarded chin.

A wild left to the temple sent Harmer into the ropes and, rebounding from them, he ran full tilt into a right which smashed against his jawbone and made him dizzy. Too high, but his weakened nerves were susceptible to jars anywhere on the head. He fell blindly into a clinch, striving to shake off the weakness that threatened to engulf him. Rourke shoved him away and floored him with a right to the body. Harmer crouched there, waiting for "nine," when the gong crashed out the end of the round.

Harmer sat gloomily silent while his handlers worked over him. He was losing about as fast as it is possible for a human to lose. Even if he stayed the limit, Rourke was sure to get the decision with the lead he had stacked up. And he knew that he could not stay the limit. There was an all-gone feeling about him. Rourke's body blows had not seemed so damaging, but their accumulated effect was beginning to become evident. His ribs were sore and bruised and he knew that he had slowed up considerably. He had left himself too open for body punishment, but if he had not done so, Rourke would have reached his chin. It looked hopeless. If only he could land that right.

The fourth round. Rourke came in like a hot blast of savagery. Left, right, he rushed Harmer back across the ring into a neutral corner. His blows were glancing off Steve's arms and shoulders, but suddenly he shifted his attack and sank his left almost to the wrist in the Sailor's body. Harmer gasped, his knees buckled, then he straightened and hooked his left viciously to Rourke's head. But Rourke had learned that he had little to fear from the left. He brushed it aside and smashed his right under the heart. Harmer winced—that blow had landed too many times—his guard involuntarily dropped. And Rourke's long curving left found his chin.

The Sailor dropped like a log. The fans began to put on overcoats and hats. The referee droned:

"—Five—six—seven—"

Harmer was rising sluggishly. That blow had not landed solidly. It glanced, all but missing entirely. Even so, it had sent waves of blackness through his brain.

At "eight" he was up, bent in a defensive crouch. The audience hesitated, then sank back in its seats. The Battler weaved about

Harmer, looking for an opening. He rushed in suddenly, feinting with his left and straightening the Sailor with a sweeping right uppercut which Harmer partly blocked. Rourke's finishing left was cocked, when Harmer with the savagery of desperation, lashed out with a right hook. His arm curved venomously through the air and the glove caromed against Rourke's quickly hunched shoulder with a force that seemed to jar the ring.

The fans gasped; Rourke's left arm dropped to his side, numbed by that terrific blow. Harmer drew back his arm and again shot it over, but this time Rourke ducked and clinched. The referee broke them, and Rourke, most of the numbness already gone from his arm, rushed in, slipped a left jab and crossed his right to the chin. Again Harmer went down.

This time it looked as if he was there to stay. At "five" he had not moved, lying as he was, flat on his back, arms flung out listlessly. At "seven" he felt a glimmering of consciousness, but seemed to be unable to move. Then, all in a flash, a fleeting instant, a voice seemed to say, coldly and without passion:

"If you don't get up, the kid will go to the penitentiary and Gloria will die from the shame."

From what deep, hidden sources of power Harmer drew strength, into what unknown and unexplored caverns of the human brain and soul, he found new energy, the Sailor never knew; nor did they know, who sat spellbound and watched him. But some way, somehow, the man with the brittle chin came into new being and found his feet just as the referee opened his mouth to say: "Ten!"

Rourke, astounded, stepped in and measured the reeling man with a left, then started his right. And at that moment the Sailor struck. Arm bent at the elbow, muscles tensed like iron, the right hook crashed through the air, with the whole weight of Harmer's heavy shoulder behind it, and behind the shoulder the full force of the body swaying at the waist, and the forward drive of the powerful legs. And for the first time that night, Harmer's right hook landed solidly.

Something cracked like a breaking tree branch and Rourke went down, not on his face but flat on his shoulder blades, driven headlong to the canvas by the force of that terrible blow. Not a limb moved as the referee counted.

Harmer reeled back against the ropes and clung there, weak and nauseated. The agony in his hand twisted his face into a staring mask. He had struck his hardest blow and his last. If Rourke rose now, he was done, because, with his knuckles shattered to pieces, he knew he would never strike another blow with that hand. He clung to the ropes with his left hand, his broken right hanging useless. And there was an intolerable torture in his left side.

"—Ten!" The referee waved to the yelling maniacs which were the audience, turned and took Harmer's right arm to lift it.

And as he did, the Sailor pitched on his face without a word.

Later Harmer lay in a bed and took it easy. He found this not hard—what with a pretty little black-haired girl anxious to provide for his every want. The door opened and young Murken breezed in, overflowing with gratitude and hero worship.

"Hey, Steve, Rourke's iron jaw wasn't what it was cracked up to be, was it? Anyway it was cracked up! You broke it in two different places with that last slam! Golly, what a clout! He was out four hours! What round was it that he busted those two ribs of yours?"

"I don't know—the last round, I guess. Just before he dropped me with that left, I think. I felt something give. Everything all right, kid?"

Young Murken flushed, dropping his eyes. Then he met Steve's gaze squarely.

"Yes, thanks to you. I was a fool, Steve! I'm not a crook naturally and you know it! I thought I had a cinch—but it's taught me something. And you can bet I won't act the fool again."

"And now suppose you prove it by running along," said Gloria. "Steve isn't in any condition to listen to your prattle, now."

The boy glanced at Harmer who reddened under his gaze, then laughed.

"Two's company," said he. "All right—I think I heard Steve raving about an engagement ring before he came to—so long!"

55

The Voice of Doom

This is the first, last and only true statement made by myself concerning my sudden and hitherto unexplained retirement from the prize ring, which took place in 1904 following my defeat by Young Slade, October 20th of that year. I have maintained a consistent silence all these years in spite of urgings by friends and misrepresentation by the newspapers. My reasons for breaking this silence at last are sufficient and need no explanation. You old-timers who remember Kid Allison and you newer ring fans who have heard of him—here is the real reason for my retirement at the very height of my fame.

I will not pretend that at my best I was championship caliber. Probably I would never have reached the heights of my profession had I continued in it. But as the old-timers know, I was a fast, tough lad, fairly clever, with as wicked a punch as any middleweight ever carried. I had fought in the smaller clubs all over the country without a loss and my manager was beginning to get offers from the better clubs—the promoters in San Francisco and New York. But he was afraid that I was not ready for the best men of the country. He wanted to "build me up" a little more, and he persuaded me to make that fateful tour of Europe which resulted in my quitting the game for good.

Yet the tour started auspiciously enough. At that time, as now, boxing was at a rather low ebb in Europe. The best British and Continental boxers were in America, drawn hither by the larger purses, and most of my opponents were rather second-class. My manager had counted on this. He wished me to fight under such conditions, so as to accustom myself to fighting before large and varied crowds, yet at the same time, he wanted me to meet men I could beat at first. I met the best men of Europe in the largest arenas and, with one exception, beat them easily. As I have said these "best men" would have been considered very second rate in America. The exception I have mentioned was Young Slade, a tough Irish middleweight and I should have beaten him except for—let me tell the whole story.

On September 20th, 1904, I fought Gunner Hanson, of the British Navy, in the Ring at London. (This Ring as all fight fans know is—or was—England's foremost fight stadium where many of the European titles have been won and lost.)

We were scheduled to fight twenty rounds. In these days of ten and fifteen round bouts, the readers will scarcely appreciate the terrific strain on men who step through twenty or thirty fast and furious rounds of battle. I will not recount the details round by round. It was a bloody, punishing fight. I found the Gunner to be the toughest man I had yet met, though he was not a very hard hitter. In the first few rounds he gave me a bad beating but my superior stamina and hitting powers (the usual advantages American fighters have over men of other races) at last began to tell and from the fourteenth to the nineteenth round he took a battering that amazed even me—I mean I was amazed that a human being could endure it. I floored him repeatedly but he always found power somewhere in him to rise before the referee could say "Ten!"

At the end of the eighteenth round he was as badly a beaten man as I have ever seen. His face was a mask of blood, he had a rib or two broken and he could scarcely lift his arms. Between the rounds I asked the referee to stop it, but he replied that he could not or would not do so until Hanson's seconds threw in the sponge and this the Gunner had forbade them to do.

I was weary myself, and cut and bruised considerably, but compared to the Gunner I was fresh. As we came out for the nineteenth round, I whipped a left to the body and he came back with a left to the face. I shot over a right hook to the side of the head and he went down. He came reeling up at the count of "Nine!" and I clinched with him and hissed: "You fool! You'd better quit before you get killed!"

With a snarl of his crushed lips and an almost insane glare in his bloodshot eyes, he shot back, savagely: "Alive or dead, I'll beat you!"

Angered, and almost nauseated myself from exhaustion, I shoved him away and crashed my right to his jaw with all my power. He shot back into the ropes and toppled headlong through them, falling with a crash to the floor outside the ring, where he was counted out. I reeled back to my corner, feeling as if my arms were made of lead, regretting the violence of that last blow, but glad that nightmarish battle was over.

But more was to come. The British boxer lay where he had fallen and a physician was summoned hastily. To my horror an examination showed that Gunner Hanson was dead! The fall from the ring had killed him, weakened as he was by the preceding battering.

To say I was remorseful and shocked would be putting it lightly. Yet I did not feel like a cold-blooded murderer, nor do I now. I had no intention of killing Hanson; my words spoken just before I struck him were not a threat. I knew men sometimes died from the effect of beatings received in the ring and I was really afraid if Hanson took any more he would go the same way. It seemed more merciful to crash over one terrific blow and end his suffering, than to continue battering at him. I did not know that we were so close to the ropes, or that my blow would drive him through them.

I was arrested and formally charged with the killing of Hanson, of course, but it was a mere technicality. The courts immediately absolved me from all blame, which was only just, for if ever a death was accidental and unintentional, that was.

Still, I was haunted by the remembrance of the Briton's bloody face as he toppled backward from my smash, and for some days went at my training in a half-hearted manner. But this mood eventually wore off and I plunged back into my work with renewed zest. This attitude may seem unduly callous to the readers but we followers of the ring learn to look upon such incidents as unavoidable and, while we regret them, we seldom allow them to ruin our lives.

I was matched next with Young Slade, and if I won this fight—which seemed almost a certainty considering our relative records—I was to be matched with the great Jack (Twin) Sullivan, in New York.

This was, in a way, my greatest chance so far, in that it was a steppingstone to greater things. With the confidence of youth I felt that all I needed was a chance at the first-raters of my profession and even believed that Jack Sullivan himself would fall before me, should we ever face in a ring.

I fought Young Slade in the Ring, October 20th, exactly a month from the date of my fight with Gunner Hanson. As I climbed over the ropes, the full memory of that terrible affair came back with a sudden rush that made me momentarily dizzy and nauseated. My eyes instinctively wandered to the point along the ropes at which he had fallen through them, and my mind's eye visualized that scene again with terrible vividness—again I could see the limp body falling backward, the arms tossing with the motion, the crimsoned face staring blankly upward. A shudder shook my whole frame and then I resolutely put the thoughts out of my mind and turned to face my opponent, who was just then crawling through the ropes—a clean-cut, powerfully built Irish lad, hard as nails but evidently rather awed by my past deeds in the ring.

The fight was brief and ferocious. As I waited in my corner for the gong, a strange nervousness gripped me, that was almost fright. I was not afraid of Young Slade—he scarcely entered into my mind. But I was in a frenzy to get the thing over with—to get out of that bloodstained ring from which Gunner Hanson had fallen to his death.

At the first tap of the gong, I rushed headlong across the ring and felled Young Slade in his own corner with a left hook to the side of the head. He bounced up without a count and sent a hard left to my midriff, followed by a right to the head which hurt. Slade could hit—was in fact the only real hitter I ever faced in Europe. But I was not to be denied. I was tougher and faster, and could hit even harder than he. I rocked him with a blasting right to the heart, and hooked both hands to the head. He reached me with a right hook to the body, but as he did so, I hooked my right to his chin and he went down. This time he took a count of nine and rose slowly and uncertainly. I was on him as he rose and slugged him back across the ring with a volley of left and right hooks to the body. The crowd was roaring but I scarcely heard them. I was fighting as I had never fought before, with a kind of insane fury, like a cornered wildcat fights. I was almost like a man in a trance—a sort of frantic dream—my only thought was to crash Slade down to defeat as quickly as possible. I was like a man fighting against Fate and Time.

I mechanically ducked Slade's wild returns, crashing my reddened gloves into his bloody face and bruised body—then suddenly an intuition told me that we were in the exact part of the ring from which I had knocked Gunner Hanson a month before. A swift side glance affirmed this feeling and a sort of wild and unexplainable frenzy took hold of me. I shot over my right with the desperate strength of a maniac, and Slade crashed into the ropes as Hanson had done. But even as the crowd, sensing a like fatality, rose with clenched hands, Slade instead of falling through them, rebounded from them and my left found his chin and crashed him to his knees.

And at that instant, as I live today I swear that I heard clearly and distinctly, a voice say: *"Alive or dead, I'll beat you!"*

The voice of the dead Gunner Hanson! Even as my crumbling brain realized the horror of this fact, blackness descended on me and I knew no more.

My seconds said that as Slade went to his knees and I stood over him, poised, tensed, ready to strike him down the instant he rose, I suddenly straightened, and flung up my head as if listening; that my face went ashen, my eyes blazed with unnamable horror, and I flung my arms wide like a man with a sudden death wound. And Young Slade, punch drunk and dazed, came reeling up with a blind, desperate and terrible swing that found my chin and dropped me senseless.

But the knockout, severe as it was, was not the thing that shadowed my life and almost made a nervous wreck of me. It was the memory of that voice—the voice of the man whose death I caused—the voice, repeating the words I had heard in the speaker's life, yet intoned with a ghostly, eerie inflection as if whispered across untold and incredible spaces and gulfs of astral being.

After that I could not fight again. The thought of anything connected with the ring set me to shuddering. Since then I have not even seen a prize fight, nor do I intend to. If any reader wishes to call on me, to interview me personally, he will find me a very courteous host but he need not bring up the subject of my last two fights and my retirement for I will very politely change the subject. And if the caller finds a man much older in appearance than he expected to find, let him not be surprized. When I recovered my senses after my first, last and only knockout, my temples were tinged with white.

There is my story. Believe it or disbelieve as you wish. I will not say that Gunner Hanson's ghost came back from the dim realms of death to wreak his vengeance on me. Perhaps I imagined it all; there is no limit to the human imagination or its power over the mind. Maybe the lurking remorse in my conscience, the inherent fear and horror that results from killing a human being even unintentionally, worked on me until it produced an unbalanced condition for the time being, and created hallucinations. I do not know. No one heard the voice but me.

Here, though, is the tale. You may believe it or not, as you wish, but be that as it may, it is my first and last word on the subject. I shall never write or speak a word about it again.

Crowd-Horror

I first saw Slade Costigan in the boxing tent of a travelling carnival. Anyone knows how these things go; every one of these wandering shows has a retinue of wrestlers and boxers, offering money to anyone who can stay so many rounds or so many minutes, fighting or wrestling. As a rule there are men planted in the audience who come forward, giving as their place of habitation some small town nearby. They enter the ring, slug or struggle as the case may be, with a great show of anger and roughness while all the deluded patrons urge them on, thinking they are encouraging home talent—then they lose in such a manner as to leave the matter in doubt enough to drive the crowd into a frenzy and assure a "return match" and a crowded house the following night. Occasionally some real native son gets the start on these fellows and the carnival athlete is forced to really exert himself. However, as an old-timer has said: "There are ways and means," and the native son very, very seldom wins, or even stays the limit.

I sat in the "athletic" tent of the carnival which was performing in the small Nevada town through which I happened to be passing, and grinned at the antics of the spieler who was volubly offering fifty dollars to anyone who could stay four rounds with "Young Firpo, the California Assassin, champion of Los Angeles and the East Indies!" Young Firpo, whose real name was probably Leary, and who was doubtless fighting in fourth-rate clubs when his illustrious namesake was an infant, stood by with a bored but contemptuous expression on his heavy, stolid features. This was an old game with him. He was a huge hairy fellow with the bulging muscles of a weightlifter.

"Now, friends," shouted the spieler, "is they any young man here that wants to risk his life in this here ring? Remember, the management ain't responsible for life or limb! Any man gets in here at his own risk and—"

At that moment the crowd set up a yell: "Costigan! Costigan! Slade's the boy to fight this bird! Get in there, Costigan! Go on, Slade!"

At last a young fellow rose from his seat, and with a rather embarrassed grin on his face, vaulted over the ropes. Young Firpo evinced some interest and from the hawklike manner in which the spieler eyed the newcomer, and from the ovation given him by the crowd, I knew that he was "on the up and up"—a local boy, in other words.

While the usual rigmarole of argument and instructions was gone through with, I wondered just how the carnival men intended saving that fifty dollars in case the boy should happen to be a match for their man. As a general thing, the ring is set close to the back of the tent, with a curtain stretched across the back, behind which are the dressing rooms. A tough local boy is worked up to this curtain in a clinch, his head suddenly pressed against it, and the razorback lurking behind for that purpose sees the bulge in the curtain and instantly smites it with a blackjack. The carnival boxer, feeling the victim go limp, releases him, striking him on the jaw at the same time. To the crowd it looks like a clean knockout. They think the boy received a body blow while fighting in close, and crumpling, was struck again as he fell.

However, in this case the ring was set in the middle of the tent with no curtain near, the dressing rooms being in another part of the tent. I was sure that something crooked would be worked, but I could not figure out just how it would be.

Costigan climbed into the ring after a short trip to the dressing room and was given a wild ovation. He was a finely built lad, about six feet in height, slim waisted and tapering of legs, with remarkably broad shoulders and heavy arms. He was dark of skin with narrow grey eyes and a shock of black hair falling over a broad forehead, and he had the true fighting face—broad across the cheek bones, with thin lips and a firm jaw. Opposed to him Young Firpo looked ponderous and slow; apelike.

Their weights were announced, Costigan 189, Young Firpo 191. The crowd jeered and hissed at the last; anyone could see that the carnival boxer weighed at least 210.

The battle was short, fierce and sensational with a bedlam-like ending.

At the first tap of the gong Costigan came in wide open and Young Firpo met him with a hard left hook to the chin. Costigan staggered, his hands dropped and the carnival boxer swung his right to the jaw. This was really a terrific blow, but strangely enough it did not seem to worry the young fellow as much as the other had. He shook his head and came plunging in again, but as he did so, Young Firpo drew back his deadly left and crashed it once more to the jaw. Costigan dropped face down, like a log. The crowd was frenzied. The referee—the spieler—leaped forward and began counting swiftly; Young Firpo standing directly over the fallen warrior.

At "five" Costigan had not moved—not a muscle twitched. At "seven" he stirred and began making aimless motions, the fighter's instinct seeking to drag him to his feet. At "eight" he reeled to his knees and his reddened, dazed eyes, wandering about, seemed suddenly to fix themselves on Young Firpo standing over him. Instantly they blazed with the fury of the killer. As the spieler opened his mouth to say "Ten!" Costigan came reeling up in a blast of breathtaking ferocity that stunned the crowd and Young Firpo for an instant. That was enough. Before the hairy giant could lift his hands, Costigan's right found his chin and smashed him down on the canvas with a force that shook the whole ring.

The astounded spieler mechanically lifted his hand to begin counting but Costigan, moving like a man in a daze, or one who is walking in his sleep, pushed him away and, stooping, tore the glove from Young Firpo's left hand and, removing something therefrom, held it up to the crowd. It was a heavy iron affair, resembling brass knuckles, and known in the parlance of the ring as a knuckle duster or iron mike. Seeing this I fairly gasped in astonishment. The force with which that iron-laden glove had landed twice on Costigan's jaw should have shattered the bone, and yet he was able to arise within ten seconds and knock his man out!

Now all was bedlam; the spieler tried to snatch the knuckle duster from Costigan's hand and one of the wrestlers, acting as Young Firpo's second, rushed across the ring and struck at the winner. The crowd, sensing the injustice to their favorite, and fired by the unreasoning mob-spirit, came surging into the ring with the avowed intention of "wrecking the blank-blank show!" As I made my way to the nearest exit I saw an infuriated townsman swing up a chair to strike the still unconscious Young Firpo. Costigan sprang forward and caught the blow on his own shoulder, the force of it hurling him to his knees. Then with a breath of relief I was on the outside and walked swiftly away, laughing as I heard the shouted commands of the special officers who were seeking to restore peace and order.

Over a year later I sat at a ringside in a small fight club on the California coast, waiting for the main event of the night. One of the habitués of the club was giving me his opinion of the fighters.

"And wait'll ya see this boy! He'll bowl Battling Harrigan over in a round or two. No boxer, but baby, how he can clout! A glutton for punishment; that's him—"

About this time the boxers entered the ring. One was a stocky blond, the other a tall dark-complexioned youngster. It was Costigan.

He had not improved much on his style since I had last seen him. As before he came tearing out of his corner wide open, hitting with both hands. The fight only lasted two rounds and it was evident from the first blow that it was only a question of time when Costigan should land his knockout blow. Harrigan fought gamely and handed out a good deal of punishment but Costigan shook off his blows as if he did not feel them and in the first minute of the second round, sank his left glove to the wrist in the blond boy's solar plexus. That was enough.

During the fight my old interest in Costigan was renewed. In spite of his senseless wide-open style, I saw that he had the makings of a champion in him. A perfect build, incredible stamina, as terrific a punch as I have ever seen, it was evident that his one failing was an absolute lack of science. I did not attach too much importance to this, as detracting from his merit. Many a boxer stumbles through his ring life and never learns anything simply because of an ignorant or negligent manager.

I went into Costigan's dressing room and accosted him. "My name is Steve Harmer. I saw you fight tonight and I saw you knock-out Young Firpo in a carnival about a year or so ago."

Costigan grinned. An eye was partly closed, his lips were bruised and there were several small cuts on his cheeks, owing the last desperate efforts of Battling Hansen.

"That was some affair, wasn't it? Regular riot! They had to call out the cops. What can I do for you?"

I sat down and looked him over.

"You look fairly intelligent," I spoke bluntly.

He seemed rather surprised, but grinned.

"I've always considered myself fairly so, if anybody in the fight game is—which I doubt sometimes," he added rather bitterly.

"You fought a senseless fight tonight."

"I know it," he answered shortly.

"With your brains and your body," I said slowly, "you should be fighting in the best rings in the country—not second-rate joints like this. Have you ever had your chance?"

"Once in San Francisco against Sailor Sloan. Once in New York against Johnny Varella. I lost the decision each time."

"Just as I figured. Varella was too clever, and Sloan too fast and tough for you to batter with your wild attack, wasn't that the way of it?"

"Yes," he admitted.

"Sure. Now listen, I'm saying this for your own good. As a boxer, you're a false alarm. Wait now, don't get sore. You're the toughest, hardest punching slugger I ever saw, but you don't use your brains.

You start your punches from the floor, leave yourself wide open at all times, forget about footwork and fall for every trick your opponent tries. You're not even a scientific slugger like Dempsey, McGovern and Ketchel—they knew enough to weave and to duck occasionally at least!

You came straight in and trust to luck to land one of your crushers and the only reason you've ever whipped anybody is because you're a freak—a regular steel-jawed iron man. But you'll crumple after awhile under the steady fire of punches, and go around cutting paper dolls. Punch drunk, that'll be you! Just another Joe Grim. You're liable to whip anybody because of your punch, but on the other hand any dub is liable to outpoint you. Look at Battling Harrigan tonight—a regular tramp. You'd have knocked him out with the first punch if you could have hit him. As it was, he beat you to a pulp before you finally landed. And you'll never amount to anything until you learn a little science."

"I know it," he said roughly. "But what of it? And how is it any of your business?"

"Who's your manager?"

"I haven't any. I gave him the bounce a few days ago."

"Listen, Slade," I said as kindly as I could, "I wouldn't be wasting my time on you if you were of the general run of iron men—small-brained sluggers who haven't intelligence enough to learn. But you have plenty of brains; you're educated—better than I am, probably. How you got into the game, I don't know, but I do know you have the heart and the punch of a champion. You can learn the fine points of the trade if you are so inclined. I don't say I can make you a second Griffo—a ring wizard. But I say this: if you'll throw in with me, try your best to learn and apply what I teach you and follow my instructions, I'll make a champion out of you. You're taking tons of unnecessary punishment. You're the next heavy champ if you'll learn to hit scientifically and keep the other fellow from mauling you to shreds while you're closing in on him."

Costigan shrugged his shoulders. I could not tell whether he was impressed or not.

"Alright," he said, rather indifferently. "As you say. I've never been knocked out yet, but this incessant battering is beginning to tell on me already. I'll try your system awhile, at least."

And that was how I came to manage "Iron" Slade Costigan. I liked the boy from the start. He was good natured, though inclined to be moody at times, courteous and modest in his speech. He was of a good family and had a good high school education, but was one of these unfortunate beings who from birth are cursed with a paranoid urge, a restless wandering disposition.

"I failed at everything else," he told me on our way to San Francisco, "and finally drifted into this game—naturally I guess. I'd had several fights in that town where you first saw me, and after the fiasco with Young Firpo I drifted East. The same old tale, though. I could whip the sluggers but the clever fellows were too much for me. I've always been a great drawing card—iron men always are until they crack," he added cynically.

I set to work to make a scientific slugger out of Slade Costigan. I have followed the game for more years than Slade owned in his entire life and I know the tricks of the trade. I dispensed with sparring partners for the time being and alone in my training camp I had him study the tactics of Dempsey, McGovern, Ketchel and Tom Sharkey. I showed him that the most effective trick of the slugger is the weave whereby he avoids his opponent's left jab and gets in under his guard. I had him practice for hours at a time on the light fast inflated-bag for speed—though slowness was not one of his faults—and on the two hundred pound sand bag to learn the secret of the short jolts by which McGovern and Dempsey ruined so many challengers. He learned with an ease which surprized me—I could not understand why he had not learned these things himself, by actual fighting in the ring. I trained him for weeks in this manner and then, to build confidence in himself, matched him with a clever but punchless second-rater in one of the smaller clubs.

The fight was so short that I could tell nothing about it—I could not decide as to whether Costigan had profited by my training or not. He finished his man with the first charge, rushing him into a corner and crashing him down with a left to the chin and an overhand right to the heart. It appeared to me that Costigan simply plunged in with all the old wide-open ferocity. True, he knocked his man out, but the boxer was thrown off guard by the suddenness of the attack and the finishing punch might have been a chance blow. No, it looked to me as if Costigan had fought along his old lines instead of following my carefully coached plan of battle.

So I retired to the training camp again with him, and brought Johnny Hilan for his sparring partner—a good clever light-heavy-weight. I absolutely forbade Costigan to slug Johnny and told them to step in a good, fast, light workout. Business called me to the city for a few days and when I returned, Johnny met me.

"Say," he said, caustically, "I thought you said this bird was nothin' but a wide-open slugger!"

"What about it?"

"Why, say, he's as good a boxer as I am! Or is now, after a few workouts! Look at this eye! He done that with the smoothest left jab I've seen since Jack Root's days. The first couple of days he was kind of wild and clumsy but lately he's been showin' me a real style!"

I was amazed. Had Johnny told me he had seen Tom Heeney do a ballet dance, I could not have been more surprized. I demanded to be shown and to my amazement watched my iron slugger glide about Johnny for four fast rounds, outstepping and outjabbing him, tying him up in the clinches and flashing a defense that showed real genius.

"Slade," I said heartily, "I've been all wrong! I've been trying to make a scientific slugger out of you. Now I'm going to make you the classiest boxer the ring has ever seen! You're a queer fellow, Slade. I never heard of a slugger before who concealed such latent cleverness. I can't understand how you've been such a tramp in the ring. It's absolutely beyond me."

He shook his head in a helpless sort of manner and I was vaguely worried to note that he did not seem at all enthusiastic. "I could always box cleverly in the training quarters," he said, "but the instant I climb into a ring, I seem to be transformed from a boxer into a… tramp." And he laughed sardonically.

"I can understand that," I answered. "The killer instinct is so strong in you that the moment you get your opponent in front of you, you have only one thought—to get to him and smash him as quick as possible—the old tigerish bloodlust. You've never taken up the art of boxing seriously. You haven't been handled right. Learning to box means self-control. You've been thinking like a slugger; you've got to learn to think like a boxer. With that ferocious tiger instinct under control, you'll be a terror."

I imported the cleverest sparring partners I could find and set to work. Costigan took naturally to his work and I was wildly enthusiastic. I believed I had stumbled onto that rarest of all heavy-weights finds—a clever boxer with a killing punch. Could I make a cool crafty boxer out of Slade, I knew that no man in the world could stand against him. Fast, aggressive, too tough to be worried by the few punches that would slip past his guard, with the power of a projectile in each hand, and the speed of light in his feet, he would tower above the general ruck of fighters like a giant above dwarfs. The manager's and fight fan's dream—the superfighter! A Corbett with the ruggedness of Jeffries and the punch of Dempsey!

All these things I imparted to Costigan but he listened silently and his only comment was a despairing, empty and self-mocking laugh that worried me deeply. But I went on with my program.

At last I deemed my man ready to take the first step in the course I had mapped out for him. Accordingly I matched him with one Joe Handler, a tough fighter, fairly clever, with a wicked punch. I impressed upon Costigan that this was his first fine chance; that if he won, it was the first step on the ladder of fame and fortune, the first foot on the trail that was to lead from second-rater to world's champion. I instructed him to box Handler, keep away from him until he saw an opening and then crash in with the short heavy smashes I had taught him. He listened, nodded and said nothing.

The night of the fight came at last and I will not attempt to give the details attendant thereto, up to the time that Costigan climbed into the ring to fight Joe Handler fifteen rounds to a decision—if the fight went that long.

"Remember," was my last urgent command. "Don't take any unnecessary punishment. Be as aggressive as you wish, but don't follow your usual procedure and walk into all the punches he sends out. Feint him out and counter when he leads."

The gong sounded. The crowd thundered. Handler strode out to the center of the ring, hands up, warily; Costigan slid out of his corner in a half crouch, with the smooth catlike tread that was his. I looked and wondered if this could be the same man who had fought Young Firpo and Battling Harrigan.

Handler led with his left but Costigan was out of reach. Again he led and this time Slade stepped inside it and hooked a short left to the body. Handler grunted and went back on his heels and instantly Costigan was on him, raining right and left hooks to body and chin. Somehow Handler blocked them and slipping blindly through the hail of gloves, clinched desperately. The referee broke them and Handler, striking out blindly, connected with a hard left to the face. Costigan stepped back from a wild right—the crowd shouted jeeringly as crowds will, mindlessly—and then to my horror Costigan went out of his mind and charged in blindly and wide open, flailing right and left! My yells were in vain. He drove Handler about the ring with the force of his onslaught, missing most of his punches or landing glancingly. The crowd was up yelling—they liked this of course. What do they care about a fighter, or whether he spends his last days maundering about with a punch-drunk brain?

Handler was so astounded by this metamorphosis that he was unable to work out a plan of defense and just before the gong Costigan floored him with a wild right swing to the side of the head. Back in his corner Slade sat with his head in his hands, paying no attention to my curses and entreaties. For the second round he came out slowly, in a boxing pose, but before the gloves touched, he went to pieces again and reverted to his old style. Handler was so weakened by the punishment he had received in the first round that he was in no shape to withstand Costigan's ferocity, and after missing seven or eight terrific swings, Slade landed a haymaking left to the jaw and Handler went down and out.

Slade sat in his dressing room in silence, his eyes on the floor. I did not berate him for I could sense that he was suffering. I slapped him on the back and said: "Cheer up, kid, better luck next time. After all, this is only the first bout."

He shook his head and let fall his hands in a despairing gesture.

"No, Steve, it'll be the same next time and always. I've been this way ever since I can remember. I'll never be anything but a tramp at the game. It was only by chance that I won—Handler was so surprized at my change of style that he left himself open. Otherwise he'd have beaten me to a pulp when I blew up and started slugging. Oh, I've had this experience before. When I first started fighting it was the same way. I'd come out sparring and dancing and then the crowd—" he shuddered suddenly and clenched his fists until the nails sank into his palms.

"The crowd! They yell and I go insane. I can hear every shout— 'Fight, you yellow tramp!' 'Get off your bicycle!' 'Stand up and fight, curse you!' The force of those thousands of mind-wills beats on me like a material flood. I've seen psychologists. Mass hypnotism, they say it is. I'm like a man in a trance. A part of my brain goes to sleep and all that remains is the wild beast urge to defend myself—to destroy my enemy. The crowd beats down my willpower and mesmerizes me."

"I've heard of such things," I said, "but I never met up with a case like that before. Still I maintain that it can be overcome. You slug naturally. We want to train you until you box naturally and instinctively. And I believe we can do it."

"I doubt it," said Costigan hopelessly. "When I'm alone in the training quarters, I can think and act as I think. But when the thunder of the crowd is beating on my brain, I'm stunned— dazed; only partly aware of what I'm doing."

I went back to the training camp with one object in mind—to drill Costigan until he boxed as naturally as he fought. To implant the science of the game so thoroughly in his reflexes that his trained motions would carry him through even if his brain "went to sleep."

The reporters pounced on Costigan's sensational knock out of Joe Handler and boosted his stock sky-high. They proclaimed him as a second Dempsey, a smashing, tearing mankiller of the West, and laughed over his trick of fooling Handler into thinking that he was a defensive boxer! That showed brains, they said, and scoffed at the idea of such a slugger trying to box anyone. Their enthusiasm was not dampened when they looked into his record and found that he had lost a fifteen-round decision to Sailor Sloan, and ten-round decisions to Johnny Varella and an unknown named Flynn.

Costigan read these things and laughed savagely. It showed him—and me—just what he might be, had he not been cursed with the unexplainable crowd-horror which prevented him from thinking while in the ring.

I was cautious in getting him his next match. He was moving in good fighting circles now and I did not wish to match him with some man who would ruin him, in case he should blow up again. Boxing and fighting, he could whip any man in the world, I felt confident, but slugging he was no match for a clever man, except for the chance of a lucky blow. I finally selected Tommy Hansen, a clever light-heavyweight, but not the possessor of a man-killing punch. The sportswriters were somewhat surprized at my preference, but the crowd who packed the arena was infinitely more so. As before, Costigan began boxing in a lively manner, but almost instantly blew up and began his wild and futile slugging.

The bout was for ten rounds. It went the full limit and Hansen, boxing cleverly, punished Costigan terrifically but because of the iron man's incredible stamina, was unable to stop him or even knock him off his feet. At the end of the slaughter, the referee decided that Costigan had gained a draw, owing to his aggressiveness and the fact that his aimless but terrible swings had twice floored Hansen for counts of nine.

The sportswriters, after they had recovered from their astonishment, trained their heavy artillery on us. They inquired sarcastically as to what kind of a man it was, who, possessing an iron jaw and walking beam arms, was unable to defeat a man fifteen pounds lighter than himself. They wound up with the conclusion that Costigan and his manager were both false alarms and that my man's defeat of Joe Handler was pure luck, which last was true, of course.

As for me, I saw the handwriting on the wall.

"Slade," I said, "my championship dreams have gone glimmering. The crowd has us whipped. I hate to quit after two starts, but I believe the psychologists were right. You've got the crowd horror and we can't break it. You're still a drawing card and might be for three or four years yet. But eventually, if you keep at this game, you're going to be rooming in a padded cell. The human brain isn't built that can stand up to the battering to which yours is subjected in fight after fight. I like you, Slade, and for your own good, I'm asking you to quit. Retire; step out and forget it. You're young yet, and you've saved your money. What you got in your last two fights will set you up in a modest business somewhere, and if you need any more I'll be glad to loan it to you."

Slade grasped my hand and shook it silently.

"Steve, you're a real friend, and you're right. It's bitter, quitting the game like this, but it's the best. My face is already more battered than many an old-timer's, and my brain will be the next. I've seen these punch-drunk wrecks that were once such fighters as I. But I want one more fight. Just one more, and I'll have enough money to go into the kind of business I want. Get me one more bout, Steve."

I argued against it, but finally gave in. Joe Handler and his manager were clamoring for a return match, and as I could get more money for my man there than any other way, I agreed after some misgivings. Handler was a hard man, though Costigan had knocked him out by chance the first start.

I let Slade go about his training as he would. I knew that no matter how much or how little he trained, or in what manner, Costigan was in for a beating and possibly a knockout at the end of a long cruel battering. These iron men of the ring are really pitiful figures. Too wild and erratic to beat a good man, too game to lie down and too tough to be knocked out like an ordinary man, they battle their uphill way through life and find nothing at the end of the terrible trail but poverty and a shadowed mentality.

I let Slade take it easy on his training and though he usually worked faithfully before a bout, I expected that he let things ride a great deal this particular time. One night a few days before the fight he came in and after hesitating awhile, and making several false starts, he said, blushing like a schoolboy: "Steve, I have a girl."

Following my manager's instinct, my first thought was to protest, then I remembered that Slade was practically through with the game, and congratulated him heartily.

"Her name's Gloria," he said. "She dances in some of the higher-class cabarets. She's a beauty. Maybe—maybe—maybe when I get started good in my business I'll ask her to marry me."

And he wandered off daydreaming. I sighed. It was pathetic to me, for I felt in my heart that Slade would fail in his "business" just as he had failed at everything else.

The night of the fight arrived and I stood in Slade's corner—I thought for the last time—murmuring some words of encouragement to him. Across the ring Joe Handler sat, glowering, grimly intent on wiping out the stain on his record.

"I'm glad Gloria isn't here," muttered Slade just as the gong sounded and I silently echoed his words. If the girl cared anything at all for the boy it would be a terrible sight for her to see the beating I knew he was in for.

The first round started. Costigan leaped from his corner in one vain effort to smother Handler and crush him before he could get set. But Handler, while determined on revenge, was taking no chances with the sledges which had knocked him out before. He backpedaled around the ring with Slade in hot chase swinging fiercely and futilely. Handler evaded his efforts, frequently beat him to the punch and threw him off-balance with a stinging left jab, and clinched when necessary. Little damage was done by either that round.

During the minute intermission, I thrust my head between the ropes and spoke a few cheering words to Slade, who grinned at me rather uncertainly, then as I stepped back, I felt someone tug at my coat. I turned to look into the face of a girl who sat in a front row seat. She was a small and slender girl, not much more than a child, with a winsome pretty face, set off by silky blond hair. This hair was cut in a very boyish bob and a round little hat perched jauntily on top, adding to her appearance of piquant youthfulness.

"Mister, Slade is going to win, isn't he?" she asked childishly, her large violet eyes gazing trustfully up at me. "You're Mister Harmer, aren't you?"

"How do I know whether he's going to win or not?" I responded rather irritably, for worrying about the boy had rasped my nerves. "What is it to you?"

"I'm Gloria," she answered nervously. "Hasn't Slade told you about me?"

"My God!" I exclaimed, "what are you doing here?"

She shrank back into her seat. "Don't tell him," she cried. "He told me not to come, but I wanted to see him whip Handler."

"You're more like to see him battered to a bloody pulp," I snarled brutally. "Why can't women stay where they belong? Don't let him see you, whatever you do. He's in for enough suffering as it is, and if he sees you, he'll go all to pieces sure enough."

I instantly regretted my unnecessary roughness. Tears sprang to her soft eyes and she twined her white hands nervously.

"You'd better leave," I said more gently. But she shook her head.

"I'm right behind Slade's corner," she said in a subdued manner. "He can't see me unless he turns right around and he isn't likely to do that, is he? Mister Harmer, please let me stay, I won't scream or anything."

"Alright." I turned back to my fighter who was just getting off his stool to answer the gong. Evidently, in the racket the crowd was making, he had heard nothing of our conversation and was unaware of the girl's presence.

At the beginning of the second round Handler settled down to business. Costigan kept charging and swinging but Handler had evidently solved his style and had little trouble in avoiding those sledgelike smashes that would have spelled defeat had they landed. Handler, himself a wicked puncher, began doing a little punching on his own, jabbing Costigan savagely with the left and before the round was over, Slade was bleeding at the nose. The third was a repetition of the second, with Handler hitting oftener and putting more steam behind his jabs. Once he crossed his right with all his power. It landed squarely but a little high, and the next instant the crowd was on its feet roaring as Handler was swept to the canvas by a glancing left hook.

He took a short count and arose unhurt but wary. He knew that Costigan was dangerous every minute and he knew too that he had the fight won if he could keep away from the slugger's haymakers. Just before the gong Costigan glanced a right off Handler's ribs that hurt and Handler sent Slade back on his heels with a vicious right cross.

The fourth round was fast and furious. Handler worked in close and let Costigan's swings go around his neck while he battered away at the slugger's body, shifting occasionally to the face. Handler had found that Costigan had but one style, and evading his swings was now mechanical and instinctive. The fifth, sixth, seventh and eighth were alike. Costigan missing and receiving terrible punishment. At the end of the seventh, he went down beneath a volley of right hooks to the head, and had to be helped up and shown his corner. I was on the point of throwing in the sponge but Costigan, both eyes partly closed, his nose smashed, and blood gushing from innumerable cuts on his face, stopped me. Oh, he had courage, that lad!

He was floored again in the eighth, this time for a count of nine, and let me tell you, when a man like Costigan stays on the floor for nine seconds it is an index to the hideous punishment he has been receiving. He reeled up, gory and scarcely human in appearance, and Handler rushing in savagely to finish him, ran into a wild right and kissed the canvas himself!

Such incidents as this one show why iron men will always be drawing cards. Nothing appeals to the crowd so much as the sight of a beaten man staggering up and flooring his conqueror. However, Handler cautiously took a count of "Nine" though he could have risen sooner, and got up minus the determination to finish Costigan that round. He changed his tactics, worked in close and gave Slade as severe a body beating as I have ever seen in any ring. At the close of the round, Costigan groped his way to his corner and dropped limply onto his stool, his face a mask of blood.

"How many more rounds?" he muttered.

"Two more, Slade," I answered. "For God's sake, let me throw in the sponge!"

"Take it standing up," he muttered like a man in a dream. "Feeling better already—last out the bout."

It was true that his recuperation was remarkable—more so than in any man I have ever known. He actually charged out for the ninth round with a show of freshness which would have broken some men's heart—and the slaughter re-commenced.

I heard a sound of sobbing and turned to see the girl Gloria. She had left her seat and was leaning against the ring at my side. Her pretty little face was streaked with tears, her foolish little hat all awry.

"Oh, why don't they stop it?" she whimpered. "Isn't there some way that Slade can whip that brute?"

"Yes," I said bitterly, as a man will sometimes pour out his heart. "Handler's leaving scores of openings if Slade could only take advantage of them. If the boy only had some blows besides a long roundhouse swing that a blind man could duck. Slade would win if he could box him!"

To my amazement, her eyes flashed suddenly, she leaped feet first into a seat, and her high shrill voice cut through the din like a knife, "Box him, Slade, *box him!*"

And before my eyes a miracle happened. At the first sound of that voice, Slade stopped short. His head turned as he sought the author of it, and instantly Handler crashed a sledgehammer right to his jaw. Costigan dropped like a log, but as the referee counted over him, he got to his knees and his blood-misted eyes swept the ringside until they rested on the girl who was standing in the seat; and remained riveted there as if he could not credit his senses.

"Slade, oh, Slade!" Her arms were outstretched, and all the pleading and love of a thousand centuries of womanhood trembled in her voice. "Box him, kid, *box him!*"

"Nine!" shouted the referee—Costigan was on his feet. The crowd screamed! I yelled. Handler's manager screeched and turned pale. Handler rushing in to deliver the finishing blow had been met with a snaky left jab that set him back on his heels and brought a flow of blood from his lips! Like a great smooth leopard Costigan was after him, and again and again the left shot to Handler's face while Costigan easily avoided the boxer's wild and bewildered returns. It was an incredible reversal of form! Now it was Handler who staggered and swung clumsily, and Costigan who poured a swift fire of jabs and hooks to head and body. Never before had such a thing happened in any ring. Had Handler had his mind about him, he might have won yet, for Costigan was weakened by his previous punishment, but just as Costigan had beaten him before by a shift from boxer to slugger, so he beat him now by a shift from slugger to boxer. Handler missed repeatedly, went down from a right and arose weakening fast. Back across the ring Slade jabbed his foe, and when Handler, rebounding from the ropes, sought desperately to clinch, Costigan sank his right four times to the midriff at close range. Handler sank to his knees and was counted out crouching and holding dazedly to Costigan's legs.

"For the love of Mike!" exclaimed a dazed reporter to me, as the crowd sat in stunned silence and then broke into bedlam. "What sort of a bird are you managing? You mean to tell me that Costigan deliberately took a beating like that to trick Handler— or what?"

"The psychologists say that the influence of the mob can be counterbalanced by one person, if you think enough of that one person," I answered, only about half-aware of what I was saying. "There's a living proof of that statement!"

And I pointed to the corner of the ring where Costigan had collapsed in the arms of Gloria who was showering him with tears and kisses, absolutely unaware of the yelling crowd or Slade's outraged handlers.

"And about this retirement business you hinted about the other day," the reporter plucked at my sleeve. "What about it? Is Costigan going to retire now?"

"I've changed my mind about that," I answered. "You can announce for Costigan and me, that I'm managing the next heavyweight world champion!"

That fight marked the beginning of a new era for Slade Costigan. How it came to be I do not know, not being a psychologist, but the horror of the crowd was a thing of the past for him, as long as Gloria was at hand to call to him when the old mists began to steal back over his brain. As he himself expressed it, it was as if her voice woke him from a deep sleep and started his drugged brain cells working again. The crowd roared and thundered as of old, but all that my boxer heard now was the beloved voice of Gloria, which outweighed all other influences.

I always had a seat reserved for the girl just behind his corner, and when the going was roughest, her voice kept him steady and keen. Perhaps it was simply his great love for her which made him instinctively follow her directions under all circumstances. Perhaps it was that her nature was stronger than his. Or perhaps it was that like all wandering, paranoid souls, his needed an anchor of some sort and she was that anchor. I do not know. I only know that with the girl in his corner, Slade Costigan was invincible. Oh, I do not mean that she shouted for him to lead with his left, shoot the right or infight! She knew nothing of the art. She called to him, telling him what I told her to tell him, and as a rule her words were absolutely meaningless to herself. But through her they reached Costigan, and when the battle was hardest and it seemed that he would break and lose his boxing sense under the strain, her war-cry of love, "Box him, kid, box him!" would quaver through the roar of the fans and bring her lover back to his right mind—and victory.

Costigan, Gloria and Harmer, his manager; the Unbeatable Triangle, the sportswriters called us, and our onrush for the title will be the talk of fight fans for the next hundred years.

With an anchor for Costigan's peculiar mind, he developed into what I had always visioned him—an irresistible superfighter. It would have been criminal to throw an ordinary man in the ring with him. He was too fast, clever and tough. Clever enough to get through any man's defense, he had the punch to deliver the k.o., which is what so many clever boxers lack. Using the short vicious jolts I had taught him, he lost none of his punching power, and gained infinitely in accuracy and speed. The toughest man could not stand up under his punches, the fastest man could not keep away from him, and though now he was seldom punished, the hardest smashes that slipped by his guard scarcely jarred him.

After he had fully recovered from the beating given him by Handler, I matched him with Tommy Hansen again and the light heavyweight did not last two rounds. Five one-round knockouts followed in a row, all against good men, and then Johnny Varella, who had once beaten Costigan, managed to stay eight rounds before a left under the heart and a right to the chin put him down for the evening.

Costigan was pointed for the title. No doubt of that; once he had found his stride he had come up the heavyweight ladder like a whirlwind and now only three men stood between him and the champion—Ace Banning, the negro marvel, Sailor Sloan and Buffalo Gonzalez, the South American. Any of these men, including Costigan, was touted to beat the champion. The heavyweight class was in a tangle. Banning had had the best of a ten round no decision bout with the champion and Sloan had lost to him on a foul, the rightness of which decision was very questionable. Gonzalez had beaten Sloan in a ten rounder, and Banning had also defeated the Sailor. Talk had been of matching Banning with Gonzalez, but Sloan in a return match had knocked Banning out. I challenged Sloan but he sidestepped the issue by declaring that he had already beaten Costigan—which was true but meant nothing, for at the time that Sloan had beaten Costigan, any good man could have turned the trick. To my continual challenges, the champion had but one answer: he would fight the man who had whipped all other challengers.

So I called his bluff and signed up for three fifteen-round bouts: with Ace Banning in San Francisco, with Sailor Sloan in Boston and with Buffalo Gonzalez in Chicago. All was going fine; I could see the title already in our grasp, then as suddenly as the Unbeatable Triangle had been formed, it was broken.

It was two nights after Costigan had outboxed Ace Banning and knocked out the Brown Ghost of Atlanta in seven rounds. As I came into our training camp, I met Gloria coming out and one glance showed me that bad weather was brewing. Her eyes flashed and she had been crying. Oh, Gloria had a will of her own, for all her childish gentleness, she was something of a little tigress when roused.

"I hate him!" she said, stamping her little foot.

"Who, Gloria?" I asked.

"Slade!"

"Why—" I was completely struck speechless.

"He's a bully and a brute!" she cried, tears starting to her eyes. "Just because I went to a dance with a fellow he don't like, he had to get rough! Look at that bruise on my arm!"

"But, honey," I soothed, "I know Slade didn't intend to hurt you. He wouldn't intentionally do anything like that. He's so strong—"

"He had no business grabbing me!" she sobbed, stamping her foot some more. "I'm through with him—forever and a day! I wouldn't come back to him if he got down on his bended knees! I'm through-h-h!"

And suddenly she threw her arms around my neck like a child, wept briefly on my bosom, jerked away, stamped her foot again—and was gone! And I could see my hopes of a championship fading with her.

I went on into the training quarters. Slade sat at a table, head sunk in his arms.

"Slade," said I, "you're a fool."

He nodded without reply.

"What's come up between you and Gloria, anyway?"

"Oh, I'm a fool as you suggested. There's a fellow been hanging around her—a regular rotter, and I asked her not to go with him.

Or rather, I tactlessly *told* her not to go with him anywhere. Girls are stubborn and I think she wanted to make me jealous. She went to a dance with the fellow tonight and when they came here afterward, I went out of my mind and threw him out after soaking him one for luck. That didn't make much of a hit with her, and we had a regular row—our first. She threw my engagement ring at me and swore she was through.

"My god, Steve, I could feel my whole universe crashing down on me when she said that! Like an awkward fool—or rather like a drowning man clutching at straws, I caught hold of her. I didn't mean anything; it was just a wild instinctive gesture like I used to make in the ring. But I hurt her of course, bruised her arm. She cried and swore that she *was* through with me now—and she means it. She won't come back."

He said this last with such a tone of despairing finality that it went straight to my heart. His fingers opened and the engagement ring he had given the girl fell upon the table. He looked at it and covered his face with his hands. And I stole away when I saw burning tears between his fingers.

I tried to find Gloria but she had left the city. Evidently she meant what she said; and I wondered how it would be with Slade to go into a hard desperate battle without her voice to aid and steady him. I don't believe that I slept an hour from that time until the fight with Sailor Sloan. I had a couple of detective agencies working day and night trying to trace the girl, but Slade said: "No use, Steve; even if you found her, she wouldn't come back."

The night of the bout with Sailor Sloan, Costigan sat in his corner with his head bowed in his hands. The great throng which packed the stadium roared and thundered—like a raging ocean of sound upon which I knew Slade Costigan's anchorless soul was drifting, against which his numbed brain was vainly struggling. Again and again I asked myself the question—would his trained reflexes carry him through or would he crack as he had cracked before?

"Slade," I hissed urgently to him, "you've got to box tonight as you've never boxed before! Remember, this is the fellow who whipped you when you were a beginner and you're out for his blood! He's as good as beaten right now if you'll box him! Remember, he's dangerous. Banning outpointed him easily the first time, then got careless in the return bout and was knocked cold. You're a better man than Banning—a better man than Sloan! But you've got to box, not slug!"

I doubt if he heard me. He threw one despairing glance at the empty seat behind his corner—for the promoter, knowing nothing of the break between Slade and Gloria, had reserved her seat as usual. Then the gong sounded and Slade crashed out of his corner where I had found him. I haven't the heart to tell of that battle. It went fourteen hideous rounds and at last Costigan, after taking punishment that nauseates me and takes the stiffening out of my knees to this day when I think of it, knocked his man out. Sloan himself more of a slugger than a boxer, punched himself out and wore himself down trying to stop the iron tiger, and after beating Costigan to a frightful red smear, crumpled and went down and out.

Both men had to be carried out of the ring and I sat by Slade's side all night while he lay in a semi-conscious state, occasionally muttering brokenly as his bruised and battered brain conjured up red visions. He lay, both eyes closed fast, his nose a crushed ruin, cut and gashed all about the head and face, now and then stirring uneasily as the pain of two broken ribs stabbed him.

"Gloria! Gloria!" he whimpered over and over again, groping out with his hands like a lost child. Again he fought over his fearful battles and his mighty fists clenched until the knuckles showed, and low bestial snarls tore through his battered lips.

Once in his delirium he muttered a sportswriter's parody of Chesterton's lines:

> "I call the muster of iron men
> From camp and ghetto and Barbary den,
> To break, and be broken God knows when,
> And only God knows why!"

Then raising himself painfully on one elbow, his burning unseeing eyes gleaming like slits of flame between the battered lids, he spoke in a low voice as if listening to the murmur of ghosts:

"Joe Grim! Battling Nelson! Mike Boden! Joe Goddard! Iron Slade Costigan!"

I sat listening and my skin crawled with a sort of ghostly horror. It was uncanny to hear the muster of those iron men of days gone by, muttered by the pulped and delirious lips of the grimmest of them all.

Costigan kept his bed for days, and showed the effects of that beating for weeks. Still I could not locate Gloria and I tried only in a half-hearted way. My soul was filled with bitterness and I hated the girl as much as I had liked her before. Simply because of a foolish row, she had deserted her lover and let him take a beating that might shadow the rest of his life.

Then one day to my amazement I came in the training quarters and found Slade punching the light bag.

"My heavens, man," I exclaimed, "you're in no shape to start training, especially if there's no need to!"

"I'm training for my fight with Gonzalez," he answered shortly.

"Gonzalez! You're not going to fight that man, or anyone else."

"Yes, I am. The contract's drawn and you've put up a ten-thousand-dollar forfeit."

"Do you think I care anything about the money?" I asked bitterly, "it's yourself I'm thinking about."

"And it's Gloria I'm thinking about," he muttered, as he continued his aimless hitting at the rebounding bag.

"Forget her!" I snarled. "She's not worth it! A woman who'd desert a boy like she did—"

He shook his head. "It was my fault and I'd give the hand off my wrist to undo what I did. But worthy or not, or no matter whose fault it was, she's in my dreams night and day. I'm like a craft drifting without ballast. I don't know where to turn. The night I fought Sloan, time after time I glanced instinctively to where she would have sat, and each time the sight of that empty seat was a knife in my heart. When the thunder of the crowd beat on my brain like hammers of fire and steel and I could feel myself slipping, I waited in vain for her voice. Somehow I thought she was there after all and through the fight I waited to hear her call. And it was the mute hope of that call that kept me on my feet after the red fogs of blindness and senselessness had closed on me and I could find Sloan among them only by the crash of his fists upon me."

"I know, boy. I knew it at the time, and I sweated pure blood for you. But you can't mean you'll fight Gonzalez! Listen, man, he's never been whipped! He's a giant, a killer, a super-slugger. He's what Sullivan would have been had Sullivan been as large a man as Jeffries. Boxing him, you have a chance; slugging he'll kill you!"

Costigan shrugged his great shoulders.

"I'll fight Gonzalez," he said stubbornly. "I'll fight him whether you have anything to do with it or not. I'll go out in a blaze of glory, at least. Steve, don't say anything more. I'm determined to close my ring career with a battle with Gonzalez and nothing you can do will alter that decision. But I'd like to have you in my corner that night."

Long ago I learned that when a boxer is so determined, it is useless to argue. With much misgivings I went about my preparations for the bout.

There was no need for me to look into the credentials of Buffalo Gonzalez. Once in a hundred years such a man flashes cometlike across the stage. Landing in New York less than fourteen months before, carrying his scanty belongings in a bandanna handkerchief and armed with the high sounding but empty title of heavyweight champion of South America, the Buffalo had soon proved his worth by smashing through all opposition and the record books showed a list of twenty straight knockouts to his credit.

Naturally, the papers worked the coming bout to the skies and much speculation was rife as to its outcome. The records of the two men were combed over and compared and at ringside the betting was practically even, with the odds slightly on Gonzalez. Men who had seen the Sloan fight were wary of placing their money on Costigan. He had knocked Sloan out while Gonzalez merely held a decision over the Sailor, but most experts agreed that Sloan would have won had he not worn himself out and smashed his knuckles on the iron jaw of Costigan. Then a sportswriter, probably to boost the odds on Costigan, came forward with what he termed inside dope; Costigan had fought Sloan on a pre-arranged scheme, had taken that terrible beating simply to throw Gonzalez off his guard! This writer recalled the two fights with Joe Handler and predicted a like shift in tactics. Apparently no one placed much significance on Gloria's absence from Slade's training camp, though some of the papers commented on it in a casual way. I had said nothing of the breakup, and beyond that single remark I made to the reporter the night Slade knocked out Handler the second time, I had said nothing of her remarkable influence on my fighter. Had I done so, I would scarcely have been believed. Sportswriters rattle off a great deal about psychology but few know or believe anything about it.

As for me, I could see only one outcome to the bout.

Gonzalez was as tough and rugged as Slade, and could hit just as hard. More, he was stronger and heavier and as great a natural slugger as I have ever seen. By that I mean that he battled with a certain natural science. Instead of coming straight in, upright and wide open like Costigan, he weaved, circled, fought from a crouch mostly, feinted and ducked. He was far from being a finished boxer, or a boxer at all, it is true. He missed frequently, left innumerable openings and knew nothing of the finer points of infighting and defense. But he was a straight and accurate hitter, remarkably fast on his feet, and thus far his stamina and punching powers had made him invincible. He would not punch himself out as had Sailor Sloan. If Costigan came in open to those sledgehammer smashes, he would be beaten down long before the Buffalo's mighty arms began to weary.

With Slade at his top form, boxing and fighting, I believed even the Buffalo would fall before him; at his old trick of useless swinging, it would be simply a massacre.

I had one hope; that in the first few rounds one or the other would crash over with a swift knockout. But of that there was little chance. The few blows Slade would be liable to land would scarcely be enough to waft Gonzalez—himself an iron man—into dreamland, while Costigan was too tough to be knocked out without incredible battering before the final blow.

Then once again the thunder of the crowd tore at us, the ring lights blazed above and the smell of canvas, resin and sweaty leather filled our nostrils. I helped Costigan through the ropes and watched him as he stood erect and flung off his bathrobe. A fine figure of a man he was; six feet and 190 pounds of lithely-muscled young manhood, with the long smooth sinews rippling along his powerful arms and mighty shoulders. Handsome too, in a sort of fierce tigerish way, despite the disfigurations of his many battles. These were not so bad as one might think, for a true iron man; few blows had left their marks permanently on him and though his nose had been broken many times, it was not altogether shapeless. I thought as I looked at him how self-confident and efficient he must have appeared to the onlookers—but to me he seemed merely pathetic, a bewildered giant laboring under a handicap he could never overcome alone, groping blindly through life and cursed by a chaotic and uncontrollable nature. He shivered as though from a cold wind when the full blast of the crowd smote him, and into his cold grey eyes stole the blank unseeing stare as of old. Again the crowd thundered his name, and again.

Then the clamor changed for another form was entering the ring. Gonzalez! A huge hairy giant he was, with the mightiest chest that had ever been seen in an American ring. His shoulders seemed like iron mountains and his arms were knotted like oaken limbs. Six feet two he stood, and he reminded me slightly of Young Firpo, whom Slade had fought so long ago, but where the carnival boxer had seemed merely bulky and ponderous, the South American gave the impression of dynamic speed and power. Every ounce of his 215-pound body was vibrant with savage energy, and from under thick black brows his small eyes gleamed and sparkled with magnetic fierceness.

The men were called to the center of the ring and given instructions, Slade listening with bowed head, like a great panther gathering himself for the charge. Then they stepped to their corners, the seconds and handlers left the ring, and as I climbed through the ropes I hesitated for a last word:

"Slade, for God's sake let me throw in the sponge if the going gets too rough."

His hand gripped mine and I felt the grasp of his iron fingers through the glove on his fist.

"No, Steve, let me go out like I've lived. The game's not worth the candle. My world's crashed about me and I guess I've been out of place all my life. Tell Gloria I still loved her to the last. The gong! Now let's see how long the greatest iron man can last against the greatest slugger!"

And like a huge leaping tiger he was out of his corner, leaving me speechless with horror, for I read in his last words a determination to die there in the ring! Oh, don't laugh at the idea of a man dying under a hail of leather gloves. It has happened before, and if there ever was a man in the world who was built for the destruction of—and intent upon the slaughter of—his opponents in the ring, it was Buffalo Gonzalez. It was said of him that he had knocked bulls off their feet with a blow of his fist, and certainly a squarely landed smash of his right would have caved in the skull of many an ordinary man. Consider, then, the prospects of standing up under a blast of those terrible blows—of running full into them again and again, as was bound to be the case of Slade Costigan.

No, I knew that unless Costigan should by some miracle be knocked out quick by one blow, that he would be carried senseless from the ring as he was the night he fought Sloan, and that this time he would never come to. Even his rugged nature sapped by the punishment of a few months ago, he could not survive such a beating as it was in Gonzalez to give him.

Over the stadium a hush fell—a sudden, brief, breathless silence, as the tiger and the buffalo met in the center of the ring. Costigan came very close to winning by a knockout in the very first exchange. Rushing in like the charge of a whirlwind, he landed first—a triphammer left to the jaw and a blasting right that dashed Gonzalez to his knees for his first trip to the canvas. The right was high; had it been a little lower I do not believe that even the Buffalo could have risen. As it was, he bounced up without a count, hurt but furious, and roaring like a wounded bull, he staggered Slade with a crashing left to the jaw. He missed a ferocious right but ducked Slade's return and landed again— under the heart with his right.

"My God," a reporter screamed at me, "has Costigan gone crazy? What does he mean trading punches with Gonzalez?"

I did not answer. How could I tell him that the boy was not only following his mazed and stunned instinct, but was also bent on his own destruction? How could I tell him of the thoughts which prompted Slade's despair—his girl gone, and with her all his hopes and ambitions? But I understood how the boy felt, crazed with the shattering of his hopes and haunted by the ghosts of all of his failures. Life meant nothing more to him and he was willing to lay it down here in the ring.

Again Gonzalez landed hard under the heart and again. He was weaving and ducking and Slade's savage smashes were glancing off his ponderous shoulders. The South American was confident in the power of his own punches and he was wild with rage and humiliation. For the first time in his life, he had felt the feel of canvas under his knees! I sighed. That incident showed me that Slade carried power enough in his fists to knock even Gonzalez out, if he could land often enough. But the man never lived who could flatten the Buffalo with one or two punches and the infrequent smashes which Slade was likely to land would not turn the trick. Costigan was being outslugged by the better slugger.

Slade whipped a ferocious left from his knees but Gonzalez blocked it and smashed his right to Costigan's mouth, bringing an instant flow of blood. A second swing—a left, hung Slade over the ropes but he came back fighting. The crowd was crazy now. Smash, smash, smash! Gonzalez' straight rights battered at Costigan's body and his long looping left hooks found Slade's temple repeatedly while the lighter man's swings glanced from the ducking Latin's arms or the top of his skull, or missed him altogether.

A right hook caught Slade off-balance and hurled him to the floor. He was up without a count and as he rose they traded crashing rights to the body. Slade was staggered but Gonzalez grunted and halted an instant in his rush. Instantly Costigan swung wildly and fiercely and by pure luck landed under the heart with his sledgehammer right. Gonzalez gasped and bent double and another minesweeping right straightened him and flung him into the ropes where he clung, dazed. Then and there Costigan should have won the fight but with the South American reeling helplessly before him, he missed swing after swing and recovering with his usual alacrity, Gonzalez lurched off the ropes and smashed Costigan to the canvas with a long overhand right. The gong sounded. We lifted Costigan to his feet and helped him back to his corner.

His handler babbled wildly: "Boy, he's fightin' wide open! You nearly got 'im that first rush! If you can duck them slams, he's yours. Why'nt ya box 'im a little?"

"Shut up!" I snarled. "The boy don't even know what you're saying!"

Slade sat, lolling back on the ropes, his eyes vacant. "Something in his left glove," he muttered. "Get him the next round though."

I knew that there was nothing in Gonzalez' gloves but his own iron fists for I had personally watched the taping of his hands and the putting on of the gloves. Costigan, practically out on his feet, thought that he was fighting Young Firpo back in the carnival tent. His seconds worked over him and he was able to answer the gong— his body and nerves responded as freshly as ever but in his eyes still flamed that blank glare that the roaring of the throng induced.

As I had thought would be the case, Gonzalez came out more cautiously. He ducked Costigan's first three or four swings, clinched and pounded Slade's body with a clublike left. As the referee broke them, Gonzalez struck and missed, was warned by the referee and answered the warning with a fierce scowl. He shot a straight left to Slade's face and as the lighter man went back on his heels, the South American, bunching himself into a compact unit of destruction, crashed through and sank his right to the wrist in Slade's body.

Not even an iron man could stand up under such a blow. Costigan dropped as if he had been shot. Somehow he managed to reel up at "Eight," and again Gonzalez dropped him, this time with a right to the face.

"One! Two! Three! Four! Five!"

Costigan was struggling to rise; the blood that trickled from his battered features reddened the canvas. The crowd was chanting in unison to the count of the referee. I reached for the sponge. Then suddenly, at my very elbow sounded a cry which halted me short.

"Box him, kid, oh box him, *box him!*"

Gloria! I whirled. She stood at my side, the foolish little hat perched high on her blonde head; one hand clutched at a rope, the other reached out in mute appeal toward the battered and gory fighter who was slowly rising in the center of the ring.

"Seven!"

At the first sound of her voice, Costigan's head had whipped about toward his corner. His eyes flared and he shook his head violently as if to clear his brain. He raked a glove across his eyes to wipe away the blood, and into those eyes, as their gaze fell on the tear-stained face of the girl, came a sudden blaze of light. The blank stare vanished; in its place gleamed a sane and self- confident expression. A sob of grateful relief burst from me.

"Nine!"

Costigan rose with a rather uncertain motion; his legs trembled, showing that the punishment he had received had taken its toll. Gonzalez came in warily, expecting the usual savage and aimless charge. But Costigan, with a catlike movement, ducked between the Buffalo's great arms and clinched, cinching the South American up so that he was helpless in spite of his superior strength. The crowd bellowed; Gonzalez swore. The referee broke them but before Gonzalez could strike, Costigan had again clinched. The crowd shouted its disapproval but Costigan gave no heed. Every moment was precious to him now, for with each passing second the strength was flowing back into his veins.

He would not run from any man, even in the direst extremity, but he could clinch and stall, and clinch he did until the crowd was frenzied, Gonzalez was wild and trembling with fury, and the referee was weary from tearing them apart. The South American was all at sea. He had been warned to expect the sudden change of Costigan from slugger to boxer or vice versa, but the actual occurrence of it bewildered him. He knew nothing of the finer arts of defense and he failed to land one solid blow the rest of the round, while Costigan did not attempt to hit him, simply slipping in and clinching, holding on and resting, while he got his strength back. The gong! And I knew Gonzalez' best chance of victory was gone, barring an accident.

Slade did not need to be helped to his corner this time and as he sat down on his stool, Gloria climbed through the ropes and fell into his arms. The handlers cursed and caught at her shoulder but I interposed, roughly I fear, for my emotions were stirred. The Irish are all inclined to be sentimental.

"Let her alone, you fool! She'll do the lad more good than all the handlers and seconds in the world!"

"Slade, Slade!" Gloria was sobbing. "I'm a selfish, damn' fool! I had to come back to you, Slade—do you still love me?"

His battered lips curled in a gentle smile. "Gloria, darling, you know I'll always love you."

"I couldn't stay away," she was crying and laughing at the same time, while the crowd looked on, struck speechless with amazement. "I had to come back!"

"Seconds out!"

I sprang up and gently disengaging the girl's clinging arms, I helped her through the ropes and turned for a single swift word:

"Is it alright, kid?"

"Alright, Steve," he grinned. "Watch this for a boxing lesson! I could whip a ringful of buffaloes now—"

The gong! Costigan roared and charged. Slade rushed to meet him, not with the senseless, wide-open plunge of the slugger, but the smooth studied charge of the perfect aggressive boxer. The Buffalo's left swing went wide and as the body, following through, caromed against Costigan's hunched shoulder, the other whipped a quick left to his solar plexus and brought the right up to the chin. Gonzalez swung savagely with both hands, then striking his stride, began to smash away with straight hammering blows for the head and body. But Costigan weaved, blocked and ducked, never giving back very much, but slipping inside the straight smashes and ducking the swings. He was too busy defending himself to retaliate for the time being, but suddenly he crashed a straight right inside Gonzalez' wide left hook and the South American grunted and went back on his heels, and a trickle of blood started from his lips. Costigan was on him before he could regain his balance and beat him back across the ring with a whirlwind of short jolting hooks to the body. At the ropes Gonzalez made a fierce rally and staggered Slade with a hard overhand right to the head but the youngster shoved him away and kept him at bay with a flashing left jab which soon had the Buffalo bleeding copiously at the nose. The gong found them fighting out of a clinch.

Costigan went out for the fourth round as fresh as he had first entered the ring. But Gonzalez was a grim and desperate fighter. Seeing victory fading before the snakelike jabs of the rejuvenated boxer who faced him, he came out to kill or be killed. His first charge was like the blast of a wind from Hell and Slade with all his renewed skill could not wholly evade it. Back across the ring he was hurled in a whirlwind of cannonball smashes that would have destroyed any but he. With his ribs pounded black and blue and a deep gash opened on his cheek bone, Costigan felt the ropes at his back and gave up boxing for the moment. As I saw him burst into a ferocious rally of slugging, I thought for an instant he had gone wild, and Gloria did also, for she shrieked at him.

But Slade knew what he was doing. A human tiger had him pinned on the ropes where his skill was useless and he must fight him off as best he could or go down to swift defeat. He went into terrific action, letting go his punches with all his power for the first time since Gloria had called him, staking all on his toughness and punch. But he was not slugging wildly as of old; chin low on his chest, body bunched into a defensive crouch, he slashed away with short terrific hooks and straight jolts. He was taking plenty of punishment but he was handing it out, too! Gonzalez had forgotten everything but his desire to smash his foe, and already his face was a red mask and his breath was coming shorter. The terrible swings he was missing were wearing him down almost as much as Slade's body punches. *Crash, crash, crash, crash!* At close range the mighty blows thundered on each other and then Gonzalez reeled back from his prey under the impetus of a sledgehammer right to the jaw, and Slade bounded from the ropes. Yet even as he did, Gonzalez reeled back and crashed a terrible overhand right through the air. The return was as sudden and unexpected as the stroke of a cobra. Costigan ducked but he was not quite quick enough. No man would have been! He took it square on the temple and went down on his face as though the force of the blow would drive him through the boards. The referee sprang forward and began to count, while Gonzalez lurched into a neutral corner, almost in as bad a way as the man he had just floored. Gloria began to cry but I felt no doubt at all in my mind. I knew Slade Costigan would be on his feet before the last count. And he was. He was shaken and dizzy but he grinned through the crimson gargoyle mask that was his face and met Gonzalez' rush with a straight left and a clinch. The South American had staked all on that first rush and had about fought himself out.

The gong found them leaning against each other, shoulder to shoulder and slugging with slow mechanical motions like clockwork automatons.

"My God," ejaculated a frenzied reporter at my elbow. "That round will go down in history! Didja see it? Fought themselves clean cut and were still on their feet at the gong! I don't see how one or the other didn't go! Isn't there any limit to the surprizes this Costigan will spring? He goes on swinging like a barroom tramp, then flashes a brand of boxing that equals Corbett and Tunney's best efforts, then he slugs again, but in an altogether different manner!"

Costigan was fast regaining his wind and strength under his seconds' care and he grinned at me when I shouted advice at him.

"Box him if you can! If you can't keep away from him, slug him like you did this round! Maybe your short straight smashes will beat him at his own game, but keep away from him if you can."

The fifth round! Gonzalez lurched up off his stool and came to the center of the ring with dragging steps and stiffly moving legs. Only his wild beast courage kept him on his feet, but he was still dangerous. He rushed like a great unwieldy monster, his great fist moving in swift arcs, his partly closed eyes glaring furiously. He could not understand this man who stood before him, who evaded his best efforts and who continued to rise after blows that would have killed an ordinary man. The punishment and the pace were telling on the Buffalo more than on Costigan.

Slade glided in and hooked both hands to the head, taking a wild left swing on the top of the skull. Gonzalez plunged after him, but ghostlike Slade sidestepped and shot a left hook to the temple as the South American missed. Gonzalez came back with a hard left to the ribs but Costigan paid him with a flurry of left jabs to the face and a hard right under the heart.

The buffalo swung wildly, missed a straight right and for the first time he was being hit without a return. With a last dying effort he reeled back in a semblance of his old ferocity, rushed Costigan back across the ring and sank in a right to the body that hurt the iron man. Slade hooked a left to the chin and a terrific right under the heart, and the swart giant's knees began to buckle. He swung uselessly—little more than a gesture it was—and a blasting right to the chin dropped him to his knees whence he slid to his back on the canvas.

Costigan went swiftly to the furthest corner, and I saw his knees tremble as he stood there. What a battle that had been! Now as the referee counted, Gonzalez turned and blindly staggered to his feet, where he stood with his trembling legs braced wide apart, his great shaggy head bowed upon his mighty chest, scarcely able to lift his hands, out on his feet, but still impelled by that ferocious courage, that wild beast instinct of battle.

Costigan slid out of his corner and approached the South American, rather uncertainly. A single blow would decide the battle but Slade wished to be spared toppling the helpless man over. He turned, spoke to the referee, and that official hesitated and then waved Gonzalez toward his corner. But the South American did not see the gesture, for as the referee raised Slade's right hand, Gonzalez pitched forward on his face and lay still, completely out.

Slade sank into his own corner, unable to climb out of the ring, and there Gloria squirmed into his arms and wept and laughed and kissed him.

"I saw the pictures of your fight with Sloan, in Boston the other night, and I hadn't realized until then how much you needed me! Oh, Slade, I thought I'd die! Kiss me, Slade, I'll never, never leave you again as long as we both live!"

Iron Men

Chapter .1.
"Like A Barroom Brawler—"

A cannonball for a left and a thunderbolt for a right! A granite jaw and a chill steel body! The ferocity of a tiger and the greatest fighting heart that ever beat in an iron-ribbed breast! That was Mike Brennon, heavyweight contender in the year 19--.

Long before the sportswriters ever heard the name of Brennon, I sat in the "athletic tent" of a carnival performing in a small Nevada town, and grinned at the antics of the barker who was volubly offering fifty dollars to anyone who could stay four rounds with "Young Firpo, the California Assassin, champeen of Los Angeles and the East Indies!" Young Firpo, whose real name was doubtless Leary and who was probably fighting in fourth-rate clubs before his illustrious namesake was ever heard of, stood by with a bored but contemptuous expression on his heavy features. This was an old game to him. He was a vast hairy fellow with the bulging muscles of a weightlifter.

"Now, friends," shouted the spieler, "is they any young man here what wants to risk his life in this here ring? Remember! The management ain't responsible for life or limb! But if anybody'll git in here at his own risk—"

I saw a rough-looking fellow start up—one of the usual "plants," of course—secretly connected with the show—but at that moment the crowd set up a yell: "Brennon! Brennon! Go on, Mike!"

At last a young fellow rose from his seat and with an embarrassed grin, vaulted over the ropes. The "plant" hesitated, Young Firpo evinced some interest, and from the hawklike manner in which the barker eyed the newcomer, and from the roar of the crowd, I knew that he was on the "up and up"—a local boy, in other words.

"You a professional boxer?" asked the barker.

"I've fought some here and in other places," answered Brennon, "but you said you barred no one."

"We don't," grunted the showman, noting the difference in the sizes of the fighters.

While the usual rigmarole of argument was gone through with, I wondered how the carnival men intended saving their money in case the boy happened to be too good for their man. The ring was set in the middle of the tent, the dressing rooms in another part. There was no curtain across the back of the ring where the local fighter could be pressed to receive the blackjack blow from the confederate behind the curtain.

Brennon, after a short trip to the dressing room, climbed into the ring and was given a wild ovation. He was a finely built lad, six feet one in height, slim waisted and tapering limbed, with remarkably broad shoulders and heavy arms. Dark, with narrow grey eyes and a shock of black hair falling over a low, broad forehead, his was the true fighting face—broad across the cheekbones, with thin lips and a firm jaw. His long smooth muscles rippled as he moved with the ease of a huge tiger. Opposed to him Young Firpo looked sluggish—apelike.

Their weights were announced, Brennon, 189, Young Firpo, 191. The crowd hissed; anyone could see that the carnival boxer weighed at least 210.

The battle was short, fierce and sensational with a bedlam-like ending. At the gong Brennon sprang from his corner and came in wide open like a barroom brawler. Young Firpo met him with a hard left hook to the chin, stopping him in his tracks. Brennon staggered and the carnival boxer swung his right flush to the jaw—a terrific blow, which strangely enough, did not seem to worry Brennon as had the other. He shook his head and plunged in again, but as he did so, his foe drew back the deadly left and crashed it once more to his jaw. Brennon dropped like a log, face first. The crowd was frenzied. The referee—the barker—began counting swiftly; Young Firpo standing directly over the fallen warrior.

At "Five!" Brennon had not twitched. At "Seven!" he stirred and began making aimless motions. At "Eight!" he reeled to his knees and his reddened, dazed eyes fixed themselves on his conqueror. Instantly they blazed with the fury of the killer. As the spieler opened his mouth to say "Ten!" Brennon reeled up in a blast of breathtaking ferocity that stunned the crowd.

Young Firpo too, seemed stunned. Face whitening, he began a hurried retreat. But Brennon was after him like a blood-crazed tiger and before he could lift his hands, Brennon's wide-looping left smashed under his heart and a sweeping right found his chin, crashing him face down on the canvas with a force that shook the whole ring.

The astounded barker mechanically began counting, but Brennon, moving like a man in a trance, pushed him away and, stooping, tore the glove from Young Firpo's limp left hand and, removing something therefrom, held it up to the crowd. It was a heavy iron affair, resembling brass knuckles, and known in the parlance of the ring as a knuckle duster. I gasped. No wonder Young Firpo had been unnerved when his victim rose! That iron-laden glove crashing twice against Brennon's jaw should have shattered the bone, yet he had been able to rise within ten seconds and finish his man with two blows!

Now all was bedlam. The spieler tried to snatch the knuckle duster from Brennon and one of Young Firpo's seconds rushed across the ring and struck at the winner. The crowd, sensing injustice to their favorite, surged into the ring with the avowed intention of "wrecking the blank-blank show!" As I made my way to the nearest exit I saw an infuriated townsman swing up a chair to strike the still prostrate Young Firpo. Brennon sprang forward and caught the blow on his own shoulder, going to his knees under it; then I was outside and as I walked away laughing, I still heard the turmoil and the shouts of the policemen.

Over a year later I saw Brennon fight again, this time in a small fight club on the West Coast. His opponent was a second-rater named Mulcahy. During the fight my old interest in Brennon was renewed. With incredible stamina, as terrific a punch as I ever saw, it was evident his one failing was an absolute lack of science. Mulcahy, though strong and tough, was a mere dub, yet he clearly outboxed Brennon for nearly two rounds, and hit him with everything he had, though his best blows did not even make the dark-browed lad wince. With the second round half a minute to go, one of Brennon's sweeping swings landed and the fight was over.

I thought to myself: that lad looks like a champion but he fights like a longshoreman; but I won't attach too much importance to that. Many a fighter stumbles through life and never learns anything simply because of an ignorant or negligent manager.

I went to Brennon's dressing room and accosted him. "My name is Steve Amber. I've seen you fight a couple of times—"

"I've heard of you," he answered without enthusiasm. "What do you want?"

Overlooking his abrupt manner I asked: "Who's your manager?"

"I haven't any."

"How would you like for me to manage you?"

"I'd as soon have you as anybody," he answered shortly, "but this was my last fight. I'm through. I'm sick of flattening dubs in fourth-rate joints."

"Tie up with me and maybe I'll get you better matches."

"No use. I had my chance twice. Once against Sailor Slade; once against Johnny Varella. I flopped. No, don't start to argue. I don't want to talk to you—or to anybody. I'm through and I want to go to bed."

"Suit yourself," I answered. "I never coax—but here's my card. If you change your mind, look me up."

Weeks stretched into months. But Mike Brennon was not a man one could forget easily. When I dreamed, as all fight fans and fighters' managers dream, of a superfighter, the form of Mike Brennon rose unbidden—a dark, brooding figure, charged with the abysmal fighting fury of the primitive.

Then one day Brennon came to me—not in a daydream but in the flesh. He stood in the office of my training camp, his crumpled hat in his hand, an eager grin on his dark face—a very different man from the morose and moody youth to whom I had talked before.

"Mr. Amber," he said directly. "If you still want me, I'd like to have you manage me."

"That's fine," I answered and he broke in:

"Can you get me a fight right away? I need money bad."

"Not so fast," I said. "I can advance you some money if you're in debt—"

He made an impatient gesture. "It's not that—can you get me a fight this week?"

"Are you in trim? How long since you've been in the ring?"

"Not since you saw me last; but I always stay in shape."

I took Brennon to my open-air ring where Spike Ganlon, a clever middleweight, was working out, and instructed them to step for four fast rounds. Brennon was eager enough and I was astonished to see him put up a very fair sort of boxing against the shifty Ganlon. True, he was far out-stepped and out-classed but that was to be expected—Ganlon being a rather prominent figure in the fistic world. But I did not like the way Mike sent in his punches. They lacked the old triphammer force and he was slower than I had remembered him to be.

However, when I had him slug the heavy bag he flashed his old form and nearly tore the bag loose from its moorings and I decided that he had been pulling his punches against Ganlon. The days that followed were full of hard work and careful coaching. Brennon listened carefully to what Ganlon and I told him, but the result was far from satisfying. He was more intelligent than the general run of fighters but he could not seem to apply practically what he learned easily in theory.

Still, I did not expect too much of him at first. I worked with him patiently for several weeks and imported a fairly clever heavyweight for his sparring partner. The first time they really let go, I was amazed and disappointed. Mike shuffled and floundered awkwardly with futile flabby blows. When a sharp jab on the nose stung him, he quit trying to box and went back to his style of wild and aimless swinging. However, these swings were the old sledgehammer type and his erratic speed had returned to him. I quickly called a halt.

"I'm wrong," I said. "I've been trying to make a boxing wizard out of you. But you're a natural slugger, though you seem to have little of the natural slugger's aptitude. Looks like you'd have learned something from your actual experience in the ring.

"Well, anyway, I'm going to make a real slugger out of you like Dempsey, Sullivan and McGovern. I know how you are; you've got the slugger's instinct. You can box fairly well with a friend when you're doing it for fun, but when you're in the ring or somebody stings you, you forget everything but your natural style. It's no discredit to a man's mentality. Dempsey was a clever boxer when he was sparring but he never boxed in the ring. And he swung, too, like you do, till De Forest taught him to hit straight.

"Still, Mike, I'll tell you frankly that at his crudest, Dempsey showed more aptitude for the game than you do. Now, this is for your own good. Dempsey, Ketchell and McGovern, even when they were just starting, used instinctive footwork and kept stepping around their men. They ducked and weaved and hit accurately. You go in straight up and wide open and a blind man could duck your swings. You've unusual speed but you don't know how to use it. But now that I know where I've been making my mistake, I'll change my tactics."

For a time it seemed as though my dreams were coming true— that Mike was a second Dempsey. In spite of his urging that I get him a fight, I kept him idle for three months—that is, he was not fighting. For hours each day I had him practice hooking the heavy bag with short smashes to straighten his punches and eliminate so much aimless swinging. He would never learn to put force behind a straight punch but I intended making him a vicious hooker like Dempsey. And I tried to teach him the weave of that Old Master and the trick of boring in, protected by a barricade of gloves and elbows until in close; and the fundamentals of footwork and feint-ing. It was not easy.

"Mike," said Ganlon to me, "is a queer nut. He's got a fighter's heart and body, but he ain't got a fighter's brain. He understands but he can't do what you teach him. He has to work for hours on the simplest trick and then he's liable to forget it. If he was a bonehead, I'd understand it. But he's brainy in other ways."

"Maybe he fought so long in second-rate clubs he formed habits he can't break."

"Partly. But it goes deeper. They's a kink in his brain."

"What do you mean, a kink?" I asked uneasily.

"I dunno. But it's somethin' that breaks down his coordination and keeps his mind from workin' with his muscles. When he tries to box he has to stop and think and in the ring you ain't got time. You see a punch comin' and in that split second you got to know what you can't do and what you can do to get outa the way and counter. 'Course you don't exactly study it all out, but you *know*, see? That is, if you're a fast boxer. If you're a wide-open slugger like Mike, you don't think nothin'. You just take the punch as a matter uh course, spit out your teeth and keep borin' in."

"But any slugger is that way," I objected. "And we are not trying to teach Mike to be clever, in the technical sense of the word."

Ganlon shook his head. "I know. But Mike's different. He ain't cut out for this game. Even these simple tricks is too complicated for him. Well, he's got to learn some defense or he'll get punched cuckoo in a few years. All the great sluggers had some. Some weaved and crouched like Dempsey; some wrapped their arms around their skull and barged in like Nelson and Paolino. Them that fought wide open didn't last no time, specially among the heavies. The padded cell and paper-doll cut-outs for most of 'em. It don't stand to reason a human skull can stand up under the beatin's it gets like that."

"You're a born croaker. Mike's rugged but intelligent. He'll learn."

"At anything else, yes—at this game—maybe."

Chapter .2.
"Bat Nelson True to Life—"

"Steve," said Brennon, "I've got to have a fight. I need the money—bad."

"Mike," said I, "it's none of my business but I don't see why you should be so desperately insistent. You've been at no expense at all, here in the camp. You said you weren't in debt and you've refused my offers to loan you—"

"What business is it of yours?" he broke in, white at the lips.

"None at all," I hastened to assure him. "Only as your manager, I've got your financial interests at heart, naturally. I apologize."

"I apologize too, Steve," he answered abruptly, his manner changing. "I should have known you weren't trying to pry into my private affairs. But I've got to have at least—"

And he named a sum of money which rather surprised me.

"There's only one way to get that much," I answered.

"Understand, I don't believe you're ready to go in with a first-string man. But since money is the object—Monk Barota is on the coast now, padding his k.o. record. He'll be looking for setups. The promoter at the Hopi A.C. is a friend of mine. I can get you a match with him at close to the figure you named. You understand that a bad defeat might ruin you. Don't say I didn't warn you. But you're in fine shape and if you fight as we've taught you, I believe you can whip him."

"I'll whip him," Mike nodded grimly.

I hoped he was more sincere in his belief than I was. I really felt in my heart that he was not ready for a first rater and had intended building him up more gradually. But there was a fierce, driving intensity about him when he spoke of the money he needed that broke down my resolution. Brennon was, in many ways, a character of terrific magnetic force. Like Sullivan, he dominated all about him, trainers, handlers and matchmakers. But only in the matter of money was he unreasonable and this quirk in his nature amounted to an obsession.

Mainly through my influence, Brennon, an entirely unknown quantity, was matched with Barota for a ten-rounder; at ringside the odds were two to one on the Italian with no takers. My last instructions to Mike were: "Remember! Use the crouch and guard Ganlon taught you! If you don't have some defense, he'll ruin you!"

The lights went out except those over the ring. The gong sounded. The crowd fell silent—that breathless momentary silence that marks the beginning of the fight. The men slid out of their corners and—

"Oh, Hades!" wailed Ganlon at my side. "He's doin' everything backwards!"

Mike wore his old uncertain manner. Under the lights, with his foe before him and the roar of the crowd deafening him, he was like a trapped jungle beast, bewildered and confused. Barota led and Mike ducked clumsily the wrong way and took the punch in the eye. That flicking left was hard for any man to avoid but Mike incessantly ducked into it.

Ganlon was cursing at my side. "After all these months of work, he forgets! You better throw in the sponge now. Look there!" as Mike tried a left of his own. "He can't even hook right. The whole house knows what's comin'. Same as writin' a letter about it."

Barota was taking his time. In spite of the fact that his foe seemed to have nothing but a scowl, no man could look into Mike Brennon's face and take him lightly. But a round of clumsy floundering and ineffectual pawing lulled his suspicions. Meanwhile he flitted around the bewildered slugger, showering him with slinging left jabs. Ganlon was nearly weeping with rage as if his pupil's inaptness somehow reflected on him.

"All I know, I taught him, and there's that wop makin' a monkey outa him!"

With the round thirty seconds to go, Barota suddenly tore in with one of his famous attacks. Mike abandoned all attempts at science and began swinging wildly and futilely. Barota worked between his flailing arms and beat a rattling barrage against Brennon's head and body. The gong stopped the punishment.

Mike's face was somewhat cut, but he was as fresh as if he had not just gone through a severe beating. He broke in on Ganlon's impassioned soliloquy to remark: "This fellow can't hit."

"Can't hit!" Ganlon nearly dropped the sponge. "Why, he's got a k.o. record as long as a subway! Ain't he just pounded you all over the ring?"

"I didn't feel his punches, anyway," answered Mike and then the gong sounded.

Barota came out fast, in a mood to bring this fight to a sudden close. He launched a swift attack, cut Mike's lips with a right and then began hammering at his body with the left-handed assault which had softened so many of his opponents for the k.o. The crowd went wild as he battered Mike around the ring but suddenly I felt Ganlon's fingers sink into my arm.

"Bat Nelson true to life!" he whispered, his voice vibrating with excitement. "The crowd thinks, and Barota thinks them left hooks is hurtin' Mike—but he ain't even feelin' 'em. He's got one chance—when Barota shoots the right—"

At this moment Barota stepped back, feinted swiftly and shot the right. He was proud of the bone-crushing quality of that right hand. A clear opening he had and every ounce of his weight went behind it. The leather-guarded knuckle, backed by spar-like arm and heavy shoulder, crashed flush against Mike's jaw. The impact was plainly heard in every part of the house. A gasp went up and nails sank deep into clenching palms. Mike swayed drunkenly but he did not fall.

Barota stopped short for a flashing instant—frozen by the realization that he had failed to even floor his man. And in that second Mike swung a wild left and landed for the first time— high on the cheekbone but Barota went down. The crowd rose screaming. Dazed, the Italian rose without a count and Mike tore into him with the ferocity of a tiger that scents the kill. Barota, blinded and dizzy, was in no condition to defend himself, yet Mike missed with both hands until a minesweeping right-hander caught his man flush on the temple and he dropped— not merely out, but senseless.

The crowd was in a frenzy but Ganlon said to me: "He's a iron man, don't you see? A natural born freak like Grim and Goddard. He'll never learn anything, not if he trains a hundred years."

Chapter .3.
"It's Your Brain—A Cog Missin'—"

The day after Mike Brennon had shocked the sporting world by his victory, he, Ganlon and I sat at breakfast and we were a far from merry gang. Ganlon read the morning papers and growled.

"The whole country's on fire," he muttered. "Sportswriters goin' cuckoo over the new find. Tellin' Barota cried and took on in his dressin' room when he come to; and talkin' about how Mike 'fooled' his man in the first round by lookin' like a dub— callin' him a second Fitzsimmons! Applesauce. But here's a old timer that knows his stuff.

"'If I am not much mistaken,'" he read, "'this Brennon is the same who looked like a deckhand against Sailor Slade in Los Angeles last year. His k.o. of Barota had all the earmarks of a fluke. He is, however, incredibly tough.'"

"Uhmhuh," said Ganlon, laying the paper down. "Quite true— Mike, I hate to say it, but as a fighter, you're a false alarm. It ain't your fault. You got the heart and the body but you got no more natural talent than a ribbon clerk and you can't learn. You got the fightin' instinct, but not the fighter's instinct—and they's a flock uh difference.

"You're just a heavyweight Joe Grim. A iron man; never was one but Jeffries who could learn anything. As such I'm advisin' you to quit the ring—now. Your kind don't come to no good end. Too many punches on the head. They get permanently punch drunk. You don't have to go around countin' your fingers; you got brains enough to succeed somewhere else.

"You got three courses to follow: first, you can go around fightin' setups at the small clubs. You can make a livin' that way and last a long time. Second, you can sign up with some of the offers you're bound to get now. Fightin' clever first-raters, you won't win much if any, but you'll be an attraction like Grim was. But you won't last. You'll crack under the incessant fire of smashes and wind up in the booby hatch. Third and best, you can take what money you got and step out. Me and Steve will gladly lend you enough to start in business in a modest way."

I nodded. Mike shook his head and spread his iron fingers out on the table in front of him. As usual he dominated the scene—a great sombre figure of unknown potentialities.

"You're right, Spike, in everything you've said. I've always known there was a deficiency somewhere. No man could be as impervious to punishment as I am and have a perfectly normal brain. Not alone at boxing; I've failed at everything else I've tried. As for boxing, the crowd dazes me for one thing. But that isn't all. I just can't remember what to do next and have to struggle through the best way I can.

"But—I can take it! That's my one hope! That's why I'm not quitting the game. At the cost of my reflexes, maybe, Nature gave me an unusual constitution. You admit I'd be a drawing card. Well, I'm like Battling Nelson—not human when it comes to taking punishment. The only man that ever hurt me was Sailor Slade— and he couldn't stop me. Nobody can now. Eventually, after years of battering, someone will knock me out. But before that time, I'm going to cash in on my ruggedness. Capitalize on the fact that no man can keep me down for the count. I'll accumulate a fortune if I'm handled right."

"Great heavens, man!" I exclaimed. "Do you realize what that means—the frightful punishment, the mutilations? You'll be fighting first-raters now—men with skill and terrific punches. You have no defense—they'll hammer you to a red pulp."

"My defense is a granite jaw and iron ribs," he answered. "I'll take them all on and wear them down."

"Maybe," I answered. "A man can wear himself down punching a granite boulder as I've seen men do with Tom Sharkey and Joe

Goddard, but what about the boulder! You were lucky with Barota. The next man will watch his step."

"They can't hurt me. And I can beat any man I can hit. Win or lose, I'll be a drawing card and that means big purses. That's what I'm after. Do you think I'd go through this Purgatory for glory, if the need wasn't great?"

"If it's poverty—" I began.

"What do you know of poverty?" he cried out in a strange passion. "Were you left in a basket on the steps of Saint Joseph's boys home almost as soon as you were born? Did you spend your childhood mixed in with five hundred others where the needs of all were so great that no one of you got more than the barest necessities? Did you pass your boyhood as a tramp and hobo worker, riding the rods and starving? I did!

"But that's neither here nor there; nor it isn't my own personal poverty so much that drove me back in the ring—but let it pass. As my manager I want you to get busy. If I can win another fight it will increase my prestige. I don't expect to win many. Later I'll pack them in just as Joe Grim did—to see if I can be knocked out. Until the fans find out I'm a freak I'll have to go on my merits. Barota wants a return match. I don't want him now or any other clever man who'll outpoint me and make me look worse than I am, even. I want the fans to see me bloody and staggering and still carrying on! That's what draws the crowd. Get me a mankiller—a puncher who'll come in and try to murder me. Get me Jack Maloney!"

"It's suicide!" I cried. "Maloney'll kill you! I won't have anything to do with it!"

"Then by heaven!" Brennon roared, heaving erect and crashing his fist down shatteringly on the table, "our ways part here! You could help me better than anyone else—you know the ballyhoo. But if you fail me—"

"If you're determined," I said huskily, my mind almost numbed by the driving force of his willpower, "I'll do all I can. But I warn you, you'll leave this game with a clouded brain."

His nervous grip nearly crushed my fingers as he said shortly: "I knew you'd stand by me. Never mind my brain; it's cased in solid iron."

As he strode out, Ganlon, slightly pale, said to me in a low voice: "A twist in his head, sure. Money—all the time. This mornin' I says to him: 'Mike, why don't you get some new shoes with the money you got from the fight?' He says: 'I can wear these a month yet.' Lord knows I'm no dude but he dresses like a wharf hand. What's he do with his money? He ain't supportin' no aged mother, it's a cinch. You heard him say he was left on a doorstep."

I shook my head. Brennon was an enigma beyond my comprehension.

The rise of Iron Mike Brennon is now ring history and of all the vivid pages in the annals of this heart stirring game, I hold that the story of this greatest of all iron men makes the most lurid, fantastic and pulse-quickening chapter.

Iron Mike Brennon! Look at him as he was when his exploits swept the country. Six feet one from his narrow feet to the black tousled shock of his hair; one hundred and ninety pounds of steel springs and whalebone. With his terrible eyes glaring from under heavy black brows, thin blood-smeared lips writhed in snarl of battle fury—still when I dream of the superfighter there rises the picture of Mike Brennon—a dream charged with bitterness. Take a man with incredible stamina and hitting power; take from him the ability to remember one iota of science in actual combat and leave out of his make-up the instincts of the natural fighter, and you have Iron Mike Brennon. A man who would have been the greatest champion of all time but for that flaw in his make-up.

His first fight, after that memorable breakfast table conversation was with Jack Maloney—one hundred and ninety-five pounds of white hot fighting fury, with a right hand like a caulking mallet. They met at San Francisco.

I set the old ballyhoo working with the aid of Ganlon and friendly scribes. The papers were full of Mike Brennon. They pointed out that he had over twenty knock outs to his credit, ignoring the fact that all of these victims except one were unknown dubs. They glossed over the fact that he had been outpointed by second-raters and beaten to a pulp by Sailor Slade. They angrily refuted charges that his k.o. of Barota was a fluke.

The stadium was packed that night. The crowd paid their money and they got its worth. Before the bell I was whispering a few instructions which I knew would be useless, when Mike cut in with fierce eagerness: "What a sell out! Look at that crowd! If I win it'll mean more sell-outs—bigger purses! Oh God, I've got to win!"

His eyes gleamed with ferocious avidity—the gong sounded— two giants crashed from their corners. Maloney came in like the great slugger he was, body crouched, chin tucked beneath his shoulder, hands high. Brennon, forgetting everything before the blast of the crowd and his own fighting fury, rushed like a longshoreman, head lifted, hands clenched at his hips, wide open—as iron men have fought since time immemorial—with one thought—to get to his foe and crush him.

Maloney landed first, a terrific left hook which spattered Brennon with blood and brought the crowd to its feet roaring. I heard a note of relief in the shouts of Maloney's manager. This bird was going to be easy, after all! Like most sluggers, when they find a man they can hit easily, Maloney had gone fighting crazy. He lashed Brennon about the ring, hitting so hard and fast that Mike had no time to get set. The few swings he did try, swished harmlessly over Maloney's bobbing head.

"He's slowin' down," muttered Ganlon as the first round drew to a close. "The old iron man game! Maloney's punchin' hisself out."

True, Jack's blows were coming not weaker but slower. No man could keep up the pace he was setting. Brennon was as strong as ever and just before the gong he staggered Maloney with a sweeping left to the body—his first blow.

Back in his corner, Ganlon wiped the blood from Mike's battered face and grinned savagely: "Joe Goddard had nothin' on you. I'm beginnin' to believe you'll beat him. You've took plenty and you'll take more; he'll come out strong but each round he'll get weaker—fought out."

The crowd thundered his acclaim as Maloney rushed out for the second. But he had sensed something they had not. He had hit this man with everything he had and had failed to even floor him. So he tore in like a wild man and again drove Brennon about the ring before a torrent of left and right hooks that sounded like the kicks of a mule. Brennon, eyes nearly closed, lips pulped, nose broken, showed no sign of distress until the latter part of the round when Maloney landed repeatedly to the jaw with his maul-like right. Then Mike's knees trembled momentarily but he straightened and cut his foe's cheek with a glancing right.

Now at the gong the crowd began to realize what was going on. The timbre of their yells changed. Fans began to inquire at the top of their voices if Maloney was losing his famed punch or if Brennon was made of solid iron.

Ganlon, wiping Brennon's gory features and offering him the smelling salts which he pushed away, said swiftly: "His legs trembled as he went back to his corner; he looked back over his shoulder like he couldn't believe it when he saw you walk to yours without a quiver. He knows he ain't lost his punch! He knows you're the first man ever stood up to him wide open—he knows you been through Hell and high water and ain't even saggin'. You got his goat. Now get him!"

The gong sounded and Maloney came in with the light of desperation in his eyes to redeem his slipping fame as a knocker-out. His blows were like a rain of sledgehammers and before that rain, Mike Brennon went down. The referee began counting. Maloney reeled back against the ropes, breath coming in great gasps—completely fought out.

"He'll get up," said Ganlon calmly.

Brennon was half-crouching on his knees, dazed, not hurt. I saw his lips move and I read their motion: "More fights—more money—"

He bounded erect. Maloney's whole body sagged. Brennon's rising took more morale out of Jack than any sort of a blow would have done. Mike, sensing his mental condition and physical weariness tore in like a tiger. Left, right, he missed, shaking off Maloney's weakening blows as if they had been slaps from a girl. At last he landed—a wide left hook to the head. Maloney tottered and a wild overhand right crashed under his cheekbone, dashing him to his knees. At "Nine!" he staggered up, but another right that a blind man in good condition could have ducked, dropped him again. The referee hesitated, then raised Mike's hand, beckoning to Maloney's seconds.

As Maloney, aided by his handlers, reeled to his corner on buckling legs, I noted the ironical fact: the winner was a gory, battered wreck, while the loser had only a single cut on his cheek. I thought of the old fights in which iron men of another day had figured: of Joe Goddard, the old Barrier champion, outlasting the great Choynsky, finishing each of their terrible battles a bloody travesty of a man, but winner. I thought of Sharkey dropping Kid McCoy—of Nelson outlasting Gans—Young Corbett— Herrera. And I sighed. For of all the men who relied on their ruggedness to carry them through, Brennon was the most wide open, the most erratic.

As I sponged his cuts in the dressing room, I could not forbear to say: "You see what fighting a first-string hitter means— you won't be able to answer the gong for months."

"Months!" he mumbled through battered lips. "You'll sign me up with Johnny Varella for a bout next week!"

Chapter .4.
The Rise of the Iron Man.

Thus was born, figuratively, Iron Mike Brennon. After the Maloney fight, fans and scribes realized what he was—an iron man—and as such his fame grew. He became a drawing card just as he had said— one of the greatest of his day. And his inordinate lust for money grew with his power as an attraction. He haggled over prices, held out for every cent he could get, but rather than pass up a fight, would always lower his price if he had to. For the first and only time in my life,

I was merely a figurehead. Brennon was the real power behind the curtain. And he insisted on fighting at least once a month.

"You'll crack three times as quickly fighting so often," I protested. "Otherwise you might last for years."

"But why stretch it out? If I can make the same amount of money fighting in a few months that I could make in that many years, what's the odds?"

"But consider the strain on you!" I cried.

"I'm not considering anything about myself," he answered roughly. "Get me a match."

The matches came readily. He had caught the crowds' fancy and no matter whom he fought, the fans flocked out. He met them all—ferocious sluggers, clever dancers, dangerous fighters who combined the qualities of slugger and boxer. When first-rate opponents were not forthcoming quick enough, he went into the sticks and pushed over second raters. As long as he was making money, no matter how much or how little, he was satisfied. What he did with that money, I did not know. He was honest, always shot square with his obligations; but beyond that he was a miser. He stayed at the training camps or at the cheapest hotels, in spite of my protests; he bought cheap clothes and allowed himself no luxuries whatever.

At first he won consistently. He was dangerous to any man. Coupled with his abnormal endurance was a mental state—a driving savage determination which dragged him off the canvas time and again. This was above and behind his natural fighting fury and he had acquired it between the time he had first retired and the next time I met him.

At the time he was in his prime, there was a wealth of material in the heavyweight ranks. And Brennon loomed among them as the one man none of them could stop. That fact alone put him on equal footing with men in every other way his superior.

Following the Maloney fight, the public clamored for a match between my iron man and Yon Van Heeren, the Durable Dutchman, considered up to that time the toughest man in the world, and who had never been knocked out, and whose only claim to fame, like

Brennon's, was his ruggedness. A certain famous sportswriter, referring to this fight as "a brawl between two barroom thugs," said: "This unfortunate affair has set the game back twenty years. No sensitive person seeing this slaughter for his or her first fight, could ever be tempted to see another, as people who do not know the game are likely to judge it by the two gorillas who, utterly devoid of science, turned the ring into the shambles."

Before the men went into the ring they made the referee promise not to stop the fight under any circumstances—an unusual proceeding, but easily understood in their case.

The fight was a strange experience to Mike; most of the punishment was on the other side. Van Heeren, six feet two and 210 pounds, was a terrific hitter but lacked Mike's dynamic speed and fury. Those sweeping haymakers which had missed so many others, crashed blindingly against the Dutchman's head or sank agonizingly into his body. At the end of the first round, his face was a gory wreck. At the end of the fourth his features had lost all human semblance and his body was a mass of reddened flesh. Toe to toe they stood, round after round, neither taking a back step. The fifth, six and seventh rounds were nightmares, in which Mike was dropped three times and Van Heeren went down twice that many times. All over the stadium women were fainting or being helped out; fans were shrieking for the fight to be stopped.

In the ninth, Van Heeren, a hideous and inhuman sight, dropped for the last time. Four ribs broken, features permanently ruined, he lay writhing, still trying to rise as the referee tolled off the "Ten!" that marked his finish as a fighting man.

Mike Brennon, clinging to the ropes, dizzy and nearly punched out for the only time in his life, stood above his victim, acknowledged king of all iron men. Aye—that fight finished Van Heeren and nearly finished boxing in that state, but it added to Brennon's fame and his real pity for the broken Dutchman was mingled with a fierce exultation of realized power. More money—more packed houses!

The world's greatest iron man! In the three years he fought under my management, he met them all except the champion of his division. He lost about as many as he won, but the only thing that could impair his drawing power was a knockout—and this seemed postponed indefinitely. He won more of his fights against the hard punchers than against light tappers who took no chances. Many a slugger, after battering him to a red ruin, blew up and fell before his aimless but merciless attack. He broke the hands and he broke the hearts of the men who tried to stop him.

The light hitters outboxed him but did not hurt him, and his wild swings were dangerous even to them. Barota outpointed him, and Jackie Finnegan, Frankie Grogan and Flash Sullivan, the light-heavy champion.

The hard hitters made the mistake of trading punches with him. Soldier Handler dropped him five times in four rounds and then stopped a right-hander that knocked him clear out of the ring and into fistic oblivion. Jose Gonzales, the great South American punched himself out on the iron tiger and went down to defeat. Gunboat Sloan battered out a red decision over him, but still believing he could achieve the impossible went in to trade punches in a return bout and lasted less than a round. Brennon finished Ricardo Diaz, the Spanish Giant, and beat down Snake Calberson after his toughness had broken the Brown Phantom's heart. Johnny Varella and several lesser lights broke their hands on him and quit. He met Whitey Broad and Kid Allison in no decision bouts, knocked out Young Hansen and fought a terrible fifteen round draw with Sailor Steve Costigan, who never rated better than a second-class man, but who gave some first-raters terrific battles.

To those who doubt that flesh and blood can endure the punishment which Brennon took, I beg you to look at the records of the ring's iron men. I point to your attention, Tom Sharkey plunging headlong into the terrible blows of Jeffries; that same Sharkey shooting over the ropes from the blows of Choynsky, headlong onto the concrete floor, yet finishing the fight a winner. I call to your attention Mike Boden who had no more defense than had Brennon, staying the limit with Choynsky; and Joe Grim taking all Fitzsimmons could hand him—was it fifteen or sixteen times he was floored? Yet he finished that fight standing. No man can understand the iron men of the ring. Theirs is a long, hard, bloody trail with oftentimes only poverty and a clouded mind at the end, but the red chapter their clan has written across the chronicles of the game will never be effaced.

And so Brennon fought on, taking all his cruel punishment, hoarding his money, saying little—as much a mystery to me as ever. Sportswriters discovered his passion for money, and raked him. Accused him of being miserly and refusing aid to his less fortunate fellows—the battered tramps who will occasionally strike up a successful fighter for a handout. This was partly true. He did sometimes give money to men who needed it desperately, but rarely.

Then he began to crack. Ganlon, his continual companion, first sensed it. Crouching beside me the night Mike fought Kid Allison, Spike whispered to me out of the corner of his mouth: "He's slowin' down. It's the beginnin' of the end."

That night Spike spoke plainly to his friend.

"Mike, you're about through. You're slippin'. Punches jar you worse than they used to. You've last lasted three years of terrible hard goin'. You got to quit."

"When I'm knocked out," said Mike stubbornly. "I haven't taken the count yet."

"But, man!" cried Ganlon sharply, "when a bird like you takes the count, it means he's a punch-drunk wreck. When the blows begin to hurt you, it means the shock of them is reachin' the brain and hurtin' it. Remember Van Heeren that you finished? He's wanderin' around, sayin' he's trainin' to fight Fitzsimmons, that's been dead for years."

A shadow crossed Mike's dark face at the mention of the Dutchman's name. The beatings he had taken had disfigured him and given him a peculiarly sinister look, which however did not rob his face of its strange dominating quality.

"I'm good for a few more fights," he answered. "I need money—"

"Always money!" I exclaimed. "You must have half a million dollars at least. I'm beginning to believe you are a miser—"

"Steve," said Ganlon suddenly, "that cuckoo Van Heeren was around here yesterday."

"What of it?"

"Mike," said Ganlon almost accusingly, "gave him a thousand dollars."

"What if I did?" cried Brennon in one of his rare inexplicable passions. "The fellow was broke—in no condition to earn any money—I finished him—why shouldn't I help him a little? Whose business is it?"

"Nobody's," I answered, "but it shows you're not a miser. And it deepens the mystery about you. Won't you tell me why you need more money?"

He made a quick impatient gesture. "There's no need. You get the matches, I do the fighting. We split the money and that's all there is to it."

"But Mike," I said as kindly as I could, "there is more to it. You've made me more money than either of the champions I've managed and if I didn't sincerely wish for your own good, I'd say, stay in the ring.

"But you ought to quit. You can even get your features fixed up—plastic face-building is a wonderful art. Fight one more time even, and you may spend your days in a padded cell."

"I'm tougher than you think," he answered. "I'm as good as I ever was and I'll prove it. Get me Sailor Slade."

"He beat you before when you were better than you are now. How do you expect—"

"I didn't have the incentive to win then, that I have now."

I nodded. What this incentive was I did not know, but I had seen him rise again and again from what looked like certain defeat—had seen him, writhing on the canvas, turn white, his eyes blaze with sudden terror as he dragged himself upright. Terror? Of losing! A terror that kept him going when even his iron body was tottering on the verge of collapse and when the old fighting frenzy had ceased to function in the numbed brain. What prompted this dread? It was a mystery I could not fathom, yet in some way it was connected with his strange money-lust, I knew.

"You'll sign me for four fights," he was saying. "With Sailor Slade, Young Hansen, Jack Slattery and Mike Costigan."

"You're out of your mind!" I exclaimed sharply. "You've picked the four most dangerous battlers in the world!"

"Hansen will be easy. I beat him once and I can do it again. I don't know about Slattery. I want to take him on last. First I've got to hurdle Slade. After him, I'll fight Costigan. He's the least scientific of the four, but the hardest hitter. If I'm slipping I want to get him before I've gone too far."

"It's suicide!" I cried. "If you've got to fight, pass up these mankillers and take on some setups. If Slade don't knock you out, he'll soften you up so Costigan will punch you right into the bughouse. He's a murderer. They call him Iron Mike, too."

"I'll pack them in," he answered heedlessly. "Slade's nearly the drawing card I am, and as for Costigan, the fans always turn out to see two iron men meet."

As usual, there was no answer to be made.

Chapter .5.
"—This is Why You've Been Crucifying Yourself—!"

It was a few nights before the Brennon-Slade fight. I had wandered into Mike's room and my eye fell on a partially completed letter on his writing table. Without any intention of spying, I idly noted that it was addressed to a girl named Marjory Walshire, at a very fashionable girls' school in New York state.

I saw that a letter from this girl lay beside the other one, and though it was an atrocious breach of manners, in my curiosity to know why a girl in a society school like that would be writing a prizefighter, I picked up the partially completed letter and glanced idly over it. The next moment I was reading it with fierce intensity, all scruples forgotten. Having finished it, I snatched up the other and ruthlessly tore it open.

I had scarcely finished reading it when Mike entered with Ganlon. His eyes blazed with sudden fury but before he could say a word, I launched an offensive of my own—for one of the few times in my life, wild with rage.

"You born fool!" I snarled. "So this is why you've been crucifying yourself!"

"What do you mean by getting into my private correspondence?" his voice was husky with fury.

I sneered. "I'm not going to enter into a discussion of etiquette. You can beat me up afterwards, but just now I'm going to have my say.

"You've been keeping some frail in a ritzy finishing school back East. Finishing school! It's nearly finished you! What kind of a dame is she, to let you go through Hell for her? I'd like for her to see your battered map now! While she's been lolling at ease in the most expensive school she could find, you've been flattening out the resin with your shoulders and soaking it down with your blood—"

"Shut up!" roared Brennon, white and shaking, "or before God, I'll kill you!"

He leaned back against the table, gripping the edge so hard his knuckles whitened as he fought for control. At last he spoke more calmly.

"Yes, that's the incentive that's kept me going. That girl is the only girl I ever loved—the only thing I ever had to love.

"Listen, do you know how lonely a kid is when he has absolutely nobody in the world to love? The priests in St. Joseph's home were kind but there were so many children—I got the beginnings of a good education. That's all.

"Out in the world it was worse. I worked, tramped, starved. I fought for everything I ever got. I have a better education than most, you say. I worked my way through high school, and read all the books in my spare time that I could beg, steal or borrow. Many a time I went hungry to buy a book—

"I drifted into the ring from fighting in carnivals and the like. I never got anywhere. After I whipped Mulcahy the night you talked to me, I quit. Drifted. Then in a little town on the Arizona desert I met Marjory Walshire.

"Poverty? She knew poverty! Working her fingers to the bone in a cafe. Good blood in her too, just as there is in me somewhere. She should have been born to the satins and velvet—instead she was born to the greasy dishes and dirty tables of a second-class cafe. I loved her and she loved me. She told me her dreams that she never believed would come true—of education—nice clothes—refined companions—everything that any girl wants.

"Where was I to turn? I could take her out of the cafe— only to introduce her to the drudgery of a laboring man's wife. So I went back into the ring. As soon as I could, I sent her to school. I've been sending her money enough to live in as well as any girl there, and I've saved too, so when she gets out of school and I have to quit the ring, we can be married and start in business that won't mean drudgery and poverty.

"Poverty is the cause of more crime, cruelty and suffering than anything else. Poverty kept me from having a home and people like other kids. You know how it is in the slums—parents toiling for a living and babies coming too fast. They can't support them all. Mine left me on St. Joseph's doorstep with a note: 'He's honest born. We love him but we can't keep him. Call him Michael Brennon.'

"Aye—and poverty can be as cruel in a small town as in a city—Marjory, who'd never been out of the town where she was born—with her soul starved and her little white hands reddened and calloused—

"It's the thought of her that's kept me on my feet when the whole world was blind and red and the fists of my opponent were like hammers beating on my shattering brain—that's dragged me off the canvas when my body was without feeling and my arms hung like lead, to strike down the man I could no longer see. And as long as she's waiting for me at the end of the long trail, there's no man on earth can make me take the count!"

His voice crashed through the room like a clarion call of victory, but my old doubts returned.

"But how can she love you so much," I exclaimed, "when she's willing for you to go through all this for her?"

"What does she know of fighting? I made her believe boxing was more or less of a dancing tapping affair. She'd heard of Corbett and Tunney, clever fellows who could step twenty rounds without a mark and she supposed I was like them. She hasn't seen me in nearly four years—not since I left the town where she worked. I've put her off when she's wanted to come and see me, or for me to come to her. When she does see my battered face it'll be a terrible shock to her but I was never very handsome anyway—"

"Do you mean to tell me," I broke in, "that she never tunes in on one of your fights, never reads an account of them, when the papers are full of your doings?"

"She don't know my real name. After I quit the game the first time, I went under the name of Mike Flynn to duck the two-by-four promoters I'd fought for, and who were always pestering me to fight for them again. The first time I saw Marjory I began to think of fighting again and I never told her differently. The money I've sent her has been in cashier's checks. To her, I'm simply Mike Flynn, a fighter she never hears of. She wouldn't recognize my picture in the papers—"

"But her letters are addressed to Mike Brennon—"

"You didn't look closely. They're addressed to Michael Flynn, care of Mike Brennon, this camp. She thinks Brennon is merely a friend of her Mike. Well, now you know why I've fought on and stinted myself. With Van Heeren, it was different. I'm responsible for his condition. I had to help him.

"These four fights now; one of them may be my last, but— I've got money but I want more. I intend that Marjory shall never want again for anything. I'm to get $100,000 for this fight. My third purse of that size. With good management, thanks to you, I've made more money than many champions. If I whip these four men, I'll fight on. If I'm knocked out, I'll have to quit. Let's drop the matter."

Chapter .6.
"The roll of the Iron Men—"

I haven't the heart to tell of the Brennon-Slade fight in detail. Even today the thought of the punishment Mike took that night takes the stiffening out of my knees. He had slipped even more than we had thought. The steel-spring legs which had carried him through so many whirlwind battles had slowed down. His sweeping haymakers crashed over with their old power but they did not continually wing through the air as of old. Blows that should not have jarred him, staggered him. The squat Sailor, wild with the thought of a knockout, threw caution to the winds. How many times he floored Mike I never dared try to remember. But Brennon was still Iron Mike. Again and again the gong saved him, and in the fourteenth round Slade went to pieces and the iron tiger he had punched into a red smear, found him in the crimson mist and blindly blasted him into unconsciousness.

Brennon collapsed in his corner after Slade was counted out and both men were carried senseless from the ring. I sat by Mike's side that night while he lay in a semi-conscious state, occasionally muttering brokenly as his bruised brain conjured up red visions. He lay, both eyes closed, his oft-broken nose a crushed ruin, cut and gashed all about the head and face, now and then stirring uneasily as the pain of three broken ribs stabbed him. For the first time he spoke the name of the girl he loved, groping out his hands like a lost child. Again he fought over his fearful battles and his mighty fists clenched until the knuckles showed white and low bestial snarls tore through his battered lips. Once in his delirium he muttered a sportswriter's parody of Chesterton's lines:

"I call the roll of the iron men
"From ship and ghetto and Barbary den,
"To break and be broken, God knows when,
"And only God knows why."

Then raising himself painfully on one elbow, his burning unseeing eyes gleaming like slits of flame between the battered lids, he spoke in a low voice as if answering and listening to the murmur of ghosts: "Joe Grim! Battling Nelson! Mike Boden! Joe Goddard! Iron Mike Brennon!"

My flesh crawled. I cannot impart to you the uncanniness of hearing the roll call of those iron men of days gone by, muttered in the stillness of night through the pulped and delirious lips of the grimmest of them all.

At last he fell silent and went into a natural slumber. As I went softly into the other room, Ganlon entered, his savage eyes blazing with fierce triumph. With him was a girl—the darling of high society she seemed, with her costly garments and air of culture, but she exhibited an elemental anxiety such as no pampered and sophisticated debutante would, or could have done.

"Where is he?" she cried desperately. "Where is Mike? I must see him!"

"He's asleep now," I said shortly, and added in my cruel bitterness. "You've done enough to him already. He wouldn't want you to see him like he is now."

She cringed as from a blow. "Oh, let me just look in the door," she begged, twining her white hands together—and I thought how often Mike's hands had been bathed in blood for her. "I won't wake him."

I hesitated and her eyes flamed; now she was the primal woman.

"Try to stop me and I'll kill you!" she cried and rushed past me into the room.

She stopped short on the threshold. Mike muttered restlessly in his sleep and turned his blind eyes toward the door but did not waken. As the girl's eyes fell on that frightfully disfigured face, she swayed drunkenly; her hands went to her temples and a low whimper like an animal in pain escaped her. Then, her face corpse-white and her eyes set in a deathly stare, she stole to the bedside and with a heartrending sob, sank to her knees, cradling that battered head in her arms.

Mike muttered but still he did not waken and at last I drew her gently away and led her into the next room, closing the door behind us. There she burst into a torrent of weeping. "I didn't know!" she kept sobbing over and over. "I didn't know fighting was like that! He told me never to go to a fight or listen to one over the radio and I obeyed him. Why, how could I know— here's one of the few letters in which he even mentioned his fights. I've kept them all—"

The date was over three years old. I read: "—Last night I stopped Jack Maloney, a foremost contender. He scarcely laid a glove on me. Don't worry about me, darling, this game is a cinch."

I laughed bitterly, remembering the gory wreck Maloney had made of Mike before he went out.

"I've been doing you an injustice," I said. "I didn't think a man could keep a girl in such ignorance as to the real state of things, but it's true. You're alright. Maybe you can persuade Mike to give up the game—we can't."

"Surely he can't think of fighting again if he lives?" she cried.

I laughed. "He won't die. He'll be laid up awhile, that's all. Now I'll take you to a hotel—"

"I'm going to stay here close to Mike," she answered passionately. "I could kill myself when I think of how he's suffered for me. Tomorrow I'm going to marry him and take him away."

After she was ensconced in a spare room I turned to Spike: "I guess you're responsible for this. You might have waited till Mike was out of bed. That was a terrible shock for her."

"I intended it should be," he snarled. "I wrote and told her did she know her boy Mike Flynn was really Mike Brennon which was swiftly bein' punched into the booby-hatch? And I gave her some graphic account of his battles. I wrote her in time for her to get here to see the fight, but she says she missed a train."

"I imagine Mike will kill you for this."

"Let him," Spike spat. "Costigan will kill him, if they fight. I've seen these iron men crack before. I was in Tom Berg's corner the night Jose Gonzales knocked him out and he died while the referee was countin' over him. Some men you got to kill to stop. Mike Brennon's one of 'em. If the girl's got a spark of real womanhood in her, she'll persuade him to quit."

Morning found the battered iron man clear of mind, his superhuman recuperative powers already asserting themselves. I brought Marjory to his bedside and before he could say anything, I left them alone. Later she came to me, her eyes red with weeping.

"I've argued and begged," she cried desperately. "And he won't give in!"

All of us surrounded Mike's bedside. "Mike," I said caustically, "you're a fool. The punches have gone to your head. You can't mean you'll fight again."

"I'm good for some more $100,000 purses," he replied with a grin.

Marjory cried out as if he had stabbed her. "Mike, for heavens' sake, for my sake—! We have more money now than we'll ever use. You haven't been fair to me, Mike. I'd have rather gone in rags and worked my fingers to the bone in the lowest kind of drudgery than to have you suffer—"

His face lighted with a rare smile. He reached out a hand amazingly gentle and took the girl's soft hand.

"White little hands," he murmured, "soft as God meant them to be, now. Why, just looking at you repays me a thousand times for all I've gone through. And what have I gone through? A few beatings. The old-timers took worse and got little or nothing."

"But there's no reason for your crucifying yourself—and me—any longer."

He shook his head with that strange abnormal stubbornness which was the worst defect in his character.

"As long as I can draw down a hundred thousand dollars a fight, I'd be a fool to quit. I'm tougher than any of you think. A hundred thousand dollars!" his eyes gleamed with the old light. "The crowd roaring! And Iron Mike Brennon taking everything that's handed out and finishing on his feet! No! No! I'll quit when I'm counted out—not before!"

"Mike!" the girl cried piercingly. "If you fight again, I'll swear I'll go away and never see you again."

His gaze beat her eyes down and her head sank on her breast. I never saw the human being—except one—who could stand the stare of Mike Brennon's magnetic eyes.

"Marjory," his deep voice vibrated with confidence, "you're just trying to bluff me into doing what you want me to do. But you're mine and you always will be. You won't leave me, now. You can't!"

She hid her tear-blinded face in her hands and whimpered weakly. He stroked her bowed head tenderly. A failure in the ring perhaps, outside, Brennon had a power over those with whom he came in contact, which none could overcome. The way he had beaten down the girl's weak pretense was almost brutal.

"Mike!" snarled Ganlon, speaking harshly and bitterly to hide his emotions; for a moment the hard-faced middleweight with his two hundred savage ring battles behind him dominated the scene: "Mike, you're crazy! You got everything a man could want—things that most men work their lives out for and never get. You're on the borderline. You couldn't whip a second rater. "Costigan's as tough as you ever was. If I thought he'd flatten you with a punch or two, I say, go to it. But he won't. He'll knock you out but it'll be after a smashin' that'll ruin you for life. You'll die or you'll go to the bug-house. What good will your money or Marjory's love do you then?"

Mike took his time about replying and again his strange influence was felt like a cloud over the group.

"Costigan's overrated. I'll show him up. He never saw the day he could take as much as I can or hit as hard."

Spike made a despairing gesture and turned away. Later he said to the girl and me: "No use arguin'. He thinks it's the money but it ain't. The game's in his blood. And he's jealous of Mike Costigan.

These iron men is terrible proud of their toughness. Remember how Van Heeren fought!"

"Win or lose, ten rounds with Costigan means Mike's finish. Each too tough to be knocked out quick. It'll be a long, bloody grind and it may finish Costigan but it'll sure finish Mike. He'll end that fight dead or punched nutty. At his best Brennon would likely have wore Costigan down like he did Van Heeren. But Mike's gone away back and Costigan is young—which in a iron man is the same as sayin' you couldn't hurt him with a piledriver."

Chapter .7.
The Fall of a King

Mike Brennon trained conscientiously as always. I discharged his sparring partners and had him punch the light bag for speed, and do a great deal of road work in a vain effort to recover some of the former steel-spring quality of his weakening legs. But I knew it was useless. It was not a matter of conditioning—his trouble lay behind him in the thousands of cruel blows his frame had absorbed. A clever boxer may get out of condition, lose fights and come back; when an iron man slips there is no comeback.

In the four months which preceded the Costigan fight, an air of gloom surrounded the camp, which affected all but Mike himself. Marjory, after days of passionate pleading, sank into a sort of apathy. That he was being bitterly cruel to the girl never occurred to Mike and we could not make him see it. He laughed at our fears as foolish, and insisted that he was practically at his prime. He swore that his fight with Slade, far from showing that he had slipped, proved that he was better than ever! For had he not beaten Slade, the most dangerous man in the ring? As for Costigan—a few rounds of savage slugging would send him down and out. Mike was aware of his fistic faults; he frankly admitted that any second rater who could avoid his swings could outpoint him; but he sincerely believed that he was still superior in ruggedness to any man who ever lived. And deep in his heart, I doubt if Mike really believed he would ever be knocked out.

One thing he insisted on; that Marjory should not see the fight. And she made one last plea for him to give up.

"No use to start all that," he answered calmly. "Think, Marjory! My fourth $100,000 purse! That's a record few champions have set! $100,000 with Flash Sullivan—Gonzales— Slade—and now Costigan! Thousands of tickets sold in advance! I've got to go on now, anyhow. And I'm a cinch to win."

As if it were yesterday I visualize the scene; the ring bathed in the white glow above it, while the great crowd that filled the huge outside bowl swept away into darkness of each side. A circle of white faces looked up from the ringside seats. Further out only a twinkling army of glowing cigarettes evidenced the multitude, and a vast rippling undertone came from the soft darkness.

"Iron Mike Brennon, 190 pounds; in this corner, Iron Mike Costigan, 195—"

Brennon sat in his corner, head bowed, a contrast to the nervous, feline-like picture he had offered when he had paced the floor in his dressing room. I wondered if he was still seeing the tear-stained face of Marjory as she kissed him in his dressing room before he came into the ring.

When the men were called to the center of the ring for instructions, Mike, to my surprize, seemed apathetic. He walked with dragging feet. However, in front of his foe he came awake with fierce energy. Iron Mike Costigan was dark also, with tousled black hair. Five feet eleven, and heavier than Brennon, what he lacked in lithe ranginess he made up for in oak and iron massiveness. The eyes of the two men burned into each other's with savage intensity. Volcanic blue for Costigan, cold steel grey for Brennon. Their sun-browned faces were set in unconscious snarls. But as they stood facing each other, Brennon's stare of concentrated cold ferocity wavered and fell momentarily before Costigan's savage blue eyes. I realized that this was the first man who had ever looked Mike down and I thought of

Corbett staring down Sullivan—of McGovern's eyes falling before Young Corbett's.

Then the men were back in their corners and the seconds and handlers were climbing through the ropes. I hissed to Mike that I was going to throw in the sponge if the going got too rough but he made no reply. He seemed to have sunk into that strange apathy again. The gong! Costigan hurtled from his corner, a compact bulk of fighting fury. Brennon came out more slowly. At my side Ganlon hissed: "What's the matter with Mike? He acts like he was drunk!"

The two Iron Mikes had met in the center of the ring. Costigan might have been slightly awed by the fame of the man he faced. At any rate he hesitated. Brennon walked toward his foe but his feet dragged.

Then Costigan suddenly launched an attack and shot a straight left to Brennon's face. As if the blow had roused him to his full tigerish fury, Mike went into action. The old sweeping haymakers began to thunder with all their ancient power. Costigan had, of course, no defense. A sweeping left-hander crashed under his heart with a sound like a caulking mallet striking a ship's side; a blasting right that whistled through the air, cannonballed against his jaw. Costigan went down as though struck by a thunderbolt.

Then even as the crowd rose, he reeled up again. But I was watching Brennon. As though that sudden burst of action had taken all the strength out of him, he sagged against the ropes, limp, cloudy-eyed. Now sensing that his foe was up, he dragged himself forward with halting and uncertain motions.

Costigan, still dizzy from that terrific knock down, was conscious of only one urge—the old instinct of the iron man— bore in and hit until somebody falls! Now he crashed through Brennon's groping arms and shot a right hook to the chin. Brennon swayed and fell, just as a drunken man falls when a prop against which he has been leaning is removed.

Over his motionless form the referee was counting "Eight—Nine—Ten!" And the ring career of Iron Mike Brennon was at an end. A stunned silence reigned and Iron Mike Costigan, new king of all iron men, leaned dazedly against the ropes, unable to believe his own senses. Mike Brennon had been knocked out!

Around the ring the typewriters of the reporters were ticking out the fall of a king: "Evidently Mike Brennon's famous iron jaw has at last turned to crockery after years of incredible bombardings—"

We carried Mike to his dressing room, still senseless. Ganlon was muttering under his breath and as soon as we had Mike safe on a cot with a physician looking to him, the middleweight vanished. Marjory had been waiting for us and now she stood white faced and silent by the cot where her lover lay.

At last he opened his eyes, and instantly he leaped erect, hands up. Then he halted, swayed and rubbed his eyes. Marjory was at his side in an instant and gently forced him back on the cot.

"What happened? Did I win?" he asked dazedly.

"You were knocked out in the first round, Mike." I felt it better to answer him directly. His eyes widened with amazement.

"I? Knocked out? Impossible!"

"Yes, Mike, you were," I assured him, expecting him to do any of the things I have seen fighters do on learning of their first knockout—weep terribly, faint, rave and curse, or rush out looking for the conqueror. But being Mike Brennon and a never-to-be-solved enigma, he did none of these things. He merely rubbed his chin and laughed cynically.

"Guess I'd gone further back than I thought. I don't remember the punch that put me out; funny thing—I've come through my last fight without a mark."

"And now you'll quit!" cried Marjory. "This is the best thing that could have happened to you! You promised you'd quit if you were knocked out, Mike!" Her voice was painful in its intensity.

"Why, I wouldn't draw half a house now," Mike was beginning ruefully, when Ganlon burst in, eyes blazing.

"Mike!" he snarled. "Steve! Don't you two boneheads see there's somethin' wrong here? Mike, when did you begin feelin' drowsy?"

Brennon started: "That's right. I'd forgotten. I began feeling queer when I climbed in the ring. I sort of woke up when the referee was talking to us, and I remember how Costigan's eyes blazed. Then when I went back to my corner I got dizzy and drunken. Then I knew I was moving out in the ring and I saw Costigan through a fog. He hit me a hummer and I woke up and started swinging and saw him go down. That's the last I remember until I came to here."

Ganlon laughed bitterly. "Sure. You was out on your feet before Costigan hit you. A girl coulda pushed you over and that's all Costigan done!"

"Doped!" I cried sharply. "Costigan's crowd—or the gambling ring—"

"Naw—Mike's been crossed by the last person you'd think of. I been doin' some detective work. Mike, just before you left your dressin' room, you drunk a small cup of tea, didn't you? Kinda unusual preparation for a hard fight, eh? But you drunk it to please somebody—"

Marjory was cowering in the corner. Mike was troubled and puzzled.

"But Spike, Marjory made that tea herself—"

"Yeah, and she doped it herself! She framed you to lose!"

Our eyes turned on the shrinking girl—amazement in mine, anger in Ganlon's and a deep hurt in Mike's.

"Marjory, why did you do that?" asked Mike, bewildered. "I might have won—"

"Yes, you might have won!" she cried in a sudden gust of desperate defiance. "After Costigan had battered you into a red ruin! Yes, I drugged the tea! It's my fault you got knocked out. You can't go back now, for you've lost your only attraction. You can't draw the crowds. I've gone through Hell since I first saw you lying on that cot after your fight with Slade—but you've only laughed at me. Now you'll have to quit. You're out of the game with a sound mind—that's all I care. I've saved you from your mad avarice and cruel pride in spite of yourself! And you can beat me now, or kill me—I don't care!"

For a moment she stood panting before us, her small fists clenched, then as no one spoke, all the fire went out of her. She wilted visibly and moved droopingly and forlornly toward the door. The wrap which enveloped her slender form slid to the floor as she fumbled at the doorknob, revealing her in a cheap gingham dress. Mike, like a man awakening from a trance started forward:

"Marjory! Where are you going? What are you doing in that rig?"

"It's the dress I was wearing when you first met me," she answered listlessly. "I wrote and got back my old job at the cafe—"

"In God's name, why?" he crossed the room with one stride, caught her slim shoulders and spun her around to face him, with unconsciously brutal force. "What do you mean?"

She collapsed suddenly into a storm of weeping. "Don't you hate me for drugging you?" she sobbed. "I didn't think you'd ever want to see me again!"

He crushed her to him hungrily. "Girl, I swear I didn't realize how it was hurting you. I thought you were foolish— willful. I couldn't see how you were suffering. But you've opened my eyes. I must have been insane! Thank God you doped me! You're right—it was pride—senseless vanity—I couldn't see it then but I do now. My eyes were blinded so I couldn't understand how cruel I was being to you. I didn't understand that I was ruining your happiness. And darling, that's all that matters now. We've got our life and love before us and if it rests with me, you're going to be happy all the rest of your life."

Ganlon beckoned me and I followed him out. For the only time since I had known him, the fierce middleweight's hard face was softened. The sentiment that lies at the base of the Irish nature, however deeply hidden sometimes, made his steely eyes almost tender.

"I had her down all wrong," he said softly. "I take back everything I might have said about her. She's a regular—and Mike—well, he's the only Iron Man I ever knew that got the right breaks at last."

The Mark of a Bloody Hand

Ring fans will recall the strange incidents which took place on the night of May 8th, 19– in the Hopi A.C. The participants in that fight were Jack Maloney, a young Irish-American, and Tony Azerello, an experienced ring man and, as his name suggests, an Italian.

I sat at ringside that night with police inspector Hanlon, a close friend of mine, and he pointed out to me a black-eyed, red-lipped young Italian girl who sat just behind Tony's corner. This girl was wildly excited, and throughout the fight, until the sudden and shocking end, she shrieked voluble encouragement to her man, and insults at the enemy, mostly in Italian.

"Malissa di Gigisetti," grunted Hanlon. "Her old man's got a bad name—Mafia—Black Hand. Hot-blooded Sicilian and danger-ous as they come. Never proved anything on her father, but—look at those eyes! Flashin' all the love a woman can hold at Tony, and all the hate a Latin woman can hold at Maloney!

"The belle of the Latin quarter, that's her. Azerello made some enemies, I reckon, when he walked in and took her away from the local boys—three or four of them was crazy to marry her. There was Luigi Savonari, for one—"

At that moment, the hard-pressed Maloney launched a desper-ate counterattack and the round ended in a wild flurry of slugging.

"Oh you Tonee!" called Malissa, springing to her feet as her boxer walked to his corner, and throwing extravagant kisses at him. "Keela da bum! Knock outa da Irish steef—"

Tony smiled with a flash of rare white teeth and kissed his glove at her. "Never you fear, babee!" he shouted over the din of the throng. "Dis bigga boy, he's easee for Tony!"

"Easy me eye!" grunted Hanlon, chewing his cigar. "Till 'Ten!' has been counted over 'im, Jack Maloney ain't nobody's cinch. He's never landed square on this wop yet."

I glanced over to Maloney's corner. His seconds were working hard over the weary young giant, whose cut and battered face gave mute evidence of the punishing power of Azerello's straight left.

"I'm afraid the Italian's too clever for the kid," I confessed. "He's won every one of the nine rounds so far, and Maloney's scarcely laid a glove on him. Say, there's one Italian who isn't cheering for Tony!"

I referred to a swart, stocky Sicilian who sat across the ring from me. This man had risen from his seat, and now he shook his fist in the direction of Azerello's corner. Even at that distance I caught a flash of astonishing hatred on his dark face.

"He must have bet heavy on Maloney," I thought, but before I could call my companion's attention to him, the gong had sounded for the tenth round and I forgot all about the unpatriotic Sicilian.

Maloney came up for this round a sorry-looking figure. His wet hair was plastered to his head, one eye was closing and there were numerous cuts on his features. The smiling, unmarked Italian, quick and lithe as a fencer, danced toward him, jabbed him delicately, stepped back out of reach of the lad's earnest swing, stepped in again. His left flashed too quickly for the eye to follow again and again. Maloney, maddened, went into a crouch and here Tony made a literally fatal mistake. He thought the American was covering up, whereas he was merely flexing his steely muscles for a leap. That sudden lunge caught Tony unprepared and for the first time that night, Maloney landed his sledgehammer right. The Italian, receiving its full terrible force squarely on the chin, shot back halfway across the ring—he seemed to be falling into the ropes—then while he was still in midair, every light in the house went out.

Instantly, all was tumult. Friends of Maloney's were screaming for the referee to count in the dark, friends of the fallen were howling for lights. At last lights were procured— then presently the lights came back on all over the house and everyone turned back for the continuance of the fight. All but Tony Azerello. He lay half under the ropes, his head resting on the edge of the ring floor where the padding was thin—and that padding was stained an ugly red. The referee did not even go to the trouble of counting him out; he felt his heart and shouted for a physician. One came and after a brief satisfaction turned to inspector Hanlon.

"The boy's in a bad way, inspector; better get him out of here. Nasty fracture and probable concussion of the brain."

At these words the listening Malissa gave a piercing scream and shoving past the guards, threw herself on the unconscious form of her lover, wailing and weeping until it was agonizing to hear. When gently lifted from him, at the arrival of a stretcher, she flew at poor Maloney with teeth and nails. Jack had stood dumfounded, and he made no defense, seeming to be in a daze. If his indignant seconds had not dragged her away, none too gently, I believe she would have torn his eyes out.

They say she sat by Tony's bedside without moving, until he died six hours later, having never regained consciousness. Then she fainted and lay like a dead woman. Passionate and temperamental, these Latin women, and when they love, they love deep.

And when they hate, they hate deep. Jack Maloney was tried in connection with Tony's death, but it was a mere formality and he was acquitted with no delay. The verdict rendered by the coroners jury was that Tony, knocked down by that terrific blow, had struck the back of his head close to the edge of the ring where the padding was too thin. The force of his fall had been sufficient to cave in the whole back of his skull.

Malissa met Maloney as he came out of the courtroom.

Her black eyes were deep, terrible, and inscrutable.

"Listen, miss," stumbled the remorseful boxer, "you oughta know I didn't go to—to do that—I'm as sorry as—"

She raised her hand to the level of his eyes, then let it fall. "You will not live the month out," she said simply, calmly, and turned away.

A couple of weeks later as I was walking down Main Street one night, a car pulled up beside the curb.

"Get in," said Inspector Hanlon. "They just picked up Maloney in an alley back of Salvador's place—somebody stabbed him, bad. All he knows is it was a wop. They all look alike to him. He hasn't much chance to live, but *this* time, I'm goin' to hang the pin where it belongs—one of old di Gigisetti's gang turned the trick, of course. I got any number of witnesses to swear they heard the girl threaten Jack the day of the trial. This vendetta business makes me sick. I got enough to contend with—"

We had drawn up before headquarters, and Hanlon motioned me to come in.

"I got a dragnet out for old Gigi and his bunch—want to see if they've got anything—"

An elderly man was waiting at the bar.

"This man wanted to see you, sir," said the chief. "He's told me a crazy tale, and I think he's bugs. But being as it had bearings on the case today, indirectly, I had the stenographer take it down."

"Who are you?" asked Hanlon.

"The new caretaker at the Hopi Athletic Club, sir, name of Karney. I took charge yesterday and last night—well—" he indicated the statement in the hands of the chief. This statement follows, in full:

The Statement of William J. Karney.
I am forty-nine years old, born in San Diego, California, and was never in Chicago until the day before yesterday, the date of my arrival. I know nothing of the Maloney-Azerello fight, or the death of the latter, except what I have heard from the members of the club since taking charge.

Last night—June 2nd—I had business in the building where the fights are held. I was in the large room where the ring is set, entirely alone from eight o'clock until ten-thirty. Sometime between ten and ten-thirty, I glanced up from my occupation and was surprized to see a tall man in boxing togs, with boxing gloves on his hands, enter the room. I supposed he was a fighter who had been sparring in the gymnasium and beyond speaking to him in a general way of greeting, I paid no attention to him. However, this man went directly to the ring, without saying a word, and I presently felt a strange chill pass over me. I rose and looked, to see him standing by the ring, staring directly at me with a sort of fixed gaze. I noted now that, though he was naturally of dark complection, he was deathly pale and his eyes burned with a strange unnatural light. Thinking he was ill, I was about to make some inquiry of him, when he raised a gloved hand and beckoned me. I went over to where he stood and asked him what he would have. He made no answer, but laid his hand on a certain ringside seat and nodded his head, as though he meant that I should examine the seat.

I was becoming rather nervous by this time, for his manner and appearance were so strange as to be almost inhuman and unnatural in aspect. I noted that *the back of his head was clotted with blood.* But when I asked him if he were hurt, he still maintained his unearthly silence, and pointed impatiently at the seat. I bent, and looking closely, discovered the blurred imprint of a hand—or rather—the tips of four fingers, in blood, on the underside of the seat. This blood was stained deeply into the wood and almost imperceptible as if it had been there for days, or possibly weeks. When I rose from my examination, the man was gone and I have not seen him since."

When this statement was read, Hanlon stared at Karney in some suspicion.

"And why come to me with this tale?"

"Because, sir, I heard awhile ago that Maloney had been stabbed, and one of the club members was showing me the stains which soaked through the padding at the edge of the ring— which padding has since been removed—from Tony's crushed skull. This seat is nearest the stains. That is, whoever was sitting in the seat at the time, was nearest to the dying boxer."

"Umm," a light began to burn in Hanlon's eyes as his superstitious Irish nature was stirred. He opened his drawer and took thence a picture showing a full-length study of a man in boxing togs—Tony Azerello.

"Have you ever seen a picture of Azerello, or did you ever see him in person?" he asked.

"No, sir."

The inspector mutely held the picture before Karney's eyes. The man went positively ghastly. His face turned white and his lips assumed a greenish tinge.

"God be our shield against the powers of evil!" he whispered hoarsely. "As Heaven is my witness, that is a picture of the man I saw last night!"

The inspector rose. "Let's go to the Hopi," he said briefly.

Karney accompanied us, unwillingly, and tremblingly he showed us the seat, with many a nervous start and glance about as if he expected ghosts to leap on him from the corners. The stains were there alright, four faint dark blots.

"Blurred considerably," grunted the inspector. "Can you get the prints?"

"When a print's left I can get it," answered the Bertillon expert whom the inspector had brought along. "Not so easy this time, though."

"Finding who sat in this seat that night is next," said Hanlon. "I—"

Memory awoke within me.

"I remember!" I exclaimed. "I saw him stand up and shake his fist at Tony! A short, very dark Sicilian he was—"

"Makes out a good case, that does!" grunted Hanlon sarcastically. "A short dark Sicilian—thousands of 'em! And what if we find him? Didn't Tony knock his brains loose on the boards as he fell? I'm after di Gigi, not an unknown 'short dark Sicilian'—but—*what are those blood stains on that seat?*"

He shook his head. "Let it rest for the minute. Harry, take those prints and see if you can find the owner. I'm goin' up to di Gigi's place. Want to go?"

Di Gigisetti, a huge, whiskered banditto of a man, received us in his rather palacious home with a cold air. Hanlon came straight to the point.

"Where's your daughter?"

"She has been in bed for hours," was the haughty reply.

"Well, look, di Gigi, somebody stabbed Jack Maloney downtown tonight, and I have good reason to know it was one of your gang—"

"Prove it!" the strong jaws came together with a vicious click.

"Oh, I know you're a big man in the Racket," snarled Hanlon, "but I want to tell you this—your daughter made public threats and—"

A catlike tread sounded on the broad stair which led up out of the hallway. I saw a short swarthy man—

"Hanlon!" I shouted involuntarily, "that's the man that sat in that seat!"

Hanlon whirled.

"Luigi Savonari! Suppose you come here and explain the blood on that seat—"

Savonari's face turned a dirty white. In view of his actions I believe he thought Hanlon knew a great deal more than he really did. At any rate, he whipped out an automatic and fired pointblank. I felt the wind of the bullet and heard the crash of Hanlon's answering shot.

The Sicilian buckled at the knees and toppled downstairs with a loose and grotesque flinging of his limbs.

"Cospetto!" roared di Gigisetti furiously. "Swine! You invade my home! Now you kill my best friend! Dio! I will stab—"

A swift patter of feet, and a frightened face peered down the stairs.

"Oh Santa Maria, they have keel Luigi!"

Hanlon blew shrilly on his police whistle as he ran to bend over Luigi Savonari. The Sicilian was still breathing, though his hue was ashen and he was unable to talk.

"The priest!" he gasped in good English. "Get the priest. I would confess."

"You won't live till he gets here," said Hanlon.

"Then I will tell you," the words came slowly and painfully. "I and only I killed Tony Azerello. He stole Malissa from me. I did not go there to kill him that night, only because I hoped Maloney would give him one dam' good beating. Then when Maloney hit him—in the tenth round—and the lights went out—I saw the saints had—delivered him into my hands. I was out of my seat, leaning against the edge—of the ring. In the darkness he fell partly through the ropes, into my very arms. His head did—not strike—the boards at all. None saw or knew. Like a flash I whipped out—my slung shot which I always carry—and struck him a deathly blow—in the back of the head. I shoved him—back in the ring—and sat down, hiding the blackjack. Then the lights came—on again. I kept my bloody hand—in my coat pocket—but I must have touched my hand to the seat—if there was blood—on it—oh Dio—!"

Luigi Savonari went limp. The girl had fainted into her bewildered father's arms.

"Saints and the prophets!" said Hanlon to me. "Here's a story for you!"

And as such I give it, in bare outline, telling only the hard facts of the matter. Maloney eventually recovered; his attacker was never apprehended. I suppose di Gigisetti still flourishes in Chicago, high in the "Racket."

But here is the strange point: *Who or what was it that showed that telltale seat to William Karney?*

I have since made the man's close acquaintance. He is the soul of veracity when sober, and, to my best knowledge, he was never drunk. He is of sound mind. None of the participants in the matter was anything to him, and I am sure he told the truth when he said he had never seen Azerello or a picture of the man. He had only lately arrived from California and was an absolute stranger in Chicago.

That being the case, is it probable that he knew the true facts of the case somehow, and took this novel way of presenting them? If he knew, how did he know? I cannot say. I simply tell the tale as it was. If William J. Karney was not lying then *the strange boxer he saw that night was the ghost of Tony Azerello come back for vengeance on his slayer.*

They Always Come Back

"Three years ago you were the foremost heavyweight contender—now you're a whiskey-soaked tramp in a Mexican saloon!"

The voice was hard and rasping, with a bitter contempt that cut like a knife. The man to whom the words were addressed flinched and blinked his liquor-reddened eyes.

"And what business is that of yours?" he demanded roughly.

"Just the fact that I hate to see a man make a hog of himself—just because I hate to see a man with championship material in him lying around in a one-horse border village!"

They made a strange contrast, those two, and the loafers and Mexicans who lounged in the rear end of the adobe saloon eyed them curiously. The man who lolled half-across the beer-stained table was young, and in spite of his ragged garments, his athletic frame was evident. His face was not a bad face, in spite of the lines of wild dissipation. The face was surprizingly finely molded with a thin-bridged regular nose that spoke of good blood. About the mouth there was a sign of weakness, at first glance. A second glance showed a keen observer that it was a sensitive mouth, rather than a weak one—an index to a certain flaw in the character that was erratic and unstable rather than bad.

The man who stood looking down on the other was a slender, wiry man of more than middle age. His lips were thin and straight, his nose beaklike, his eyes hard and bitter. He was dressed in a manner costly but plain and seemed out of place in this sordid dive.

"Three years ago," continued his inexorable voice, "you were touted for the next heavyweight champion. Jack Maloney—a classy boxer and a terrible puncher. The man with the mallet right! You slashed through opposition like a second Dempsey. Starting at eighteen, you cleaned up your division and at the age of twenty-one, you were beating at the doors of the title. Twenty-one! An age at which most men are fighting in the preliminaries for ten dollars a round. And you were drawing down the thousands. In three years you came up from nowhere. You were fast as a cat, keen, brainy and tough. You hit like the blow of a caulking mallet. You were wined, dined and petted as the favorite of society—the classy pride of the ring!

"Then what happened? You were matched with Iron Mike Brennon, then an unknown. He stopped you in three rounds. You went all to pieces. You lost your guts. You were knocked out in your next start by Soldier Handler, a hard-hitting second-rater. Then you quit the ring; disappeared. You went to the gutter. You'd lost your nerve; turned yellow—"

"That's a lie!" Maloney was stung out of his indifference.

"Alright, I won't say you were yellow. But you'd lost your guts. You took to booze fighting. Went to the gutter. Went broke. Now, in three years you've made a no-stop flight from Broadway to this dump."

Maloney's mighty fists clenched into iron knots on the table. His eyes flamed through the tousled mass of his black hair.

"I ought to kill you," he said huskily, inflamed by the stuff he had been drinking. "Just because you've managed a few champions you think you can talk to a man any way. You don't manage me."

"I'm not in the habit of managing whiskey-soaks," sneered the other. "The men I managed may not have been as fast or as hard-hitting as you were, but they were men. They didn't go all to pieces just because somebody hung a k.o. sign on their chin."

Suddenly he changed his manner and sat down opposite the ex-fighter.

"You're still young, Maloney," said he slowly. "Why don't you try to come back?"

"Fight again?" Maloney shuddered as from a nightmare memory. "Ugh!"

"You've brooded over that knockout until it's become an obsession with you. Get yourself in shape again—"

"No! No! I couldn't. I don't want to try—to even think about it."

"Then you've no more guts than I thought," the bitter rasp had come back in the voice. "I thought—"

"Listen!" the other cried with a desperate note in his voice. "What do you know of my trouble? You never fought in your life."

"No," the other admitted, "but I know you fighters better than most of you know yourselves. And I know you could come back if you had the guts."

"Sit down," Maloney ordered huskily. "I'll tell you my side of it."

"Alright, I'll listen to your tale of woe—and buy you a drink, too," the older man added with a cutting sneer.

Maloney's eyes momentarily flashed, but he had sunk too low to be over-resentful of anything beyond a direct insult. He motioned to the bartender, gulped down the fiery draught and said savagely:

"Guts! Bah! What do you know of a man who has the heart knocked out of him? Listen, I was all you said and more. Till I met Brennon. I thought I was invincible. I wore myself out punching him. I ruined myself—"

"And why?" broke in the other. "You mean you were ruined mentally. You came out of that fight with only one mark. A cut on your cheekbone, and a few bruises. I've seen fights in which the winner was carried out of the ring. You took that defeat to heart. Just because you couldn't stop Brennon, you lost all your nerve, permanently.

"And why couldn't you stop him? Because he's a freak. An iron-jawed, steel-bellied gorilla that can't be knocked out! No man's ever turned the trick, and won't until he cracks from the continual punishment. Remember Joe Grim, what Gans, Fitzsimmons and Johnson failed to stop! But you punched yourself out and took the count. And you let it beat you! Bah! Your vanity couldn't stand the shock. You'd gotten to the point where you didn't believe any man could hurt you.

"If you'd had the stuff it takes to make a real man, that beating would have done you good—taken some of the conceit out of you. As it was, it ruined you."

"Listen!" there was fury and agony in Maloney's tone; he was drunk but his mind was lucid. "Listen! I'll try to tell you—

"I'd never met a man like Brennon. I didn't credit much those stories I'd heard of Grim, Goddard and Boden—those old-time iron men. I didn't believe the man lived who could stand up to my punches.

"Then I met Brennon at the Hopi A.C. in San Diego. I'd heard he was tough—been knocking over a bunch of second raters on the coast till Steve Harmer took him over and began getting him good matches.

"At the first I was impressed by the ferocity of Brennon's face and the steady glare of his eyes. I half expected him to be awed by my name and k.o. record, but he glared at me as if I were one of the second raters he had been pushing over. Or rather, as if he were a tiger and I a bison he was going to tear limb from limb. I tell you, the fellow isn't human! He's made of solid iron and there's room in his skull for only one thought—the killer instinct!

"At the gong he came out of his corner wide open; no defense at all. And he knew nothing about scientific hitting. He lifted his swings from the floor, in the old rough-house style. I went in to finish him quick. I expected to flatten him with the first rush, but when I landed my first blow, a left hook to the body, I got the surprize of my life. Brennon didn't even flinch; instead of sinking wrist deep into his body, my fist rebounded just as if I had struck a metal boiler instead of a human body!

"I tell you, he was almost as hard as steel. But I didn't stop to worry; I began throwing rights and lefts to the body and head with everything I had. I was the first first-class man Brennon had met, the papers said. That was his introduction into the first-rate ranks, and I gave him a baptism of fire and blood.

"I battered him all over the ring without a return. He didn't even know enough to duck or wrap his arms around his jaw. Blood spattered all over us; I closed one of his eyes nearly shut. But he wouldn't go down. And just before the gong, when I thought he must be weakening, he suddenly landed one of those wide-sweeping left-handers under my heart. It felt for a second as if he had caved me in. Took my breath away. But it wasn't the blow that sent me to my corner so discouraged; it was the fact that for three solid minutes he'd taken everything I could hand out, and was apparently as strong as ever.

"Between rounds my manager and handlers urged me to go slow; they were getting afraid that I'd fight myself out. But my pride was stung. I'd trained perfectly, but I was beginning to feel fatigued. None of my fights had been at such a pace as this! Just imagine battering away with all your power for three minutes straight! And consider the fact that Brennon had taken every blow I started! I could scarcely believe it, but at the gong here he came with his wild beast eyes glaring in his bloody face.

"I threw caution to the winds. Mike Brennon must have gone through hell in that second round. Near the end of it, his nose was smashed flat, both eyes closed to mere slits, his face one red mask of pulped flesh and blood. But through the slits of his eyelids his eyes still blazed with their old light—I tell you, you have to kill a man like Iron Mike Brennon to stop him! He's tougher than Battling Nelson was.

"I felt myself slipping. My blows were coming slower, I knew. My arms seemed to be turning to lead; my legs were trembling, my chest heaving. I rallied with one more ferocious attack just before the gong, and crashed my right four times to his jaw. Think of that! And I'd knocked men out with one blow of the right many a time, to the side of the head or face! For the first time Brennon reeled. His knees buckled, but just as I thought 'He's going!' he straightened and glanced a right from my cheekbone. It opened a cut and for a second I was blinded by a flash of white light in my brain. Oh, I'd been hit before. Hit hard; knocked down. But never such blows as those; and what was worse was the knowledge that I couldn't hit Brennon hard enough to weaken him.

"My knees trembled as I walked back to my corner, and I looked over my shoulder to see if Brennon was showing the effects of his beating. I shouldn't have done that. When I saw him walk to his corner without a quiver, something went out of me. I had an all-gone feeling. As I sank onto my stool, I heard the crowd yelling: 'Hey, whatsa matter, Jack? Lost your punch? How come you ain't stopped this tramp? This boy must be made outa iron!'

"I began to wonder if I had lost my punch. My brain reeled. This was a nightmare! I, the hardest puncher since Dempsey's days, had pounded this wide-open dub for two solid rounds without even weakening him! Surely there must be some limit to his endurance! There must be an end even to his incredible vitality!

"My manager was begging me to box him, take my time! Be content to outpoint him. I scarcely heard. I was in a panic. The factor that sent me out to kill or be killed wasn't so much wounded vanity as you think—it was more fear than anything else! Yes, fear! Just like a man penned in with a tiger who must kill or die!

"I gathered my waning powers and tore out for the third round like a wild man. Brennon with his longshoreman's style was easy to hit. He fought straight up and wide open. I fought like a man in trance. Left, right! My left hand broke on his head but I didn't notice it. I threw my right again and again, with a wild desperation. Every ounce of weight, power and fighting fury went behind that right hand at every blow. When it landed it sounded like the blows of a caulking mallet. And Brennon reeled, wavered—went down!

"When he fell, all my unnatural fury went out of me; I staggered back against the ropes, completely fought out—an exhausted shell of a man. The referee was counting. Then to my utter horror, Brennon shook his head and began to get his feet under him. I nearly fainted. I thought I'd finished him—I knew I was done. And he was getting up! The ring floated before my eyes.

"Then Brennon was up and coming for me. I tottered away from the ropes on buckling legs and lifted arms that were no stronger than a girl's. I was all gone—out on my feet. Even then he missed— missed—missed. At last he crashed a leaping left-hander to my head. There was a flash of white light again, I reeled and he smashed a terrible swing under my cheekbone. The lights went out. They said I came up again at the count of nine, and he floored me the second time before I was counted out. I don't know. I don't remember any-thing after that fearful right-hander that first dropped me."

A momentary silence fell. Maloney's bloodshot eyes burned unseeingly and when he continued he seemed to be talking more to himself than to his hearer.

"That fight made Iron Mike Brennon," he said huskily at last. "It broke me. My mind was in a chaotic whirl. I couldn't get down to training. I couldn't settle on anything. I stayed out of the ring for four months, then went back in against Soldier Handler. I was all at sea. I hit with my old force but I had no timing or accuracy. Every time I started a blow the vision of Iron Mike Brennon's bloody and snarling face rose up before me. I was wild and awkward. Every time I saw a blow coming, the memory of Brennon's terrific knock-out smashes made me flinch and back away. The crowd booed me, hissed me, called me yellow. At last, in the fifth round I went down and out from the swings of a man I should have stopped in the first rush. The sportswriters said I quit. Maybe I did. I could hear the referee counting over me; I wasn't unconscious but I couldn't drag myself to my feet."

Grendon moved restlessly. His quick nervous energy made it impossible for him to keep still long at a time.

"It's the mind," said he. "Your superiority complex got a jolt. You should have recovered by this time. It wouldn't be impossible for you to get back in shape. I saw the Handler fight. You were like a man dazed or drugged. Even so he staggered every time you landed, and it took him five rounds to beat you down, in the condition you were in. You were not in shape, mentally or physically.

"As for Brennon," the harsh rasping note stole in again, "you said you were in shape for him. You weren't. You thought you'd trained. You'd been going through the motions but your heart wasn't in your work. You were too sure of yourself. And that same conceit whipped you—you fought yourself out and when Brennon dropped you—as he might have dropped any man that ever lived—you didn't have the stuff to take it and come back.

"Once more I ask you—will you let me take you and put you back in the ring?"

Maloney's sole answer was to turn his back on his interrogator and reach for the bottle of tequila which the bartender had left on the table. He felt the cold eyes of Grendon on him for a few moments, then was vaguely aware that the manager had gone.

Maloney had been drinking hard three years. Today he plunged into his old vice with a sort of desperation, to drown the old ghosts which Grendon had conjured up. In a short time he was too muddled to even wonder why the bartender kept bringing the liquor for which he, Maloney, had no money to pay.

He swiftly passed into the hazy semi-consciousness of extreme intoxication and as he hovered on the borderline of complete oblivion, he was dimly aware of a commotion. There were shouts, a fall of chairs, the crash of broken bottles— something struck him a powerful blow and he struck back. Or at least that was his intention but he was so far gone in drink that he never knew whether he put the thought into action or not.

Jack Maloney awoke with a thirst and a splitting headache. Neither particularly worried him, since the last few years this had been a common phenomenon on waking. But he at last realized that he was in strange surroundings. A pitcher of water close at hand first occupied his attention, then he looked about him. He was in a small room, walled, floored and roofed of 'dobe. There was one door which was closed; one small heavily-barred window.

The ex-fighter lurched and tried the door. It was locked. Slowly the truth dawned on him. He was in jail. A sort of panic struck him. He knew the horrors of these Mexican jails in whose vermin-ridden cells men die forgotten. He pounded on the door and shouted loudly.

Steps sounded outside in the corridor and presently the door swung open. Two heavy-faced Mexican soldiers, heavily armed, stood on either side of a third man.

"Grendon!" Maloney exclaimed. "What's all this mean?"

There was no sympathy in Grendon's cold eyes.

"Don't you remember last night?

Maloney passed an uncertain hand over his throbbing brow.

"I don't remember anything after our talk."

"No," Grendon rasped, "you were drunk as a swine. Anyway, after I left, a row started in that joint where you were and when the police came in to stop it, one of them bumped into you and you knocked him stiff. It's a serious offense to strike an officer in this part of Mexico. You've been given a heavy fine."

"I haven't any money," said the ex-fighter. "Pay my fine and I'll pay you back."

"Pay out five hundred dollars, American money, for a rum-soaked ruin?" Grendon's voice was more bitter than Maloney had ever heard it.

"Five hundred dollars!" Maloney was dumfounded.

"Sure. And if you can't pay it, you'll lay it out—and not in this cool cell either. These soldiers have come to take you to the bullpen, they tell me. You know what a few months there means."

Maloney shuddered. He had looked into these "bullpens," had seen the men imprisoned there, the maundering wrecks that milled ceaselessly to and fro beneath the merciless sun. For a Mexican bullpen is simply a jail with high walls and no roof. No breeze can blow upon the men there; only the semi-tropical sun beats down upon their defenseless bodies all day long. There is no shade; nowhere to sit or lie save on the hard flag stones or the packed dirt floor, in the broiling sunshine. Men go insane there and die gibbering."

"You won't leave a man of your own race for a fate like that?" the fighter cried desperately.

"No?" Grendon sneered. "Watch me!" Then seeing the utter despair on Maloney's face, he said:

"The alcalde happens to be a friend of mine. I'll do this much for you. There's a sort of one-horse fight club here, run by an American gambler, as you probably know. Alright. A Mexican heavyweight by the name of Diaz is in town, looking for a match. They'll let you out of jail to fight him. You'll get nothing of course, but I'll bet five hundred dollars on you *and you'll win!* If you don't, it's the bullpen."

Maloney cried out in horror: "Fight? After three years of idleness and dissipation? Why, I couldn't even spar a round! I've no wind, stamina or punch. A child could push me over."

"Alright," Grendon rapped. "Suit yourself; maybe you'll have an easier time in the bullpen, anyhow." He turned away.

"Wait!" Maloney shouted in desperation. "I'll fight! But how can I expect to win?"

"A man can do anything he has to," Grendon answered grimly. "I'll go arrange things. They won't let you out of this cell till Diaz is in the ring. Till then you might while away the time thinking about the sun on the bare walls of the bullpen!"

Maloney lay face down on the dirt floor; his aching head forgotten. How could he even stand up to a fighter, even such a dub as this Mexican most undoubtedly was? Much less, how could he win? Then the vision of the bullpen rose up in his mind. The thought of the fight nauseated him; the thought of the prison crazed him.

Time passed; at last the door opened and two Mexican guards entered. They motioned him to precede them, and they followed close behind, their bayonets barely touching his back.

In the ring, in the squalid, little sheet iron fight stadium, Diaz lolled in his corner and awaited the coming of the dub he was to slaughter. Diaz was sure of himself; he had been told that they were taking a white man out of the jail to meet him, and surely no fighter of any consequence could be in a jail in this tiny border town which owed its sole existence to the thirst of the white men across the river, and which even Diaz held in contempt. He had not even taken the trouble to learn the name of his opponent.

He glanced up languidly. A black-haired American was climbing unsteadily through the ropes, aided by a wiry man of late middle age whom Diaz with a start recognized as the great Grendon himself. Diaz' heart skipped a beat. What was the manager of champions doing here, and why was he seconding a fourth rater? Something wrong here!

Diaz stole a look at the other fighter with quickened interest. He looked closer, with unbelief in his eyes. Then his swarthy color faded to a dirty white and he spoke swiftly and passionately to his manager.

Jack Maloney felt an involuntary shudder go through him as he looked about at the old familiar sight—the ropes of the ring, the stained canvas, the shouting crowd. Again there rose dizzily a bygone vision—a vaster, more pretentious ring, a huger throng— and a black-haired battler who writhed broken, at the feet of a gory slugger. Then another vision blotted this out—a vision of a roofless Hades where men went staring crazy.

He glanced at his opponent, a second-rate Mexican he had never heard of. He saw recognition flare in Diaz' eyes, saw the pallor on the dark face. A faint pride stirred in him. As low as he had sunk, the very memory of his name was enough to frighten this second rater. Bitterness flooded him at the thought on his past glory and his present degradation.

The referee called the men to the center of the ring and gave them the usual unheard instructions. Diaz was beginning to get back some of his confidence. His manager had told him that this man was the same who had been lying about the saloons for months, and he himself knew that Maloney had not fought for three years. The lines of dissipation in the American's face and the lack of training evident in his whole frame cheered him; but he must be careful. Must take no chances and be sure that this man was harmless before risking anything. Diaz had once fought a preliminary to one of Maloney's fights and the memory was still fresh in his mind, of the sledgelike smashes that had flattened the man's opponent on that occasion.

The men went back to their corners and as Grendon climbed through the ropes he hissed one parting word: "I've sunk five hundred dollars on you! Win and you're a free man; lose and it's the bullpen!"

The gong sounded. Maloney rose and walked slowly toward the middle of the ring. Diaz came out even more slowly and carefully. Maloney scarcely saw him; in his mind he saw a snarling blood-stained demon who rushed and smote like the very spirit of the primitive.

A moment the men circled each other. At last Diaz led half-heartedly; his left got home under Maloney's heart and the Mexican, awed by his own audacity, involuntarily closed his eyes, expecting to be blasted out of existence instantly. But Maloney made no attempt to return the blow. It had not been hard, but the feel of it brought back in a nauseating wave all his old fears; again in that instant he relived his nightmare battle with Brennon, his slaughter by Soldier Handler.

Finding himself still alive, the Mexican repeated his lead. This time Maloney countered with his own left and Diaz, shrinking away from it, was surprised to feel it glance lightly from his shoulder. No force there. Diaz' intelligence told him that the once-great Maloney was only a shell of himself; but his instinctive fears kept him from rushing in to make a quick finish of it.

He attacked warily, jabbing at Maloney's face, then as the American retreated heavily, he followed up his advantage with a right to the body that carried force. Maloney felt as if a keen knife had cut off his breath for a fleeting instant. Already he was beginning to feel the effects of his lack of training. His knees were beginning to tremble, his breath to come in gasps. And the first round had scarcely progressed a minute.

Only Diaz' caution kept him from flattening his opponent in the first round. He kept a steady stream of straight lefts in Maloney's face, blows that cut and hurt but did not stun, and occasionally he drove his right hard to the body, knowing that Maloney was in no shape to take punishment there.

The white man was already in a bad way. Those right-handers sank deep in his flabby midriff; sweat soaked his body, his gloves and trunks, and it seemed his heart would burst with the exertions of his labored breathing. Worse than all, the blows that rained steadily upon him brought up the memories of those last two fights—

Diaz grew in confidence. So far his opponent had not laid a glove on him. The great Maloney was staggering before his blows! This would be a tale to tell to admirers! As this feeling grew, Diaz increased the savagery of his attack. Just before the gong Maloney went down, partly from the increasing force of the Mexican's blows, partly from his own exhaustion.

He came to himself in his corner. Grendon was working over him with all the skill of an old-time handler, but Maloney gasped: "I'm through. I can't even get up off my stool."

Grendon reached for the sponge to toss it in. His eyes were bitter.

"All right, the bullpen for you. This fourth-rate spig's punched you right into it."

At that moment the gong sounded. From whence his renewal of strength came, Maloney never knew. He always secretly believed it was a flare of momentary insanity and perhaps he was right. But at Grendon's words, a fearful chaos of hatred flamed up in his brain; hatred for Grendon who was consigning him to a living death, hatred for the Mexican soldiers who stood about to see that he did not escape, hatred for Iron Mike Brennon who was the prime cause of all his trouble. And naturally, all his hate centered on the man in the ring with him.

Diaz came rushing from his corner like a great tiger. He was wild with the killer instinct, inflamed with the desire to stretch this once-great battler at his feet. But he met a different man. Somehow Maloney heaved up off his stool, knocking the sponge out of Grendon's hand. His legs seemed dead but he lurched forward and as Diaz plunged savagely in, Maloney steadied him with a straight left to the face, and crashed his right under the heart, with a force which even surprized himself.

Diaz staggered, whitened. For the first time in his life he had run full into the blow of a real hitter and the sensation left him weakened and nauseated. He felt as if he had been caved in; as if his heart had momentarily stopped. No longer did he dally with a desire to see the great Maloney stretched at his feet. He only desired to avoid utter destruction.

He commenced a hasty retreat and Maloney, realizing that his strength was swiftly fading, and with the bullpen before his eyes, lurched desperately after him. Diaz was still unmanned by that blow under the heart and on the ropes Maloney caught him. And there, holding the ropes with his left hand to keep him on his feet, Maloney crashed another right-hander over, this time to the jaw, and Diaz dropped for the full count.

As the referee said "Ten!" Maloney dropped likewise, his fading thought being that he was going to die of fatigue.

He came to himself to see Grendon bending over him, and if the manager felt any satisfaction, his face did not show it.

"Alright, hustle out of it," he rapped harshly. "We're leaving town. I paid your fine."

"You can go to hell," snarled Maloney, sitting up, all his hatred of Grendon blazing in his eyes. "I fought my bout like you said and I'm grateful for what you did—getting me the fight. Otherwise I owe you nothing."

"You owe me five hundred dollars," Grendon retorted. "The stakeholder skipped with the money I bet on you. I paid your fine out of my own pocket. That way I've lost a thousand dollars on you, but we will just call it five hundred. And you're going to work it out for me."

"Work it out?"

"Fight it out, if you like the word better. That fight showed one thing; you're not as far gone as I thought. You still know how to hit and you've got more than a shadow of your old punch. Close, careful training will sweat the booze out of your system and get you back in shape. You'll never be much, maybe, but you can slap down a flock of pushovers and pay back my money."

"I won't do it," Maloney answered shortly. "I went through Hades last night. I won't do it again for anybody."

"Maloney," said Grendon looking at him piercingly, "you hate me, don't you?"

"As much as one man could hate another," answered Maloney with his characteristic honesty.

Grendon seemed not displeased. In fact he grinned thinly. "Alright, do you want to go through life knowing you're obligated to a man you hate?"

Maloney's black-crowned head jerked up and his eyes glinted into Grendon's hawklike gaze.

"I'll do it," he said abruptly. "You ought to make your money back off me in one fight. Then we're through, understand."

Grendon's only answer was a wintry smile.

Thus came Jack Maloney, once a coming champion, now a has-been, to the managerial care of "Iceberg" Grendon. No words of love passed between them; their conversation was limited to short abrupt advice or requests on the part of the manager and shorter replies on the part of the fighter.

After the affair at the border town, they went directly to the coast and took ship for Australia, Grendon's native land. Maloney having no money, Grendon paid all expenses, and the fighter wondered that he should spend so much, merely to assure himself of the payment of five hundred dollars. Grendon seemed not at all parsimonious except in this matter and Maloney decided that the man hated him as much as he hated Grendon and was merely taking this revenge. He remembered that in his early career he had knocked out one of Grendon's protégés and though the Australian was not a man to harbor grudges, Maloney, for lack of a better reason, decided that Grendon had never forgiven him. He determined to pay back not only the five hundred that Grendon had spent paying his fine, but the five hundred which the crooked stake holder had stolen. After that—Maloney's fists slowly clenched as the black tide of his hate surged through his brain.

Grendon had a training camp in the country back of Sydney and there Maloney plunged into the work of conditioning himself.

Grendon proved himself a first-class trainer, whatever else his faults. He made Maloney go easy at first, start very gradually to building up his long-abused body, and Maloney, realizing his manager's wisdom and experience, followed his instructions to the letter.

Months passed; slowly Maloney was rounding into shape. He was training harder now, and his muscles were vibrant with strength and life. He felt no craving for liquor. He had never been a natural sot, had drunk only to drown his dreams. He could do miles of roadwork now without discomfort and when he struck the heavy punching bag it leaped and tossed like a ship on a windy sea. In the daily bouts with his sparring partners he felt that his timing and speed had come back to a remarkable extent. Speed and punch—the secret of his earlier successes— and now he strove to regain them. The punch that numbed and shocked the toughest fighter, the speed that carried him through the guard of cleverer men. Maloney had never been a really clever boxer in the fullest sense of the word. He had been more of the slugger; but his defense was not to be sniffed at and his shifty footwork would have done credit to many a more crafty boxer. Speed to catch his man and the punch to finish him!

At last when he believed he was ready to face a fairly good opponent, Grendon kept him at light training a month longer. In a way Maloney was eager to fight and get it over. His labor had been one of hatred, not love, and the sooner he could fling the money he owed into Grendon's face with a curse, the better it would suit him. But when he thought of entering the ring again, the old red ghost came back and left him weak and trembling.

Still, he was secretly grateful for one thing; he was no longer a whiskey-soaked hobo, but a man. Like all natural athletes, he reveled in the feel of his new strength and vibrancy—in the smooth flowing muscles and the work of the great clean lungs. He decided that he would never again sink into the gutter—he was still young, scarcely twenty-five years old. He would get some sort of a job and if he could not be a fighter, he would at least be a man.

Then at last Grendon announced that he had gotten Maloney a match.

"An American by the name of Leary," said Grendon. "You ought to draw a good crowd, if the fight fans down under remember you. And they always turn out to see a couple of Americans battle. I don't know what's the matter with Australia; she turns out so few fighters worthy of the name these days. I remember when Young Griffo, Hall, Murphy—"

Maloney gave him no heed. The vanished glories of Australia's fistic past was the one subject on which Grendon was prone to grow garrulous.

The old all-gone feeling came back when Maloney stood in the ring that night in Sydney. The crowd, some of them remembering him, had given him quite a hand but he was remembering—

With an effort he jerked himself out of his crimson reveries and looked across at his opponent—a rangy red-headed fellow, taller than himself but lighter. The announcer was saying:

"—Jack Maloney, America, weight 195; Red Leary, also of America, weight 180—"

At the gong Grendon hissed: "Remember my five hundred—and that you hate me!" And Maloney found time to wonder at the avariciousness of the man.

Leary, like Diaz, knew Maloney of old and like the Mexican, he had no desire to serve as a steppingstone on the comeback road of a former great one. But differently from Diaz, he attacked instantly, though warily. Grendon had taught Maloney more of the real art of boxing than he had ever known before and now as he blocked and sidestepped the rangy boxer's leads, Maloney realized that he was a better boxer than ever before. But the knowledge is not all—the heart must be in the game—and with no horror of bullpens before his eyes, not even his hatred of Grendon could keep the old red memories from Maloney.

He retired on the defensive, flinched involuntarily from blows that did not hurt, and could not seem to untrack himself. The first round was slow; toward the end Leary drew first blood with a volley of straight lefts to the face. Maloney scarcely felt them and retaliated with a whistling left hook which Leary cleverly blocked.

"Can't you untrack yourself?" rasped Grendon back in his corner. "You're in perfect shape; his best blows are not hurting you. You're hitting as hard as you ever did in your life. But you don't hit often enough. You've been on the run since the tap of the gong. This second rater is going to outpoint you if you don't take a chance." Then, as Maloney made no reply, Grendon snarled bitterly. "Bah!

Your heart's not in your work. You're going to take a whipping just from pure lack of guts."

Maloney went out brooding over his manager's words and Leary, taking advantage of his abstraction, smashed a wicked left hook to the body and staggered his man with a sweeping right to the body. Stung out of his apathy, Maloney came back with a hard left hook to the ribs, knocking Leary into the ropes and bringing the crowd to its feet yelling. But the burst of action was brief. As Leary rebounded from the ropes, Maloney seemed to see Mike Brennon's shadow wavering between and the heart went out of him. His reason told him that the blow he had dealt Leary had not landed solidly enough to knock down any trained man, but his blind unreasoning inhibitions clamored that here was the old tale all over again—a man whom his blows could not hurt.

Thus passed the second, third and fourth rounds, and the sixth and seventh rounds. Leary boxing carefully, taking no chances, piling up an enormous lead, with Maloney defending in his half-hearted manner. Then came the eighth round. Maloney came up as fresh as he had been at the first gong. He felt no fatigue whatever. But Leary saw only his cut and blood-stained features. He did not know that Maloney, tough and in perfect trim, had scarcely felt the jabs which had marked him. Leary believed that Maloney's lack of aggressiveness was from weakness. "They never come back!" And as he rushed out for the eighth, Leary suddenly discarded his former intention of winning on points and went savagely in for a knockout.

The crowd rose roaring; it was in hopes of this that they had sat so patiently through the fight. Maloney found himself the center of a whirlwind. Leary, though no match in hitting power for his opponent, carried a wicked punch and knew how to use it. Throwing caution to the winds he battered Maloney all over the ring and floored him in a neutral corner.

Maloney took a count of nine though he could have risen sooner. He was dizzy, not hurt. As he rose, Leary was on him, wild with the instinct of the kill. Maloney missed a vicious left, landed hard under the heart with the same hand and took a volley of lefts and rights to the head as he backed away, covering up.

Leary gave him no rest. He feinted him out of his position, ducked a venomous right and crashed his own right to Maloney's jaw. Again he landed. Maloney was dizzy; out on his feet. Suddenly it seemed that he was fighting, not Red Leary, but Iron Mike Brennon. Through the blood which veiled his eyes, he seemed to see Brennon's snarling face floating before him.

Suddenly Jack Maloney went crazy. He had suffered enough from this phantom. At last his instinct was fight, and not run. He had forgotten all about Leary. Now he bunched himself into a solid cannonball of destruction and shot forward, blasting his terrible right hand full into the ghostly face which mocked him. And that blind smash found Red Leary's jaw.

Maloney, waking as from a nightmare, heard the referee counting and saw at his feet the limp form of his victim.

Grendon came to him in his dressing room.

"Here is your part of the purse; five hundred and fifty-five dollars."

Maloney snatched it from his hand. "Now then, here's your money, you—"

Grendon seemed not to notice him; he drew from his pocket a newspaper cutting. "Read this."

The date of the paper was a month old. The paper itself had been torn and was pasted together in a crude manner. Maloney read it and cried out incredulously: "Mike Brennon knocked out! Why, this can't be true! It says, 'Red Leary knocked out Iron Mike Brennon tonight in the first round of a scheduled fifteen frame go. It was Leary's last fight before leaving for Australia.' Why—"

He sat down, his brain reeling. He had whipped the man who knocked out the terrible Mike Brennon. A wild feeling of exultation swept over him. He whirled on Grendon, his hatred of the man submerged in his new emotion.

"You'll keep on managing me! You'll get me some more fights! If I whipped the man who whipped Brennon, I can whip any of them! Including Brennon!"

"Handler's in England," said Grendon with a strange eager gleam in his cold eyes. "Do you think you can take him?"

Maloney laughed like a boy. A terrible load seemed lifted from his shoulders and only then did he realize how black and terrible it had been, distorting his entire viewpoint on life.

"I can take a roomful of him! Grendon, you're managing the next champion! First Handler! Then Brennon! Then whoever stands between me and the title! I'll flatten them all!"

"And, say," as Grendon started for the door, "here's your money."

"Keep it!" Grendon rapped. "I never accept money from my fighters. Keep it and pay me back by winning the title!"

Fight fans of London will remember the Maloney-Handler battle as long as they live, after the memories of longer, harder-contested struggles have passed into oblivion. It was short but it was sensational—the kind of fight which brings fans to their feet holding their breath and which sends them away babbling deliriously.

Before the gong sounded, Maloney sat in his corner, fresh and glowing with health after his long sea-trip, vibrant with fierce energy, which many took for nervousness. Across from him Handler sneered confidently. Had not he stopped this youth three years before? Maloney had been better then, surely. The burly Soldier had heard of his life since then. What if he had pushed over a couple of dubs since he started his comeback? Handler laughed confidently; he himself was at the height of his career.

At the gong Maloney shot from his corner like a thunderbolt. And like a thunderbolt he smote the astounded Soldier. Gone were all the red ghosts that once lurked in Maloney's brain, chaining his limbs. Again he was Jack Maloney, the Virginia Thunderbolt.

Handler had scarcely time to get out of his corner before the whirlwind struck. A sizzling straight left rocked his head back and as his jaw came up from behind the hunched and protecting shoulder, Maloney's fearful right crashed over. Only a born hitter can deliver a blow like that; the whole body working in unison, the mighty shoulder following the drive of the arm, the body pivoting at the waist, the feet thrusting powerfully upward and forward—and all done in the flash of a split second.

Handler dropped face down, nor did he move until he was brought to in his dressing room. His first words have come down the years with other ring classics:

"Baby!" caressing his chin, "that galoot don't hit! He explodes!"

Two more fights followed in England; to Maloney they were mere incidents, stepstones on his upward trail. His eventual goal was the title, he felt, but even that was subordinated to his desire to meet Iron Mike Brennon again. For this he lived.

Shortly after he knocked out Soldier Handler, he was matched with Tom Walshire, the champion of England. The clever Briton eluded the wrath to come for nine rounds but Maloney was not to be denied, and in the tenth he cornered Walshire and smashed him to the canvas for the full count.

Gunboat Sloan followed. The Gunner was past his prime, but he still had his old-time ring craft and a left hand as deadly as a crossbow bolt. Boxing superbly, he kept Maloney at bay for four rounds and in the fifth landed that terrible left flush to the jaw. Maloney's knees buckled, but even while the crowd held their breath expecting his fall, he lurched headlong into the Gunner and brought him down with an inside right under the heart.

It was a few days after this victory that Maloney rushed into Grendon's room. The relations of the two men had changed subtly. Grendon's manner had altered after Maloney's decision to continue in the ring, and Maloney's feeling had changed from hatred to a grudging admiration. He had stayed with Grendon because he realized that the man was one the cleverest pilots in the game and could aid him in his climb. At last he had come to have a secret liking for the Australian and had often wondered if the man's cold hard attitude were not a mask to hide his real sensitive nature.

But now as he entered Grendon's room, his brain was in a turmoil.

"Look here!" he waved a newspaper in his manager's face. "Last night in America, Iron Mike Brennon was knocked out by a fellow they call Iron Mike Costigan! In the first round! And the paper says that's the first time Brennon has been flattened!"

Grendon nodded.

"But you told me," stammered the fighter, all at sea, "you told me that Red Leary, whom I whipped in Sydney, had knocked Brennon out! The knowledge that I'd whipped Leary has been what's holding me up!"

Grendon shook his head. "More than that, Jack. You needed something then, to brace you. Now you're able to go on your own."

Maloney frowned and cogitated, then suddenly threw back his shoulders and grinned with the pleasant arrogance of youth.

"You're right; I'm over all that stuff. I realize that it was just mental—just an inhibition or complex or something that I'm rid of. I'll go on and fight—"

He halted, suddenly realizing something of which he had not thought before.

"Brennon must be terribly battered, or he couldn't have been knocked out."

"The last time I saw him," said Grendon, "months before I first met you in Mexico, he was a battered wreck. Nearly ready for the padded cell. Anybody could have pushed him over in this last fight. That's the way these iron men go; they seem invincible for years, then they crack suddenly."

Maloney shook his head pityingly. "I've hated him for three years. I don't hate him any longer and I don't want to fight him. Anyway, the paper says he's retiring. If he wasn't, I wouldn't push over a punch-drunk ruin—say, get me Costigan, the fellow that knocked him out!"

"But Jack, he's an iron man too! Just a counterpart of the Brennon who knocked you out nearly four years ago."

"No matter—and Grendon, I want to say that at last I appreciate everything you've done for me. I was a hog and you made me a man against your will. What your original object was I don't know—"

"Why, Jack," Grendon's hard eyes were strangely soft, "years ago when you were just a hard-slugging kid, I kept my eye on you; wanted to manage you but couldn't buy your contract. I've always liked you as a fighter; of late I've come to like you as a man.

"When I found you wasting your life in that little border town, I wanted to see if you were capable of getting out of the gutter, even with help. I told you that time that the alcalde in the town was my friend. He was and is. I framed the whole thing. You didn't sock an officer; you were too drunk to do anything, or remember anything. I didn't bet any money on you. There wasn't any fine to pay.

"I admit it was cruel, sending you in against Diaz in your condition. But I wanted to find out if you had anything left. Even if he flattened you with the first punch, I didn't intend leaving you there to rot in those low-class dives.

"But you showed me in that fight that you still had your super-human physical ability. I don't believe the man ever lived before who could have knocked out a fighter in good condition, after having gone through what you'd been through! And I saw your heart was in the right place, too. Nothing wrong there. The same old fighting heart. But it was your mind. You needed a bracer.

"I was afraid to show you the paper about Leary and Brennon before the fight and if you'd lost, I'd never have used it. But you see the result."

"How'd you frame that?" Maloney asked.

Grendon smiled. "You noticed how the paper was torn? I simply tore out a few words and pasted the torn edges together. The original lines were: 'Red Leary *was knocked out by* Iron Mike Brennon in one round.'"

Maloney laughed. "It served the purpose. It made me regain my confidence. Now I'll never lose it again if I live to be a hundred. And now I want a match with Costigan."

"Jack, you'll gain nothing by fighting this iron man; just now he's at his prime. Dempsey couldn't knock him out, neither could Fitzsimmons. If you beat him you'll gain considerable prestige, but if he beats you, you're ruined. These iron men are the worst opponents in the world for nervous, sensitive fighters like you. Pass him up and take on a fast, clever fellow like yourself."

Maloney shook his head. "I'm older now. I won't make a fool out of myself again. I won't punch myself out on Costigan as I did on Brennon, but I want to beat the man who beat the man who broke me. Till then, I won't have regained my fullest self-respect and self-confidence."

This is an item which appeared in the newspapers a month later: "Jack Maloney, whose sensational rise and fall four years ago was the talk of the sporting world, rose another step on the fistic ladder which he is remounting when he outpointed Iron Mike Costigan, the conqueror of Iron Mike Brennon. Maloney seems to have regained all the speed and punch which four years ago caused sportswriters to christen him the Virginia Thunderbolt, and to predict his early accession of the heavyweight crown, and has gained in boxing skill.

"This was Maloney's first battle in an American ring since he began his comeback campaign. He held the upper-hand throughout the bout, taking every round of the fifteen-round go, and in the last frame sent Costigan twice to the canvas for counts of nine. Only Mike's superhuman endurance and vitality saved him from the first knockout of his career, and it seemed that if it had gone a few more rounds, he would have taken the count in spite of his ruggedness which is of a quality to make Joe Grim jealous. Maloney, though he did not score a knockout, deserves praise for superb work, and seems a cinch for the title."

The Trail of the Snake

Mistah Snake Wamberson, doomed to obscurity as a whole, was possessed of one doubtful notoriety; people were always pointing him out as a burning example of what a man might be if he had some slight quality he didn't have. What Snake didn't have was a fighting heart. He looked like a champion until he got in a ring with a tough man. Then he looked either a Marathon runner or a rug, according to the speed of the opponent.

In outward appearance Snake was the ideal gladiator. Five feet ten, and 190 pounds of shiny ebony muscles rippling under his glossy hide like great smooth cables, he was. He was broad shouldered, narrow hipped, heavy limbed. He was not musclebound and the fact that his muscles had a tendency to knot like a wrestler's only added to the impressiveness of his appearance. He had a broad-shouldered, narrow-hipped, heavy-limbed fighter's body and he had a fighter's face. When he drew his heavy brows down over his wicked black eyes, an act which caused his woolly scalp to crawl down on his low slanting forehead, and when his thick lips writhed back from his gleaming white teeth, then Snake Wamberson was a fearsome spectacle. However this scowl was present only when he was sure of winning. Opposed to a dangerous man his ebony features assumed a greyish tint of pure horror.

Snake couldn't help it. Lack of courage is a defect which can often be no more supplied than a missing leg can be supplied to the physical body. Figuratively speaking and to mix metaphors, a wooden leg can be supplied but it is not the real article. Snake's metaphorical wooden leg, or false courage, was vanity and laziness. His splendid body had trapped him into the ring game; his detestation of manual labor and the occasional applause of his race kept him there. He was crafty; he managed to fight the rankest novices usually. He was fairly clever and he hit like a mule kicking, when he did hit—but he was so dishearteningly careful of who he was hitting.

At the time this chronicle opens he was in San Francisco, fighting two or three times a month at the cheaper clubs fringing a district known unofficially as Little Harlem, against carefully picked opponents—carefully picked on Mistah Wamberson's part. He had an uncanny knowledge of darktown doings and he rarely went into a ring with a man whom he did not know by report at least. At that he was kept busy. It is surprizing the number of hams, both black and white who aspire to the fistic game.

Snake's daylight hours were spent in desultory training and in lounging around the eating houses, blind pigs and pool rooms of his race, where his flashy manner of dressing and his loud talk and braggadocio made him a center of attraction. Clothes were his weakness; he spent the greater part of his ring earnings on apparel, mainly trusting to his skill at the rattling bones to keep his capacious stomach filled.

Then came a day when old Man Fate snuck up from the rear and planted a number twelve boot just aft of Mistah Wamberson's self-esteem. Snake had showed up at the office of one of the cheap clubs at which he regularly performed.

The promoter eyed him with disfavor. He was a hard-boiled baby of the old school and the conviction had been growing on him of late that Snake lacked a certain requisite of a fighter. The promoter smiled ogreishly and rubbed his hands together. Snake watched him with some nervousness; he had learned that when a promoter rubs his hands together, trouble is hatching for somebody.

"Well, Snake," said the promoter, "the Seattle Terror's run out on us."

"Yessuh," said Snake, expanding his 48-inch chest slightly. "Ah 'spects dat boy am already back in Seattle washin' dishes at de ole joint." Snake had, as usual, made subtle enquiries as to the status of his prospective foe.

"An' I'm goin' to do you a big favor, Snake," purred the promoter, licking his lips. "I'm goin' to give you a white man to lick."

Snake started and swallowed his Adam's apple. This didn't listen so good!

"Uh—ah-wh-white man, suh?" he quavered, "Mistah Harger, Ah ain't feel so well—"

"Arragghh?" snarled the promoter in a questioning tone like a hungry panther. "Yeah? Now listen here, you overgrown hunk of tar, I'm sick of your runarounds. Three times you've pulled out on me because you didn't like the looks of your dancin' partner. Yeah, three times! Me, that's been like a father to you. Once it was a sprained wrist; then it was a sprained shoulder; then it was a sprained ankle. If you open your head before I tell you to, it'll be a sprained neck!"

"Yessuh, Mistah Harger," murmured the subdued Snake.

"You ain't got nothin' to fear," said Harger subtly, biting off the end of a villainous cigar.

"This fellow is just a big raw sailor boy whose ship is docked for awhile. He don't know nothin'."

"Sailuh boy?" That sounded far from hot. Sailuhs was usually tough babies.

"Yeah," Harger bent over the lighted match in his cupped hands to hide the demoniac gleam in his eye. "It's a cinch; I doubt if they'll be more'n one punch landed. On your way now."

Snake gingerly took his hat, pausing at the door for another hesitant word: "Mistah Harger, suh, what am dis boy's name, suh?"

"Whata you care?" roared Harger. "How'm I to keep up with the name of every bum in the business? On yer way!"

The door closed and the Wamberson footfalls dwindled away in the distance. Harger leaned back and laughed till the tears ran down his cheeks.

"One punch is right! The big hunk of coal dust! He's through here as an attraction anyway, and he's cost me money, runnin' out on me. What a surprize I got for him!"

Yea, verily, Mistah Harger was an egg with a twenty-minute shell.

Meanwhile Snake had taken heart; he was inspired to swagger. His philosophy was always swagger before the fight; afterwards there might be no excuse to swagger. Now he strutted into the Parisian Poolroom and with a swish of his Malacca cane, importantly informed the habitués: "Well, boys, dat Seattle Terroh done run out on me. 'Spect he hyuh 'bout mah tarribull right hook. Yeah, boy! Ah done clean up de coluhed population uh dis naybuhood anyways. Mistuh Harger done impo't me a white boxuh!"

The listeners were visibly impressed. Snake expanded in the glow of admiration. Let others find their thrill in the blaze of the ring—that was but secondary—a means to an end—here was where Snake got his kick!

"Who dis white boy, Snake?" asked one of his friends.

Snake thought quickly; he wanted to impress his acquaintances, but he mustn't pull it too strong. He would name some well-known second-rater, who might conceivably be fighting a main event in a club like Harger's—a name flashed through his mind.

"He name am Costigan," he said importantly. "Steve Costigan, de battlin' sailuh."

After the fight, thought Snake, if assailed by men who knew the Sailor, he could swear that Costigan had been matched with him and had run out the last moment as had the Terror. Anyway, Snake lived in the Now, and posed minute by minute. "Costigan!" the name was breathed in awed whispers. It was a name well-known along the West Coast and in many an Asiatic port, wherever the merchant ship *Sea Girl* touched; Steve Costigan, the toughest ham-and-egger that never graduated from the second-rate ranks.

"You-all ain't nevah whipped a white man that good, has you Snake?" one asked.

Snake gave him a pained and pitying look. "Boy, git wise to yo'sel'. Ah ain't 'ppreciated round hyuh. Ain't Ah cleaned up dis neck uh de woods? Ah tell you, Mistah Harger 'preciates me—he's gittin' me de toughest boy he could find, jus' fo' a wuk out."

Poor Snake! Little did he reck the close truth of his words. Mistah Wamberson climbed into the ring for his last appearance at the club of Mistah Harger, which worthy was at present chewing an evil-looking cigar and grinning like a pleased wolf.

The coluhed faction was out en masse to see their tribesman triumph over his white foe. They shook the house with whoops as Snake flexed his muscles, expanded his huge chest and did a war dance to warm himself. He nodded to them and waved a hand to a certain flashy high brown baby who regarded him as her particular property. Then he backed into his corner, turned and began to dip, gripping the ropes. He loved the drama of this moment when all eyes were on him. He exerted his great strength with a preoccupied expression as though unaware that he was nearly tearing the ropes loose. Snake was aware that his opponent had entered the ring but he did not look at him. That was one of his tricks. He heard the name of Costigan shouted repeatedly and chuckled. He had lied so convincingly that the word had spread and the bulk of the crowd thought that this raw unknown was Costigan. He chuckled. The referee called them to the center of the ring for instructions and Snake sidled over, exchanging smiles and glances with the high brown girl who was calling endearments at him. He did not even glance at the white man while the referee was talking. Of course he saw him out of the tail of his eye but he paid no real attention. He was too much engrossed with his own acting; too drunk with the admiring shouts of his followers. He gave the impression of despising his foe too much to notice him or heed the referee—a picture of superb self-confidence.

Snake rippled back to his corner; the lights went off; the gong sounded. Snake whirled and came plunging out—to get the greatest shock of his life to date! In midair he froze with horror though the momentum of his plunge carried him on. The terrible scowl was wiped from his face to be replaced by an expression similar to that of a man who has unwittingly stepped into a cage with a Bengal tiger. The man charging across the ring was as heavy as Snake, but taller. From his lean feet to his cauliflowered ears, he looked the fighter. From under heavy black brows a pair or ferocious blue Irish eyes blazed at the horrified black man.

It *was* Costigan!

This fact burst in Snake's head like a bombshell. Sailor Costigan, a man utterly lacking in the finer points of the game, which fact kept him in the ham-and-egg class, but a man harder to hurt than a chunk of iron, and the most murderous puncher on the West Coast! Snake's eyes batted; this jolt handed him by Fate and Mistah Harger was in a fair way to reduce him to gibbering lunacy. But there was no time to gibber at present.

Costigan, following his only style, met the erratic Snake in mid-ring. Mistah Wamberson had been unable to check his rash rush and he was too shocked to keep his hands up. There was nothing to stop Costigan's left hook which hummed as it shot through the air. *Wham!* Mistah Wamberson stopped that deadly missile with great accuracy, on his features. It was high but unduly potent.

The chocolate-hued pride of Little Harlem turned a complete somersault before lighting on the back of his neck with a jar that shook the building. Mistah Harger wept with demoniacal joy.

As for Snake, he had been dimly aware that a powder house had exploded with stupendous pyrotechnics, in the midst of which he had been belted across the head with a battleship. Simultaneously came oblivion. Entirely out, some dim sub-conscious instinct prompted Mistah Wamberson to gather together his buckling legs and rise. This alone proves how completely out he was.

Costigan noted the rise of his victim with irritation but no surprise. He was of a school whose followers make it a point to always get up, regardless of the circumstances, and he himself had been described as a galoot who made it a habit to fight twenty rounds after having been knocked cold. He expected no less of others.

As he slid out of the corner to which he had retired, poising his murderous right, his victim suddenly regained some of his senses. To his utter horror he found himself on his feet. Panic swept his soul. His reflexes or something had betrayed him and put him in position to again be socked by the Celtic demon in front of him. His goggling eyes fixed with grisly anticipation on the charging white man. Snake acted instantly.

Two things happened simultaneously. Costigan sprang in tiger-ishly and hooked a terrible right for the jaw; Snake dropped like a man struck dead. Costigan stepped back amazed and shocked. He knew, the referee, Harger and most of the crowd knew, that that right hook had missed by at least a foot. Snake hugged the canvas, with bulging eyes while the referee counted disgustedly over him. Mistah Harger chewed his cigar and swore bloodthirstily at the fact that he was deprived of seeing more punishment dealt to his erratic protégé. The crowd hissed and jeered.

Costigan muttered under his breath. He was shocked and outraged; his sense of the eternal fitness of things was jarred to its very foundations. That any man, white or black, should deliberately quit, should fall below a punch whose wind he scarcely felt, was to him too heinous a thing to contemplate. He felt dimly that simply because he was in the ring at the time, some of the infamy or the loathsome outrage might rebound on him. Therefore he glared fero-ciously at Mistah Wamberson and the recumbent gladiator found his glare disquieting in the extreme.

The count was finished; Snake, regardless of the platitudes of the mob, bounded suddenly to his feet, shot through the ropes like a startled fawn and flickered down the aisle to his dressing room like a black streak. It needed no oracle beyond the bloodlusting screams of the maddened fans to tell him that he was through as an attraction at that fight club. As he ghosted through the ropes without looking back, he heard a venomous swish! and something like the near pas-sage of a red-hot brick fanned the back of his neck, from which he rightly conjectured that Mistah Costigan was displaying his irritation with another of his man-killing right hooks. As he drifted through a back door at full speed, with his street clothes under his arm, Snake found time to marvel at the astounding fortune which had been his to twice escape the devastating effect of the Costigan right.

Dawn found the pride of Little Harlem far from the scene of his ignominy. The voices of his coluhed brethren at the ringside had left little to his imagination—so Snake Wamberson brought his dove-colored hat, his high-tan shoes, his lavender socks, his sport suit and his 48-inch chest into the colored community of a small but thriving city in Alabama.

The fighting bee had not yet stung these dusky citizens. Careful questioning told Snake that he had nothing to fear from anyone here, so he posed and swaggered. He soon captured the fancy of a certain high brown baby, superior in pulchritude to the 'Frisco belle, and thereby hangs a tale.

Picture Mistah Wamberson holding forth in the Genteel Poolroom to a crowd of admiring listeners.

"—and Ah says: 'Huccum Mistah Wills calls hisse'f coluhed champeen when he ain' nevah met me?' An' de pahmoteh he say: 'Snake, dat am jest de trouble! You is too good! De fust ratehs ain' gwine meet you!' Ah say: 'Mistah Pahmoteh, does you-all gets me Harry Wills, Kid Norfawk or Gawge Godfrey, Ah fights um fo' money, mahbles or matches!' Ah says."

"Golly Moses!" breathed one Sam Gupson awedly. "Wouldn't none er dem big boys fight wid you, Snake?"

"Well," said Snake truthfully, "dey ain't done it. So I had to take on de toughest white boys dey could find."

"Say, Snake," broke in a gimlet-eyed, hard-faced and usually silent individual known eloquently as Dirk Knife Bill, "seem lak Ah hyuh you done get knock' out by Sailuh Costigan in one roun' fo' you come hyuh."

Snake winced. Dirk Knife Bill had underground ways of hearing things; and it might not be safe to call him a liar. Snake glared at him and swelled out his chest but Bill did not seem overly impressed.

"One roun'? Git wise to yo-se'f, Dirk Knife—*twenty*-one rounds. Why, boy, listen: dat white boy much as admitted hisse'f Ah licked him. Between de fust an' de twentieth roun' Ah drop him eighteen times! Dat boy sho' tough! But Ah coulda finished him de fust roun' only fo' Ah go in, Mistah Harger, de pahmoteh, he say to me, he say: 'Snake, you got to let dis boy stay de limit so de crowd gits its money's worth.' So Ah hold dis boy up and he'p him up after Ah knocks him down, an' den in the twenty-fust roun' Ah slip in de blood on de canvas and fall down wid mah ahm stickin' through de ropes. A couple er three fellows done grab mah ahm an' hold me down while dey count me out. A frame if dey was ever one! After de fight Mistah Costigan he say to me, he say: 'Snake, you is de best man Ah ever fought. Ah wouldn't git in de same ring wid you again for no money!'"

Snake glanced around him importantly. Even the saturnine Dirk Knife was evidently impressed.

"Well," said the hero, rising suddenly and looking ostentatiously at his watch, "Ah got to be goin'. Ah got a date."

"Wid who-all am you got dat date wid, Mistah Wamberson?" nervously asked a chubby youth whose fat round good-natured face was overcast with gloom.

Mistah Wamberson eyed him without approval.

"Well, Mistah Tommy Wicks, that ain't concuhnin' you none. Wheah Ah steps in, yo' interest steps out. If you-all is buhnin' up to know with whom Ah is datin' out with, it's Miss Astoria Bassums—which it don't take me to tell you, boy, that you is *out!*"

With which parting shot Mistah Wamberson twirled his Malacca cane and swaggered forth into the day. Behind him an admiring peal of laughter heralded his going. They were laughing with him and at Mistah Wicks who sat slumped down in gloom. Tommy was a vast, unstable youth whose timidity equaled his bulk.

"Astoria was mah gal," he gulped, "till dat fellah come into town. Ah don' see what womens sees in fellahs like dat. Ah was all set to marry dat gal—she good as tooken me already. Ah done make fust payment on house down on Johnsing Street. Now—"

"Looks like, boy," said Dirk Knife with little sympathy, "yo' goose am cook'. Dat prize-fightuh ain't gwine marry Astoria but he gwine spoil her fo' easy goin' no-count fellahs like what you is. Womens crave publicity and dey like a man what's in de eyes of de crowd."

"You big boy, Tommy," suggested Sam Gupson, "whyn't you-all train up and fight dis boy yo'-se'f?"

Mistah Wicks shuddered violently at the mere thought.

Well, there was no doubt about it—Astoria had fallen hard for the dazzling notoriety—as recounted by himself—of Snake Wamberson. She basked in the reflected glory of his company. There was no one in Darktown to give him the direct lie. To most of the simple inhabitants, 'Frisco, and San Diego, and Seattle were dim and legendary places. Such names as Harry Wills, George Godfrey, Panther Horton they were faintly familiar with, as they were familiar with such names as Sam Langford, Joe Jeanette and Jack Johnson— all huge mythical figures veiled in a glimmering mist of glory and unreality. They knew nothing of the thousands following the game. Snake told them of his glories and they believed him. They believed him so thoroughly that he almost got to believing them himself and added to the telling day by day. He blossomed, he expanded in the adulation bestowed on him. As he paced his measured way along the streets the admiring whispers which reached his ears were like wine to him.

"Dat Mistah Snake Wamberson, de great prize-fightuh!"

This glory was shed on all who were closely associated with him. And so Astoria shivered with ecstasy at his attentions, and smiled on him lovingly. And spoke sharply to her former suitor who came mooning about.

"Why'nt you-all go do somethin' big and glorifious like what Mistah Wamberson done do?"

"Well, Astoria," pleaded Tommy, "us can't all be prize- fightuhs. Ah got good job—"

"Snf!" sniffed Miss Astoria. "Good job! You-all talk 'bout money! Snake done tole me he get fo'ty thousand dollahs fo' one fight!"

Tommy shrivelled but tried a faint comeback: "Den huccum he borrowin' money from Sam Gupson and Dirk Knife Bill?"

"He done lose lot uh money on hoss racin'," answered Miss Astoria. "He drop hun'ned thousan' dolluhs on Kentucky Dehby. Dat ain' nothin' to him. Right away big pahmoteh out on de Coast send fo' him to fight Mistah Godfrey and he make back de hun'ned thousan'. Go long, boy," said Miss Astoria with hauteur. "Don' tell me. Anybody see dat man got money. Look at he clothes! Whyn't you-all dress like what he do?"

"Well, gee whiz, Astoria," protested the badgered Tommy, "Ah got to eat, ain' Ah? Ah ain' got no hun'ned thousan' dolluhs to blow on clothes."

"No, Ah say yo' ain't," snapped Miss Astoria, "and yet you wants me to marry up wid you-alls. Huh."

"Befo' dis fellah come you was right lovin' wid me, Astoria," mourned Tommy. "Now you ain' got no kind word fo' me."

"Well," said Astoria, softening slightly, "Ah got nothin' 'gainst you, Tommy, but you ain' notorishus like what Snake am. Ah laks a fightin' man. Whyn't you be a fightuh, Tommy? You and Snake could have a fightin' match right hyuh to kinda staht you off, lak."

"Staht me off? Finish me off, you means."

"Is you scairt?" sniffed Miss Astoria. "You bigger'n him."

Tommy miserably realized his inability to explain to his lady love that mere size had little to do with the matter.

"Ah's fat; dat boy's hahd. Weight Ah got on mah stummick he got on he shouldahs."

"You's jest afeered on him."

"But Astoria, dat's boy's business is fightin'!"

"Well," was her Parthian shot, "on yo' way. Till you does somethin' by which Ah kin be proud of you by, don' come caterwaulin' 'roun' me."

Tommy disconsolately sought his friend Sammy Gupson and that giant intellect immediately began revolving.

"What Ah thinks, Tommy," said the oracle, "is dis—Astoria ain' really in love wid dat big cheese, she jest think she am. She plumb dazzled by him. Now de thin' for you to do is dispel de delusion."

"Do which?"

"Show him up."

"How?"

"Lick him!"

Tommy groaned deep, long and loud. "You and Astoria is done gone off yo' beans. Dat what she say—is *you*-all tryin' to git me kilt?"

"She say fight dat big boy?" cried Sammy exultantly. "What Ah tell you? She crave fo' you-all to take her away f'um him, only she don't know it. Wimmens like mens to fight oveh um—cave man stuff."

"Uh huh," grunted Tommy. "Ah gits cave-mannish wid dat Wamberson boy and Ah leaves mah corpse behine me when I climbs outen de ring."

"Aw, use yo' haid," urged Sam. "Does he git licked after all he big talk, he ain't gwine show his face 'roun' hyuh no mo.' Now lissen, Ah done thunk it out—is you fo'got yo' sister which went to N'y Awleens and got married—"

Tommy started with sudden recollection and a gleam shone in his eye as the voice of the conspirator sank to a sinister whisper…

"Let de real festivities commence, boys, de king am arrove!" thus Mistah Wamberson greeted the earnest workers in the back room of the Genteel Poolroom. The click of rattling bones halted momentarily. Sam Gupson came sliding around the room in a distinctly serpentine manner, displeasing to Mistah Wamberson.

"Snake, we is done found you a opponent!" chortled Mistah Gupson.

"You is found me a which?" Mistah Wamberson's eyes batted and his reactions were not altogether pleasant.

"A man which craves to mingle wid you in fistic entuhtainment. We done decided to go in fo' de game hyuh in Chop Suey. Ouah lodge, de Gran' High Exalted Mogal uh de Fo'th Dimension, is gwine stage de show. We's awready buildin' de ring—"

"Uh huh," said Mistah Wamberson noncommittally. "And who dis misguided gent what craves to mingle wid me?"

"Tommy Wicks!"

"Who?" Snake staggered; his eyes batted rapidly. "Tommy Wicks."

Snake threw back his head and laughed till the rafters shook. He staggered over to a chair, fell carelessly into it and laughed some more. With tears rolling down his cheeks, he gasped: "Sho' Ah know dat boy was lackin' in de uppah story but Ah ain' know he dat bad."

"Well, Snake," Sam carelessly fingered an ample roll of bills, "Tommy he trainin' mighty close and Ah willin' to bet a little on him. He ain' think you so much, an' he mighty soah 'count uh Astoria. He believe he gwine lick you, so strong he give me some money to bet on hisse'f."

Snake's eyes narrowed. He was not altogether a fool. He knew few men will put up money for the sake of friendship. Then he reflected: Sammy had never seen a prizefight; to a shrimp like Sammy doubtless Tommy's huge flabby bulk looked awe-inspiring. Sheer size means a lot to the untutored. And maybe—though it scarcely seemed possible—Tommy had a reputation as a tough back-alley fighter. Snake had no fear of such, in or out of the ring—they always rushed with a wild right swing, and never could take it in the kitchen. It was the tough boxers Snake feared. And Tommy now, train him down as fine as Mistah Wamberson was trained and he would not be any more than a light heavyweight. Anyway, Snake made the plunge. He couldn't resist. It looked such a cinch! His brows drew down in a horrible scowl.

"Awright, Ah fights him. He ain' gwine into dis in ignorance. He know me."

"Ah takes all or any paht uh dat Wicks' money," broke in Dirk Knife Bill, pushing forward. Snake caught his shoulder and whispered in his ear:

"Lend me fifty dolluhs to bet on muhse'f. Ah pays you back outen de winnin's."

Dirk Knife, pockets bulging at present, complied. Dirk Knife often had more money on him than he would have cared to try to account for—to a chief of police, say.

"Ah bets fifty dolluhs Ah wins," bellowed Snake importantly.

"Gimme some odds," urged Sam.

"What odds you-all wants?" scowled Snake. "Two to one!"

"Faih enough," growled Snake, his vanity overcoming his judgment.

At those heavy odds all the Wicks' money was covered in a hurry. Only three men were betting on Tommy besides himself—Sam, Fish Toms and Little Joe. The stakes were given to Ace Johnson to hold—a saturnine, silent gambler, who was as deadly as he was reticent.

"Undehstand," said Sam. "Dese bets is win or lose; us is bettin' Snake *loses*. If its a draw, de bets is off."

The others agreed and a sudden thought struck Snake. "How 'bout de chu'ch element? Mighty 'ligious folks 'round hyuh; maybe de eldahs won't like it."

Sam's face split in a wide grin. "Ah already fix dat. We payin' Deacon Sacker ten dolluhs to referee. He ain' nevah seen no prizefight, but—"

"Kin he count up to 'Ten' he alright wid me," grunted Mistah Wamberson. "How we split de gate?"

"All de lodge axes is jest expense-money outen de proceeds. De rest you-all splits, seventy-five—twenty-five."

A broad, luscious grin wandered around Mistah Wamberson's ebon countenance. *Miss Luck, you has sent me uh whole flock uh lambs fo' shearin'!*

The dance hall of de Gran' High Exalted Moguls of de Fo'th Dimension, temporarily converted into a fight arena, was crowded with the dusky elite of Chop Suey, as well as with the more humble element. On this night the doors were flung wide and nonmembers could enter for the paltry sum of fo' bits, which amount was also taken from the dues of the members, as in the case of other entertainments heretofore.

Snake, as he came up the aisle with the wild acclaim of the crowd ringing in his ears, completely forgot any lingering suspicion which might have been lurking at the back of his mind. It was a full house, no question. Maybe this would develop into a regular thing, with Snake as the main attraction. The countryside was full of boys who thought they could fight—and who never had seen a glove.

Snake was taking no chance of a run-around this time. A sneaking glance into Tommy's improvised dressing room had shown him that Mistah Wicks was there, with his fighting togs on. Maybe he'd been training but he didn't look it. Snake swaggered into the ring, shook his clasped hands at the howling throng and went through his usual procedure, drinking in the gasps and exclamations of delight that welled upward when he flung off his bathrobe and disclosed his impressive physical development. Snake hauled at the ropes and glanced at his corner, where ensconced amid a formidable array of towels, sponges and buckets, were Dirk Knife and his fellows. He glanced at Deacon Sacker, a near-sighted ancient who mooned about the ring like an absent-minded billy-goat in a strange stable. Then he was aware of another entrance into the ring.

The yells of the crowd soared heavenward, altered strangely and ceased suddenly. Snake, chilled with a sudden premonition, glanced across the ring.

He froze. He gasped violently for air. An icy hand slid up and down his palpitating spine. Not Tommy Wicks, round and flabby with his babyish face, was climbing through the ropes, but a tall, rangy stranger—a bronzed tiger with a snarling hawk face. That build—that face—where—who—? Mistah Wamberson made a convulsive attempt to leave the ring.

"Snake—wheah-at you gwine?" Dirk Knife Bill was in front of Snake, his gimlet eyes boring into that worthy's shaking soul.

"Dirk Knife, Ah ain't feel so well—" gurgled Mistah Wamberson. Dirk Knife leaned toward him with an insidious motion and Snake's bulging eyes fixed on Bill's right hand. This hand, casually inserted into his shirt, was resting on the hilt of the dread weapon which gave Bill his name. Snake could see the glint of the blade. Bill's pet was not technically a dirk; the Southern darkies call any sort of a dagger a dirk knife; Bill's weapon was a long vicious stiletto—long, narrow bladed, three edged and diamond keen of point.

Dirk Knife's low voice was as piercing as his dagger: "Sam Gupson done pull a fast one on us. Ah dunno what. But does you lose or quit, Ace gives ouah money to dem. Dey was bettin' on you to lose! Dey didn't specify who to, to Ace. We done fall fo' it. Now you git in dah, and you fight *and you win!*"

Snake reeled back from a diamond-pointed doom, to face one almost as bad—if not worse. Keeping himself erect by holding on to the ropes and unable to take his gaze from the basilisk eyes of the terror in front of him, Snake swayed, about ready to collapse. The faces of the crowd swam before him in a mist; his world had crashed about him. Reality had become a nightmare. Was nothing stable or reliable? He doubted his sanity. He closed his eyes, as if to dispel the hallucination. He opened them. No! It was real! In the opposite corner sat Panther Horton!

Dimly he heard the urbane Sam announcing to the crowd: "—Mistah Tommy Wicks done sprain he ankle in he dressin' room jest now and this gem'man agree to take he place. Ladies and gem'men, Ah presents Mistah Panther Horton! You is all hyuhd about him."

Heard of Panther Horton? For a moment the dusky fans sat dumfounded, then they broke forth into a pandemonium which even brought a flicker of a smile to the Panther's thin lips.

Snake's brain was crumbling, he felt. This couldn't be! Through the chaos that was his mind, flashed a horrific picture: a battered, bloody travesty of a man writhing on the canvas— above him, a lean bronze barbarian, crouched like a tiger—a frenzied throng shouting a name in wild acclaim: "Horton! Horton! Horton!"

And piercing his horror and dismay, riding paramount even of his fear of Horton and of Dirk Knife's stiletto for the moment, was a flaming curiosity to know the why and wherefore of this unthought atrocity—what Panther Horton was doing in this makeshift arena, appearing against an unknown second-rater—Panther Horton, whose meteoric rise in the fistic world was swiftly supplanting the waning star of Wills and the rest of the old squad—who seemed headed for a title bout at the rate he was going, who performed in the biggest fight arenas in the country for fabulous purses and to packed houses.

The gong! Snake had not been aware that gloves had been put on his hands. There was no calling them to the center of the ring for instructions—Deacon Sacker knew nothing to tell the fighters and had only a vague idea of what he was supposed to do, though he had been carefully coached by Sam and Snake, as to the duties of a referee.

Snake felt himself violently propelled from his corner and he wobbled toward the Panther who came in smoothly, grinning most wolfishly. Even though death, destruction and utter damnation were his instant lot, Snake *must* know why Horton was here.

A left like a red-hot poker licked into Snake's face and like a man in his sleep he threw his arms awkwardly about his foe and held on with a death grip.

"M-m-mistah—mistah—Horton!" he gibbered, wild eyed, "w-wh-what you-all doin' hyuh?"

The Panther sneered cruelly and lovingly sank his free hand deep and lingeringly into Snake's midriff.

"You wants to know, eh?" he sneered. "Alright, black boy, Ah tells you before Ah takes you apaht and scatters yo' pieces to de fo' winds! Ah thinks mo' of mah wife den Ah does anything else in de world! Anything she wants me to do, Ah does! Even to comin' way down hyuh in de sticks, to frail de livin' daylights out uh a sorry, triflin', no-'count rat what's tryin' to steal a kid-boy's gal!"

Snake gagged and sagged; Horton had empathized each adjective with a short venomous jolt to Snake's suffering midriff. But Snake held on grimly.

"B-b-but, Mistah Horton, Ah don' see—"

"You won't see nothin' when Ah git through wid you," opined the Panther. "Mah wife is Tommy Wicks' sistah, an' when he sent word to me what was goin' on, Ah come. Now git loose f'um me, black boy, Ah craves action."

And so saying, Horton jerked loose and threw the reluctant warrior from him with so much force that Snake sprawled on the canvas. Deacon Sacker, who had been mildly eying the proceedings, ambled over uncertainly and in response to the howls of the crowd, began counting methodically over the fallen hero.

Snake's eyes roved. He saw Horton hovering close by, waiting for him to get up and be murdered. He glanced at his corner and saw in Dirk Knife's eyes a meaning gleam; in Dirk Knife's hand a meaner gleam. Snake's horror-stricken gaze wavered down the long slim blade which Dirk Knife had fully withdrawn. What a dilemma! He couldn't win—and he couldn't lose! *Miss Luck, wheah is you? If Ah lays heah, Dirk Knife cahvs mah gizzahd; if Ah gits up, de Panther rips mah head off!*

Snake gingerly rose from his haven of temporary refuge. Horton sneered and poked Snake in the eye with a long left, crossing a racking right to the belly. Snake bent double and as he straightened, he swung a wild right. There was no thought to the blow. It was purely an act of desperate terror. But it caught Horton off guard. It crashed against his head and the pride of Harlem saw a flock of stars. Enraged, he forgot his intention of prolonging the sport and brought his right up from the floor in a sweeping haymaker which stopped its flight right under the Wamberson cheekbone. Snake's feet left the floor and his body described a perfect arc backward across the ring. He landed in the ropes near his own corner. His knees were hooked over the middle rope, his outflung arms entangled with the upper one. So Mistah Wamberson sagged, partly in, partly out of the ring, his back to the crowd.

Deacon Sacker blinked; no course of action suggested itself to him, so he did nothing. Horton slid across the ring and stood just in front of his victim, who hung, facing inward. Horton's hands were down, a cruel sneer on his lips.

"Come on, boy, ontangle yo'se'f and git back in hyuh. Ah ain' through wid you."

Some slight sense drifted back into the addled Wamberson brain. Realization of his position swept over him. Quick as thought he partly straightened, whipping one foot free of the rope, to plant it on the edge of the platform. Quick as he was, another was quicker. Even as he made this motion, before the crowd had time to see that he intended leaving the ring entirely rather than re-entering it, Snake heard the hiss of Dirk Knife behind him, and felt a keen point sink agonizingly a full inch into the fleshy part of his hip.

With a piercing howl Mistah Wamberson shot back into the ring. His action was without his conscious volition; it was entirely involuntary—and was as suddenly unexpected and devastating as the discharge of a catapult.

Panther Horton had expected no such sudden move. He was standing directly in front of the much-abused Snake. He was caught flatfooted. Mistah Wamberson's adamantine head sank like a battering ram, up to the ears, in Mistah Horton's relaxed stomach. Snake, floundering wildly to his feet, realized that he was trampling an inert body in his haste. Closer examination revealed the body to be that of Mistah Horton. The Panther was as out as a man can be, who has just been unexpectedly hit in the stomach by an iron-headed 190-pound battering ram.

Snake staggered to the farthest corner, a gibbering lunatic. The crowd was going into hysterics. Deacon Sacker scratched his head; his sight was none too good; he did not know exactly what had happened. But there was a man on the floor and Dirk Knife Bill was screaming at him to count. So count he did, while the dumfounded victor gazed on with glassy eyes, and the anguished howls of the conspirators cut through the din of the frantic mob.

A figure approached Miss Astoria Bassums, hat in hand. "You-all waitin' fo' somebody, Astoria?"

"Ah's waitin' fo' Snake, he say he meet me hyuh; dass what he say 'fo' de bout. Ah ain' seen um since de fight."

"He done left town, Astoria," said Tommy Wicks. "Dirk Knife say he left right after de fight, and Dirk Knife say he ain' comin' back."

Miss Astoria sighed. After all, such glittering triumph as had been hers through her association with Mistah Wamberson was too good to last. And now, since her fickle suitor had deserted her to return to the great outside world, what better than to return to her faithful worshipper who, after all, had a good job and was a catch any Chop Suey girl might desire? Astoria had no illusions about Snake coming back; when men-folks left like that, they generally stayed left. She smiled on Tommy, whose honest heart leaped.

"Tommy, less us go look at dat house down on Johnsing street—"

"Golly Moses, Astoria, dat soun' like ole times! Ah reckon," said Tommy as he took the willing arm of his fair one. "Mistah Wamberson have big fight offahs now. Dirk Knife say he can't affohd stay 'roun' hyuh after beatin' Panther, 'cause dis mean big money to him."

Tommy quoted Dirk Knife alone, here. The saturnine one had allowed his imagination to ramble when accounting for the sudden departure of his friend. Only Dirk Knife knew exactly what had happened at the ringside—and Dirk Knife was noted for keeping his own council.

Snake had said nothing of big money or future fights. In fact he had said little except gibberish between the second, when leaning on the ropes, he realized that he had laid out Panther Horton, and the second he grabbed a fast freight headed East. Only the direst financial necessity had caused him to stop long enough to collect his bets and winnings and pay Dirk Knife his fifty.

The thought of being within a hundred miles of the place when Horton came to caused goose pimples to rise on Mistah Wamberson. What he craved was distance and lots of it. It needed no vivid imagination to tell him what would happen to him if the Panther ever got his hands on him. With cold clammy sweat standing out all over him, Snake passionately swore to devote the rest of his life in avoiding Mistah Horton.

Miles and miles and miles away from the scene of his dumfounding victory, and rapidly increasing that distance, Snake was just getting over his panic to the point where he could uncross his eyes and make his hair lay down, about the time that, back in Chop Suey, the fickle Astoria Bassums was murmuring contentedly to Tommy Wicks, flat broke but happy:

"Anyways, Tommy, Ah don' know if Ah coulda been happy wid such a fierce man as what Snake was; he so war-like Ah sceered uh him mahself."

Poems

Kid Lavigne is Dead

Hang up the battered gloves; Lavigne is dead.
Bold and erect he went into the dark.
The crown is withered and the crowds are fled,
The empty ring stands bare and lone — yet hark:
The ghostly roar of many a phantom throng
Floats down the dusty years, forgotten long.

Hot blazed the lights above the crimson ring
Where there he reigned in his full prime, a king.
The throngs' acclaim roared up beneath their sheen
And whispered down the night: "Lavigne! Lavigne!"
Red splashed the blood and fierce the crashing blows,
Men staggered to the mat and reeling rose.
Crowns glittered there in splendor, won or lost,
And bones were shattered as the sledges crossed.

Swift as a leopard, strong and fiercely lean,
Champions knew the prowess of Lavigne.
The giant dwarf Joe Walcott saw him loom
And broken, bloody, reeled before his doom.
Handler and Everhardt and rugged Burge
Saw at the last his snarling face emerge
From bloody mists that veiled their dimming sight
Ere they sank down into unlighted night.

Strong men and bold, lay vanquished at his feet,
Mighty was he in triumph and defeat.
Far fade the echoes of the ringside's cheers
And all is lost in mists of dust-dead years.
Cold breaks the dawn; the East is ghastly red.
Hang up the broken gloves; Lavigne is dead.

"Aw Come On and Fight!"

His first was a left that broke my nose,
His right ripped off my ear;
The red blood splashed beneath our blows
Till we stood in a crimson smear.

He cracked three ribs with his smashing right,
His left hooks gashed my head;
I saw the ring aswim in a light
Hazy and dim and red.

He split my brow and the lid dropped down
Like a curtain over the eye;
At every shove of his wet red glove
I saw the crimson fly.

On my hands and knees in a scarlet pool
I heard the referee toll,
And the crowd roared: "Kill the yellow bum!"
Like the sea along a shoal.

I sprang, I struck, I crushed his skull
With a sudden desperate swing,
He died with his eyes to the glaring lights
And his back to the canvassed ring.

The referee counted above the dead,
I swayed and clung to the ropes,
And the crowd roared: "Yellow! Both of 'em's bums!"
Like the seas on the beaches' slopes.

The Cooling of Spike McRue

(With Apologies to R. W. Service and John L. Sullivan)

A couple of hams were having a mill
In Gallegher's old saloon.
With long left jabs and round house rights
They were playing a merry tune.
One was the Bowery Terror, Murderous Spike McRue,
The other the pride of the whole East Side,
Benny, the Battling Jew.

When out of the night where the fly cops were,
Into the cheering crowd,
A stranger pummeled his way within,
And he laughed both long and loud.
"Now who is he," said Monk McKee
"Interferrin' wi' our sport?"
With a single clout he knocked Monk out
And he gave a scornful snort.

He'd weigh a scant two hundred pounds,
Yet the crowd was still as a louse
As he smashed a sledgehammer fist on the bar
And bellowed for drinks on the house.
And, "Boys," said he, "you don't know me,
And I don't give a ding.
But Spike, that bloke — just watch my smoke."
And he bounded into the ring.

Benny he ducked and the stranger swung,
And Benny he hit the floor.
The stranger tore into Spike McRue
And the crowd began to roar.
'Twas a left that lashed and a right that smashed,
And a left and a right again,
And shoulders flat Spike hit the mat
When he took it fair on the chin.

The crowd it cheered but the stranger sneered,
As he stepped to the waiting bar
And took a swig of whiskey, neat,
And lighted a long cigar.
And "Boys," said he, "I don't know ye,
And there's none of youse worth a damn,
But you all know John L. Sullivan,
And that's the guy I am."

While knocked out flat on the trampled mat,
Lay Murderous Spike McRue,
With his feet in the classical Yiddish face
Of Benny the Battling Jew.

Fables for Little Folks

He was six foot four and wide as a door
And he weighed two hundred pounds
And he laughed as he spoke, "I'll cool that bloke.
I'll flatten him in two rounds."
Ah, the crowd they cheered, but the crowd they jeered
When his foeman stepped in the ring;
They hissed and jowled and the giant scowled
And rushed with a roundhouse swing.
Yes, he came full tilt but the beans were spilt
For the smaller man timed him fair
And knocked him out with a left hand clout
And the crowd gave him the air.
So the moral is this: make your foeman miss
And never lead with your right,
But the first that you're to do is be sure
That it's not Jack Dempsey you fight.

The Champ

The champion sneered, the crowds they jeered,
And to the crowd said he,
"In all this land is there a man
Will go three rounds with me?"
Up then I leaped, "You bum," quoth I,
The champion loud jeered,
And like a crowd, full long and loud,
The audience they cheered.

And then into the ring we came
And he rushed swift at me.
His nose I slammed, his jaw I whammed
And mixed it merrily.
A swing I landed on his jaw,
The crowd did yell and stamp,
The referee did count him out
And I was aye the champ.

Ah, amateur, this gink hath been
A champ before your day,
And therefore lend me fifteen cents
And I will go my way.

Slugger's Vow

How your right thudded on my jaw.
Gad, what a punch you have!
Also that left jab
To the nose was a pippin.
The referee is counting
But I care not at all.
Presently I shall get up and
Knock you for a row of South
African pickaninies.

And Dempsey Climbed Into the Ring

(originally untitled)

And Dempsey climbed into the ring and the crowd sneered.
And Carl Morris climbed in the ring and the crowd yelled,
"Sock his damned jaw!"
And Dempsey hit Carl, by Hell!
And Carl hit the floor, by Hell!
And the crowd yelled, "You're the boy, Jack!"

In the Ring

Over the place the lights go out,
Except for the cluster above the ring;
The crowd begins to thunder and shout;
At the tap of the gong I whirl and spring.
And I hear the snarl of my chargin' foe,
The Cobra Kid from Old Mexico.
And the ropes ain't there, and the crowd ain't there;
It's me and him, in the ring-lights' glare;
Like cavemen foes in an age of stone
On the ridge of the silent world alone.
He ducks my lead as he surges in
And his left hook crashes against my chin,
And he shuts my eye with a round-house slam
That feels like the bunt of a batterin' ram.
The lights are swimmin' and so is the ring;
Blind I fall in clinch and cling;
The referee grunts as he tears us apart,
And I ram a left in under the heart.
And he batters me back across the ring —
Jab and uppercut, hook and swing —
A torrent of smashes that never slack —
I feel the ropes against my back.
Hard to the head he cannonades
And I hit the mat on my shoulder-blades.
My brain's full of fog, my mouth's full of brine,
But I hear the referee countin', "Nine!"
And up I reel, though my legs won't work
And the ring-lights swim in a crimson murk.

The Cobra rushes, set for the spill,
Wild and wide open, blind for the kill.
And desperate, reelin', I shoot my right,
The last blind blow of a losin' fight.
And my right connects and his head goes back,
Till it looks, begod, like his neck would crack.
New strength surges through every vein
And the panther wakes in my punch drunk brain.
His knees, they buckle, his white lips part
As I blast my right in under the heart.
His jaw falls slack, his eyes, they blink,
As deep in his belly my left I sink;

Then every ounce of my beef goes in
To the right I heave to his sagging chin.
The leather bursts and the hand gives way,
But it's the end of a perfect day.
He hasn't stirred at the count of ten,
The referee lifts my hand and then
I hear the yells of the crowd again.

Fighting the Anaconda Kid

(originally untitled)

They matched me up that night with a bird that was a fright,
The Anaconda Kid from Amsterdam,
His face was like a fable, his wrist a hawser's cable;
His shoulder was a gable, his arm a battering ram.
He rushed me from the bell like a roaring ape from Hell
And I put a wicked left against his chin,
But his left hand found me and his right swing crowned me
And the fogs closed round me and the ring began to spin.
A surf was roaring loud which I reckoned was the crowd
Gone cookoo as babies in their cribs.
At the gong my knees were knocking, I was weaving,
    ducking, blocking,
I went to my corner rocking with a couple broken ribs.
For the second gory round he came roaring with a bound
Seeing he had victory in his grasp,
I let go my right and duck him —
    just above the belt it took him
And I know that I have shook him for he halted with a gasp.
He dropped his guard a second —
    long enough for me I reckoned —
And the crowd went crazy where they sat
For my left hand battered and my right hand shattered
Till the red blood splattered on the great grey mat.
Oh, how they did yell and whoop when I knocked him
    for a loop
Just about a couple counts before the bell.
They'd have gave as loud a bellow had I been the losing
    fellow —

God, a crowd is yellow — yellow —
   all of them can go to Hell.

Down the Ages

Forever down the ages
I watch the fighters go
Down through the bygone centuries,
Silently, row on row.
Men of the mighty shoulders,
Sinewy arms and wrists,
Whose pride and whose profession
Was the cunning of the fists.

Sluggers and panthers and sprinters,
I mark them as they go,
And I mark the kings among them
By the kingship that they show.
Wiry and light of stature,
Dark eye and swarthy face,
The best of England's finest,
The Gypsy, superb Jem Mace.

Strong and mighty of stature,
Thrilled with the battle joy,
Rugged, powerful, fearless,
Heenan, the Benecia Boy.
Morissey, Sayers, McCaffrey,
All of them men of might,

John L. Sullivan

Bellowing, blustering, old John L.
Fearing nothing 'tween sky and hell!
Rushing, roaring, swinging his right,
Smashing, crashing, forcing the fight.
Battering foes until they fell,
Tilt your glasses to old John L.!

Mitchell he knocked, from the ring clear out!
Dropped Kilrain with a single clout!
Laflin he beat and Burke he flayed,
Knocked out the Maori Giant, Slade!
Packed in each fist, damnation and hell!
Tilt your glasses to old John L.!

Old John L.'s in town today
He's hitting it down the Great White way.
Look at his swallow tail coat, silk hat!
Mustache too, say he's on a bat!
Living it in, that you can tell,
Tilt your glasses to old John L.!

He's cleaned out the roughest, toughest saloon,
He's licked O'Rourke and Jem McClune,
Sampled every saloon on the streets,
Buying drinks for all he meets,
He's taking the bowery in pell-mell!
Tilt your glasses to old John L.!

Stick in your head in that grog-shop door,
Look at him! Listen to his roar!
"Set out the whiskey, Jimmy, ye bum!
Belly the bar, ye half bred scum!
I can lick any guy from here to hell!
Tilt your glasses to old John L.!"

The world moves on and the ring moves too,
Old fighters have long given way to new.
But here's a health to the olden days,
To the wild old, mad old, bad old ways,
When a fight was a fight and not a sell,
And tilt your glasses to old John L.

Jack Dempsey

Through the California mountains
And many a wooded vale
The wind from seaward whispers
The name of the Nonpareil.
O'er many a peak snow covered,
O'er many a woodland fair
The sea-breeze murmurs the wonderful tale
Of the lad from County Clare.
But never the wind from seaward
And never the brooks of the vale
Can speak the half of the glory,
The due of the Nonpareil.
Champion of all champions,
Greatest in all times' bounds,
The lad who held Fitzsimmons
For thirteen gory rounds.
But the ring's red history passes
In a swiftly roving tale,
And there's few who now remember
The name of the Nonpareil.
But here's to the greatest of fighters,
To a name that never shall fail,
To the name of the first Jack Dempsey,
The wonderful Nonpareil!

The Duckers of Crosses

(originally untitled)

We are the duckers of crosses,
We are the swingers of swings.
We count our gains and our losses
In all of the fourth-rate rings.
We are the bums and the slackers
Swiggers of Ancient Crow.
Yet the fans pay sixteen smackers
To see us knocked for a row.
Bout losers and bout forsakers
They hand us a-many slams,
For we are the set-ups and fakers,
We are the fourth-rate hams!
We are the takers of slams and blips!
Jester and ring-side clown!
But sometimes we go with our trunks on our hips
And jerk us a title down!
Taking bouts that champs are shying,
Where the ring gong clangs and thrums
Where the swinging mitts are flying —
We are the fourth-rate bums!

All the Crowd

(originally untitled)

All the crowd
Meek and proud
Yellin' loud,
"Knock him out!"
Queer,
How clear
I hear
Every shout.
Sure, show!
Let 'em know
Every blow,
Every clout.
First a left,
All my heft,
His guard's reft,
Great fun.
Then a right,
Full might.
My fight.
I've won.

When You Were a Set-Up and I Was a Ham

When you were a set-up and I was a ham,
In James J. Corbett's day,
And toe to toe and blow to blow
We mixed it in a fray,
Or skittered with many a roundhouse right
'Mid the ropes of a third-rate ring
My soul was rife with the joy of strife
As I matched you swing for swing.

And happy we swung and happy we slugged
And happy I knocked you out.
And shoulders flat you hit the mat
With the force of that swinging clout.
And champions came and champions went
And battled with might and main
Till we grew in might and signed for the fight
And climbed in the ring again.

We were heavyweights, rough and tough,
But cautious at first in the fight;
We sparred at ease while the crowd yelled "Cheese!"
Or jabbed with a wary right.
Duck and side-step on dancing feet,
(Golly but you looked dumb!)
While the angry crowd in accents loud
Remarked that we were bum.

Then happy we rushed and happy we slugged
And happy I hit the floor;
'Twas a peach of a clout and they counted me out
The while the crowd did roar.
And that was a dozen years ago
In a ring that no man knows,
Yet here tonight in a title fight
We are matching swats and blows.

Your right is as strong as a battering ram,
Your left is a peach, you bet,
Your swings are few, your gloves are new,
Your footwork great, and yet,
Your jaw is red from my rights to the head,
Your nose from my lefts is flat.
Though my jaw's a sight from your lunging right,
Five times you've hit the mat.

Then as we linger at battle here,
With many a roundhouse slam,
Let us swing anew as in times when you
Were a set-up and I was a ham.

Appendix 1:
Early tales, variants and fragments

The Spirit of Brian Boru

Sven Vendenssen was a son of the Vikings. Tall, wide of shoulder and huge of arm, with muscles bulging all over him, yet he was lithe and quick as a tiger. "The Battling Swede" fitted him well. I sat in a ringside seat the night he knocked out the heavyweight champion and when Slade told me that the Swede would be my next man, I felt that I would never hold the title.

When I heard he had accepted my challenge, I shrugged my shoulders. It seemed to me that I would soon be out of the fighting game.

"You'll have a tough fight, Larry," Slade said, "but it was either challenge the champ or get out of the game. Do your best and hit low, just above the belt."

Just before I went into the ring, my sister Claire put her arms around me and said, smiling up into my face: "Don't weaken, Larry. Remember, you come of the race of Brian Boru and he licked the Swedes a thousand times. 'Tis a shame that a Swede should hold the title for America when by rights it should be Irish. Remember Brian Boru!"

I thought of her words as I entered the ring.

The Swede didn't keep me waiting long. He strolled in as casually as if he were entering a barroom, wearing a sneering, confident grin that I hated. I watched him curiously, with a strange detached feeling. I hardly heard O'Shane announcing:

"—Sven Vendenssen, the Battling Swede, Heavywoight champion of the woild, weight _ Larry Sloan, weight _"

Then we were in the middle of the ring, the Swede towering over me, grinning. He was a big man, as I have said. One of the biggest men that ever held the title. He was nearly as tall as Willard, fully as heavy as Sullivan.

Yet for all his bulk he moved as quick as a cat.

As for me, my feet dragged, my arms seemed heavy. For the first three rounds I never landed a blow and wondered why he did not knock me out and be done with it.

As I rested in my corner at the end of the third round, Slade hissed in my ear: "What's the matter with you? Are you drunk? Don't you see the big boche is playin' with you? Get goin', you dumbbell!"

My mind seemed to be working sluggishly. I was conscious of a feeling of resentment against the Swede which was intensified as he stalked from his corner—grinning. How I hated that grin!

The crowd was disgusted and was giving vent to its feeling.

"Go on, Swede, knock him out!"

"He's yellow. Go get 'im, Swede!"

"Aw, the big boob's asleep on 'is feet."

Yes, the Swede was playing with me. Why should he not feel confident?

He stood at least five inches taller than I, was a good fifty pounds heavier, and had a longer reach.

He got home a blow that smashed me full in the face. It seemed the jolt cleared up my mind for all my strength and skill seemed to come back to me.

The Swede was standing in front of me, grinning sneeringly.

And into the center of that grin I drove my fist.

The surprize of the sudden "comeback" took him off his guard and for a few seconds I drove him around the ring and once nearly got him on the ropes.

Then he rallied. His grin had vanished; his face was a mask of fury. His stiff, yellow hair bristled and his small, light eyes glared with a savage ferocity.

His blows were terrible. For all his quickness I was the swifter and I managed to avoid most of them, but some landed. For three rounds I held my own, by a scant margin. Then, the eighth round he got home a blow on my chest that sent me to the mat, breathless and half-stunned. I managed to stagger up and clinch, holding until I got some of my wind back. But that slowed me up and only for one thing I would have gotten the "k.o." that round.

He rushed me across the ring, swinging with right and left for my jaw. I sidestepped to avoid the ropes; he feinted with his left and then launched a terrific swing with his right. Ordinarily I could have ducked or guarded but I was still weak from the body blow.

I could neither dodge nor ward. But the luck of the Irish was with me for my foot slipped and I fell to my knee, his arm passing over me as I fell.

The force of the blow swung him off his balance and before he could regain it, I was up and landed a straight punch to the body, followed by a left swing to the jaw. I actually knocked him down but he hardly touched the mat before he bounded up, going stronger than before.

At the beginning of the ninth round I failed to land a left hook and got a straight right to the jaw that put me to the mat. I got up at the count of seven but was weak and dazed. The Swede was everywhere.

He danced, sidestepped, ducked, and I could no more hit him than I could fly. He hit me everywhere. I was down twice again and against the ropes a dozen times in that round. Smash, smash, smash! with terrible regularity. His fists found my jaw, my face, my wind. Once his glove struck me on the side of the head and knocked me to the mat by the sheer force of the blow.

The Swede was a monster. I couldn't hit him and when I did my hardest blows did not even jolt him.

His blows were like battering rams. When they did not knock me down they jarred me to my heels.

When the gong rang for the tenth round I could hardly walk to the center of the ring. The Swede met me before I had taken two steps. He was grinning again, seemingly untouched.

One of my eyes was closed and his gloves had cut my face in a dozen places.

He laughed mockingly and struck for my body. I guarded mechanically and his fist crashed against my jaw. I seemed to fall headfirst into a black night, which was lighted momentarily by a million stars.

Then a thick gray mist closed over me, through which I could faintly hear the referee's voice:

"—Three—four—"

And another voice: "Larry, Larry!"

The mist rolled away on each side and I saw her—my sister Claire.

"Larry, remember Brian Boru!"

Then the mist settled down again. But only for an instant. Again it rolled away but this time I saw neither my sister, nor the referee, nor the Swede. I was looking upon a sandy coast, upon a sea that dashed against it. A battle raged there. Just off the coast ships were riding. Long, low, black ships, with shields along the sides and dragons carved upon the prows. Dragons and serpents.

Men swarmed from these ships and rushed ashore. Big, fair-haired men, with fierce, light eyes and helmets with horns upon them. They swung swords and battleaxes and roared a heathen war-cry.

And the man who led them was a giant with a face like Sven Vendenssen. Men were rushing to meet them. Big men, too, apparently more civilized. A tall, broad-shouldered man led them, a long sword in his hand, his hair flowing free.

The charging lines met! The swords of the two chieftains clashed! Then the Viking went down and his men broke and fled back to their ships. And high above the roar of battle sounded: "Erin go bragh! Brian Boru!"

"—Seven—eight—"

I reeled to my feet and smashed the astonished Swede in the jaw. New strength raced through me. I felt as fresh as though I had just started. I took a full swing in the face and laughed.

And I drove the Battling Swede back and back and beat him to the mat until he lay still and took the count.

Then the crowd was making the welkin ring and my sister was crying in my arms.

"I knew you could do it, Larry. But 'twas Brian Boru that helped you. Brian Boru and Ireland."

A Man of Peace

(originally untitled)

If Slade O'Shane had been a few inches taller and a few pounds larger, it is quite likely that he would have lived an ordinary boyhood, and grown up to be an ordinary man, going ordinary ways.

But in the first place he was of an unusual build, considering his environment, where men under six feet and two hundred pounds were so scarce as to almost constitute a rarity.

He was born in the country of the big timber and everything there was on a big scale. Giant trees, great rivers, huge craggy mountains that seemed to push up the sky; the whole country was like, not a Titan's playground, but a Titan's workground. As if the Giants of the Ages had combined to hurl together and to build the big timber country on a monstrous barbaric splendor that was breathtaking. The men of the country betook something of the proportions of the land. And none more so than the men of Despree Settlement on Wild River close to the lumber camps of old Ezra Jenson.

Old Ezra was an old timber man himself, a tough, whiskered old scoundrel and since big business has its vanities even as men, it was old Ezra's proud boast that he hired no man who tipped the beam at less than a hundred and seventy-five. There was an emperor once who had the same conceit.

Almost entirely he drew his workers from Despree Settlement. Not a lad of the settlement had other ideas than to go to work at Jenson's lumber camps, as soon as he was large enough to handle a peavey. It was almost a tradition; even as the size of the men of Despree Settlement was a tradition to be upheld. The people of Despree boasted that a man of Despree had never been turned down because in height, weight and strength he failed to come up to the standards of old Ezra Jenson.

And amongst that community, where bulk and strength was almost essential to existence, came Slade O'Shane.

From the first his size was noticeable. His playmates rapidly outstripped him in growth and he was perforce obliged to play with younger children, and because perhaps Nature's atonement for having stunted him in size, he advanced far more rapidly mentally than did the others. He withdrew to himself. For, mentally superior to those of his own age, he could find no companionship among those younger than himself.

As for the boys of his age, tradition played as much a part in their callow lives as it did in the lives of the older people of Despree, and they despised and ignored the smaller boy, even as the older people were ashamed of him.

As he grew older, he withdrew more and more into himself, finding some companionship among the few Indians who lived a semi-nomadic life and cared nothing for the standards of old Ezra Jenson.

Slade was ten when he found that there were more disadvantages attached to lack of size than contempt and ostracism. That was when he resented the remarks of a boy of his own age, but much larger. Slade was given a most complete beating, and the contempt in which he had been held increased proportionately. For, like all the world, Despree liked a winner and looked on the loser with a supreme scorn.

So Slade sat down and thought the thing over, as was his manner. He perceived that all through life he must step aside to let the bigger men take the road, unless he found some way to counterbalance his disadvantage as to height and weight. It did not occur to him that he might find a place in the outer world, since if he thought of it at all he supposed the outer world to be merely a larger pattern of Despree Settlement.

But he could arrive at no conclusion until old Ezra Jenson came to Despree. That was a great day for the settlement and they all turned out to give a royal welcome to the man who was no less than a demi-god to them.

Slade was surprized; he was astonished. He had always imagined old Ezra Jenson to be a great, roaring giant of a man; a huge, hairy-chested mastodon of a man, with arms like bunches of steel cables and fists like caulking hammers.

And the man himself! Small, wizened, whiskered like a gray rat, stooped and squeaky of voice! Slade was dumfounded.

He noted how servile were the big men who drew their pay from old Ezra. How quick they hastened to do his irascible bidding. With what flattering attention they waited upon his every word and how uncomfortable most of them seemed to be in his presence.

That gave Slade a new idea: that size is not entirely essential to success. That the Powers that Be give a little man something to make up the difference.

Remained only to find what he had that the others of Despree did not. It did not come to him until, watching from a covert among the big timbers one day, he saw a weasel rout a great lumbering lout of a grizzly cub.

Then the great idea came to him. Speed! That was the keynote word! He couldn't achieve great strength, he thought, but he could train himself to become as fast and as ferine as the weasel. As some Indian blood ran in him and because he had sought quiet in the wild until he was part of the wild, he took the right route to desire instinctively. Incessantly he trained his muscles for speed and endurance. Running, jumping, climbing trees, swimming, wrestling with his Indian friends, and retiring more and more to himself, he became every day less like a youth of Despree Settlement and more like a true waif of the wild.

At fourteen, when most of the boys he knew stood close to six feet and were getting their first lesson on the river, in the wood cuttings and on the log drives, Slade scarcely topped five feet and weighed less than a hundred pounds. But he was steel springs and whalebone. This was not known until the boy who beat him the first time, years before, tried the trick again. He stood head and shoulders taller than Slade but he was licked before he started. Slade swarmed all over him, battering him with blows, not hard, but faster than a cat strikes. The big boys' clumsy swings merely met air and Slade, furiously exultant, punched, kicked and scratched until the bigger boy admitted that he was licked.

Slade had many battles after that, for the boys simply could not see how so small a youth could fight. They had to be convinced, one by one, and Slade, with years of petty persecution behind him, was more than ready to convince them. At first.

But after his first few victories he failed to thrill at the thud of his fists on his opponents' face, as he had at first. He was, by nature, a peace-loving youth and his training of mind and muscle had been purely defensive. Added to his own nature, the quiet of the wild wherein he had roamed most of his life had bred a desire of peace into his soul.

But once he made himself the name of a fighter, he found himself compelled to uphold it. The men of the river and the timber were giants, they did giants' work and fought for sport. They fought skillfully, savagely, but they fought for the love of it and a whipping did not mean anything to them.

With Slade it was different. His high-strung, proud nature refused to permit him to allow an insult to go unchallenged, and though he fought, he hated it. But he fought like a demon when he did fight.

Always there was some man to test his courage. He sought only peace, but he found only war. As he grew older, he met more rugged, more skilled men. The men of the lumber camps fought terrifically in their rough-and-tumble style, and occasionally a French timber-runner drifted in. These were tough as steel, quick as cats, cool and skilled as wolves.

But if they were wolves and the lumbermen were wolverines, Slade was a wildcat. He fought and he won and as he fought he learned. From the lumberjacks he learned the tricks of thumb and elbow and heel, and crude wrestling. From the Frenchmen he learned how to use his feet skilfully at that most vicious of all fighting arts, la savate.

And at seventeen he learned the tricks of the skilled fists. A derelict ex-light heavyweight wandered into Despree. He had been a celebrity in his day and he still possessed much of his old time skill.

"Never licked outside de ring," was his boast. "An' never woulda been licked there if it hadn't been for th' skirts and booze."

In their first battle, he knocked Slade down seven times. Half-senseless, Slade kept reeling back for more, slim boy against a big man, and at last he dropped the boxer with a kick under the chin.

The fighter was unconvinced. The second battle was brought to a close by Slade throwing the fighter heavily, and following up his advantage, lumberjack style, by butting the man in the solar plexus.

The boxer was outraged by what he considered a breach of fighting etiquette.

He sought Slade and expostulated.

"Fight fair, kid. Stop that kicking and wrestling and I'll knock you for a row."

So the third fight was fought somewhat according to the standard ring rules. But Slade had learned some from his two previous fights. He was no match for the ex-fighter in skill, size and strength, but he far outclassed him in speed and endurance. Again and again the lad was felled with punches that should have rendered him helpless, but he kept coming back, and by sheer speed he landed his punches. He centered his attack on the boxer's body and soon years of dissipation began to tell and at last Slade won.

Again the boxer sought Slade but this time for a different reason.

"If I can't lick you I'll teach you so no man can lick you," he said, the fierce vanity of the man showing. "You're a born champ, kid. You sling your mitts faster and harder than Ad Wolgast at his best and you can take more than Battling Nelson. Better let me manage you, kid, I'll make a champ outa you."

The idea of fighting for money was somehow repellent to Slade. But he saw the advantages of learning to fight scientifically. The boxer taught him all he knew, all the tricks, foul and fair, of the ring, also a great number of jiu-jitsu tricks and straight wrestling which he had picked up as a fighting man will. Slade never liked the man. Never liked his debauches, his drunkenness, his general character. Nevertheless, he kept his opinions to himself and learned and applied all the boxer could teach him.

With skill combined with his natural ability, Slade won his fights with an ease that was almost ridiculous.

He had early learned the folly of seeking to win by sheer brute force. His mind was never clearer than when he was fighting. He possessed that first attribute of champions, coordination between mind and muscle, to the highest degree.

And with all these qualities, he hated war and loved peace.

But still fighters came.

So at last he heeded the silent voice that drew him ever away from man's domains. On a late summer day he turned his back on Despree, who was glad to see him go.

He was then eighteen and had his full growth. Five feet, six and three-fourth inches he stood, and he weighed one hundred and thirty pounds, stripped. He could lift twice his own weight with either hand, could leap higher than his own head from a standing position, could bend backwards and pick up a bandanna without moving his feet. No exertion ever wearied or winded him. He could run miles on miles at full speed, could swim like a beaver, dive like an otter and climb like a flying squirrel.

He wandered up past the Canadian line and saw many things. There were more lumber camps and he avoided them, when he found that there were men there always ready to try a stranger. On up into British Columbia. And at last he paused awhile at a little settlement much like Despree. There he tarried awhile until the big man of the settlement took notice of the quiet stranger and decided to demonstrate his superiority. Slade left him with a broken arm and again took up his way. At a lumber camp, two timber tramps picked a row with him, and on the Fraser he was forced to thrash a rowdy French bateau-man.

By that time Slade was almost despairing of ever finding a place where men would not require him to fight them. So, as he had sought quiet by retiring to himself at Despree, so he went further and further north. He had no special goal in view. He supported himself by doing a little work along the route and where the forests were thick, he fed himself. All the training of his earlier boyhood stood him in good stead, and behind that training the centuries of forest running that was his by virtue of the Indian blood that was his. For, while Slade was half-Irish, of the other half, one-fourth was French and the other pure Cree.

He wintered upon the Great Slave and with the coming of spring he headed north again. Eventually he came to the land of the Great Barrens and there he built a cabin. How long he stayed there, he did not know, for men lose track of time amid the silences of the Great Snow Plains. But the years passed. And more and more Slade became a part of the wild. Civilization, even that represented by Despree, slipped gradually from him. He did not become degenerate, degraded; the might, the greatness, the silence of the Great Places entered into him; became as much a part of him as his hands. The Arctic Lights painted mighty pictures for him in the sky. The song of the wolfpack stirred vague impulses, primal, mighty, in his soul. He roamed like a wolf; the land was his. There he could think, could dream, could wonder at things without interruption. Men go crazed among the Great Barrens, but to Slade it was as though he had known the land, that it was his land, his native land; and that instead of being new, he had but just returned to it. So much a part of it was he that he did not even talk to himself as men do among such lands.

And yet there came a time when a vague discontent stirred in him. Of such is man. Five times the stunted trees far to the southward had sported fresh, green leaves, when Slade wandered a far greater distance to the south than was his wont. Among the great forests.

It was spring. As the sap flowed through the trees, gathering momentum with the fresh warmth of the sun, so the blood in Slade thrilled with a strange longing. Suddenly there came over him a great yearning for men, for people, for comradeship. It was the primal, the mighty tribal call, as powerful, as primitive as the everlasting hills. Like the warm Chinook melting the snows, so the urge melted the reserve, the hermit nature, of Slade O'Shane. And wondering at himself, he turned his footsteps south.

He came among the people of the south and he felt strange, out of place. The speech of man came not easily to him. People wondered at him, and wondering, disliked him, for people are prone to dislike what they cannot understand. He sought comradeship but he did not know how to get it.

It was on the Saskatchewan that he encountered the same annoyance that had driven him from Despree, in the shape of a French riverman on a spree. For an instant he wondered if the peaceful years had left him flabby and slow; but the life of a wolf had only toughened and steeled those ferine muscles, had only quickened those lynx eyes. He kicked and punched the rowdy into submission in three minutes, without having been touched himself.

His craving for peace and companionship greater than ever, he wandered still further south, through Manitoba, and again crossed the line.

He wandered among cities and wondered greatly at what he saw; he learned that city men did not molest him, but that there was no friendship to be found there. And the Great Silences that had become a part of him drove him again out to the wilderness places of the world. He could not endure the bustle, the hurry, the everlasting noises.

He wandered south by west and learned to ride, rope and brand. The branding was distasteful to him; he had lived too close to the wild to be a success at anything which included so much cruelty, even though necessary. Eventually he found his place as horse wrangler upon a ranch in Wyoming.

But he was not satisfied. The happy-go-lucky punchers did not understand the silent stranger and from avoiding him they began to ride him. One day the foreman went too far. A few minutes later the big cowboy was dazedly rubbing a pair of black eyes and a broken nose, wondering how a man could so suddenly turn into a buzzsaw, and Slade was riding down the Colorado trail, headed south again.

Slade never stayed where he fought. Experience had taught him that the moment his ability was known, other men, fighters themselves and doubting that so small a man could be so powerful, would come and force him to demonstrate.

Eventually he wandered across the Border and believed at last that he had found the land of peace which he sought. The great deserts stretching away to sky-towering mountains, immense in the distance, made him think of the great snow-lands. He was almost content. The people were a simple, kindly folk, and they took a liking to the dark, silent man. Most of his time he spent wandering over the desert, working a little at some of the rancheros. But occasionally he rode to town, to mingle with the crowds in barroom and dancehall, buying drinks for others but never drinking; watching others dance but never dancing.

It was at Juarez, where he went only occasionally, that he heard first of Red Sloan.

He was leaning on a bar, casually listening to a group of Americans.

"I hear Red Sloan's landed at Vera Cruz."

"Ship?"

"Yes," with a chuckle. "As stoker."

"A fine seaman and a fine skipper if he'd only stay sober."

"Oh, he stays sober when he's at sea."

"So I've heard."

"Yes. But drunk or sober, he's a fighting man if there ever lived one."

"Rather." This from a lean, broad-shouldered young man lounging against the bar. "I had a row with him in Manila. There was just one punch hit and I'm no baby. I never saw or felt the swat he put me away with, but they said it was a left to the jaw that travelled just about three inches."

"What kind of a fellow is this Sloan, anyway?" Several answered.

"A big, lean-hipped, broad-shouldered, red-haired battler. Skipper when he's sober, wanderer when he's not. Stands exactly six two and weighs a little less than two hundred."

"Would have made a fortune in the ring. He's a born champion. But he has funny notions of fighting. Says fighting's like loving. A gift of the gods, and that it's degrading and blasphemous to fight for money. But fight! If you can imagine a man with the strength of a Sharkey or Jeffries, the speed and fighting mind of Corbett, and the knockout kick of Fitzsimmons in his punches, then you can get an idea of what kind of a man Red Sloan is."

"But speed's his main asset. So many of these big fellows are so slow. Sloan's like a great cat. He's never been licked yet."

"He's fought a few good heavyweights just for the sport of it. Licked them, too. Wouldn't take any money for it."

The crowd shook their heads, unable to understand a man that would refuse money for anything.

"His only fault is that he won't devote any time to learning the real science of the game. He's a fine boxer for a non-professional, but he's always so far outclassed his opponents that he never really needed to use his science. A charge and a punch, that's about all he needed."

"Yes, that's so. It's my opinion that he could beat any man in the ring today except maybe the champ. But he'd have more difficulty with the small clever fellows like Jack O'Brien or Kid McCoy than he would with the big ones."

"I doubt it. Big as he is, he's too fast for any of them. And he can take as much as Sharkey, or Jeffries himself. But what do you think about this new welterweight, Micky Walker, that's coming along?"

The talk drifted away from Sloan and Slade walked away.

So the time passed and Slade still tarried, not exactly contented, but somewhat approaching content.

He made friends among the Mexicans, learned their language to an extent.

Some of the time he spent among them, but mostly he rode the desert under the great white stars, or lay in the shade of some stunted desert tree, watching the sun devils dance over the sands.

He was a man apart. A lone, lean wolf.

Men could not understand him, neither could he understand men.

Then just as Big Business, in the form of old Ezra Jenson, had shaped and formed his boyhood and younger life, so now Big Business again took a hand in the career of Slade O'Shane.

The reason thereof was this.

A certain large arms corporation found itself with a great store of arms on its hands owing to the failure of what had looked like a promising revolution in South America. The arms must be disposed of, or the corporation stood to be out a small fortune. Corporations do not care to be out small fortunes.

So one of its higher men conceived what he and his colleagues considered a brilliant idea. He had a plan by which to dispose of the arms at even a larger profit than would have been possible had not the plans of a general in the army of Venezuela gone awry. But to make this plan a success, it was essential that there be a revolution just south of the Rio Grande. Some men are like that. There was money to be made, the highest, most noble art of all arts; and if anyone had hinted that there was a certain lack of morals or decency in the project, both the man and his colleagues would have been offended and would have felt righteously angry.

But governments are remarkably stupid in some ways and an obstacle was encountered in the way of the laws concerning gun-running. And with so large a shipment, it was evident that some special way would have to be provided to smuggle the arms across. And that is where Red Sloan came in. For Sloan, sea captain and adventurer, had his part to play, as he always had when there were stirring times.

The big man of the corporation had discussed the thing with Captain Jose Ferdinando de Garille, officer in the army of His Excellency, the President of the Republic of Mexico, and a man with ambitions of his own.

The plan which they decided upon was this: on a certain night the arms should be smuggled across the river at a spot which was least likely to be patrolled. But to make assurance sure, that patriot and self-styled friend of the people, Don Lopez Miguel y Antone del Martinez, was to lend his aid. Don Lopez, with whom the traitorous Captain was playing hand and glove, was at the time residing among the mountains, to escape unwelcome attentions from the Federal troops. As a bandit chief, Don Lopez was what might be termed a flop, but as plans were going he bade fair to be a link in the tangled chain of Mexican politics.

On the night set upon, Don Lopez was to emerge from his retreat and feint a raid upon a small border town, just on the American side, so as to draw the troops patrolling the border away from the particular place the big man of the Corporation and Captain de Garille had chosen.

As the government was greatly pleased at the peace that had reigned in Mexico for an unusual length of time, and as corporations do not always escape suspicion, the border was being closely patrolled. That is not the usual habit in peace times, but the government had learned somewhat. It would take an unusually spectacular raid to leave the border clear but as to that, Don Lopez could be depended on.

However, as the attentions of the Federals had practically cut off lines of communication between Don Lopez and the Captain, there remained the task of getting word to him. And that was no such slight task, as might be supposed. The Federal government was especially desirous of getting Don Lopez, and contrary to the usual rule, the peons themselves were against him. The government was easy on them and Don Lopez was not.

"Leave it to me," said de Garille. "I have even now the man in mind. A gringo of the very red hair, one *señor* Sloan. He is now w'at you call broke an' probably also dronk. He has wander' from the coast and is now in a certain small village not far from here. Theese man is afraid of nossink. The arms are hidden perfect not many miles from the Border? Bueno. I do not know how you got them there an' it would have been better if you had land' them somewhere on the coast. But no matter. The night we mention I will be at the place with enough men and wagons to haul all at one load. Perfect? Bueno."

And Captain de Garille chuckled to himself and wondered if the big man of the Corporation had ever thought where he, the Captain, would get the money with which to pay that enormous sum. The Captain had ideas of his own, also ambitions.

And mark now how the plans of destiny are formed. Just as a certain soldier high in the councils of de Garille rode into a certain squalid Mexican town, a lousy, unshaven creature named Juan, having spent his few pesos for mescal, made his way into an old 'dobe hut to sleep off the result. As the hut was occasionally used for a stable, there was a quantity of straw on the floor, and this he pulled about him.

He was awakened sometime later by voices, and as he roused from his drunk, he thanked all the saints that he was apparently unseen. It was dark in the corners of the hut and with his ragged garments and the straw huddled around him, he looked much like what the two men had taken him for, a heap of discarded garments. Conspirators should be more careful.

One of the men was one of Captain de Garille's officers and the other was the American who had been taking his ease in the village for a while, commandeering food and whiskey from the Mexicans. Juan knew of him by hearsay. The men were speaking Spanish.

"And so, *señor*, we will do this?"

"For another hundred."

"But consider—"

"And payment in advance."

"But how do we know—"

There was an instant's silence and Juan, though he dared not risk discovery by looking, could sense the meaning; in his mind's eye he could see Red Sloan leaning across the rude table, the devil's own smile playing on his face, fierce, powerful eyes blazing into the others.

"Better stop there, leut! Any fool knows that Red Sloan keeps his word."

"To be sure," the voice was greasily conciliatory, "you misunderstood me, *señor*. To be sure, *señor*, it shall be as you say. And you understand what you are to do?"

"Sure. On the night a fire is lit on the Peak of the Hidalgos, I am to ride to the mountains where Lopez is supposed to be hiding and tell him: 'An empire rides South.' And you're to pay me five hundred dollars, American. But why choose me?"

"Because, *señor*, the country swarms with Federal spies and no one would suspect you. A cordon of troops patrol the desert close to the mountains, and they arrest anyone whom they think might be connected with Don Lopez. In the night he rides through them, but no one else can, unless it be yourself. Then, too, you are an American citizen—" the Mexican could hardly keep the sneer out of his voice, "—and just now the government is especially desirous of keeping the friendship of America."

"They've got the right idea," was Sloan's reply, as the men walked out of the hut. A few minutes later Juan peered warily about and then scurried out of the hut and off through the dusk.

Juan desired to talk. But he desired to impart his gossip to one who would not betray him. He bethought himself of his one Americano friend, a small, dark *señor* who said little and had bought him mescal on occasion.

As the Mexican made his way through the village, another thought came to him. His hair positively bristled at the mere thought of putting the plan into execution himself, but the dark *señor* did not seem to be afraid of anything. Bueno.

Slade was riding slowly, letting his horse wander as it would, watching the stars, when Juan accosted him.

"*Señor*, there is money to be made. Listen." Rapidly he told what he had heard. "Now if the *señor* were to go to Capitan de Garille, or to *señor* Sloan and say, "For so many pesos I will be silent?" The Mexican paused meaningly.

Slade caught his meaning. "You might go yourself and make that proposition."

"No, no!" Juan gestured hastily. "*Señor* Sloan would eat me! But the *señor* might pay Juan just a small amount, eh? Just a few pesos?"

Slade absently handed him the few coins he possessed and rode on; Juan watched him, not exactly understanding, but grateful for the money.

Slade was annoyed. He thought he had found a country of peace and it seemed that it was to be but a nation of war. Slade was shrewd in his way. He had heard the talk of the plazas and the haciendas and he had a fair knowledge of Mexican politics. He knew that a shipment of arms meant revolution. He hated war. Therefore he would have to move on. And he did not wish to move on. More, the old proud stubbornness began to take hold of him. He began to know a sullen, slow rage against the forces that seemed trying to thrust him into war against his will. That crystallized determination.

A few nights later, Red Sloan, glancing toward the east, saw the faint glint of a flame high on the Peak of the Hidalgo. Dawn found him riding south. His destination lay a good day's ride away and, more seaman than anything else, he was not best at riding, although the horse furnished him by Capitan de Garille was of the finest.

Few but Sloan would have attempted to ride through the widespread cordon of Federal troops in open daylight; none but he could have accomplished it.

One patrol, not of *rurales*, but of soldiers, accosted him.

"Me!" he laughed. "Why, I'm going to visit my old friend Don Lopez, sure. Want to see how he's coming with his banditting."

They laughed at the wit of the *señor*. Men liked Sloan. "Ah, I had forgotten the ranchero of Don Ferdinand Lopez lies in that direction," remarked the officer with a knowing wink. "The *señorita*, eh?"

Sloan's eyes flashed for an instant and then he shrugged his shoulders. If the greaser wanted to fool himself that way, all right. Anyway, with five hundred dollars he'd be out of the country before they could catch him, if anything came of his visit to Don Lopez. He was annoyed that his conscience bothered him somewhat as to the revolution. A man of the world should have no conscience, Sloan thought.

The sun was riding low in the cloudless sky when he came to the first low hills, beyond which, among the mountains, Don Lopez was purported to be lurking. And as he rode up the trail he saw a small man seated on a mustang just ahead, horse and rider motionless.

Sloan wondered if it could be one of Don Lopez' wild riders. But the man was white. His hand rested on the saddle horn and in it was a Colt .45.

Sloan rode up and stopped. The other spoke.

"Game's up, Sloan."

Sloan's reply was characteristic. "Who the hell are you?"

"No matter."

Slade was eyeing Sloan wonderingly. He had imagined the man to be something on the order of the boxer he had fought at Despree; a big, hulking savage of a man, with coarse, red hair, jutting jaw, low brutish forehead and great gorilla-like hands.

The real Sloan was the very opposite. His face was the face of a fighter, it is true, lean jawed and thin lipped. But no lines of dissipation showed there and the forehead was high and broad and the gray eyes were those of a dreamer. He had taken off his hat to fan himself, and his red hair showed as fine fibered as a woman's. The sun touched it into lambent flame. It was no ordinary red, that hair. There was no tinge of gold about it; it was as if it expressed the character of the man.

Square shouldered, lean of hip, waist and thigh, mighty chested, with long arms, powerful wrists and long narrow hands, he was the typical fighting man. Such was Red Sloan, born on the Isles of Aran and raised all over the world.

"Yes, the game's up, Sloan," Slade repeated; he was not talkative as a rule, but he wished to talk, to let Sloan know just how he had been outguessed. The man aroused a strange antagonistic feeling in Slade.

"Stay where you are," Slade directed. "Late tonight a shipment of arms is to be brought to the Border. Capitan de Garille will be there to receive them. Don Lopez is to decoy the troopers away."

Sloan said nothing, awaiting his chance to seize the revolver.

"I lit that fire on the Hidalgos, Sloan. And I had the devil's own job of slipping past the Federals. De Garille will know that you've started for Don Lopez, thinking he had it lighted; I saw to it that he learned of it. He'll send word that the shipment of arms be brought to the line, not knowing what else to do. He'll think one of his own men gave the fire signal too soon. Don Lopez will not be informed; I'll see to that. The troops will capture the lot: the arms, the Capitan de Garille, men, horses and all. The revolution is off. And I did it all."

A note of triumph new to him thrilled his voice. "You rat," said Sloan coolly.

Slade made no reply.

"And what do you think you're going to do now?"

"Ride you back to the line and chase you across."

Sloan's eyes glinted. Few men dared talk to him like that. "You are like Hades. I've been on horseback all day." And he coolly dismounted, threw his horse's bridle and sat down. Slade sat in his saddle, watching him. A feeling of strange helplessness was bothering him. The force of Sloan's dominant personality was making itself manifest.

"Better get down and rest yourself," suggested Sloan presently, "unless you're afraid."

Angered, Slade dismounted warily, never taking his eye off Sloan. He sat down on a rock opposite him, Sloan measured the distance between them. Not too far for a quick leap, but the gun in Slade's hand rested on his thigh, trained directly at Sloan. But he held it awkwardly, as if unused to firearms.

After awhile Slade broke the silence: "Time enough. Get on your horse, Sloan."

He rose. A pebble slipped under his foot, throwing him off his balance. The gun muzzle wavered for a fleeting instant. And in that instant Sloan leaped quick as a snake strikes and wrenched the gun from Slade's hand. Wrenched it away and threw it far out across the sands.

"Now, you little rat, I'm going to give you the beating of your life." He laughed with a fierce enjoyment.

Slade stepped back. He was bewildered. He could have stopped Sloan forever; there had been time to jerk back the muzzle and fire, even as Sloan leaped. But the swift suddenness of the bold attack had thrown him off guard for the first time in his life.

He looked at Sloan and a strange feeling of panic came over him. He had fought small fast men and big slow men, but never a man who combined such evident strength with such flashing speed. Sloan was what Slade had been, had Slade been larger. Again he felt strangely helpless. He backed away slowly before Sloan, his feet instinctively feeling for ground where no rocks would hamper his motions. Then with a contemptuous gesture, Sloan swung his right.

It was intended more as a heavy cuff than a punch but even so it would have felled most men. And, his fighting mind working mechanically, Slade went into swift action, even as the arm of Sloan began its preliminary movement.

Sloan stopped short, surprized. He fingered his nose, looking at Slade in some wonder. He saw that he had to deal with a boxer, not a mere rough-and-tumbler. And to lead to a boxer with the right hand is more than folly; it is sheer stupidity. Sloan felt as though a whiplash had flicked him, three times. That was the wonder of it. A man expects to receive a left counter when he leads with a right but Slade had hit thrice, left, right and left, before Sloan could get his arm back.

But Sloan had met fast men before and always his speed exceeded theirs when he had got started. So he chuckled as Slade stripped himself to the waist, though he noted Slade's narrow waist and sloping, sinewy shoulders, with admiration. And because of the strange chivalry of the man, he too stripped, which, though Slade did not know it, was the greatest compliment Sloan could have rendered. For Sloan merely pretended to think that he had a real battle on his hands, whereas he expected to win as he had before. With a rush and a punch.

As they squared off, a close observer, had there been one, would have noted a strange likeness between the two, in spite of the difference in size. Lean hipped, sinewy, both possessing the long, smooth muscles that betoken speed and endurance, yet there was a greater semblance. There was an intangible something about both that set them each aside from other men. Just as a lean lone wolf is set aside from a pack of jackals.

Sloan wasted no time in preliminary feinting. He stepped in, hooking his left for the jaw. Slade parried it with his right elbow, but even so the force of the punch turned him halfway around, and Sloan's straight right, following up like a flash of light, sent him to the ground with the breath knocked nearly out of him. Sloan stepped back. To his surprize, Slade rose instantly, not even taking the space of rest that Sloan would have allowed him.

Slade had learned that it was folly to seek to parry Sloan's terrific punches. So when Sloan rushed, Slade ducked his vicious left hook, whipped a left to Sloan's body and sprang out of reach. Baffled, Sloan rushed again. This time Slade met him with a straight left that leaped quick as a cat strikes, swayed under his wicked right counter and leaped away. Then with a flash of incredible speed Sloan was after him, and Slade only partially parried the terrific punch that again felled him.

Again Slade arose. For the first time in his fighting life, he began to hate his foe. Again that helpless sensation. But this time it was blown away by a sudden gust of ferine rage. Slade was in the clutch of that most savage, most merciless of furies, the hate of the weak for the strong, of the small for the mighty.

And that rage drove him to superhuman efforts. Before Sloan could even think, Slade was upon him, with a whirlwind of hooks and uppercuts that battered him from belt to crown. Then away, Sloan's savage swing meeting only the air. Sloan rushed, hooking his left for the body, driving his right for the jaw. His arms flailed the air and Slade whipped a left to his body as he slid away. Sloan was after him, swinging left and right for the head; Slade ducked the left and slipped inside the right swing. His forehead almost touching Sloan's chin, Slade put every ounce of his weight and strength into a right uppercut. Sloan's head jerked back but otherwise he seemed not to feel a punch that would have knocked most men senseless. Slade leaped away, and as Sloan followed, he feinted, then ducked under Sloan's extended left to swing left and right to Sloan's body. Though he smote with all his force, Sloan did not even stagger, and his right, catching Slade on the jaw, knocked him fully a dozen feet away. Slade rose slowly, shaking his head to clear it. He was swaying away from that punch, else it would have knocked him senseless.

He was uncertain. Sloan had taken his best punches without even wincing. There was but one thing for him to do. He must keep out of Sloan's reach, trusting to his own endurance, letting Sloan wear himself down with his own efforts.

He had the advantage of skill and, he believed, of endurance. Sloan's only dissipation was whisky, and Slade never touched it. Then, too, he was faster than Sloan by a fleeting whisper.

Sloan rushed. That was all he knew. His skill lay in his attack. Slade avoided him, scarcely striking a punch, and when he did, only quick, short left jabs that carried no weight but annoyed and bewildered.

Sidestepping straight lefts, ducking right hooks, slipping straight rights and swaying back from left hooks, Slade made Sloan miss, miss, miss with monotonous regularity.

Sloan was rapidly becoming furious. Never before had he met a man, big or little, that he could not hit. He stopped suddenly, feinted, and then pounced as a cat pounces, his left fairly swishing the air. Slade slipped easily inside and, at close range, Sloan drove his right savagely for the body. But, catlike, Slade's hand caught the inside of his elbow and the punch was wild. For a few seconds they infought. Slade stayed close in, allowing Sloan's vicious head-punches to swish about his neck, catching Sloan's arms and deflecting his body punches almost before they started. Then slipping out of a clinch he sprang away again.

It was becoming a battle of endurance. The pace was terrific but Slade showed not the slightest sign of fatigue and Sloan's speed and fury was in no way abated.

Sloan was missing most of his punches, and such as landed were glancing, as Slade swayed away from them; riding them, in the parlance of the ring. Sloan apparently scarcely felt the short straight punches which Slade occasionally landed.

Once, one of Sloan's savage lefts felled Slade and Sloan stood, poised, waiting for him to arise and continue the fight. The fact that he could have mounted and ridden away did not enter his mind. He had forgotten Don Lopez, forgotten Captain de Garille. He only knew that before him was the only man who had ever stood before him in battle as Slade had, only knew that he must batter that man into insensibility. Slade bounded to his feet.

Again that fierce dance went on.

Sloan was a red-haired fury, Slade a dancing shadow.

Sloan rushed, rushed, rushed. To hit that shifting dancing figure! Just once, just once.

He began to swing wild. From short, vicious punches he changed to wild, flailing swings, terrific if landed, but easy to avoid. Slade began to fight closer, to land more punches. Through the short summer dusk they fought, scarcely noticing the rise of the early moon, except that it gave them light.

Each felt defeat. Slade had landed his best punches again and again and still Sloan showed no signs of weakening. He seemed a giant impervious to punishment. There seemed no beating him down.

Sloan was furiously desperate. Slade's dancing figure leaped and shifted before him and he swung, swung, swung. His opponent was a fiend, a dancing demon. He was faster than Sloan by only a fleeting margin, yet that was enough. Sloan's punches missed only by hair widths, but they missed, or else merely grazed Slade.

Slade shifted within a long swing, hooked his left, then his right, to Sloan's jaw; ducked and swung both hands to the solar plexus. Sloan's body muscles were impervious to punches. His jaw only bruised Slade's knuckle. Blood trickled from upon his jaw, his face was bruised and battered, yet the giant seemed scarcely to notice it.

What could he do against such a man? Slade felt defeated. There were tricks—but he did not like the idea of using them. He must fight fair.

It was Sloan who suddenly changed the mode. He swung a long left at Slade's head. Slade moved his head back a few inches, saw that the swing would be short. It swished past his chin and he stepped in to swing a punch at close range. The next instant he was sprawled on the ground, half-stunned, Sloan's left elbow, swinging back in a terrific back hand movement, had caught him full in the jaw. It was an old trick of the ring.

Sloan stepped back, eyes slits of fury. He was in a red wrath at Slade, at himself. Stung to desperation he had played the first foul trick of his life and his fine-strung Celtic soul was fairly a-shriek with humiliated rage.

With human inconsistency, all that fury centered upon Slade. Slade had made him outrage his own sense of decency, and from then, anything went.

Slowly and uncertainly Slade got on his feet. Sloan was upon him, driving his elbow against his chest as he closed, with an upward jerk of his wrist. Slade reeled, then thrust his left elbow inside Sloan's right, even as he struck. Sloan caught his right arm and in an instant the arm was in chancery, bent across Sloan's left forearm, Sloan's right pressing it down to break it like a dry stick. Slade's right flashed up, the edge of his hand striking under Sloan's nose, jerking his head back. Slade's heel crashed against Sloan's ankle almost simultaneously, and as Sloan involuntarily relaxed the pressure, the smaller man wrenched free with a terrific effort and bounded away.

Sloan paused. Slade was poised lightly in front of him, weight distributed equally on each side, left foot slightly to the rear. Not a boxing pose at all. If it was to be a match of savate, Sloan was willing. He knew a little of the art, and he had picked up quite a bit of jiu-jitsu, also.

Slade leaped like a wolf, his left foot swishing in a vicious arc. Sloan disdained to dodge and Slade's toe took him at the edge of the ribs, staggering him. He launched a kick at Slade's body and Slade guarded hastily, jerking his left foot back and up to rest on his thigh, bent leg thrust out. A difficult parry but effective. Sloan's shin met the toughest part of Slade's leg with terrific force, throwing Slade off his feet. That parry had broken many a man's leg, but it merely bruised Sloan's,

He hurled himself forward and Slade was not able to evade him. They crashed to the ground, Sloan's clutching fingers ripping the skin from Slade's arms, Slade butting Sloan in the face.

Sloan drove his elbow into Slade's ribs, twisting his wrist. Slade gouged at Sloan's eyes. All semblance of civilization was stripped from them. It was stark, savage, primordial battle. Sloan's groping thumbs found Slade's eyes, forced his head back. Slade kicked savagely and Sloan gasped. Slade struck aside the gouging hands and drove his forehead ruthlessly into the giant's face. They reeled up, and toe to toe struck wild blows, then clinched and fell headlong. Time and space faded away from Slade. The battle was a thing of the centuries. It had always been; there was nothing else in the whole universe. His right arm broke like a twig between Sloan's hands but he scarcely noticed it. Vaguely, through a haze, he saw Sloan's face, framed in the moonlight, the grin of a gorilla on the giant's face. The thin lips were drawn back from teeth that gleamed in the moonlight. The one good eye flamed concentrated hate. Like a man in a dream Slade struck at that face.

Sloan closed, grasping him with taloned hands, encircling his body with steel-like arms. He set himself to crush Slade as a gorilla crushes its victim. Slade's mind cleared slowly. He forked savagely at Sloan's eyes.

The giant swayed back, trying to jerk his head out of reach, then with a burst of furious exertion, swung the smaller man high into the air and hurled him headlong with terrific force. Sand somewhat cushioned the jolt but even so the breath was knocked from Slade's body and he lay stunned. Then, only half-conscious, he began to slowly crawl to his feet.

He did not know what he was doing. Men call it the fighter's instinct that brings a man to his feet again and again in the face of certain defeat. With Slade it was more. It was the unconquerable spirit of the wild, the unbreakable soul of Nature, the keynote, the very essence of life itself, life, dominant, mighty, unyielding, that drove him, crawling like a crippled wolf, to face Sloan. His right arm was useless, and he knew that at least one rib was broken. The desert spun dizzily, the moon reeling back and forth across the sky in eccentric arcs. He weaved unsteadily to his feet, shook his head to clear it.

Sloan stood, swaying, arms dangling, his breath coming in gasps. His teeth gleamed from the battered mask that was his face. He stepped uncertainly toward Slade, hands grasping, groping.

And Slade, reeling, half-senseless, steeled muscle and mind for one last terrific effort. He staggered toward Sloan.

And the giant knew that he faced defeat. Vaguely he sensed some of the quality of the man. Sloan was a giant among men, a superman; but Slade was not a man. He was a wolf; the materialized substance of elemental Nature. His was the essence of the blizzard, the shrieking river-rapids, the barbaric, sombre mountains, the yell of the wolf pack, the screech of the panther. Sloan was unconquerable by man; it was as though the wild herself, with her Great Silences, her mighty conflicts, her primal, elemental struggles, had formed and shaped and molded one of her own children for the sole purpose of defeating him. It was not Slade alone that Sloan fought. He fought the land of the big timber, the Great Barrens; he battled the very essence of Primal Power.

Face to face they stood, and Sloan struck out, vaguely. Slade parried the blow, struck with his good hand for Sloan's jaw. Struck again and again. Sloan reeled, but he would not fall. Stubbornly he kept his feet, trying to return the blows. The indomitable courage of the man did not fail him. Even yet he was not beaten. He still possessed power enough to fell a man, did one of his wild punches land. Slade swayed forward, striking Sloan across the Adam's apple with the edge of his hand. Sloan swayed and Slade, bending at the hips, launched his heel for the giant's jaw. Again, and again. Sloan slumped slowly to the ground and lay there.

Slade stood, reeling for a moment. Then he pitched headlong.

Miles away on the river, a certain big man of a certain big corporation was trying to explain the purity of his intentions to a number of bored troopers, while across the river Capitan de Garille was spurring in the general direction of Mexico City, and cursing the names of Red Sloan and Don Lopez by all the saints and devils in the vocabulary.

Miles in the other direction, among the mountains to the south, Don Lopez slept the sleep of the innocent, nor dreamed that the plans of an empire had been frustrated by a man, the top of whose head would not reach Don Lopez's chin.

Dawn rose over the desert. Dawn picked out two figures sitting upon rocks, where the plains began to slope up to the mountains. Dawn touched the hair of one with a lambent flame.

"Another tooth," remarked he, ruefully. "That's three. How about yourself, Slade, me lad?"

"One. But they're all loose."

Sloan eyed him wonderingly. "They'll never believe this, my lad. I can't understand it myself. I was never licked before."

Slade shrugged his shoulders.

"And still I can't understand why you did it."

"You fellows would have started a war. I hate war. All I want is peace."

"And you licked the toughest scrapper of the Seven Seas to get it! Slade, my lad, you're a strange fellow. Belike there's Irish in you? I thought so."

All the hate Slade had felt was gone. The first liking he had felt for Sloan had returned. Suddenly, without being asked, he spoke. He told Sloan of his early life, of his battles, and his wanderings. Diffidently, half-afraid of being laughed at, he told Sloan of his love of peace, the love that was a passion with him, almost a driving obsession.

And Sloan listened and understood. He threw an arm about Slade's shoulder, big brother fashion.

"Slade, my lad, I like you more and more. On my saddle is five hundred dollars which I'm going to return to de Garille. Then, the sea! Come with me, my lad. I gambled away me ship when I was drunk, but I'll build up a fortune again. I've done it before, Peace! I'll give you peace. No man fights on Red Sloan's ship. I've held a skipper's ticket and I've owned me own ship before and I can do it again. I've wanted a pard. A lone wolf like meself. You're the lad."

"Great," said Slade O'Shane.

The Atavist

(unfinished, originally untitled)

"Dev," his friends called him, and that stood for Devil as often as it did Devlin, which was his proper name. In the ring they called him Devil Devlin and that cognomen suited him better than the name to which he had been christened. Universally hailed as the greatest welterweight since the days of Joe Walcott, his phenomenal rise had been due largely to chance.

It was in the frenzied days following the Armistice that Jimmy Kelliher, strolling down Broadway and marveling at the fact that he was back in America and alive, caught sight of a familiar figure wandering through the crowded mazes ahead of him. Instantly a chain of recollections sprang to mind: trenches— flare-lit nights of fury—bayonet brushes with Huns on the front lines and fist brawls with M.P.s at canteens and estaminets.

"Dev!" He whom Kelliher addressed turned suddenly, revealing a lean, bronzed face, and a pair of narrow, steely grey eyes.

"I'll be—Jimmy! Put 'er there!"

"What are you doing here? I thought your range was a long way west of Broadway."

Devlin shrugged his shoulders. He was a lean, rangy youth of medium height, remarkably strongly built.

"Search me, 'bo. I rode the Arizona ranges before the war but somehow I couldn't go back to punchin' cows after goin' over the top. And since then—I dunno, Jimmy. I can't settle down, somehow. Gotta keep on the move—" he gestured vaguely, failing to put into words what he so strongly felt.

Kelliher understood. Devlin was in the grasp of that unrest felt by so many after the red glory they had been through. Kelliher himself knew it. It was as though they had outlived their day, had skimmed life dry. Civilian life seemed so unutterably tedious, so monotonous. Not alone Devlin and Kelliher, but thousands of ex-service men. Life seemed stale without thrill or excitement. Civilian pleasures cloyed.

"What are you doing now, Dev?"

"Nuthin'. Just meanderin' around over the country."

"Broke?"

"Flatterin' Hades."

Kelliher paused, in a quandary. There was a strong tie of friendship between the two.

"Say, Dev, let's go to a cabaret and then take in the show at the East Side Club tonight. There's going to be some good bouts."

"Sure, anything. Prizefights, yuh mean?"

"That's it."

Devlin evinced only a polite interest in the dancers and the music at the fashionable cabaret to which Kelliher steered their course. Somehow he seemed out of place. Indeed, to Kelliher's imaginative mind, Devlin had always seemed out of place anywhere but in the trenches and even there his khaki uniform seemed somehow incongruous. Kelliher searched his mind for a situation into which he could imagine Devlin fitting exactly. There was a nebulous thought floating around at the back of his mind, a word which seemed to describe the Westerner exactly, but Kelliher could not grasp it.

"Hey, Kelliher!" The ex-soldier turned to meet the outstretched hand of a portly, florid, flashily clad man who fairly exuded an air of jovial prosperity.

"Why, how are you, Stanton? Meet my buddy, Steve Devlin, Stan. Dev, this is the fellow who's promoting that show tonight that I was telling you about."

"Yeah, and it looks like a flop. I got two palookas matched for the semifinals, one of the main bout battlers ran out on me, and the substitute I got wouldn't draw butterflies in a rose garden. If I can't get a flock of hefty prelims, the fans'll hand me the mitten."

"Have you got all the preliminary fighters matched up?" asked Kelliher idly.

"No. I'm lookin' for one now, to meet Battlin' Barto, welterweight comer."

"Say!" Kelliher turned to Devlin. "If I remember right, you whipped all the bullies in the regiment and beat up every M.P. you had an altercation with. Did you ever box any?"

"Never had a pair of gloves on but once in my life," Devlin answered. "The fellows put up a kind of makeshift ring in a canteen back of the lines and we was going to have a tournament. They matched me with a Greek who'd been a fourth-rate glove-slinger."

"Who won? How did you like the game?"

"I dunno," confessed Devlin. "Fact is, we'd just squared off when a shell landed right on top the canteen and blew it all to Hades."

"Say, listen!" interposed Stanton. "If you're suggesting that I use Devlin in the prelims, that's off. Barron would break him to pieces."

"Don't be so quick on the trigger, mister," Devlin snarled, his expression changing suddenly. "Nobody's asked you for a job. And as for breakin' me, I'm not so easy broken as I may look."

"No offense," Stanton said hurriedly, "but—"

"But listen, Stan," Kelliher interrupted eagerly. "It would go big! Dev's tough, and Barron's nothing but a wild slugger. Dev's fast enough to go four rounds with him, even if he don't know anything about boxing. And listen, think of all the servicemen running loose in New York now! Advertise Dev as the champion of his regiment, (which he was, bare fisted if not officially), and watch them turn out!"

Perhaps it was because Stanton did not wish to offend Kelliher who was wealthy and had been something of a noted sportsman before the war. Perhaps it was merely the inscrutable workings of Destiny. However it be, Stanton suddenly changed his mind.

"You in pretty good condition?"

"I always am," Dev answered shortly. He had taken a dislike to Stanton.

"That's fine. Come around to the gym now and I'll show you some tricks."

Devlin shook his head. "Naw, I couldn't learn enough science to beat Barron between now and tonight. I want to grab off some sleep."

But probably he picked up a good deal watching the slow first preliminary while Stanton cursed soulfully beneath his breath and the fans hissed long, loud and viciously.

With the donning of the trunks, Devlin's whole nature seemed to change subtly and suddenly. His lean, good-natured face took on an expression of ferocity. His eyes narrowed. When he spoke it was to fling a laconic word over his shoulder. And this was not playacting. Kelliher remembered the ferocity of Devlin in action. Ordinarily, he had been a quiet, unobtrusive sort of a fellow, reserved but friendly. But crouching behind the sandbags, awaiting the word to go over the top, he seemed another man, a fierce-eyed, snarling savage. There was some latent primitive ferocity in Devlin's soul that came to the fore only in battle.

Stripped for action, he was really an impressive figure. Five feet, eight and three-fourth inches he stood, and he scaled in at 146 pounds, though because of his build he seemed much lighter. Lean but powerful legs upheld a body wonderful in its symmetry. Lean hipped and waisted, strong chested, remarkably broad of shoulders, long arms—he was a splendid fighting build. The muscles, long and springy, rippled under his bronzed skin as he moved. The triceps and shoulder muscles were especially developed, speaking of terrific hitting power. And he stepped with the smooth ease of a leopard.

He showed none of the usual nervousness of the beginner when he vaulted lithely over the ropes. And the moment his feet touched the mat, he paused, a strange expression upon his face. He rubbed his shoe soles on the mat, stepped forward and tested the ropes. It was as though Devlin had but come into his own, that at last he realized that he was in his own element, was somehow dimly aware of it. Just why he did those things, Devlin himself could not have told. But Kelliher knew that there was one of the rarest of all rare characters, a natural ring man who, without past experience to guide him, yet followed his instincts alright.

He vouchsafed the crowd only a single, casual glance, a longer glance at his burly, beetle-browed opponent.

"Shake hands? Nuthin' doin'," he retorted curtly.

"Huh?" the referee stared. "You gotta grudge against this bird?"

"Naw, but I gotta hate anybody I fight. And I ain't shakin' hands, see?"

"All right. Get to your corners, then. Hully gosh!" And aside to the announcer: "What booby hatch did this bird leave?"

At Devlin's corner, Stanton and the handlers spoke hurried advice.

"Remember, let go your left first, don't swing your right. Keep boring in between his arms. Get inside his swings. He's a slugger and it's meetin' him at his own game, but you ain't clever enough to keep away from him. Get in close and slam away at his body."

Bong! Barron sprang from his corner, a confident sneer on his swart face. Devlin flashed from his, a terrific energy fairly emanating from him, crouching head down. They met in the center of the ring. Head down Devlin leaped in—and full into the smashing force of Barron's left. Into a single punch that stopped him, straightened him and flung him halfway across the ring and onto the mat.

The referee sprang forward but even before he could begin a count, Devlin was up and flashing across the ring. His swings fanned the air as Barron ducked and a terrific right to the chin hurled him again upon his back.

"Take a count!" yelled Stanton, but his shout was unheeded. Devlin was on his feet and charging. The fans were upon their feet, cheering, yelling. That was the kind of action they wanted.

With a savage determination Devlin was boring in. A left to the face spattered him with blood but he gave no heed. With a savage, driving determination that made the fans gasp, he slammed away at Barron with both hands, leaving himself wide open, taking a terrific beating to land one punch. A right to the jaw that resounded over the house failed to slow him. And then his left smashed against Barron's chin. Barron sagged, started a nosedive, but almost instantly a swinging right changed his direction and his shoulders hit the mat with a crash.

"—And out!" The referee bellowed and the fans rose as one man to acclaim the winner, who weaved to his corner, dizzy but indomitable. And Kelliher, staring at the man before him, caught the nebulous thought that he had been seeking. Swaying on his feet stood Devlin, blood spattered and sweaty and grim, his eyes blazing through his tousled hair, thin lips still asnarl with the battle fury.

"Atavar!" exclaimed Kelliher. "That's what you are, Dev! I've been trying to think of a word to suit you! You're atavistic! A reversion to the primitive man of the Stone Age! That garb is the only one I ever saw you in that suited you!"

And from the ring-side throng came a chubby man with an incongruously predatory nose.

"Listen," he said, "I'm 'Lynx' Sloan, manager of three world-champions in my time. You've got the makings of a real fighter in you. How about signing up with me?"

Devlin grinned. His fighting savagery had vanished.

"Glove fightin' will seem pretty tame after cannon fightin' but I guess I'll go with you."

And so Devlin entered the game to which he had been born. His rise was meteoric. Wise handling and crafty managing aided, but mostly he rose through his own indomitable fighting spirit. He took to the game as a wolf cub takes to the trail. In a short time he became, from an unscientific rusher, a skilled, crafty ring man. He remained a slugger, but the most scientific one seen in many a day. His powers of taking punishment were incredible. He was as fast as lightning and carried terrific hitting power in each hand. He possessed to the finest degree that rare, unexplainable essence known as the "knockout kick." Bob Fitzsimmons had that quality, and few others. Devlin's punches were the most scientific parts of his armament. They travelled only a few inches and they dropped what they hit. He did not need to get set; travelling at his highest rate of speed, suddenly his mitt would flash forward, from any angle and the recipient thereof would usually take the count. He was a Walcott, combined with Kid McCoy.

In a short year he had battled his way through the ranks of logical contenders and the welterweight champion was forced to acknowledge his challenge. That battle was a classic; the champion was a ring wizard, a very light hitter, but a fast, remarkably scientific boxer and he made Devlin miss with monotonous regularity. Then in the eleventh round, the terrific pace told and Devlin brought the bout to a quick conclusion with a left to the body and a right to the chin.

Devlin proved a fighting champion. He took them as they came, first come, first served. A challenge was all that was necessary. The money part of the game he gave little consideration; Sloan saw to that and all Devlin stipulated was that his manager should not demand such exorbitant sums as to interfere with the fights. For Devlin was that type of fighter so rarely met with in modern years, the John L. Sullivan type, to whom money was a lesser consideration than the joy and the glory of battle.

He trained scrupulously, nor did he dissipate. Wine, gambling and the like failed to interest him, and women bored him. Kelliher remembered that in France he had been the same way.

In less than a year, he had gone through the ranks of welter contenders so thoroughly that there was practically no competition.

The night he won the title, he signed for a bout with Jack Comsky, a first rater from whom he had already won a decision before he gained the title. Devlin won by a knockout in the seventh round and a short time later faced Willie Hermann, then Battling Kay, then Rube Rosenstein, then Billy McCoy. McCoy stayed the limit, though losing the decision, and clamored for a return match. Devlin obliged and knocked him out in the first minute of the first round. Having disposed of all the first raters, some of them twice, he gave the best of the second raters a chance. Then, unable to find worthy opponents in his class, he turned his attention to the middleweights.

Sloan, a shrewd manager, was extremely loath to match Devlin against a man out of his class, but Devlin not only insisted upon it, but refused to take a setup. So he was matched with Johnny Burrone, a good, clever middleweight and the fans turned out en masse to see how the welter champion would perform against a heavier, taller man. Burrone, with his physical advantages, did not go down beneath Devlin's first headlong charge.

Toe to toe they slugged and suddenly Burrone whipped over a terrific right that sprawled Devlin in the center of the ring. He came weaving up and was sent down again, rose and was floored and it lacked just twelve seconds of the bell, when reeling up, half-senseless, he staked all upon a wild, desperate attack, and landed his first solid blow. It was a crashing right to the jaw and Burrone went down for the count.

But that bout taught Devlin a lesson. That no matter how fast and strong a boxer may be, it is not wise to trade punches and slug with a larger man. So he paid more attention to learning the finer points of the game than he had before. He became, not less aggressive, but more crafty. As a result, he met and defeated most of the leading middleweights, though never scaling above 150 himself. He repeatedly challenged the middleweight champion but the titleholder evaded him.

It was nearly three years after he had met Kelliher in New York that he called a council. Kelliher, his constant companion, was there, and Sloan and that Moghul of fight promoters, "Smooth" Magurk.

"Listen," said Devlin, "I've got to have a match with Tommy Jansen, the middle champ."

"Yeah," mused Sloan, "there's no mazuma much in the welter class."

"There's no fights," said Devlin. "Right now, besides, I weigh 151½ pounds and I have to go some to make the welter limit, because I'm in my best fighting trim right now. I've been fighting welters at catch weights but the commission's been ranting about it. Maybe I can make the weight a few more times, but if I keep it up, it's going to weaken me. Look what happened to Joe Gans.

"I can beat Jansen—easy. If I can get a match with him, I'll relinquish my welterweight title."

"But how can I force him into the ring?" marveled Sloan. "Ain't I tried for months?"

"Try again," ordered Devlin and Sloan did.

Jansen and his manager listened languidly and with little interest to Sloan's inducements.

"There's plenty of good boys in my class," said Jansen grandly. "I ain't wastin' my time on no welterweights. I believe in givin' the deservin' boys in my own class first chance. That's me—fair and square."Sloan snorted his disgust.

"Bah! You ain't had a bout in a year and then nuthin' but setups."

Jansen disdained to reply.

"Now listen," wheedled Sloan. "We're willin' to give you seventy percent of the gate receipts, outside the guarantee! How's that for liberal?"

Jansen's manager glanced uncertainly at the champion.

That worthy yawned and rose.

"I gotta date with a peach," he remarked. "If you got time, Moe, to waste on this person, it's all right with me. But I ain't."

Devlin pondered when the interview was reported to him.

"Offer him the house and a side bet of ten thousand dollars," he suggested.

Sloan jumped out of his chair.

"I won't do it!" he shouted.

"Aw, keep your shirt on," Devlin answered impatiently. "I could make the money back on the title in no time."

"Yeah, but suppose you didn't win."

"Yeah, but I will."

"Why not offer to meet him, winner take all?" suggested Kelliher. "Appeal to his sporting sense, as it were."

"He ain't got no sporting sense," replied Sloan. "He never was much and he's held the title for four years simply by meeting setups"

"Try it again, anyway," said Devlin. Sloan tried publicity.

He played upon one incessant theme—that Jansen was afraid to meet his man. The reporters took it up and the public demanded a match. The commission ordered Jansen to defend his title. And Jansen double-crossed them there, for he took on a leading middleweight whose moral code was as shifty as his defense, and who readily agreed to throw the fight—for a consideration.

Devlin raged. He could not understand a fighter who would not fight.

Sloan sought Jansen and his manager.

"Jansen," he said, "you're a cheese champ. Devlin would knock you off your props in the first frame and you know it. If you won't fight, why don't you retire 'undefeated' and give the boys a chance?"

"Gwan," said Jansen unperturbed. "Why don't he defend his own title? He's got one already, ain't he? I ain't selfish, me. You don't see me tryin' to grab the heavyweight belt, do you? What about Jimmy Britton? Why don't Devlin give him a chance?"

Devlin gave Britton a chance. Jimmy was a clever young welterweight who had come up the contender ranks like a forest fire. He had been developed since Devlin won the title and there was some point to what Jansen said. Some of the clever ones picked Britton to out-box Devlin, but the champion was not the wild slugger that had won the title. Making the weight weakened him, for he had had to simply boil himself in Turkish baths, but even so he elected to out-box the challenger and for ten rounds he made the youngster look foolish. Then in the tenth round he grew weary of the play and with one blazing rush and a blinding whirl of gloves, he sent Britton down for the count.

"All right," said Jansen. "Looks like your man is as good as a good third rater, anyhow. I tell you what; you sign him on for a bout with Ghost Donovan; then if he wins I'll give him a chance at my title."

"Ghost Donovan!" raged Sloan. "Who the Hell ever heard of a middleweight contender having to beat the light heavy champion before he can get a chance at the middleweight title?"

"That's all right," said Jansen's manager, unperturbed. "If he beats Donovan and beats my man too, he'll have two titles. Regular Bob Fitzsimmons, hey, Sloan?"

Jansen laughed.

Sloan reported to Devlin, fairly effervescing profanity. Devlin meditated. Suddenly an ugly expression crossed his face.

"Donovan!" he said, and his tone held an ugly timbre.

"That's the dude I saw at the Beach. With a frail! Blah!"

"Maybe, but he ain't no dude," answered Sloan, "nor he ain't no cheese champ like Jansen. He likes nice clothes and all but—"

"But nothin'!" snarled Devlin with a venom his friends had seldom seen him display. "Any galoot that trails around with a flock of skirts—and him pretendin' to be a battler!"

"He's no woman chaser," remarked Kelliher. "I happen to know. But there's a little Irish girl that's just about the world to him—"

Devlin fairly snarled in irritation. Fighters are temperamental, especially sluggers, and though Devlin was much less so than most, he had erratic traits and he had conceived an unreasoning but no less powerful antipathy for the Irish champion. Balked ambition might have had something to do with it, but mainly it was this: Devlin was, hair to heels, a fighter of the John L. Sullivan type; not a brawler and a roisterer, but one who believed that a fighter should uphold certain traditions of the game. He always wore clothes more or less in keeping with his profession as he imagined it; he never attempted to get into high society or the movies; and the softer sentiments had no place in his rugged bosom. And to his ferocious, Spartan temperament, a fighter who moved in the best of society, dressed like a Beau Brummell and courted a society girl unashamed, was a dude, a pretender, a man to be despised. Devlin might have forgiven Donovan if he had been less successful in the ring, but the Irishman's success there outraged the welterweight champion's sense of fitness.

Wherefore he slammed the table, said rude things about Donovan and requested Sloan to:

"Get me a match with this bog-trottin' blarneyer."

"But listen, Dev, you ain't figuring on takin' Jansen up?"

"Jansen be damned! I'm callin' his bluff and anyway, you get me a bout with Donovan."

"But Dev—"

"You hear me. If you want to keep on bein' my manager, you'll get me that bout."

The commission hesitated over the match for awhile but finally gave way to the urging of the papers and public opinion.

A word as to Ghost Donovan. After years of Italian, Jewish and European-American champions, it seemed that the Green Isle had at last produced a worthy follower in the footsteps of Jack Dempsey, the Nonpareil and Jack McAuliffe. Born on the grey Atlantic coast, among the dim mountains of Kerry, he had early followed the calling of his race, and had finally landed in America, strong, clean limbed, with the tang of the salt seas and the strength of ocean winds. His rise had been as meteoric as Devlin's; like Devlin he boasted a record unmarred by defeat. He was a wonderful boxer, equal to the great James J. Corbett, some of the old-timers said; fast on his feet and with his hands, remarkably scientific, he possessed to the highest degree that coordination that makes a champion. Nor was he merely a wonderfully speedy boxer; he was possessed of unfathomed courage, an ability to endure terrific punishment, and a terrific right-hand punch to go with his crafty left. He had gained the light heavyweight title and held it against all comers; had out-pointed the heavyweight champion in a terrific no-decision match and had sought in vain for a return bout.

The fans hailed the forthcoming match with delight.

Somehow, Devlin's antipathy for Donovan got abroad and of course increased interest greatly. Fans revel in a grudge bout. As for Donovan, he was perfectly willing for a bout. He too was a fighting champion and of late had been unable to get any good matches. The papers hinted that one reason for his acquiescence was because of the fact that he was soon to be married, and wished to acquire all the money he could before that time. Retirement was in the wind, the papers hinted. Devlin snarled and trained with such furious energy that Sloan cautioned him against burning himself out before the match.

"Gettin' hisself hitched!" snarled Devlin, and rising to unsuspected heights through his aversion, he swaggered up and down the training quarters in an impromptu impersonation to the great delight of his rough sparring partners and handlers.

"Deah me!" he intoned in what he considered an exact reproduction of a society woman's voice, as he minced back and forth.

"Deah me, Mr. Donovan, you must have tea with us this aftawnoon, don't you know!' 'Why really, Mrs. Heavykale, I have a date at the stadium with one of those rough Swede stevedores, be jabbers!' 'Deah me, you don't say! Then come immediately aftaw and *do* wear your pink silk trunks, they look so cunning!"

Devlin's idea of high society or society of any kind was gathered from ten cent movies which he occasionally frequented, but his mimicry passed as real Thespian talent among the ex- wharfhands and lumberjacks who composed his stable, and they roared their appreciation and swore the stage had missed a real find when Devlin took up boxing.

Of course, his aping found its way into the papers, but Donovan showed no resentment; in fact, he was inclined to laugh at Devlin's uncouth antics, which enraged the welterweight champion even more.

But as the day set for the bout approached, Devlin ceased his mimicking. His hate was too fiery, his unreasoning rage too ferocious to admit of any sport. He battered his sparring partners with such vicious fury that some of them resigned. The sportswriters commented on this fact and some remarked that Devlin would be wild and erratic in the ring because of his rage. But the real fans, who had studied him, knew that Devlin was one of those rare types who can be hellishly angry and yet keep their heads. Devlin fought best when his fury was white hot.

It was no pose, his declaring that he must hate any man he fought. He did hate them. From the moment he stepped into the ring until the final gong, his hatred for his opponent, no matter who it might be, was a living, flaming thing. But never before had he carried his hatred outside the ring.

Donovan was the opposite; a rushing, aggressive fighter, but a man of icy temperament, craftier and more skillful than Devlin. A real ring wizard.

Women came to Donovan's training camp and admired him openly, which really embarrassed him. No women came to Devlin's camp. Devlin saw to that.

[. . .]

Cupid vs. Pollux

As I am coming up the steps of the fraternity house, I meet Tarantula Soons, a soph with an ingrown disposition and a goggle eye.

"You're lookin' for Spike, I take it?" said he, and upon me admittin' the fact, he gives me a curious look and remarks that Spike is in his room.

I go up and all the way up the stairs, I hear somebody chanting a love song in a voice that is incitement to justifiable homicide. Strange as it seems, the atrocity is emanating from Spike's room, and as I enter, I see Spike himself, seated on a divan, and singing somethin' about lovers' moons and soft red lips. His eyes are turned soulfully toward the ceiling and he is putting great feeling in the outrageous bellow which he imagines is the height of melody. To say I am surprized is putting it mildly and as Spike turns and says, "Steve, ain't love wonderful?" you could have knocked me over with a piledriver. Besides standing six feet and seven inches and scaling upwards of 270 pounds, Spike has a map that makes Firpo look like an ad for the fashionable man, and is neitherto about as sentimental as a rhinoceros.

"Yeh? And who is she?" I ask sarcastically, but he only sighs amorously and quotes poetry. At that I fizz over.

"So that's why you ain't to the gym training!" I yawp. "You big chunka nothin', the tournament for the intercollegiate boxin' titles come off tomorrow and here you are, you overgrown walrus, sentimentallin' around like a three-year-old yearlin' calf."

"Gwan," says he, tossing a haymakin' right to my jaw in an absent-minded manner, "I can put over any of them palukas without no trainin'."

"Yes," I sneers, climbin' to my wobbling feet, "and when you stack up against Monk Gallranan you won't need any trainin'. That's a cinch."

"Boxin'," says the infatuated boob, "is degradin'. I bet *she* thinks so, I don't know whether I'll even enter the tourneyment or not."

"Hey!" I yells. "After all the work I've done gettin' you in shape. You figurin' on throwin' the college down?"

"Aw, go take a run around the block" says Spike, drawing back his lip in an ugly manner.

"Gwan, you boneheaded elephant!" says I, drivin' my left to the wrist in his solar plexus, and the battle was on. Anyway, at the conclusion, I yelled up to him from the foot of the stairs

[A portion of the text is missing at this point]

where the college will be too small for you."

His sole answer was to slam the door so hard that he shook the house, but the next day when I was lookin' for a substitute for the heavyweight entries, the big yam appears, with a smug and self-satisfied look on his map.

"I've decided to fight, Steve," he says grandly, "*she* will have a ringside seat and all women adore physical strength and power when allied to manly beauty."

"All right," says I, "Get into your ring togs. Your bout is the main event of the day and will come last."

This managing a college boxing show is no cinch. If things go wrong, the manager gets the blame and if they don't, the fighters get the hand. I remember once I even substituted for a welterweight entry who didn't show up. Just to give the fans a run for their money, I lowered my guard the third round and invited my antagonist to hit me—he did—they were four hours bringing me to, and the fact that it was discovered he had a horseshoe concealed in his glove, didn't increase my regard of the game. They've got the horseshoe in the museum now, but it isn't much to look at as a horseshoe, being bent all out of shape where it came in contact with my jaw.

But to get back to the tournament. The college Spike and I represented had indifferent fortune in the first bouts, our featherweight entry won the decision on points and our flyweight tied with a fellow from St. Janice's. As usual, heavyweights being scarce, Spike and Monk Gallranan from Burke's University were the only entries. This gorilla was nearly as tall and heavy as Spike, and didn't make the football team on account of his habit of breaking the arms and legs of the team in practice scrimmage, he is even more prehistoric look-ing than Spike, so you can imagine what those two cavemen looked like when they squared off together. Spike was jubilant, however, at the chance of distinguishing himself in an athletic way, he having always been too lazy to come out for football and the like. And his girl was there in a seat on the front row. The bout didn't last long, so I don't know of a better way than to give it round by round. What those two saps didn't know about the finer points of boxin' would fill several encyclopedias, but I'd had a second rate, for giving Spike some secret instruction on infightin', and I expected him to win by close range work, infightin' bein' a lost art on the average amateur.

Round 1

Spike missed a left for the head and Monk sent a left to the body. Spike put a right to the face and got three left jabs to the nose in return. They traded rights to the body, and Monk staggered Spike with a sizzlin' left to the wind. Monk missed with a right and they clinch. Spike nailed Monk with a straight right to the jaw at the break. Monk whipped a left to the head and a right to the body and Spike rocked him back on his heels with a straight left to the face.

Round 2

Monk missed a right but slammed a left to the jaw. They clinched and Spike roughed in close. Monk staggered Spike on the break with a right to the jaw. Monk drove Spike across the ring with lefts and rights to head and body. Spike covered up then kicked through with a right uppercut to the jaw that nearly tore Monk's head off. Monk clinched and Spike punished him with short straight rights to the body. Just at the gong Spike staggered Monk with a left hook to the jaw.

Round 3

Monk blocked Spike's left lead and uppercut him three times to the jaw. Spike swung wild and Monk staggered him with a straight right to the jaw. Another straight right started him to bleeding at the lips. Spike came out of it with a fierce rally and drove Monk to the ropes with a series of short left hooks to the wind and head. Monk launched an attack of his own and battered Spike to the middle of the ring where they stood toe to toe, trading smashes to head and body. Monk started a fierce rush and a straight left for the jaw. Spike ducked, let the punch slide over his shoulder and crossed his right to Monk's jaw, and Monk hit the mat. Just as the referee reached "Nine" the gong sounded.

Monk's seconds worked over him but he was still groggy as he came out for the fourth round. I shouted for Spike to finish him quick, but be careful.

Round 4

Spike stepped up, warily; they sparred for a second, then Spike stepped in and sank his left to the wrist in Monk's solar plexus, following up with a right to the button that would have knocked down a house. Monk hit the mat and lay still.

Then Spike, the boob, turns his back on his fallen foeman and walks over to the ropes smilin' and bowin'. He opens his mouth to say somethin' to his girl—the crowd yells, "Look out, you big stiff!" and Monk, who has risen meanwhile, beating the count, lifts his right from the floor and places it squarely beneath Spike's sagging jaw. The referee could have counted a million.

But afterwards Spike says to me, sitting on the ring floor, still in his ring togs, he says, "Steve, girls is a lotta hokum. I'm offa 'em," he says.

Says I, "Then if you've found that out, it's worth the soakin' you got," I says.

The Spirit of Tom Molyneaux

(alternate, published version)

by John Taverel: One of the greatest managers
in the history of the fight game

Readers of this magazine will probably remember Ace Jessel, the big negro boxer whom I managed a few years ago. He was an ebony giant, four inches over six feet tall, with a fighting weight of 230 pounds. He moved with the smooth ease of a gigantic leopard and his pliant steel muscles rippled under his shiny skin. A clever boxer for so large a man, he carried the smashing jolt of a triphammer in each huge fist.

It was my belief that he was the equal of any man in the ring at that time—except for one fatal defect. He lacked the killer instinct. He had courage in plenty, as he proved on more than one occasion—but he was content to box mostly, outpointing his opponents and piling up just enough lead to keep from losing.

Every so often the crowds booed him, but their taunts only broadened his good-natured grin. However, his fights continued to draw a big gate, because, on the rare occasions when he was stung out of a defensive role or when he was matched with a clever man whom he had to knockout in order to win, the fans saw a real fight that thrilled their blood. Even so, time and again he stepped away from a sagging foe, giving the beaten man time to recover and return to the attack—while the crowd raved and I tore my hair.

The one abiding loyalty in Ace's happy-go-lucky life was a fanatical worship of Tom Molyneaux, first champion of America and a sturdy fighting man of color; according to some authorities, the greatest black ring-man that ever lived.

Tom Molyneaux died in Ireland a hundred years ago but the memory of his valiant deeds in America and Europe was Ace Jessel's direct incentive to action. As a boy, toiling on the wharves, he had heard an account of Tom's life and battles and the story had started him on the fistic trail.

Ace's most highly prized possession was a painted portrait of the old battler. He had discovered this—a rare find indeed, since even woodcuts of Molyneaux are rare—among the collection of a London sportsman, and had prevailed on the owner to sell it. Paying for it had taken every cent that Ace made in four fights but he counted it cheap at the price. He removed the original frame and replaced it with a frame of solid silver, which, considering the portrait was full length and life size, was more than extravagant.

But no honor was too great for "Mistah Tom" and Ace merely increased the number of his bouts to meet the cost.

Finally my brains and Ace's mallet fists had cleared us a road to the top of the game. Ace loomed up as a heavyweight menace and the champion's manager was ready to sign with us— when an unexpected obstacle blocked our path.

A form hove into view on the fistic horizon that dwarfed and overshadowed all other contenders, including my man. This was "Mankiller Gomez," and he was all that his name implies. Gomez was his ring name, given him by the Spaniard who discovered him and brought him to America. He was a full-blooded Senegalese from the West Coast of Africa.

Once in a century, ring fans see a man like Gomez in action— a born killer who crashes through the general ruck of fighters as a buffalo crashes through a thicket of dead wood. He was a savage, a tiger. What he lacked in actual skill, he made up by ferocity of attack, by ruggedness of body and smashing power of arm. From the time he landed in New York, with a long list of European victories behind him, it was inevitable that he should batter down all opposition—and at last the white champion looked to see the black savage looming above the broken forms of his victims. The champion saw the writing on the wall, but the public was clamoring for a match and whatever his faults, the titleholder was a fighting champion.

Ace Jessel, who alone of all the foremost challengers had not met Gomez, was shoved into discard, and as early summer dawned on New York, a title was lost and won, and Mankiller Gomez, son of the black jungle, rose up as king of all fighting men.

The sporting world and the public at large hated and feared the new champion. Boxing fans like savagery in the ring, but Gomez did not confine his ferocity to the ring. His soul was abysmal. He was apelike, primordial—the very spirit of that morass of barbarism from which mankind has so tortuously climbed, and toward which men look with so much suspicion.

There went forth a search for a White Hope, but the result was always the same. Challenger after challenger went down before the terrible onslaught of the Mankiller and at last only one man remained who had not crossed gloves with Gomez— Ace Jessel.

I hesitated to throw my man in with a battler like Gomez, for my fondness for the great good-natured negro was more than the friendship of manager for fighter. Ace was something more than a meal ticket to me, for I knew the real nobility underlying Ace's black skin, and I hated to see him battered into a senseless ruin by a man I knew in my heart to be more than Jessel's match. I wanted to wait a while, to let Gomez wear himself out with his terrific battles and the dissipations that were sure to follow the savage's success. These super-sluggers never last long, any more than a jungle native can withstand the temptations of civilization.

But the slump that follows a really great titleholder's gaining the belt was on, and matches were scarce. The public was clamoring for a title fight, sportswriters were raising Cain and accusing Ace of cowardice, promoters were offering alluring purses, and at last I signed for a fifteen-round go between Mankiller Gomez and Ace Jessel.

At the training quarters I turned to Ace.

"Ace, do you think you can whip him?"

"Mistah John," Ace answered, meeting my eye with a straight gaze, "I'll do mah best, but I's mighty afeard I caint do it. Dat man ain't human."

This was bad; a man is more than half-whipped when he goes into the ring in that frame of mind.

Later I went to Ace's room for something and halted in the doorway in amazement. I had heard the battler talking in a low voice as I came up, but had supposed one of the handlers or sparring partners was in the room with him. Now I saw that he was alone. He was standing before his idol—the portrait of Tom Molyneaux.

"Mistah Tom," he was saying humbly, "I ain't nevah met no man yet what could even knock me off mah feet, but I reckon dat niggah can. I's gwine to need help mighty bad, Mistah Tom."

I felt almost as if I had interrupted a religious rite. It was uncanny; had it not been for Ace's evident deep sincerity, I would have felt it to be unholy. But to Ace, Tom Molyneaux was something more than a saint.

I stood in the doorway in silence, watching the strange tableau. The unknown artist had painted the picture of Molyneaux with remarkable skill. The short black figure stood out boldly from the faded canvas. The breath of bygone days, he seemed, clad in the long tights of that other day, the powerful legs braced far apart, the knotted arms held stiff and high— just as Molyneaux had appeared when he fought Tom Cribb of England over a hundred years ago.

Ace Jessel stood before the painted figure, his head sunk upon his mighty chest as if listening to some dim whisper inside his soul. And as I watched, a curious and fantastic idea came to me—the memory of an age-old superstition.

You know it has been said by students of the occult that statues and portraits have power to draw departed souls back from the void of eternity. I wondered if Ace had heard of this superstition and hoped to conjure his idol's spirit out of the realms of the dead, for advice and aid. I shrugged my shoulders at this ridiculous idea and turned away. As I did, I glanced again at the picture before which Ace still stood like a great image of black basalt, and was aware of a peculiar illusion; the canvas seemed to ripple slightly, like the surface of a lake across which a faint breeze is blowing. . . .

When the day of the fight arrived, I watched Ace nervously. I was more afraid than ever that I had made a mistake in permitting circumstances to force my man into the ring with Gomez. However,

I was backing Ace to the limit— and I was ready to do anything under heaven to help him win that fight.

The great crowd cheered Ace to the echo as he climbed into the ring; cheered again, but not so heartily, as Gomez appeared. They afforded a strange contrast, those two negroes, alike in color but so different in all other respects!

Ace was tall, clean-limbed and rangy, long and smooth of muscle, clear of eye and broad of forehead.

Gomez seemed stocky by comparison, though he stood a good six feet two. Where Jessel's sinews were long and smooth like great cables, his were knotty and bulging. His calves, thighs, arms and shoulders stood out in great bunches of muscles. His small bullet head was set squarely between gigantic shoulders, and his forehead was so low that his kinky wool seemed to grow just above his small, bloodshot eyes. On his chest was a thick grizzle of matted black hair.

He grinned insolently, thumped his breast and flexed his mighty arms with the assurance of the savage. Ace, in his corner, grinned at the crowd, but an ashy tint was on his dusky face and his knees were trembling.

The usual formalities were carried out: instructions given by the referee, weights announced—230 for Ace, 248 for Gomez. Then over the great stadium the lights went off except those over the ring where two black giants faced each other like men alone on the ridge of the world.

At the gong Gomez whirled in his corner and came out with a breathtaking roar of pure ferocity. Ace, frightened though he must have been, rushed to meet him with the courage of a cave man charging a gorilla. They met headlong in the center of the ring.

The first blow was the Mankiller's, a left swing that glanced from Ace's ribs. Ace came back with a long left to the face and a stinging right to the body. Gomez "bulled in," swinging both hands; and Ace, after one futile attempt to mix it with him, gave back. The champion drove him across the ring, sending a savage left to the body as Ace clinched. As they broke, Gomez shot a terrible right to the chin and Ace reeled into the ropes.

A great "Ahhh!" went up from the crowd as the champion plunged after him like a famished wolf, but Ace managed to get between the lashing arms and clinch, shaking his head to clear it. Gomez sent in a left, which Ace's clutching arms partly smothered, and the referee warned the Senegalese.

At the break Ace stepped back, jabbing swiftly and cleverly with his left. The round ended with the champion bellowing like a buffalo, trying to get past the rapier-like arm.

Between rounds I cautioned Ace to keep away from infighting as much as possible, where Gomez' superior strength would count heavily, and to use his footwork to avoid punishment.

The second round started much like the first, Gomez rushing and Ace using all his skill to stave him off and avoid those terrible smashes. It's hard to get a shifty boxer like Ace in a corner, when he is fresh and unweakened, and at long range he had the advantage over Gomez, whose one idea was to get in close and batter down his foes by sheer strength and ferocity. Still, in spite of Ace's speed and skill, just before the gong sounded Gomez got the range and sank a vicious left in Ace's midriff and the tall negro weaved slightly as he returned to his corner.

I felt that it was the beginning of the end. The vitality and power of Gomez seemed endless; there was no wearing him down and it would not take many such blows to rob Ace of his speed of foot and accuracy of eye. If forced to stand and trade punches, he was finished.

Gomez came plunging out for the third round with murder in his eye. He ducked a straight left, took a hard right uppercut square in the face and hooked both hands to Ace's body, then straightened with a terrific right to the chin, which Ace robbed of most of its force by swaying with the blow.

While the champion was still off-balance, Ace measure him coolly and shot in a fierce right hook, flush on the chin. Gomez' head flew back as if hinged to his shoulders and he was stopped in his tracks! But even as the crowd rose, hands clenched, lips parted, hoping he would go down, the champion shook his bullet head and came in, roaring. The round ended with both men locked in a clinch in the center of the ring.

At the beginning of the fourth round Gomez drove Ace about the ring almost at will. Stung and desperate, Ace made a stand in a neutral corner and sent Gomez back on his heels with a left and right to the body, but he received a savage left in the face in return. Then suddenly the champion crashed through with a deadly left to the solar plexus, and as Ace staggered, shot a killing right to the chin. Ace fell back into the ropes, instinctively raising his hands. Gomez' short, fierce smashes were partly blocked by his shielding gloves—and suddenly, pinned on the ropes as he was, and still dazed from the Mankiller's attack, Ace went into terrific action and, slugging toe to toe with the champion, beat him off and drove him back across the ring!

The crowd went mad. Ace was fighting as he had never fought before, but I waited miserably for the end. I knew no man could stand the pace the champion was setting.

Battling along the ropes, Ace sent a savage left to the body and a right and left to the face, but was repaid by a right-hand smash to the ribs that made him wince in spite of himself. Just at the gong, Gomez landed another of those deadly left-handers to the body.

Ace's handlers worked over him swiftly, but I saw that the tall black was weakening.

"Ace, can't you keep away from those body smashes?" I asked.

"Mistah John, suh, I'll try," he answered.

The gong!

Ace came in with a rush, his magnificent body vibrating with dynamic energy. Gomez met him, his iron muscles bunching into a compact fighting unit. *Crash—crash*—and again, *crash!* A clinch. As they broke, Gomez drew back his great right arm and launched a terrible blow to Ace's mouth. The tall negro reeled— went down. Then without stopping for the count which I was screaming for him to take, he gathered his long, steely legs under him and was up with a bound, blood gushing down his black chest. Gomez leaped in and Ace, with the fury of desperation, met him with a terrific right, square to the jaw. And Gomez crashed to the canvas on his shoulder blades!

The crowd rose screaming! In the space of ten seconds both men had been floored for the first time in the life of each!

"One! Two! Three! Four!" The referee's arm rose and fell.

Gomez was up, unhurt, wild with fury. Roaring like a wild beast, he plunged in, brushed aside Ace's hammering arms and crashed his right hand with the full weight of his mighty shoulder behind it, full into Ace's midriff. Ace went an ashy color—he swayed like a tall tree, and Gomez beat him to his knees with rights and lefts which sounded like the blows of caulking mallets.

"One! Two! Three! Four—"

Ace was writhing on the canvas, trying to get up. The roar of the fans was an ocean of noise which drowned all thought.

"—Five! Six! Seven—"

Ace was up! Gomez came charging across the stained canvas, gibbering his pagan fury. His blows beat upon the staggering challenger like a hail of sledges. A left—a right—another left which Ace had not the strength to duck.

He went down again.

"One! Two! Three! Four! Five! Six! Seven! Eight—"

Again Ace was up, weaving, staring blankly, helpless. A swinging left hurled him back into the ropes and, rebounding from them, he went to his knees—then the gong sounded!

As his handlers and I sprang into the ring Ace groped blindly for his corner and dropped limply upon the stool.

"Ace, he's too much for you," I said.

A weak grin spread over Ace's face and his indomitable spirit shone in his bloodshot eyes.

"Mistah John, please, suh, don't throw in de sponge. If I mus' take it, I takes it standin'. Dat boy caint last at dis pace all night, suh."

No—but neither could Ace Jessel, in spite of his remarkable vitality and his marvelous recuperative powers, which sent him into the next round with a show of renewed strength and freshness.

The sixth and seventh were comparatively tame. Perhaps Gomez really was fatigued from the terrific pace he had been setting. At any rate, Ace managed to make it more or less of a sparring match at long range and the crowd was treated to an exhibition illustrating how long a brainy boxer can stand off and keep away from a slugger bent solely on his destruction. Even I marveled at the brand of boxing which Ace was showing, though I knew that Gomez was fighting cautiously for him. The champion had sampled the power of Ace's right hand in that frenzied fifth round and perhaps he was wary of a trick. For the first time in his life he had sprawled on the canvas. He was content to rest a couple of rounds, take his time and gather his energies for a final onslaught.

This began as the gong sounded for the eighth round. Gomez launched his usual sledgehammer attack, drove Ace about the ring and floored him in a neutral corner. His style of fighting was such that when he was determined to annihilate a foe, skill, speed and science could do no more than postpone the eventual outcome. Ace took the count of nine and rose, backpedaling.

But Gomez was after him; the champion missed twice with his left and then sank a right under the heart that turned Ace ashy. A left to the jaw made his knees buckle and he clinched desperately.

On the breakaway Ace sent a straight left to the face and right hook to the chin, but the blows lacked force. Gomez shook them off and sank his left wrist deep in Ace's midsection. Ace again clinched but the champion shoved him away and drove him across the ring with savage hooks to the body. At the gong they were slugging along the ropes.

Ace reeled to the wrong corner and when his handlers led him to his own, he sank down on the stool, his legs trembling and his great dusky chest heaving from his exertions. I glanced across at the champion, who was glowering at his foe. He too was showing signs of the fray, but he was much fresher than Ace. The referee walked over, looked hesitantly at Ace, and then spoke to me.

Through the mists that veiled his muddled brain, Ace realized the significance of these words and struggled to rise, a kind of fear showing in his eyes.

"Mistah John, don' let him stop it, suh! Don' let him do it; I ain't hu't nuthin' like dat would hu't me!"

The referee shrugged his shoulders and walked back to the center of the ring.

There was little use giving advice to Ace. He was too battered to understand—in his numbed brain there was room only for one thought—to fight and fight, and keep on fighting—the old primal instinct that is stronger than all things except death.

At the sound of the gong he reeled out to meet his doom with an indomitable courage that brought the crowd to its feet yelling. He struck, a wild aimless left, and the champion plunged in, hitting with both hands until Ace went down. At "nine" he was up, backpedaling instinctively until Gomez reached him with a long straight right and sent him down again. Again he took "nine" before he reeled up and now the crowd was silent. Not one voice was raised in an urge for the kill. This was butchery—primitive slaughter—but the courage of Ace Jessel took their breath as it gripped my heart.

Ace fell blindly into a clinch, and another and another, till the Mankiller, furious, shook him off and sank his right to the body. Ace's ribs gave way like rotten wood, with a dry crack heard distinctly all over the stadium. A strangled cry went up from the crowd and Ace gasped thickly and fell to his knees.

"—Seven! Eight—" The great black form was still writhing on the canvas.

"—Nine!" And then a miracle happened; Ace was on his feet, swaying, jaw sagging, arms hanging limply.

Gomez glared at him, as if unable to understand how his foe could have risen again, then came plunging in to finish him. Ace was in dire straits. Blood blinded him. Both eyes were nearly closed, and when he breathed through his smashed nose, a red haze surrounded him. Deep cuts gashed cheek and cheekbones and his left side was a mass of torn flesh. He was going on fighting instinct alone now, and never again would any man doubt that Ace Jessel had a fighting heart.

Yet a fighting heart alone is not enough when the body is broken and battered, and mists of unconsciousness veil the brain. Before Gomez' terrific onslaught, Ace went down—broken— and the crowd knew that this time it was final.

When a man has taken the beating that Ace had taken, something more than body and heart must come into the game to carry him through. Something to inspire and stimulate him— to fire him to heights of superhuman effort!

Before leaving the training quarters, I had, unknown to Ace, removed the picture of Tom Molyneaux from its frame, rolled it up carefully and brought it to the stadium with me. I now took this, and as Ace's dazed eyes instinctively sought his corner, I held the portrait up, just outside the glare of the ring lights, so while illumined by them it appeared illusive and dim. It may be thought that I acted wrongly and selfishly, to thus seek to bring a broken man to his feet for more punishment—but the outsider cannot fathom the souls of the children of the fight game, to whom winning is greater than life, and losing, worse than death.

All eyes were glued on the prostrate form in the center of the ring, on the exhausted champion sagging against the ropes, on the referee's arm which rose and fell with the regularity of doom. I doubt if four men in the audience saw my action—but Ace Jessel saw!

I caught the gleam that came into his bloodshot eyes. I saw him shake his head violently. I saw him begin sluggishly to gather his long legs under him, while the drone of the referee rose as it neared its climax.

And as I live today, *the picture in my hands shook suddenly and violently!*

A cold wind passed like death across me and I heard the man next to me shiver involuntarily as he drew his coat closer about him. But it was no cold wind that gripped my soul as I looked, wide eyed and staring, into the ring where the greatest drama of the boxing world was being enacted.

Ace, struggling, got his elbows under him. Bloody mists masked his vision; then, far away but coming nearer, he saw a form looming through the fog. A man—a short, massive black man, barrel chested and mighty limbed, clad in the long tights of another day—stood beside him in the ring! It was Tom Molyneaux, stepping down through the dead years to aid his worshiper—Tom Molyneaux, attired and ready as when he fought Tom Cribb so long ago!

And Jessel was up! The crowd went insane and screaming. A supernatural might fired his weary limbs and lit his dazed brain. Let Gomez do his worst now—how could he beat a man for whom the ghost of the greatest of all black warriors was fighting?

For to Ace Jessel, falling on the astounded Mankiller like a blast from the Arctic, Tom Molyneaux's mighty arm was about his waist, Tom's eye guided his blows, Tom's bare fists fell with Ace's on the head and body of the champion.

The Mankiller was dazed by his opponent's sudden comeback— he was bewildered by the uncanny strength of the man who should have been fainting on the canvas. And before he could rally, he was beaten down by the long, straight smashes sent in with the speed and power of a piledriver. The last blow, a straight right, would have felled an ox—and it felled Gomez for the long count.

As the astonished referee lifted Ace's hand, proclaiming him champion, the tall negro smiled and collapsed, mumbling the words, "Thanks, Mistah Tom."

Yes, to all concerned, Ace's comeback seemed inhuman and unnatural—though no one saw the phantom figure except Tom—and one other. I am not going to claim that I saw the ghost myself— because I didn't, though I did feel the uncanny movement of that picture. If it hadn't been for the strange thing that happened just after the fight, I would say that the whole affair might be naturally explained—that Ace's strength was miraculously renewed by a delusion resulting from his glimpse of the picture. For after all, who knows the strange depths of the human soul and to what apparently superhuman heights the body may be lifted by the mind?

But after the bout the referee, a steely-nerved, cold-eyed sportsman of the old school, said to me:

"Listen here! Am I crazy—or was there a fourth man in that ring when Ace Jessel dropped Gomez? For a minute I thought I saw a broad, squat, funny-looking negro standing there beside Ace! Don't grin, you bum! It wasn't that picture you were holding up—I saw that, too. It was a real man—and he looked like the one in the picture. He was standing there a moment—and then he was gone! God! That fight must have got on my nerves."

And these are the cold facts, told without any attempt to distort the truth or mislead the reader. I leave the problem up to you:

Was it Ace's numbed brain that created the hallucination of ghostly aid—or did the phantom of Tom Molyneaux actually stand beside him, as he believes to this day?

As far as I am concerned, the old superstition is justified. I believe firmly today that a portrait is a door through which astral beings may pass back and forth between this world and the next—whatever the next world may be—and that a great, unselfish love is strong enough to summon the spirits of the dead to the aid of the living.

"I had just hung..."

(untitled fragment)

I had just hung my sparring partner, Battling O'Toole, over the ropes with a neat left to the lug, when I hear a feminine voice exclaim:

"Oh, how superb! And what a figure!"

I look around to see who the unknown skirt is spieling about and to my intense surprize my glance falls on a dame who is standing as close to the ring as she can get, her hands clasped ecstatically, and her eyes fixed on me with a burning intensity which makes me nervous. I am not used to being thus oggled by strange dames. This damsel is a eye soother if I ever see one, being golden haired and violet eyed, with clothes that are about as suited to her present surroundings as I would be suited to a Chinese tea party. Classy, what I mean; the high society racket, get me? The social life, see?

While I gaze at her in open mouthed astonishment, she rises on her toes, thrusts her small and pretty nose between the ropes and says:

"Oh mister prizefighter, won't you—"

A slight interruption occurs at this point. Battling O'Toole is dizzy and therefore dangerous. I have jarred his scant supply of brains and the only instinct he has at present is to assassinate whoever happens to be in the ring with him. The fact that it is supposed to be a mild workout means nothing to O'Toole in his present condition. He is one of these birds who make a rule of fighting twenty rounds after they are knocked stiff. At present he knows he is in a ring and that is enough. I am leaning forward with the eagerness to hear what the dame is about to say when the reeling O'Toole connects with an aimless left swing which nearly gives me fallen insteps and nearly jolts my brains loose from the back of my skull. With a slight roar of annoyance I take O'Toole on the chin with my right and the benighted slugger vanishes over the ropes on the opposite side of the ring, his ungainly feet flapping drearily for an instant above the top strand, while the infuriated yells of the crap shooters who are making hay on that side announce that he has fallen into their game.

Leaving my handlers to bring him to, I lean over the ropes and with the greatest of politeness I ask:

"Lady, what was you fixin' to say when that bezark butted in on you?"

"Aren't you Iron Mike Costigan who fought a draw with the champion?" says she eagerly. With the modest blush I admit I am.

"I'm Marilyn Taverel," says she. "I saw the pictures of your fight with the champion, and it thrilled me more than anything I ever saw in my life—oh, pardon me—" she drags forward a frail-looking bird that I hadn't even noticed. "This is Tommy Densington," says she in an offhand sort of way, and the bird stuck out his hand like he was afraid I'd take it off.

I climb through the ropes and this dame feels of my triceps and looks me over considerably like I was a prize racehorse.

"Goodness, such muscles!" says she. "How much do you weigh, Mr. Costigan?"

"Two hundred and five, stripped," says I with the pride, expanding my bellows so she can see what a forty-eight inch chest looks like. At this moment up strolls, with a sinister air, my manager, Shifty O'Leary. This blight stays awake at night figuring out ways and means of crimping my style and putting a damper on my innocent pleasures, and the only reason we have not parted company long ago is because we know too much on each other.

"The heavy bag for you, Costigan," says this bezark. "How come—you slowin' down on your work?"

Giving him a glance which causes him to lose color and step backward with the haste, I say: "Miss Taverel, meet this bird; his name is O'Leary and at present he has the honor to be managing me."

"I'm so glad to meet you, Mr. O'Leary," says the dame. "I was just telling Mr. Costigan how I enjoyed the movie of his fight with the champion. That was so thrilling when he dropped the champion in the tenth round."

"Yah," says Shifty nastily. "The champ got his feet tangled up and fell over the referee—Mike, are you goin' to get to punchin' the bag or ain't you?"

"Listen, crumb," says I with the bloodthirsty snarl, "what I'm goin' to punch, if you don't shut up, ain't no bag, get me?"

The Ferocious Ape

(incomplete, originally untitled)

"They is only two reasons why fans pack a fight stadium; they like a fighter or they hate him. Gimme a boxer which is either loved or hated wildly. These natural crowd pleasers always gets a hand but it's the hate or the love which makes the turnstiles click."

Thus brooded and meditated my manager Abe Garfinkle, sitting in our room and gazing out the window on Finnegan's alley.

"Our money," said Abe, "is gettin' low. And your hand won't allow you to fight for a couple of months yet, at least. Hadst you followed my instructions and belted that Swede in the pantry instead of on the hatrack, we would now be eatin' regular."

"I flattened him, didn't I?" I asked with the slight annoyance.

"You knocked him out, but you also knocked us out of eatin' regular. I had a flock of fights lined up for you—but enough; I have an idee. Do you know any fighter which is a regular caveman for looks? Even more horribly primitive than what you are?"

"I know very few which approach me for manly beauty," I answered with calm dignity, "but if you want a real specimen of how low the human race can sink, I will go fetch you Ape Mahoney who blew into town yesterday lookin' for a match. This palooka would make Bull Montana run for cover, and when he was fightin' on the East Coast, the managers of the other fighters tried to make him wear a mask, claimin' his horrible map ruined their men's nerve."

"Has he ever fought in California before?"

"Naw; he's never been here before. I met him in New York last year. He ain't known off the East Coast; and likely won't never be."

"All wrong, Steve," said Abe pensively. "Go bring me this gorilla; if he is the type, he'll be known all over the United States shortly."

I went forth in search of Mahoney and knowing his habits, made straight for the nearest billiards hall. Sure enough there was the Ape, trying to shoot a billiard ball without breaking his cue. Which was practically impossible owing to his incredible strength. The habitués of the joint was standing around in awe, talking in hushed whispers. They was as tough an aggregation as I ever saw, but they looked like Sunday School boys by the side of Ape Mahoney. Honest, that boy looked—but you wouldn't believe me; you'd have to see it yourself.

He greeted me with pleasure and after he'd pulverized my hand shaking it, and given me broken insteps slapping me on the back, I imparted the news to him that my manager, Abe Garfinkle, wanted to see him. This cheered Ape up for he saw a match in the offing and as usual, he needed money.

I ushered him into the regal presence and a glow of gratitude burned in Garfinkle's eyes as he took in the flattened nose, misshapen features and ferocious appearance in general of my huge friend.

"Now listen, Mahoney," said Abe. "I'm goin' to bring you fame and fortune, but you got to do exactly like I say. I already got a match for you—or rather I can get it. Steve was goin' to fight One-Round Handler at the Lead Pipe A.C. tonight, but he hurt his left last week and to date they ain't got no substitute. You're goin' to be it. But first off I want to know, are you goin' to do just exactly like I say?"

"Sure," answered Mahoney who would of fought the Statue of Liberty for ten dollars.

"Alright," said Abe. "Wait here with Steve while I go make arrangements."

We indulged in pinochle till Abe returned and he was rubbing his hands together with satisfaction.

"The first step to fame and fortune is practically stepped," said he. "Everything is arranged. One thing I like about these second-rate fight clubs, you can put things by that wouldn't go nowheres else. And you can start makin' a name for yourself there.

"Now then, fellows, here's the dope. Ape, I'm goin' to make you the worst hated man on the West Coast! No, don't interrupt. The fans would never love you; therefore they got to hate you enough to come to see you perform. If they hate you enough they'll overlook the fact that you're a terrible dub and as a drawing card you can get matches you wouldn't never get otherwise.

"Now, then, this is the idea—" And for a half hour solid Abe talked while Mahoney set there with that ferociously vacant look on his terrible map, only partly aware of all that Garfinkle was driving at.

They was a good-sized crowd at the Lead Pipe A.C. that night. They always was no matter who fought, for they was always a chance of the fight show ending in a free-for-all and the Lead Pipe neighborhood was tough—with capitals. They liked their fighters tough and for once they was satisfied.

Carefully coached by me and Abe, Mahoney carried out his part fine. The referee and One-Round Handler was in on it, or we couldn't have put it over. First, Handler clumb in the ring and looked about him. Then there come a terrible roar from the dressing room and Mahoney came flying down the aisle, his bathrobe fluttering from his shoulders. Me and Garfinkle was right behind him and Abe was yelling: "Look out for him! Don't nobody git in his way! He's out for blood!"

We caught him as he clumb through the ropes and after a struggle which looked mighty real to the dumfounded audience, we forced him onto his stool. A moment later he broke away, raced across the ring and attacked Handler in his own corner. One-Round, no slouch of a actor hisself, yelled bloody murder and with the aid of the referee and Handler's seconds, we dragged Mahoney from his victim and held him in his corner till the gong sounded. By this time the audience was clean coo-koo and when the bout started they got wilder and wilder till somebody sent in a riot call and the police broke up the show.

At the gong, Mahoney, following Abe's instructions, made a flying tackle at Handler and laid him low; then he proceeded to kick, gouge and butt him—or at least he appeared to do so. The referee dragged them apart and they went at it hammer and tongs and Mahoney lowered his head and butted Handler clean out of the ring. This really irritated One-Round and he clumb back and soaked Mahoney a corker on the nose. Ape give a bellow and floored Handler and then remembering that he was supposed to imitate a caveman, began to kick his prostrate foe in the pants.

Even the hard-boiled crowd that frequented the Lead Pipe was shocked and horrified at the actions of this primeval man which had somehow got in the ring, and having shrieked their lungs out for the referee to stop the bout and give it to Handler on a foul, they took matters into their own hands and swarmed into the ring. At this moment the police arrived and Ape enhanced his glory by knocking a cop kicking.

We all went to the station and spent a night in the hoosegow, but the publicity we got was worth it. A police reporter pounced on the doings and give Ape a long write up in his paper next day. He told about interviewing the caveman in his cell, and how Mahoney would snarl and plunge at the bars every time he saw a uniform pass. He wound up with: "This man seems to be an atavist; a reversion to some remote ancestor of the cave days. One look at his face would convince the average man that he is not altogether human."

That last crack burnt Mahoney up and it was all we could do to keep him from going down and wrecking the newspaper office. But it was a great advertising for him and us. You see, Abe had figured out that Mahoney's foul fighting tactics would make him hated by the crowd, and his caveman publicity would make him a curiosity. Therefore, some would come to see him get whipped, some merely to see him. And that's the way it turned out.

"Next fight will be on the level," said Abe, "and you'll have to ease up a little on the rough stuff. Snarl and roar and all that, and fight as rough and foul as you can, but see if you can't get away with it. Losing a fight on a foul won't hurt you much as a drawin' card, but the more we win, the better."

We went up in Oregon next and matched Mahoney with Tom Hansen. It was a success. The crowd come near lynching us all, and after Mahoney put Tom on the canvas with a knockout kick on the shin, they rose en masse and threw all three of us out of the stadium bodily. But Abe was enraptured.

"Oh, baby!" said he. "What a name Ape's gettin'. What a crowd 'ull turn out for his next fight!"

And they did, seeing, much to our surprize, Mahoney knock out Armand Nogales in the second round. The referee was more lenient than the last one had been and Nogales took considerable punishment in the way of clawing and kicking before he went out. And so we built a name and fame for Ape Mahoney. From a unknown second-rater of the Atlantic Seaboard, he become the best drawing card on the West Coast. Great crowds packed the stadium where he performed, rooting wildly for the other fellow, roaring their distaste for Ape, weeping when he flattened his man, or cheering horribly when he was disqualified for throwing the other fellow out of the ring or stomping him when he was on the canvas.

It began to be hard to find a man who would meet Ape; they liked the crowds he drawed but they looked with distaste on the idea of getting maybe a leg pulled off by this inhuman gorilla.

As for Ape, it was hard to keep him on his path. He'd forget and get sociable with some fellow when he should have answered questions with low, sinister snarls, as Abe told him. A lot of his ferocity in the ring was real, but outside it he was the best-natured man in the world and it was hard for him to act like a cannibal when not actually fighting. Why, I remember once me and him was coming down the street late in a tough neighborhood when a hard-looking galoot bumped into Mahoney.

"Look where you're goin', you ham!" roared this individual and swung on Ape's jaw. Mahoney just looked at him with the hurt dignity; it took a sizable swat to make him sore.

"You got no business pokin' me," said he, and I quick broke in.

"Great Moses, feller, ain't you got no brains? Don't you know this is Ape Mahoney?"

The fellow fainted without another word and I grabbed the dumfounded Mahoney by the arms and commenced yelling for help. A crowd run up and I yelled: "Carry the body away before

Mahoney gits loose from me! He cooled this feller with one punch because he didn't like his face and now he wants to collect the pelt!"

The crowd promptly scattered in all directions, horror struck, and me and Mahoney continued our homeward way. He was sore at me but it give us a lot of free advertisement.

Reporters was always hanging around and you should of heard the line Garfinkle handed them; how Mahoney run away from his parents at the age of two and was raised in the Rockies by a female mountain lion. How he lived with the wild animals and et uncooked meat until the age of twenty when he was captured by a band of explorers and brung to civilization. The marks on his face, Garfinkle explained, was caused by his battles with the denizens of the wild. He admitted that he fought some in New York before he come West, but maintained that he, Abe Garfinkle, had been the wild man's manager ever since he had emerged from his mountain lair.

How much of this tripe the reporters believed, I don't know, but they give him some terrific write-ups. When they come to the training quarters, Garfinkle always had Ape prowl around, snarling and answering questions very shortly and gruffly, and tearing his sparring partners apart. He tried to get Ape to eat some meat which wasn't cooked, but Mahoney balked. And it made him sore because Abe headed him off every time he started to tell the reporters about the gang fights he had in the Bowery when he was a kid.

Garfinkle had a friend which was a animal trainer and had a huge ape which was gentle as anything, and did tricks on the stage. Garfinkle had this ape over and every now and then when the reporters come, Mahoney would wrestle with this ape and pretend that ordinary human sparring partners wasn't tough enough for him. The ape wouldn't hurt Mahoney, appeared to look on him as a lost brother, but Mahoney was horribly afraid of him, and after the reporters had went, he would run away from the ape and lock hisself in his room where he would lie panting with the cold sweat standing out on him all over.

Mahoney was mighty fond of kids and for some reason they seemed to take to the overgrown orang-outan and the training quarters was infested with them. Garfinkle used to keep his weather eye out for reporters and when he saw them coming he'd scurry and chase the babies offa Ape's lap and from around his knee. But one time he slipped up. A gang come on to us unexpected.

It was the day after Mahoney had knocked out Spike Moriarty, after both of them had took enough punishment to kill a regiment, and Mahoney had finally put over the k.o. after he was too dizzy to claw and kick.

"Show us this caveman," said they. "Lead us to this man-eatin' savage. Have you got him in a cage or is it safe for us to approach him on the outside?"

"Follow me," said Garfinkle, "but walk softly and think of moral subjects. Try to compose your minds as you'd like 'em to be if you was to suddenly enter the next world. Mahoney is restless and uncertain; and if one uh you gets the nose bleed, let every man look out for hisself! The smell uh gore drives him into a frenzy and no life is safe around him!"

Cold sweat broke out on the reporters' brows but if they left without an interview they'd lose their jobs so they followed me and Garfinkle. As we approached the room where Mahoney was supposed to be either tearing a punching bag apart, or brooding on murder and bloodshed, we heard a ferocious voice recite: "Eenie, meenie, minie, mo—"

With a horrible suspicion in my mind I halted and I saw Garfinkle's face go white; but the reporters pushed on past us and flung open the door. There sat Ape Mahoney revealed. He was sitting on a stool, with a child on each knee; one of them had made a chain of daisies and he had this around his neck. He was counting the toes of one of the kids, and reciting nursery rhymes to them.

We stood dumfounded, while he stopped short and glared at us. Then Abe Garfinkle's great mind began functioning again. He laid a finger to his lips and closed the door.

"You see him in one of his rarer gentle moods. Wild as a lion with grown men, sometimes the soothing touch of a little child will calm his most vi'lent rages."

"Chili sauce," says a hardboiled cub. "Looks to me like he's stopped too many punches with that ivory ball he calls his head. Ain't we goin' to get to interview him?"

"I dares not interrupt his privacy," said Garfinkle. "If you will beard the lion in his den, you does it at your own risk."

The bluff worked. The reporters left. Abe did a war dance on his hat and raved.

"The overgrown ham! After all this work uh buildin' him up! Lemme at him!"

He rushed back into the room but before he could speak, Mahoney lifted a huge hand, with what he supposed was a gentle smile on his frightful features.

"Shhh! The little darlin's is asleep!"

Abe put his hand to his brow and staggered out of the room with a low scream of anguish.

The reporters evidently decided to follow his lead, though, for they wrote a lot of hooey about Mahoney's one human trait bein' his affection for kids.

"This ferocious brute," they wrote, "is mild and gentle beneath the soothing touch of a baby's hand. Who knows? Mayhap the denial of brothers and sisters in his early youth lies at the bottom of this. Or can it be—" and so on and so on.

This tickled Mahoney. "Great," says he. "Sure, I like kids, even if I was the youngest of a family of eleven."

Abe didn't like it. "Not so good. A lot of people will warm to you readin' this and decide you're just a diamond in the rough after all. I don't want 'em to think you got *one* good trait! If they get to likin' you, the gate receipts 'ull fall off. You ain't the type uh fighter which can draw a crowd by popularity. Next time, I want you to lose on a foul. You won your last three fights. This time I want you to throw your man and get on him and manage to kick him in the face a couple of times, before you're dragged off."

This was did and a roar of protest was raised. People forgot the child incident and Mahoney was as cordially hated as before. The gate receipts grew and all was merry.

"Spike Morissey was as tough a kid . . ."

(untitled fragment)

Spike Morissey was as tough a kid as ever came to Menton College. He was a slums product, a true example of the survival of the fittest, a characteristic type of production from a place where a child must be a combination of John L. Sullivan and a Rocky Mountain wildcat to reach the age of maturity.

Such an environment is an ideal breeding place for prizefighters and yeggs but scarcely the thing for a future teacher, banker or missionary. When most college-boys-to-be were learning to knock home runs and make end runs, Spike was learning to bounce an antique egg off a policeman's nose and get away with it. From the time he could toddle down to the corner saloon for a schooner of lager, he was more interested in left hooks than in culture.

Why he ever came to college, or how he got through the ward schools, no one ever knew, probably not even Spike. But to Menton College he came, sneering, aggressive, making no attempt to conceal his contempt for everything connected with the institute. He could not understand his classmates, nor could they understand him. He spoke in the jargon of the streets, and his thoughts and ideas were mature and sophisticated enough for a man of twice his age. He was wise with a warped wisdom gained in a hard school, and as untutored as a savage.

"Cake eaters" was his term for practically all the youths he met, a scornful term, made more biting by the drooping sneer with which he let the word slide from the corner of his thin lips.

"Cake eaters."

To his classmates he was an object of wonder and contempt. They had grown up in a different world. When most of them were learning to dance, Spike had been perfecting a right cross to the jaw of a personal friend. There were, of course, bullies and tough fellows among their crowd, but they were all transcended—pushed into the background. Here was the real tough, the gangster—doubtless the future yegg, could his ambitions be realized.

"The tale has always been doubted . . ."

(untitled fragment)

The tale has always been doubted and scoffed at, and probably always will be. But there is really no reason for the sneers that greeted its first telling and later repetition. The first, remarkable, prelude occurred in full view of a throng of several thousand people, who were, perforce, compelled to believe their eyes, even though they refused to credit the plain narrative as to what followed.

The man to whom the most strange experience occurred, is not at all one who would be like to make up such a narrative, being, outside his chosen trade, a very commonplace person indeed, of little imagination, and no trend whatever toward the occult. Nor was there any obvious reason for supposing it to be a plan for sensational publicity. Indeed, the happening has never been explained. And though the public laughed to scorn the narrative of the man, no one has managed to explain how it is that one who before the occurrence had only the rudiments of an education, and to whom history and astronomy were as profound as the fourth dimension, is now acknowledged as one of the foremost authorities on both subjects.

Briefly, the strange occurrence took place in this manner. The man, O'Rourke, as he is known, was at the time a prizefighter of rather second class. It was in his battle with the light heavyweight champion that his strange disappearance took place. It was in the very first round and O'Rourke had rushed the champion into his corner. There the champion made a rally, and as O'Rourke instinctively lowered his guard to block a powerful left to the body, the champion hooked a right to his jaw with considerable force. Then the strange thing occurred. O'Rourke simply vanished from view, as if he had been a candle flame blown out! Thinking he had broken through the floor of the arena, the referee rushed forward, but no such thing had happened. There was no break in the floor, neither was there a secret door. O'Rourke had simply vanished, without a trace, before the eyes of several thousand people.

The Ghost Behind the Gloves

(unfinished)

Shifty Tremayne grinned but there was desperation behind that grin. His gloved hands fenced and stabbed with their old cunning, but blood trickled down his face and a faint, red-tinged haze waved across his eyes.

The lad in front of him, a white ghost in Shifty's dimming sight, shot out a sudden jab that was a fire-pointed lance against Tremayne's battered lips, and swung heavily with the right.

Shifty ducked mechanically, his muddled brain failing him but his reflexes sending him through instinctive motion. And mechanically, gropingly, he found his foe, clinched and held on. The roar of the fans came to him like the surf on a long beach. They were yelling with the bloodlust, yelling for the winner to shove him away and finish him.

And the boy was trying to do that very thing, but Shifty had him clinched and helpless. Not for nothing had he won his nickname and now, even dazed as he was, the inexperienced youth was no match for him in cleverness.

The referee broke them with a powerful surge of his arms and Shifty ducked instantly, out-thinking his antagonist, knowing that the boy would swing his right as soon as they were clear. That right he must avoid at all costs; it was what had started him on the road to downfall. The left was a stabbing lance but the right carried the force of a triphammer.

Shifty clinched again, digging his chin into his foe's left shoulder. His brain was clearing. The old lynxlike craft was coming back. He sneered as he felt the gasping heaving wrenches of the youngster in his efforts to break away and send over the sleep maker. Shifty's pride was stung; it had seemed so easy to smash down this youth, this Young Slattery who was unknown outside the mining district where he fought. He had sparred along easily, sneering, mocking, making a monkey of the boy with the superior skill he had acquired in four years of hard fighting in many rings. Then suddenly it happened; Slattery's right, swung with the force of hurt vanity, had crashed through Tremayne's guard and sent the Shifty to the canvas. Tremayne had risen at the count of nine, dazed, on the defensive.

Now he snarled at the bellowing crowd, over Slattery's sweating shoulder and his crafty, vicious brain worked swiftly. Another break, a swing which Tremayne ducked, and then Shifty feinted twice and sent a right to the body. His glove crashed against Slattery's left elbow and almost simultaneously Slattery's right curved to his temple—a little high but the mists began to close again.

Slattery's best trick, Shifty knew now, blocking a right to the body and countering with a right to the head. And he realized that he was too weak to keep the slugging youngster at bay. He took a light left to the face, caught Slattery's right arm and clinched, working in very close. The referee loomed over the struggling two, hiding them from sight for an instant—then the screaming crowd rose from their seats.

Young Slattery was writhing on the canvas and Shifty stepped back, a wicked sneer on his hardened face. The crowd yelled jeeringly—an old trick, they supposed. Shifty had struck a body blow in the clinch, they thought, an unsportsmanlike thing, to be sure, but according to the special rules, not a flagrant foul. They had not seen Shifty's knee come up, nor had the referee, momentarily blinded by an apparently accidental backward flirt of Shifty's hand, as he strove to part the two.

Slattery struggled up before "ten" had been reached, not thinking of charging foul, in his angry youth only thinking of reaching his foe and tearing him to pieces. He rushed across the ring wildly, dazed and weakened, to be met by a diabolically cool, viciously merciless boxing master. What little of skill he had deserted him beneath the steady rain of jabs and hooks which battered him.

The boy's wild swings met only thin air or glanced from Shifty's shoulders and elbows, while ducking, blocking, weaving, Shifty hammered him into a staggering halt, and then flailed him back across the ring. Tremayne's mind was clear now but he was taking no chances with that wicked right; blows showered on Slattery's head and body in an endless stream. Eyes nearly closed, nose broken, cheeks cut, reeling, Slattery, with magnificent courage, sought to stem the tide of defeat. Shifty sneered, marking the desperation in the boy's bloody countenance. He [. . .]

Lobo Volante

(unfinished fragment, originally untitled)

A revolution by itself, *señors*, is bad enough, but when you mix it up with a spitfire Latin girl, a know-nothing boxing referee and a mankiller like this Lobo Volante—then, *Santa Maria!*—it is what you *gringos* call one *caliente* time in the old town!

This Lobo Volante was one *diablo*. He was Indian and Spanish and French and *Dios* only know what else—and all devil. I don't know where he came from or where he started fighting but the first I knew of him, he was fighting in small fight clubs in Colombia and knocking out three or four men every night. Oh yes, the fight is all the rage in South America now and by golly, *señors*, you'd be surprized to find arenas in villages you wouldn't think of, yes, sir. This Lobo business had been fighting in some of the larger towns up in Central America but he had to leave on account of smuggling and gunrunning. He came down into Colombia and for a while, it was rumored he was with the great bandit chief, General Gonzales Segrano, that called himself the Scourge of the Jungle. Then next I hear of him, *Santa Maria!* he is performing in little inland towns again.

What his real name is, I don't know and probably nobody, neither. Lobo Volante means Winged Wolf, which he was not called because he looked like a wolf only in disposition, but because they said he fought like these jungle eagles that the *gringoes* call harpy eagles. The natives call them Lobo Volantes, and they are so strong that they can kill a mountain lion. They have short heavy wings and this fighter was short and stocky, and a incredible strong man.

Me and Kid Allison which is a seaman on the ship I am fireman on, was taking shore leave in __ when come word to him from a little inland town that they would pay him a hundred dollars, American money, to fight this Lobo Volante there. Kid Allison was all for it.

Night Encounter

(incomplete, originally untitled)

The night was as dark as the inside of a black man's hand; heavy wet clouds hanging right down in a fellow's face, but I knowed they was a moon up there somewheres on account of every now and then they would be a sort of rift in the darkness, like a cloud had busted or something and let the moonshine trickle through.

I'm the original hard-luck baby; don't tell me. I know! I was born in the dark of the moon and seventeen black cats sung me to sleep. If I reach for a four-leaf clover I catch a wasp, and if I heave a horseshoe over my shoulder I crown a cop. Otherwise, why shouldst I have got lost from the patrol that night? No reason in the world for it. We was moving along, crawling on our bellies, ducking flares, getting our clothes tore on loose barbed wire—mud to our eyebrows. Fine night to send honest working men out scouting, eh? Some shavetail's idea. They was a lull on the sector that night, like they sometimes is, even in the grandmammy of all wars. Both sides gathering their energies for a splash, while John Private on each side grabbed a little sleep, put ointment on his bruises, wrote his girl he was winning the war, and shot craps in two foot of water—maybe. Most of him was standing along the parapet expecting raiding parties any minute.

We was supposed to reconnoiter around over toward the enemy's lines and find out if they had got any letters from the Kaiser or something. It was so still for the front lines it made me right nervous. Now and then a flare went up and we flattened. Away off to the left and further away to the right come an occasional low mutter of artillery, but right here it was as quiet as Monaghan's Bar the night after.

We was moving along as I said before, single file, each man feeling the man ahead of him, when my puttee strap come undone. If they is anything that runs me nuts it's part of my

clothes dragging in the mud and catching ahold of things. I stood it for a few minutes, valiantly resisting the impulses to yell and tear my hair, then I give up. I stopped, saying nothing, and fixed the thing.

As I done so, I heard the soft *scrush-scrush!* of the rest of the gang slithering through the mud like so many snakes, and figured it would be a cinch to catch up with them. And it mighta been, had not I wandered slightly off my course as I crawled after them. *Blop!* I went headfirst into a ditch which some misbegotten son of a so forth and so on had dug for no good or sufficient reason, and which was partly full of water and the muddiest mud I ever fell into.

I lay still, expecting a barrage or a mass attack or might near anything. I had made so much noise I figured I'd woke up the dollar-a-year men in the offices at Washington. But nothing happened and after awhile I got nerve enough to push my heart back down where it belonged, and stuck my head out. The clouds was clearing up a little but it was still dark. I dug the mud out of my eyes and was aware of a most peculiar sensation. I was plumb turned around! The fall and the fright had gone to my head as it were and for the time being I'd lost all sense of direction. They was not a light anywhere except the flashes of cannon fire away off on the horizon, and no rockets was going up now from either trench. Which way was my trench? I couldn't tell; everything looked just alike in the dark. Get me right, you babies who think a man couldn't get lost in No Man's Land with trenches on each side. I was raised in cities and I'm a helpless babe in the wilderness. Furthermore, whilst I probably wouldst find myself eventually, if I made a mistake it would be one of them you make but once in a lifetime. And how was I to locate my pards without waking up the whole German army, I ast you?

I set me down in the mud and broodingly meditated over the jam I was in. I tried to reason the thing out logically, and the more I reasoned the more fluticated I became till at last I give it up before I started trying to square the circle. All I could see was to squat there till daylight come or the moon come out bright, and then race the Boche bullets back to my trench. The more I thought of this, the less I liked the idea. I would make a very ungainly figure hurdling shell holes with seven thousand Germans making wisecracks and shooting at me. So finally in desperation I arose on my hands and knees, and having reduced my scouting equipment to a .45 caliber pistol, I started out at random.

How far I crawled, I don't know. At last it began to lighten up a little and I saw a dark bulk looming just ahead of me. I recognized it as what was left of a woods, and immediately oriented myself. Somehow or other I had wandered clean out of bounds. No Man's Land proper was behind me, with the American trenches to the right and the German trenches to the left. In front of me was some German dugouts which had been vacated on account of our artillery having shelled them all to pieces, and beyond them, that is, almost parallel to where I was, but a considerable distance further away, was some more German trenches stretching away in a oblique manner. These was shot up, too, but afforded shelter for snipers and a occasional machinegun nest as we had found.

Now the moon began to come out at a alarming rate and my hide began to crawl as I thought of the bloodthirsty snipers waiting for a sight of something to drill. I hustled for the busted-up woods as fast as I could go, and hadst no more than got among them when the moon come out proper. Now as I was laying there on my belly taking advantage of all the shelter I could, I heard a noise off to the left. I listened and pretty soon I heard it again. Then the blasted moon went behind a cloud again and everything got dark and spooky. The splintered trees with their bare branches looked like ghosts and my hide commenced to crawl again. And then I caught a fleeting glimpse of something broad and bulky through the trees. I got to my knees slow and careful and began moving in the direction of the critter, and finally heard the noises again. No doubt about it this time; a man was in front of me, hidden in the shadows. I waited in doubt. I could tell about where he was, and this time I couldn't consider the two armies. This was between him and me, unless they was a gang with him. If I was rushed I'd have to shoot and if I woke everybody up, I couldn't be shot no deader by a couple of hundred men than by one. I could locate him by the sound and now and then see a dark blob shifting around among the shadows. Whoever he was, he wasn't very cautious or else he was powerful heavy-footed. Once or twice I believe I could have plugged him, but I didn't want to fire unless I had to. Outside of waking up everything along the sector, the question was to shoot and risk plugging one of my own pards, or not shooting and risking getting plugged by a German.

Then the bird musta heard me, because I couldn't see the blob no more and everything got quiet. They was a perfectly gigantic tree stump nearby which the tree had been cut in half by a shell as clean as a saw could have did it. I glode very stealthy and wary to it, and crouched there waiting for a sound or sight. Then I heard something—on the other side of the stump!

I began to crawl around slow, with my gun stuck out in front of me. I kept hearing stealthy noises, but seen nothing, though I made the entire round of the stump. Then I felt tracks in the mud besides the ones I made, and the truth was bore in upon me. They was some other fellow on the other side of the tree which was crawling in the same direction I was. As this thought gripped me, my hair stood up and I was briefly nauseated. I began to back away slow and easy on my hands and knees, when a sudden noise made me turn my head. That instant the moon come out again and to my horror I seen a man behind me, in the same position I was, on his hands and knees, pointing the other way, but looking over his shoulder at me. At that instant I recognized the uniform and the coal-scuttle helmet. A German!

We bounced up at the same tine, covering each other, me with my pistol and him with a rifle which had a bayonet on the end. Then as we stood there, hesitating, he says:

"Steve Slade, by golly!"

"Dutchy Heinbock!" said I, plumb flabbergasted. "What you doin' here?"

"I'm a soldier," said he. "What you think?"

"Point that gun some other way," said I. "You was always careless with weppings."

"I can't, Steve," he answered apologetically. "It's the rules of this here game. One of the first rules of war is allus point your gat at the enemy—"

"You call me a enemy," I snarled. "Me that has stole your marbles and give you many a black eye in Monaghan's Alley when we was both kids?"

"I got no hard feelin's, Steve," answered he, "but accordin' to the rules of war I got to tell you, you're my prisoner. I got the drop on you, Steve."

"I don't see how you figure it," I retorted. "Looks like I got the same on you. You're my prisoner, Dutchy Heinbock! And how come you in the German army anyway?"

"I'm a German, I guess," he answered sulkily. "I was born—"

"Yeah, you're a German," I sneered. "So much so that you can talk English a couple of times better'n you can talk German. Don't start soundin' off to me! I know your history as good as you know it—up to the last few years. You was born in Berlin at a early age, but your family come to America when you was only a few months old. You went to the Tenth Ward School and me and you had about seven hundred fights. Then when you was fourteen, your family moved back to Germany. You didn't like it there and come back to America when you was about eighteen, and you started working in Hans Groper's bakery, and fightin' as a lightweight on the side.

"You stayed in America a few years and growed and put on weight and developed into a full-fledged middleweight and as such went back to Germany for some unknown reason. That was nearly four years ago and I hadn't heard nothing of you since."

"I went back to visit my family," said Dutchy, "an' they persuaded me to enlist. America wasn't in the war then. Anyways, I guess I done right. I'm German and my place is in the ranks of—"

"Aw, shut up!" I snarled. "A fine soldier you are! How many battles you been in?"

"I cleaned out a saloon full of drunk hussars," said he, his eyes lighting, "and—"

"Sign off!" I said. "I bet you been in the guardhouse nine-tenths of the time. I'm goin' to haul you back to where you belong—the American army."

"Don't you start nothin' with me, Steve," said the deluded wretch. "You see this gun? I got it pointin' right square at your wishbone and my finger's on the trigger—"

Wham! I felt the wind of the bullet as I ducked.

"Dutchy Heinbock," I said with the deepest indignation, "what you mean by shootin' at me?"

"I didn't go to do it, Steve," said he. "Honest, it was accidental. I guess my finger musta slipped or somethin'. I never kin tell when these things is cocked or not. I was allus clumsy about guns—remember the time I shot Abie Goldberg in the breeches?"

"A fine sample of German discipline you are," I said with the mounting anger. "The Prussian Guard'll never wipe out the blot you've put on 'em. Don't know when your gun is cocked— don't look down the barrel, fool! You'll blow your worthless brains out!"

"I was just tryin' to see what made it explode that way—"

"Throw that gun away," I ordered. "You're a menace to innocent bystanders. If you stay in this war much longer, you'll shoot somebody. I'm going to bend this pistol over your solid bone head and drag you back to the American lines."

"You hit me with that gun and I'll jab you in the pants with this bayonet," said Dutchy. "I guess I got a right—"

"Shut up!" I ordered bitterly. "You ain't got no right to do nothin'. And keep quiet a minute. I just happened to think that we're in the vicinity of two hard-boiled armies lustin' for gore. It's a miracle that shot of yours ain't started the war goin'."

We listened. The hot dark night pressed on us, for the moon had went behind a cloud again. Far away came the mutter of artillery.

"Fool's luck," I muttered. "Dutchy Heinbock, are you comin' peaceably or do I hang one on your chin and drag you?"

[. . .]

"Lemme die in peace, you blank-blank!" said Dutchy irritably. "You should not of kicked me. I am very sensitive to bein' booted on the shin. This is a hell of a come-off! I'm in a good way to get plugged by my own army."

"What about me, you boneheaded so forth and so on?" I asked indignantly. "If I'd a had any idee about what I was gettin' into when I joined this war—! The fire's slackenin' up, Dutchy, let's get to that house and get our melee over with before the main one starts. This lull can't last always. And this time don't you even think about a gun."

"How was I to know it would explode just from throwin' it down?" he asked. "These Mausers ain't supposed to do that, but lemme tell you, a gat will do anything. Gi' me a pair uh four ounce gloves an'—"

"And a referee that thinks a slam anywhere below the eyebrows is a foul," I sneered nastily. "Let's get goin'. I'll show you whether I fouled you that night in Los Angeles or not."

Maybe my managers was all right when they said I was first class ivory from the eyes up and nothing else. Anyway I followed Dutchy Heinbock through the mud and the darkness till we got to the old chateau. I reckon it was a mansion in its day, but that day was long past. Most of the top floor was tore clean off, the walls sagged, the roof had dropped in and altogether it was about as ruined an affair as I ever see.

"Hey," said I, "the whole thing will fall in on us if I hit you with my right."

"Naw, it won't fall if you hit me with a maul," said Dutchy. "The basement ceiling is braced with steel and concrete. Come on. Foller me."

"Wait a minute," said I. "This is all wrong. One side or the other is bound to be watchin' this place."

"Why? They's no reason to. It don't control nothin'. Come on."

He led the way. I followed. I been following some sap into trouble all my life, seems like. We went through a busted door and groped our way down a rickety flight of stairs in total darkness. I thought several times I was going to pitch headlong down 'em, but I managed, being slightly annoyed by Dutchy's protests of me kicking him in the back when I was only trying to keep my balance by throwing out my leg.

At last we reached the bottom of the stairs and I recognized the feel of a concrete floor under my heavy army shoes. Dutchy told me to stand still while he lit a lamp.

"Very good," I said, "but do you realize that the minute a light is seen in this dump, seven million tons of steel will probably descend on it?"

"Stay in your pants," he answered very calmly. "This is a very deep basement. I have closed the door that leads onto the stair goin' up, and the only outside winders is heavily shuttered. When this house was occupied by German troops, this basement was fixed up kinda on the order of a refuge from bombers. A bomb falling on what's left of the roof upstairs wouldst probably blow this joint clean through to China, but anyway, it's light proof. Watch!"

At that moment a flare sprung up in the darkness and I saw Dutchy's face all strange and ghostly looking. The next minute he had lighted a large candle which was stuck in the wall and I got my first glimpse of the place he had chose for our affair. It was a large bare basement with a cement floor and I noticed that the walls and ceiling was heavily braced with steel. It was so deep that moisture formed on the stone walls, and altogether it was a damp, dank and cheerless place, though I reckon before the war it was full of the juice of cheer, judging from the remnants of wine barrels scattered hither and yon over the floor.

"Le's get goin'," I suggested. "This dump gives me the all-overs. It's plumb full of ghosts of feudal lords which drunk theirselves to death. And too many men has died here right recent for me to feel at ease around here. This is a nice time uh night to come here. I don't hardly feel alive, myself."

"You're too impressionistic," said Dutchy, who has the nervous system of a warthog. "This is the safest place on the whole front and we likely won't be troubled by anybody."

As he was speaking, he was rummaging around amongst some debris in the corner, and he presently drawed forth a set of gloves—considerable the worst for wear, stained and battered, but still good old fighting-size gloves. My hands itched as I looked at them and the old eager nervousness come back to me, just like I was waiting for the gong back in the old Barbary A.C. or Flaherty's fight club in San Diego. I could almost smell the resin and the canvas, and hear the crowd yelling—when I remembered I was two thousand miles from San Diego, right between two armies which was just resting up before they started cutting out each other's hearts again. But the thought of the old days was like a knife in my liver.

"You kin take your choice of either pair," Dutchy was saying. "These stains," he added casually, "was caused by what was left of a officer fallin' on my pack right after a shell had busted him. I shoved off the remains as quick as I could, but the blood soaked through to the gloves. I wish these fellers wouldst be careful where they fall."

"Shut up," I snarled, "you cold-blooded kraut—"

"A feller can't be in a war as long as I've been without gettin' kinda callous," he answered. "It's git hard or die. But lets git goin', now if ever. No way of keepin' time. We 'ull just have to dispense with rounds. We 'ull fight till one of us goes out. When one falls, the other'n 'ull count over him, if he's able."

"Alright." I drawed the gloves on over my bare hands, feeling rather strange without taping them that way. I neglected to say we had stripped to our shoes, socks and pants, and I had hung my gun belt on the wall.

We started for each other slow and wary, our shadows wavering like black giants on the cold slimy walls, in the flickering light of the candle. I felt the hard concrete under my feet, and knowed how it would feel to land on it.

I knowed Dutchy was a slow starter. He was rough and hard, but he got off to a slow start. That being the case, I crashed into him suddenly and with everything I had, trying to batter him down before he could get set. I come in like a whirlwind, rammed a terrific left to his body and blasted a right flush to the jaw. *Wham!* Dutchy's heels went up and he come down on his shoulder blades hard enough to bust the ordinary human. But Dutchy was no ordinary human. He was the toughest middleweight I ever saw in my life.

I started counting: "One! Two! Three! Four!—"

At "Nine!" he bounced up and dived headfirst into a clinch. While there he hammered me to the body with his left.

"You foul me and I'll shove my thumb in your eye!" I snarled.

"You do, and I'll kick you in the abdomen!" he grunted and action thereafter was too swift for conversation.

Dutchy and me was very evenly matched. We was both of the slugging, aggressive school, hard hitters and tough. We was both fairly clever for sluggers though I had the edge on him there. I went for his body, because I knowed he had a granite jaw if any human ever did, and I had no desire to risk breaking my hand on his head unless I was reasonably sure of landing solid.

I hooked both hands to his body while he worked a straight left to my face that soon had me bleeding profusely at the nose. Angered, I drove his head back with a right uppercut, and he came back with a terrific right to the temple. *Bam!* He connected to the head with a roundhouse left swing and I seen stars. I snarled and opened a cut over his cheekbone with a venomous left and followed up with a solid right under the heart which made him gasp. He shot both hands to my face and I clinched and lammed him on the ribs with my right till his left side was red.

We broke, and stepping back from a right hook, I fell over a barrel hoop. Dutchy instantly began counting, and while I was not hurt, I let him get to "Nine" before I got up, and then rose, considerably better for the rest.

As I bounded up Dutchy rushed in with a left and right to the body and I missed a wicked left for the chin. I sank a left to the body and glanced a right off his ribs, while he hooked me severely on the chin with both hands.

Hummmmmm! Far away the heavy guns began to mutter sullenly, but we was

[. . .]

you fair—and what's more, don't you hear that racket? That means the war has opened up again! Let's get outa here and get back to our trenches!"

Dutchy went over to where his clothes was, still grumbling and arguing. I went for mine and started to take off the gloves. I was facing Dutchy, with my back to the door that let out onto the basement stairs. Suddenly I heard this door open, and a premonition scooted up and down my spine like a cold wind. I whirled.

There in front of us stood a tall man in the uniform of a German officer—and he had one of these here Luger pistols in his hand. His eyes were narrowed like he couldn't figure it all out—how one of his men and one of the enemy should be found in this basement, stripped and beat up as we was. He could tell that Dutchy was in his army by his pants, of course. Then the officer seemed to come to a decision. His gun came up and the muzzle centered on my breast. I was froze—helpless— stunned—incapable of thought even. I could read death in that black muzzle and them cold eyes above it. And in that instant Dutchy screamed "Don't shoot!" and leaped between us.

I heard the gun crack on the instant and Dutchy reeled back against me as if hit by a terrific blow. Yes, harder than any blow he had ever got in the ring. I caught at him, but he slipped between my arms and crumpled to the floor where he lay in a widening lake of blood. For a second the German officer stared at the prostrate form, too froze with surprize to shoot again, and in that second I leaped across Dutchy and crashed my right against that officer's jaw with everything I had behind it. His heels shot up and from the way his skull hit the concrete, I knowed he wouldn't get up. His skull wasn't as hard as Dutchy's.

And the next second—*crash!* The ceiling splintered above me and a piece of a rafter or something laid my scalp open to the bone. I could hear the house going to pieces over me, as I stooped and got Dutchy over my shoulder. The candle guttered and went out just as I reached the stairs and how I ever got up 'em with that dead weight on my shoulders, is more'n I know. I was like a man in a dream, drenched with blood, dazed, only partly aware of what it was all about. As I come through the broken door up above I thought for a minute that I had got kilt and was in Hell. The whole sky was lit by terrific flashes and bursts of flames which flared up out of the earth it seemed like, and showed me the tangled, torn woods and the shattered barbed wire entanglements.

I staggered blindly away in the general direction of the American trenches, and I hadn't gone thirty steps, when they come a screech in the air like a locomotive flying through the sky and the house went up in flame and smoke behind me. I reeled on through the falling debris, and for the rest I don't remember much. Shells were hitting all around me, I was stunned by the roar and the noise and the only feelings I had was to keep Dutchy on my shoulders and keep going.

That journey was a inferno of noise and fire, a crisscrossed pattern of flame and blackness. The air was full of little singing things, like bees, and twice they kissed me and it burned worse than fire and cut like a knife. I felt a warm moisture on my chest and arms and thought it was a sweat, but inside I was cold as ice, and when the flash of the bursting shells give me a look at myself I seen it was red all over. But I didn't give it a thought; I was staggering along, tripping over wire and corpses, falling into shell holes and getting tangled in entanglements—I said at the start I didn't remember much about it, and I should of stuck to that statement. But at the last I heard yelling in a familiar language and then I reeled up on a mound and tumbled headlong into a trench, me and Dutchy all tangled up together.

"It's Steve!" I heard somebody yell. "Shot all to pieces! And he's got a prisoner! Golly, what a battle he musta had! Lookit the black eyes on 'em! And look on their hands!"

I didn't have time to think what the thoughts of the A.E.F. musta been to see a half-naked private suddenly loom outa the night with a enemy, similarly attired, acrost his shoulders, with boxing gloves on! I had only time to mumble: "Take care uh Dutchy, boys, he saved my life!" And then I went clean out.

I passed through a lot of stages of delirium, I guess, but when I finally come to my right mind, I didn't believe what I saw. I was lying in a clean fresh bed with real white sheets on it, and across from me in one similar was Dutchy.

He looked like I felt—considerable weak and pale, but he grinned at me.

"I thought you was dead," said I.

"I knowed you wasn't," he said. "Anybody that kin git up after I floor 'em ain't to be finished by common, ordinary bullets—of which you got seven or eight in you while totin' me to the trenches."

"Now you're here," said I, "you're goin' to stay. Or we tangle again, see?"

"I'm stayin'," he grunted, "not because I'm afeard uh you, understand, but because I hear peace is been declared. I'm goin' back to America and I hope we can get Mr. Flaherty to rematch us at the old Hopi A.C."

"Dutchy," said I presently, "how come you hop in the way and take that slug for me?"

"Aw," he said, kinda embarrassed, "I dunno. Forgit it. It was the only thing I coulda done under the circumstances. You don't reckon I'd let you git killed without havin' first whipped you, do you?"

"Dutchy," said I, "you're a plumb liar. You risked your life to save me—because—aw, just because, I reckon. An' Dutchy, that time I flattened you in Los Angeles, I reckon the referee was right. That punch was pretty low at that."

"Aw, forgit it," said he. "The punch woulda been fair only I jumped into the air just as it landed."

The Folly of Conceit

(unfinished, originally untitled)

I was born in a little village in the Wicklow mountains, in the province of Leinster, Ireland. The people of Wicklow are a fierce and independent breed, part Celtic and part Danish and they have always been foremost in the revolutions which have torn Ireland for a thousand years.

I do not remember anything about the country or the people because when I was only a few months old, our family had to leave Ireland under a cloud. An attempt was made on the life of an English landlord and though none of my immediate family had any knowledge of the deed, we were implicated and my parents thought it best to slip out of Ireland and come to America.

My parents settled in a farming community in North Carolina and there I grew up. The countryside around us was settled thickly with Irish emigrants, many of whom came from the same county that we did. There were also many Scotch people there and as Celtic people are proverbially turbulent, I had many fights with the sons of the neighbors. Perhaps this developed my natural liking for the sport, beside giving me quickness and toughness and adding to the muscles developed by hard farmwork.

But I did not like farmwork. My mother's people were more Danish than Irish and most of the men in her family were sailors. So when I was fifteen I left the farm and ran away to sea, shipping as mess boy aboard a sailing vessel which plied between the Atlantic seaboard and the West Indies. At fifteen I was as big as most men and very tough and strong. I stayed at sea three years, and then came ashore and entered the ring.

I had done plenty of fighting aboard ship and in foreign ports with the crews of other ships, and a passenger on the ship, a Mr.

Harmer, had been interested in me and he persuaded me to try the fighting game. At this time I was eighteen years old, was five feet and ten inches tall, weighed 160 pounds and was strong as a bull— stronger than most heavyweights.

I had never dissipated or led a riotous life which may seem strange to many people who are familiar with the looseness of many sailors and the evil that attends the waterfront of seaports. But the fact was, I was just a big happy-go-lucky kid, who knew remarkably little of life in spite of the fact that I had rubbed shoulders with all the rawer sides of life. The painted women of the waterfront repelled me with their shrill voices and skull-like faces; coming of a European peasant breed I was thrifty for a boy—that is, I spent my money freely but I would not gamble it away because I wanted some return for it. And as for drink— well, I loved to fight and engage in all kinds of athletic sport; I was inordinately proud of my fine body and too proud—too vain, if you wish—to do anything that would impair it. I knew what liquor did to strong men and I let it alone as if it was venom. This caused my mess mates to jeer at me a great deal and I had a great many fights about it.

At any rate, this is the truth—I sailed the seas for three years and touched at the vilest ports on the Atlantic and the Gulf of Mexico, and my mess mates were often the scum of the earth, yet when I came ashore from my last cruise, I swear I was as clean, mentally, physically and morally, as any man that ever lived. I attribute this to two things: the teachings of as fine and religious a mother as any man ever had, and my love of athletics. This last has kept many a young man in the straight and narrow path. I will admit that in some of our colleges today, especially, too much importance is being put on athletics but on the whole they are the best thing for a young man.

Well, my success in the ring was phenomenal at first. I was quick, brainy and tough, and I had a shrewd manager. I won my first eight fights by knockouts and my manager, Mr. Harmer, began matching me with first class opponents. Against this stiffer opposition I found the going pretty tough but I smashed through, mainly by my punching power, and out of a total of ten fights fought after

Harmer began to look for better men, I scored two knockouts, won seven decisions and fought a draw with the great Johnny Lucas who was at that time the foremost challenger for the middleweight crown.

Naturally, my success went a great deal toward turning my head. There were the usual line of hangers-on who follow every successful fighter, and they were forever telling me how good I was, and how I was the next champion, sure, and repeating every word I said as if I was a miracle of wit and wisdom—flattering me in order to share my good fortune, of course, and laughing in their sleeve at me for the fool I was.

Well, Mr. Harmer kept the women away—for there always is a certain class of women who take up with fighters. I had money—more money than I had ever thought existed when I was working on the farm and pulling sheet ropes on the merchantman. I dressed in good clothes—rather flashy in fact!—I bought many books and tried to educate myself—for though I had finished a grammar school before I left home, the education a country grammar school gives you is not very complete, and I was ashamed of my ignorance before so many suave and polished men of the world with whom I came into contact.

I learned to speak a very different brand of English than I had been accustomed to speaking. But for all this, I did not neglect my training. I was prouder of my physical achievements than ever. I was matched with the Cornish Nonpareil, Jack Penhryn, following my draw with Johnny Lucas, and in event of my winning I was assured of a return match with Lucas.

"Now this is your chance, O'Hanlon!" exclaimed Harmer, his eyes blazing with excitement. "Lucas' manager is dickering the champion but the match isn't made by a long shot! Your holding Johnny to a draw hurt his drawing power with the crowds a little. A big percent of the fans think you can take him if you get another chance. But you've got to hurdle Penhryn and don't think that Cornishman is easy. If you lick him, we get Lucas—you'll whip him next time, I know you will. The champion's manager is holding off, waiting to see how it comes out—oh, I know this game! Don't tell me! If you whip Penhryn, you'll be even a bigger drawing card than you are now—give it an international flavor. If you whip Lucas, then, you're a cinch for a title match!"

"I'm a cinch then," I said with a swagger. "I can whip both those birds, and the champion too, in the same ring."

Harmer looked at me a minute with his keen cold grey eyes.

"Another thing, O'Hanlon," he said. "You're getting a little too cocky lately. You weren't that way when you started fighting. Don't let success go to your head. Yes, you've done well—mighty well. You're only twenty now—in two years you've gone further than many men go in ten. But for that very reason you ought to watch your step; you can lose in a month now what it's taken two years to gain. You're Irish and the Irish always stand defeat better than winning. They fight harder when they're losing—it's when they've won they let down and start going easy. If you win in this game, you've got to stay top notch every minute."

"Well, not so fast," I snapped, a trifle miffed. "I'm not passing up anything, am I? Don't I train strictly, and haven't I won my fights? What more do you want?"

"I want you to keep on doing that. I don't like the class of friends you have hanging around you. I don't like the way you've been running around to cabarets in your off time—"

"Now listen here," I said in the thoughtless vanity of youth, "my friends are my own business, see? And what I do when I'm not training or fighting is my own business, see?"

"Well, it's my business if you go to abusing yourself or making a fool out of yourself for it affects you in the ring where *I'm* concerned—"

"My, great God!" I exclaimed in a fury. "Have I ever done anything to be called down this way? Let up on me! I've never drunk or dissipated but you round on me like I never did anything else! Let up on me! Shut up! Get out! Go take a walk and cool off! I'm sick of your racket!"

"Alright," was his parting admonition. "Remember—rave all you want to—but you've got to train as you never did before for

Penhryn; he's more dangerous than Lucas was, even, because he hits harder. This is the crossroads of life for you—one way leads to the title and fortune and the other leads to the gutter. It's up to you. I won't be back until tomorrow; but you be in bed by nine and if any of your rat-eyed 'friends' come around, take my advice and kick them out."

I snorted in contempt and went into the gym to punch the bag. To my credit, I went through my training routine faithfully that day, but Harmer's remarks still nettled me. After all, I was an unbalanced kid—I had attained such financial success as comes to most men late in life, when they have enough experience to keep their heads. Harmer was my only equalizer and I didn't have enough sense to know it. I realized his shrewdness in matchmaking and training had largely made me what I was—I was grateful to him—but—oh, well, who can explain the workings of a boy's mind?

I was in a surly mood all day and this was noticed by a fellow called "Slick" Baden, a hatchet-faced narrow-eyed man who had the reputation of being a sport and who hung around me a great deal—one of the flatterers I have mentioned before.

"Kid," said he—and I can see him now as he said it, with his derby cocked over one eye and a cigarette hanging from the corner of his mouth, "you need a little recreation. You're goin' to go stale, first thing you know."

"Aw," I growled, "I'm in silk—harder than nails."

"Yeah," he agreed, puffing his cigarette, "but you won't be, by the time the fight comes off, next month. You'll be dried out like a mummy—oh, I've seen 'em over-trained before. I've seen 'em so shaky and nervous they was whipped before they started. Harmer's trainin' you to death. Regular slave driver. Come on— let's step out tonight."

"I guess I better not," I hesitated. "Harmer said I ought to be in bed at nine—"

"Oh, alright," said Slick with an indifferent wave of his hand, "If you're *afraid* of him—"

"Look out what you say!" I shouted just like a ten-year old kid, "I'm not afraid of any man in the world, but I've got to be in shape to fight Penhryn. He's no snap."

"No, but you will be, if you keep on edge this way. You been snappin' and snarlin' all day. That ain't like you, Kid, and it's a sign a man's gettin' over the edge."

Well, in my heart I knew the cause of my grouchiness was my irritation at Harmer, but, boy-like, I began to persuade myself that Slick was right and I was over-training.

"Come on," he said, "we'll just run down to the Frenchman's—you don't have to even sniff a drink or even dance, or eat anything. We'll just mingle with the crowd a while and let you get this fight off your mind and kinda rest up, see? We'll get back no later than twelve, at the most. Harmer won't ever know nothin' about it, and it'll help you a lot, Kid."

Well, in the end I agreed and we went to the Frenchman's, a roadhouse that had a rather shady reputation. While we were sitting at our table, watching the dancers, a waiter came up and touched me on the shoulder.

"Are you Kid O'Hanlon?" he asked. I told him I was and he said:

"A lady told me to ask you to come over and join her party—you and your friend."

"Where is she?" I asked, for I was always nervous and bashful around women and was not much disposed to accept that invitation. The waiter pointed to a table away over close to a window, rather secluded from the rest, and I saw there were four people, two men and two women. The men were tall, handsome gentlemen, dressed in evening clothes with all the air of big-businessmen. The women were dressed in silk evening dresses with costly fur wraps and they fairly shone and sparkled with the rich garments they wore. One was a blond, the other a brunette and this one I noticed especially. She was tall, slender and refined looking, with very black hair and eyes. She was looking at me and when she saw I was looking, she smiled and beckoned me.

I turned to Slick to ask him what to do, and to my amazement I saw he seemed greatly excited.

"Gee whiz, Kid," he exclaimed in a low, tense whisper, "that's Joan Cromwell, the society belle of the town! Her old man's worth millions—and that's Tom Marks, the millionaire racetrack owner with her. It's exits for us, Kid, we ain't the kind to be seen in *that* company!"

That made me stubborn just as he might have known it would.

"Why shouldn't we be seen in their company?" I asked. "She's inviting us—and I never heard of any of them before, while it seems they have heard of me."

I got up and pulling Slick, still resisting, to his feet, I followed the waiter across the room. The minute I got to Joan Cromwell's table I wished I'd taken Slick's advice because when the girl looked at me with her deep dark mysterious eyes, I felt like falling through the floor with embarrassment.

"You're Kid O'Hanlon, the great Irish boxer, aren't you?" she said. "I'm wild about boxers. I saw you fight Johnny Lucas. You should have had the decision, I thought. I just had to meet you, and I didn't know anyone who could introduce us, so—? Do you think I'm very unconventional and terrible?"

"Nothing you'd do could be wrong, Miss Cromwell," I managed to stammer with the flattery that comes natural to an Irishman.

She smiled. "Won't you please sit down, you and your friend? Oh, I forgot, pardon me. Mr. O'Hanlon, this is Miss Kathryn Hampstead, and Mr. Marks, and Mr. Skelly."

I acknowledged the introductions and introduced Slick, who appeared to be even more ill at ease than I was. And all the time we were at their table, he sat up stiff and straight as a poker and replied in monosyllables. If I had had any sense I would have seen something was wrong, because I had seen Slick in all sorts of companies before and he had never shown any embarrassment, being a rather brassy sort of a fellow anyway.

As for me, I scarcely remember anything of the conversation. I know that Joan asked me about my fights and got me to talking about myself—which is a sure way to flatter any man. I was fascinated by her—the first society woman I had ever known. She was so different from the painted women of the seaports, and from the simple country girls I had known as a boy. My senses swam when she looked into my eyes, the strange unfamiliar fragrance of her perfume filled my nostrils and altogether I was in a kind of delirium in her presence.

Vaguely I knew that at last Slick was pulling at my sleeve and insisting that I go, and it was getting late. Joan gave me her hand and said in a low voice: "I must see more of you. May I not pick you up on the road tomorrow?"

I agreed eagerly and Slick and I took our departure. On the way home I expanded on Joan's good looks and refined and cultured manner. Slick was not so enthusiastic.

"That dame's just a rich man's spoiled daughter," he said. "She's had everything she wanted and she's fed up on the regular dancin' and yachtin' and all that high-society people do. She's lookin' for a new thrill. You ain't any more than a fine racehorse to her—just a new toy to amuse herself with. In a couple of months she'll get tired of the fight game and boxers, and she'll forget you ever lived."

Of course this was the best way in the world to keep up a stubborn youth's interest. Like a young fool, I replied with some heat, for like all young idealistic men I resented Slick's worldly cynicism. It was about two o'clock, as I noticed, when we arrived at the training quarters and got to bed.

Harmer returned next day and nothing was said to him about my visit to the Frenchman's. But all morning I went through my routine in a lackadaisical manner, all my mind being on seeing Joan that evening. I went out on the road in the latter part of the afternoon and insisted on going alone myself. As Harmer knew that he could—or could have heretofore—trust me in training, he made no objection, so I went out on the road by myself and hardly had I gotten out of sight of the camp when a fine roadster purred past, stopped and my mind reeled again at the sight of Joan.

I climbed in beside her and she drove over hill and dale, while we talked, or rather while I talked and she encouraged me with clever questions or carefully turned compliments on my physical prowess. So vain I was, so young and foolish I was, I imagined any woman could easily be attracted by me and I boasted shamelessly of my achievements. After a couple of hours, she brought me back close to the camp and I took my departure, making her first promise she would meet me in that manner the next day. She demurred at first.

"You know I want to, Kid," she said, leaning toward me and gazing into my eyes with her great dark ones, "but it might not be good for you. Don't you boxers have to take a certain amount of road-work each day? If you ride around with me it won't help you much."

I laughed. "Don't you worry, Miss Cromwell. I'm trained to the notch now. I could go into a ring and whip any middleweight in the world right this minute."

"I believe you could, too," she breathed, and then she promised to meet me.

So it went for a week. Every day I would go out alone for my road work and every day Joan would meet me out of sight of the camp and we would take up an hour or two in riding about and talking. I honestly tried to make up for this lack of real work, by strenuous sessions at the light and heavy punching bags and with my sparring partners, and I could not tell that I was affected anyway—but hard and constant road work is necessary in a real fight. You will not feel the need of it punching a bag or sparring with partners but in a long, grueling battle the lack of it means a lack of endurance and stamina. Even Harmer, keen trainer as he was, could not tell, from my slugging bees with my sparring mates, that I was neglecting my footwork, and from the way I worked in the gym, he thought I was giving all my best attentions to training and he praised me highly, which made me feel guilty. But this feeling was forgotten when I thought of Joan. I was by this time madly in love with her. Yet I had never spoken a word of love. With all my vanity I was still a big overgrown youth with the bashfulness and timidity of youth. I dreamed, though, of declaring my love for her someday—preferably after I had won the title—and of course she would accept! I even dallied with giving up the ring and going into some dignified business with the aid her father would undoubtedly give me! But I decided that it would be more manly to wait until I could lay the title at her feet—and meanwhile I noticed an alarming flabbiness in my waistline. Harmer noted this, too, and was worried.

More, it seemed to me that my punches were losing something of their speed and accuracy. This was natural— overwork in one respect and underwork in another. Harmer had me cut down on my bag punching, pully work, rope skipping and boxing and he worried a great deal over the fact that my legs were not as slim and hard as they should be.

"It's just like you weren't doing any road work," he said, knitting his brows in perplexity. "But I know you're not neglecting that—"

I reddened with a momentary shame to think how he trusted me and how, with all his nagging, he did not believe me capable of neglecting my training. One of the handlers spoke up about this time and said he believed I was just putting on natural weight. I was pretty tall for a middleweight, he said, and he believed I was going to grow into a heavyweight. Harmer shook his head, said that was bad because I had to make the weight for the Penhryn fight, but it couldn't be helped. He told me to wear a heavy sweater when I ran and to swing half-pound dumbbells.

It was a week just before the date of the fight. The fans were wild with excitement. Nearly all the ringside seats had been bought up ahead of time, the buyers paying from ten to twenty-five dollars a seat. The fight was advertised as the battle of the century, of course, and given an international interest. I was not champion of America, neither was Penhryn the champion of England, but each of us was looked upon as the logical successor to those titles, and probably to the world title. I was described by the reporters as "the shiftiest, hardest hitting slugger since Stanley Ketchel," and Penhryn as, "the Cornish Wonder—a second, cleverer Fitzsimmons."

Reports from our spies in the Cornishman's camp showed him to be in first-class condition—and I was most certainly not.

Harmer was desperate. At last he took to sending someone out on the road with me and I did not get to meet Joan. I found out then how desperately in need of road work I was. Inside of a mile I was panting and my knees trembled. For a moment a rush of panic overwhelmed me, then in my insane self-confidence, I laughed at the idea. I would make it a quick, rushing fight. While Penhryn stood off and sparred in his English manner, I would crash in and blast him out of existence in the manner of the terrible Ketchel, to whom sportswriters compared me.

Two days before the fight! Harmer sent me out on the road with a trainer. I had written Joan a note; I gave the trainer the slip and got in her car. As we whizzed down a side road we passed the trainer and I saw his mouth gape as he recognized me. But I didn't care.

My pulses throbbed. Joan! She was sitting beside me—her perfume was in my nostrils. Suddenly I threw my arms around her and crushed her to my breast; she did not resist. It seemed to me that she even snuggled closer to me while I poured hot passionate words into her ears. Disjointedly I told her of my love and my hopes and asked her to be my wife.

She had stopped the car and now she turned and hesitantly put her arms about me. "I like you too; Kid—but you'll have to give me time—you've taken me all of a sudden. I had no idea you felt this way about it."

"Is there any other man?" I asked with a sudden pang of jealousy.

She shook her head. "No other man—Kid—I don't know whether I love you or not. Give me a little time, won't you, please? Wait until after the fight—I'll give you my answer then."

"Won't you give me a little hope?" I asked distractedly. I come of the blood of the fierce Wicklow hill people; when we love, we love deeply and terribly, and when we hate—but that is another tale.

Suddenly she turned to me and for the first time spoke my first name:

"Patrick!" she whispered—"I love you!" And her lips met mine.

"But—!" she eluded me as I sought to crush her to my breast again. "I don't know my own mind—I don't know whether I'd be fair to myself and you in marrying you! Wait—wait—please give me time—I must have time to think. Just now let's not talk about it anymore. Let's just enjoy ourselves, as if this were the last day we were to be together."

I winced. "Don't talk like that Joan, it's bad luck, and besides—"

She pinched my cheek gently. "I was just joking. Come on—let's spin over to Dad's hunting lodge for a lark."

At the hunting lodge, some miles out in the country, we stopped. The place was deserted, save for an old caretaker, a villain-ous-looking old scoundrel whose looks rather surprized me. Joan insisted that we go in and soon we were dancing in the big front room to the tune of a Victrola. Then Joan went to a cupboard and brought out a bottle, and a cocktail shaker.

"Just a little nip to celebrate your coming victory," she said. "I don't drink—seldom ever—but this is a special occasion. You don't mind if I mix up a cocktail, do you?"

Mind? Anything she did was right, as far as I was concerned. I was flattered that she considered my likes and dislikes in the matter. She shook up the cocktail, with me watching every move she made and feasting my eyes on the beauty of her. It never occurred to me to taste the drink even, until she poured a glass full and handed it to me.

"Why, no, Joan," I said. "I can't drink, you know." She looked embarrassed and a little hurt.

"Of course—how thoughtless of me! But such a teeny-weeny little sip—and it has scarcely any whiskey at all in it. I—I thought you'd like it because I made it myself—"

Suddenly she bent her head and touched her lips to the edge of the glass. Then looked up at me with a coy smile: "There now—won't you just taste it?"

What man could resist? I swallowed the contents with no fur-ther parley. You know as a man is, whose system is absolutely free of any alcoholic taint—who has never indulged in intoxicants in his life. The merest amount of whiskey rushes to his head. This it did with me. The cocktail, I know now, was unusually strong, I did not know that then, for I had not noticed the amount of whiskey she mixed in. I did not know that the warm glow I felt was induced by the alcohol I instantly felt the need of another, and when she was not looking, poured myself a glass from the mixer. A small voice down inside of me warned me I was doing wrong, but the voice of the whiskey drowned it out—I grew super-confident—became noisy and boastful.

I noticed Joan eyeing me in a peculiar manner and when I wanted another drink she refused to let me have it. She tried to keep me from drinking and in a playful scuffle I took the mixer away from her and drained another glassful of the stuff. She argued in vain with me. I told her I could whip any man in the world, in any condition, and as I really grew drunk, my Irish brogue thickened, and Irish instincts rose and I remember cursing Penhryn for a Cornish rogue, a Sassenach sycophant and a Cromwellian, and swearing to break his head in the first round.

Things grew vague and hazy. How much I drank I do not know. After the cocktail shaker was empty, I drank straight whiskey from the bottle. I remember trying to dance with Joan who was strangely acquiescent, and stumbling over my feet; I remember hearing her say: "Kid, you're drunk; this will help you."

As in a haze I saw her holding out a glass full of some sort of amber liquid.

I drank, being aware of a pungent aromatic taste. Then I knew nothing more.

When I came to myself I felt sick and bad generally. My head throbbed in an unendurable manner and I could not think straight. I wondered where I was and what had happened. I sat up and found myself to be in a clean bed in a rather expensive-looking room. I shouted but no one answered. Gradually the events came back to me and I blushed with shame. My first thought was of Joan. She must have become disgusted at my drunkenness. I rose shakily, finding myself to be fully dressed.

My legs seemed numb but as I moved about circulation slowly returned to me. If I had been an experienced drinker I would have realized that there had been something more than mere intoxication the matter with me. I opened the door and went out. There was no one in the hunting lodge. I went out into the sunlight; it was about ten o'clock. How long I had been unconscious or asleep I had no idea.

I hailed a passing automobile and rode into town. At the edge I stopped where my training camp was. I entered the quarters. Harmer was pacing the floor, tearing his hair. He seemed to have aged years. The trainers and handlers sprang up as I entered. Harmer rushed over to me, running his hands over me as if to be sure I was all there.

"Where have you been? Are you hurt? What happened?" Then before I could reply he shrieked: "You've been drunk— laying out in a gutter somewhere! Oh, you cursed fool! And I've been scouring the country for you all night! Oh, my God—and within thirty-six hours you've got to climb in the ring with the most dangerous fighter in the country! You look like you'd been through a sawmill! I won't have you fight this way—I'll call it off—"

The promoter was there; his brow was black. "You can't call it off!" he snapped. "And the crowd won't accept a substitute. The tickets are all sold out. This little rat—I don't know what he's been into, but he's got to get in there and fight, win or lose!"

"And he'll lose," raved Harmer. "Look at him! He's in no shape to fight anybody! Oh God, all our hopes for a title gone up Salt Creek because the young fool—oh, boy, why did you do this?"

I shook my head. I had nothing to say. Harmer grew furious again.

"And another thing," he fairly screamed, "your trainer told me how you gave him the slip yesterday and went sailing off with some high-brow dame! So that's why you've been putting on weight and getting soft-legged! Been passing up your roadwork to buzz a ritzy frail! Who is she?"

"That's none of your business," I snarled, finding my voice at last. "And you'll speak with some respect when you talk of her. She's going to be my wife!"

He looked at me and the anger faded out of his keen old eyes, leaving only sadness and pity.

"Peel and climb on the scales," was all he said. I did so; in my underwear I weighed 165 pounds.

"Five pounds overweight," grunted the promoter. "That's $10,000 taken flight, Harmer—that was your forfeit to Penhryn's manager."

Harmer merely nodded. "I'll pay it. To boil that extra weight off the Kid now would weaken him and maybe damage his constitution permanently."

I was stung with shame.

"You won't pay it!" I cried. "I'll get in the baths and steam if off and steam the alcohol out of me at the same time. And what's more, I'll whip Penhryn, in condition or not."

I had rather pass over the hours preceding the fight. I had never had to boil fat off me before and I had no idea what a task it was. For hours I sweated in a Turkish bath and I felt as if my vitality was slowly oozing from me with the perspiration that poured from every pore. But at least I saved Harmer's money. When I stepped on the scales before the fight I weighed 159½ pounds.

No doubt I had soaked the alcohol from my system but I was far from being in shape. The forced reducing weakened me more than I cared to admit, and I still felt queer and sluggish— for a reason I'll divulge later. A nerve kept jerking and throbbing in my temple and my feet dragged in spite of myself.

Well, at last I was in the ring, listening to the deafening roar of the fifty thousand odd people there. I saw the pain in Harmer's eyes as he looked me over and then glanced at Penhryn in the opposite corner, but he had spoken no word of blame to me since that first outburst.

"Kid," he said passionately, "rush him from the first bell! If you don't finish him in the first four rounds, you're through. And if the going gets too rough, look for the towel."

I shook my head. "No, Mr. Harmer, don't throw in the towel. That would break my heart. If I must take a licking, let me take it standing. But don't worry; I'll finish this Cornishman in five rounds or maybe less."

For in spite of all, I had no doubt in my mind as to the outcome of the fight. I was going to win! I looked over at Penhryn, 160 pounds of splendid manhood. He was built somewhat like his famous countryman, Bob Fitzsimmons, being light in the legs and broad in the shoulders. Also, like the great Fitzsimmons he was freckled and these freckles stood out in bold contrast to his extremely white skin.

"Kid O'Hanlon, the Irish-American Hope," the referee was shouting. "And in this corner, Jack Penhryn, the Cornish Nonpareil—weights—"

"Watch his shift," Harmer was whispering urgently in my ear, "the old Fitzsimmons trick—" The gong sounded for seconds out.

The lights went off except for those just over the ring. Again the gong clanged. I bounded out of my corner intent on making the fight a one round affair. Penhryn came out more cautiously. He must have fathomed my intention and was taking no chances with my terrific right hand. But for all his caution I almost blasted him with my first rush. Moving with all my usual speed I was on him before he could get set and I drove him back across the ring in a perfect frantic whirlwind of blows, one of which, a right hook, crashing through his guard, dumped him on the canvas for a knock down. He was not hurt however, and he took the count of nine, resting coolly on one knee.

I waited in the furtherest corner, trembling with eagerness. Already I could feel my vitality slowly ebbing. I was in no shape to fight a rushing, slugging battle, yet I must throw caution to the winds and go in, using up all my waning powers to win a quick knockout. Let him elude me for five rounds and I knew I would collapse.

So when he rose I tore madly into him again. He backpedalled rapidly and I followed, raining blows on his elbows and shoulders as he covered up. Faintly through the terrific din I could hear Harmer screaming for me to feint him out and straighten him up.

I stepped back and began feinting, stepping in and out swiftly but not hitting, and then Penhryn raised his head slightly from his crooked, sheltering arms, and tried a vicious left for my solar plexus. I blocked it, at the same time stepping in and crashing a terrific right uppercut to his jaw. The force of the blow jerked him erect out of his crouch and instantly I hooked a sizzling left to his jaw. His eyes went glassy, his knees buckled and he tried to fall into a clinch. I brushed his clutching hands aside and crashed my right to his jaw. He crumpled and the referee began counting over him. At "Nine!" the gong sounded and the Cornishman's seconds jumped in the ring and carried him to his corner.

As I sat in mine, I noticed my chest heaving slightly—a bad sign at the end of the first round. In spite of the terrific pace I should have been breathing as naturally as if I had been sleeping instead of fighting. Harmer was massaging my body muscles while he talked, but I scarcely noticed what he was saying. My eyes were roving over the ringside seeking for Joan and when I failed to see her, my heart sank to my shoes and something went out of me more than the fight had caused. I could not understand.

"You're fighting a great fight, boy," Harmer was saying. "Oh, if you were in shape he'd never stand a chance—"

At the gong I went out fast and hard, but I knew I was slipping. Penhryn, a good game man, was tired of running and now in spite of the yells from his corner, he stood up to me. Toe to toe in the middle of the ring we traded punches until the crowd went wild and Penhryn, finding himself outclassed in sheer hitting power, backed away with blood trickling from his lips.

He began boxing again and sank a wicked left into my midriff. Instantly my lack of proper condition told. A racking pain went through me and I felt momentarily as though the marrow had melted in my leg bones. I rallied and lashed out wildly connecting with a right to the mouth which spattered the Cornishman with blood. At the gong I was battering Penhryn along the ropes but my blows were getting, not weaker, but wilder. I lacked accuracy and the Cornishman was beginning to realize this.

Iron Men

(first version)

Chapter .1.
"Like a Barroom Brawler—"

A cannonball for a left and a thunderbolt for a right! A granite jaw and an iron body that could not be dented! The ferocity of a tiger and the greatest fighting heart that ever beat in a steel-ribbed breast! That was Mike Brennon, heavyweight contender in the year 19-- .

I saw him first in the boxing tent of a travelling carnival, long before any fight fan or sportswriters had ever heard the name of Brennon. This carnival, like many wandering shows of that type, had a retinue of wrestlers and boxers—pork-and-beaners who had passed their prime or hard-eyed kids who were too young for the game. As usual the spieler was offering a prize to anyone who could stay so many rounds or minutes with the show athletes, boxing or wrestling. As a rule there are men planted in the audience who come forward giving fictitious names and claiming to reside in the town in which the carnival is showing.

These men enter the ring, slug or struggle as the case may be with a great show of roughness and anger, while the deluded patrons urge them on, thinking they are encouraging home talent. Then they lose in such a manner as to leave the matter in doubt enough to drive the crowd into a frenzy and assure a "return match" and a crowded house the next night. Occasionally some real native son gets the start on the plant and the carnival fighter is forced to really exert himself. However, as an old-timer has said, "There are ways and means," and the native son very seldom stays the limit.

I sat in the "athletic tent" of the carnival which was performing in the small Nevada town through which I happened to be passing, and grinned at the antics of the spieler who was volubly offering fifty dollars to anyone who could stay four rounds with "Young Firpo, the California Assassin, champion of Los Angeles and the East Indies!" Young Firpo, whose real name was doubtless Leary and who was probably fighting in fourth rate clubs before his illustrious name sake was ever heard of, stood by with a bored but contemptuous expression on his heavy stolid features. This was an old game to him. He was a vast hairy fellow with the bulging muscles of a weightlifter.

"Now, friends," shouted the spieler, "is they any young man here what wants to risk his life in this here ring? We bar no man! Step up, fellers! This is the man that give Johnny Risko his hardest battle, the one who made the present champeen quit in a private workout! Remember, the management ain't responsible for life or limb! Any man that takes up this offer gits in here at his own risk and—"

At that moment the crowd set up a yell: "Brennon! Mike Brennon! Mike's the boy to fight this bird! Go on, Brennon!"

At last a young fellow rose from his seat and with a rather embarrassed grin on his face, vaulted over the ropes. Young Firpo evinced some interest and from the hawklike manner in which the spieler eyed the newcomer, and from the ovation given him by the crowd, I knew that he was "on the up and up"—a local boy, in other words.

"You a professional boxer?" asked the spieler.

"I've fought a few times in the club here," answered Brennon, "but you said you barred nobody."

"We don't," grunted the spieler, taking in the difference in size between his man and the local lad.

While the usual rigmarole of argument and instructions was gone through with, I wondered just how the carnival men intended saving that fifty dollars in case the boy should happen to be a match for their man. As a general rule the ring is set close to the back of the tent, with a curtain stretched across the back, behind which are the dressing rooms. A tough local boy is worked up to this curtain in a clinch, his head suddenly pressed against it, and the razorback lurking behind for that purpose sees the bulge in the curtain and instantly smites it with a blackjack. The carnival boxer, feeling the victim go limp, releases him, striking him on the jaw at the same time. To the crowd it looks like a clean knockout. If they notice the boy crumple before the final punch they think he received a short body blow while infighting.

However, in this case the ring was set in the middle of the tent with no curtain near, the dressing rooms being in another part of the tent. I was sure that something crooked would be tried through I could not figure out just what it would be.

Brennon, after a short trip to the dressing room, climbed into the ring and was given a wild ovation. He was a finely built lad, a good six feet one in height, slim waisted and tapering of legs, with remarkably broad shoulders and heavy arms. He was dark of skin with narrow grey eyes and a shock of black hair falling over a broad forehead, and he had the true fighting face— broad across the cheek bones, with thin lips and a firm jaw. His long, smooth muscles rippled beautifully as he moved with the ease of a huge leopard. Opposed to him Young Firpo looked ponderous and slow; apelike.

Their weights were announced, Brennon 189, Young Firpo 191. The crowd jeered and hissed at the last; anyone could see that the carnival boxer weighed at least 210.

The battle was short, fierce and sensational, with a bedlam-like ending. At the first tap of the gong Brennon sprang from his corner and came in wide open, like a barroom brawler. Young Firpo met him with a hard left hook to the chin, stopping him in his tracks. Brennon's hands dropped, he staggered and the carnival boxer swung his right flush to the jaw. This was really a terrific blow but strangely enough it did not seem to worry the young fellow as much as the other had. He shook his head and came plunging in again but as he did so, his foe drew back his deadly left and crashed it once more to the jaw. Brennon dropped face first, like a log. The crowd was frenzied. The referee—the spieler—leaped forward and began counting swiftly; Young Firpo standing directly over the fallen warrior.

At five Brennon had not moved. Not a muscle twitched. At "seven" he stirred and began making aimless motions, the fighter's instinct in his brain seeking to drag him to his feet. At "eight" he reeled to his knees and his reddened dazed eyes, wandering about, seemed suddenly to fix themselves on Young Firpo standing over him. Instantly they blazed with the fury of the killer. As the spieler opened his mouth to say "Ten!" Brennon came reeling up in a blast of breathtaking ferocity that stunned the crowd.

Young Firpo too, seemed stunned. His jaw went slack, his face whitened and he began a hurried retreat. Brennon was after him like a blood-crazed tiger and before Young Firpo could lift his hands, Brennon's wide looping left crashed under his heart, and as the carnival boxer's knees buckled, a sweeping right found his chin and crashed him down on the canvas with a force that shook the whole ring.

The astounded spieler mechanically lifted his hand to begin counting, but Brennon, moving like a man in a daze, or one who is walking in his sleep, pushed him away and stooping, tore the glove from Young Firpo's limp left hand. Removing something therefrom, he held it up to the crowd. It was a heavy iron affair, resembling brass knuckles, and known in the parlance of the ring as a knuckle duster. Seeing this I gasped. No wonder Brennon had gone down as though struck by a triphammer. And no wonder Young Firpo had been unnerved when his victim rose! The force with which that iron-laden glove had landed twice on Brennon's jaw should have shattered the bone, and yet he had been able to arise within ten seconds and knock his man out with two blows!

Now all was bedlam. The spieler tried to snatch the knuckle duster from Brennon's hand and one of the wrestlers, acting as Young Firpo's second, rushed across the ring and struck at the winner. The crowd, sensing injustice to their favorite and fired with the unreasoning mob-spirit, surged into the ring with the avowed intention of "wrecking the blank-blank show!" As I made my way to the nearest exit, I saw an infuriated townsman swing up a chair to strike the still unconscious Young Firpo. Brennon sprang forward and caught the blow on his own shoulder, the force of it dashing him to his knees. Then with a breath of relief I was on the outside, and as I walked away, laughing, I heard the shouted commands of the special officers who were seeking to restore peace and order.

Over a year later I sat at the ringside of a small fight club on the California coast, waiting for the main event of the night. One of the habitués of the club was giving me his opinion of the fighters.

"And wait'll ya see this boy. He'll bowl Bat Mulcahy over in a coupla rounds. No boxer, but baby how he can clout! And as for takin' it! Imagine Bat Nelson and Tom Sharkey and Joe Goddard all mixed together, and triple the result! A glutton for punishment; that's him—"

About this time the boxers entered the ring. One was a stocky blond caveman, the other a tall dark complectioned youngster. It was Brennon.

He had not improved on his style. As before, he came tearing out of his corner, wild and wide open, hitting with both hands. Mulcahy had no skill to speak of, was even more a dub than Young Firpo had been, yet he managed to last nearly two rounds and to hand out a raft of punishment before one of those sweeping blows landed. It was a left which sank to the wrist in the blond boy's midriff and it was enough.

During the fight my old interest in Brennon was renewed. In spite of his senseless, wide-open style, I saw that he had the makings of a champion in him. A perfect build, incredible stamina—Mulcahy's best blows had not even made him wince— as terrific a punch as I have ever seen, it was evident that his one failing was an absolute lack of science. Apparently he had everything but the instinct which makes some fighters do things right in the ring, even lacking proper instruction. He looked like a champion but he had the style of a longshoreman. Still, I did not attach much importance to this, as detracting from his general merit. Many a fighter stumbles through his ring life and never learns anything simply because of an ignorant or negligent manager.

I went to Brennon's dressing room and accosted him. "My name is Steve Amber. I saw you fight tonight and I saw you knock out a dub by the name of Young Firpo in a carnival in Gantsley, Nevada, about a year ago."

"I've heard of you," answered Brennon without enthusiasm. "What do you want?"

Overlooking his abrupt manner, I said: "Who's your manager?"

"I haven't any."

"How would you like for me to manage you?"

"I'd as soon have you as anybody," he answered shortly. "But this was my last fight. I'm through. I'm fed up on knocking out dubs in fourth-rate joints."

"Tie up with me and maybe I'll get you better matches."

"No use. I had my chance twice. Once in Los Angeles against Sailor Slade; once in New York against Johnny Varella. I flopped. I couldn't get a fight at either of the clubs where I fought, now."

"No!" he raised his hand as I started to speak. "No use to argue. I don't want to talk—to you or anybody. I'm through with the game and I want to go to bed."

"Alright," I answered. "Suit yourself. I never was one to coax. But here's my card and if you change your mind, look me up. You might do worse for a manager."

The weeks stretched into months; I was busy with my affairs and the memory of Mike Brennon faded. But he was not a man one could forget, having ever seen him. When I dreamed, as all fight fans and fighters' managers dream, of a super-fighter, the form of Mike Brennon rose unbidden—a dark, brooding figure, charged with the abysmal fighting fury of the primitive.

And then one day Mike Brennon came to me—not in a daydream but in the flesh. For some reason I could scarcely believe my eyes as I saw him standing before me, in the office of my training camp, his crumpled hat in his hand, an eager grin on his dark face. Something had changed him; he was very different from the morose and moody youth to whom I had talked in the dressing room of the coast fight club.

"Mr. Amber," said he, "if you still want me, I'd like to have you manage me."

"That's fine," I answered, and before I could continue, he broke in:

"Can you get me a fight, right away? I need the money bad."

"Not so fast," I answered. "I can advance you some money if you've got some debts—"

"No," he made a quick gesture. "It's something else—can you get me a fight within a few days?"

"Are you in trim?" I asked. "How long since you've been in the ring?"

"Not since you saw me last. But I always stay in shape."

"I'll see."

I took Brennon to my open-air ring where Spike Ganlon, a clever middleweight was working out and instructed them to step four fast rounds. Brennon seemed eager to get to business and I was astonished to see him put up a very fair sort of boxing against the shifty Ganlon. True he was far outstepped and out-boxed, but that was to be expected, Ganlon being a rather prominent figure in the fistic world and Brennon an unknown slugger. Still I did not like the way Mike sent in his punches; he was fairly accurate but his punches lacked the triphammer force which had attracted me to him before.

However, when I had him slug the heavy bag he nearly tore it loose from its moorings, and I decided that he had been pulling his punches against Ganlon. I taught him all the tricks of the trade as I have learned them in my years of experience, and Ganlon, who took a great liking to Mike, added his practical tutelage in the days that followed. But the result was far from satisfying. Brennon was more intelligent than the general run of fighters, but he could not seem to apply what we had taught him. He understood the principle and the theory but it was hard for him to practice the actuality.

Still, I did not expect too much of him at first; I worked with him patiently for a few weeks and when I sent him against his first opponent in the semi-windup of a fight in the Hopi, A.C., San Diego, I felt that I had a man whose terrific hitting, coupled with a fair boxing defense, would carry him to victory.

The opponent I had selected for him was not particularly formidable—one Joe Nogales, a clever but punchless Mexican heavyweight, whose windmill style of milling had prompted sportswriters to dub him an overgrown Harry Greb. I wanted to build self-confidence in my man, also to test his actual ability in the ring before I sent him against a dangerous puncher. You cannot always make a classy fighting man out of a wide-open slugger, especially in the short time I had had Brennon under my wing, and I found—but of that later.

As I climbed through the ropes that night, I repeated my instructions to Mike to feel his foe out and remain on the defensive the first round. I did this to find out how much he remembered of what Ganlon and I had taught him.

The gong sounded and following my instructions, Brennon came out cautiously feinting in a rather awkward manner. Nogales danced around him, jabbed several times, while Brennon shuffled about, apparently growing more clumsy and uncertain every second. I swore amazedly. Mike was certainly no ring leopard now—or rather he looked like a leopard hindered by chains on all his legs.

Nogales continued his dancing tactics, finally decided his foe had nothing and swarmed all over Brennon. Mike seemed to do everything wrong. He blocked in an ineffective and slouchy manner, his footwork was bad, he missed often and when he landed there was no kick to his blows. The gong found him pinned in a neutral corner, jabbing vainly at the bobbing, weaving Nogales, while the crowd booed.

"My gosh," marveled Ganlon, who was acting as Mike's handler, "you do everything backwards! What's the matter, kid, you box three times as good in the trainin' camp!"

"You want me to box him this round?" asked Mike.

"Go after him any way you want to," I answered. "You're doing no good this way. I made a mistake, sending you back in the ring before you were seasoned."

The gong sounded. Nogales had decided the man he faced was harmless and he came bouncing out into the center of the ring inclined to make a farce out of the fight. He spread his arms wide, made fantastic gestures and grotesque faces—it was at that moment that the thunderbolt struck him.

At the tap of the gong Brennon had gathered himself like a tiger about to leap upon his prey. The air of repression fell away from him, and as Nogales came dancing toward him, he shot out of his corner as though propelled by a giant steel spring.

Wham! Nogales was entirely off his guard—wide open, and occupied with his comedian tricks. A blind man could have hit him. Brennon's left, starting at the floor, crashed like the crack of doom against the Mexican's chin, and Nogales, lifted clean off his feet, shot back across the ring, rebounded from the ropes and lay sprawled, face down, blasted into senselessness by that terrible swing. The crowd went crazy.

On the way back to our training quarters, I said: "When I'm wrong I'm the first to admit it. I was trying to make a boxer out of you. But you're a natural slugger, though you've never showed any of the natural slugger's aptitude. You hit the widest, wildest swings of any man I ever saw. Looks like you'd have learned something from your actual experience in the ring. Look at Nogales—if it hadn't been for pure luck, likely he'd have outpointed you. But he got to acting the fool. A stevedore could have hit him."

"But not that hard," said Ganlon jubilantly. "Oh baby, what a clout!"

"Sure it was hard; but it must have travelled a couple of miles before it landed. And it would never have landed if Nogales had been minding his business. Mike, I'm going to make a slugger out of you—I mean a real slugger, like Dempsey, Sullivan and McGovern. A scientific slugger. You've got all their instincts; I understand how you feel. You can box in a fair manner in the training camps but when you get into the ring, where it's a matter of life and death so to speak, you forget everything but your natural style of fighting. Dempsey was a good boxer when he was sparring with his sparring partners, but he never boxed in the ring. He swung too, until DeForest taught him to hit straight. Still, I'll tell you frankly that at his crudest Dempsey showed more aptitude for the game than you do—now, this sounds brutal but I'm saying it for your own good. Dempsey, and Ketchell and McGovern too, for that matter, used instinctive footwork and kept stepping around their men. They ducked and weaved and hit short punches. You never go any way but straight forward—judging from the three fights I've seen. You're as fast as Dempsey was when he was coming up, but you don't seem to know how to use your speed.

"I'm saying all this so you'll realize how important it is for you to master your trade as we teach you. I'm going to make you a second Dempsey."

And for a time it seemed as if my dreams were coming true. In spite of Mike's urging that I get him another fight immediately, I kept him idle for four months. By idle, I mean he was not fighting in the ring. Otherwise he was busy enough. I had him practice hooking the heavy bag with short smashes to straighten his punches and eliminate so much of his wide and useless swinging. He would never learn to put any force behind a straight punch, I saw, but I intended making him a wicked hooker, like Dempsey. It was slow, hard work.

"Mike," said Ganlon one day, "is a queer nut. He's got a fighter's heart, and a fighter's body but he just ain't got a fighter's brain. It don't work right. He understands, but he can't practice what he understands. The simplest trick, he has to work on for hours every day—and then he's liable to forget it. If he was a bonehead, I'd understand it. But he ain't; he's got more brains in other ways than any man I ever saw."

"Maybe it's because he fought so long in second-rate clubs, with his wild style that he formed habits he can't break." I suggested.

"That's partly it; but it goes deeper. I tell ya, Mike Brennon's the hardest hitter, and the toughest fighter I ever saw, but they's a kink in his brain and he ain't cut out for this game."

"What do you mean, a kink?" I asked uneasily.

"I dunno. But it's somethin' that breaks down his coordination and keeps his mind from workin' with his muscle. When he tries to box clever, he has to stop and think and in the ring you ain't got time—you got to act mechanical. You see a left comin' at you and between the time it starts and the time it's to land ain't a split fraction of a second. But in that time you think: here's a jab I can't beat with mine. I can't block cause that'd leave me open for his right, I'm too close to snap back—I'll slip it, and as it goes over my shoulder I'll sink my right to his ribs. You got to think that in a flash; 'course you don't really study it all out, but you *know* it, see? That is, if you're a fast boxer; if you're just a wide open slugger like Mike you don't think nothin'. You just take the jab in the map as a matter uh course, spit out a mouthful and keep borin' in."

"But any slugger is that way," I objected.

Ganlon shook his head. "I know. But I tell yuh Mike is different. He ain't cut out for a boxer. If he don't learn a defense, he'll get punched cuckoo in sight of a few years. All the great sluggers had some kind of a defense. Some crouched and weaved like Dempsey and Ketchell and McGovern; some wrapped their arms around their skulls and barged in like Nelson and Paolino. Them that fought wide open didn't last no time especially among the heavies. And when they're through, they're through! The padded cell and the paper-doll cut-outs for most of 'em. It don't stand to reason a human skull can stand up under the beatin's it gets that way."

"You're a born croaker," I said, slightly worried. "Mike's not a slow brained gorilla with a ten-inch skull wall. He's rugged but intelligent. He'll learn."

"At anything else, yes," was Ganlon's parting shot. "At this game—maybe."

Chapter .2.
"Bat Nelson true to life!—"

"Listen, Steve," said Brennon, bearding me in my den so to speak, "I've got to have a fight. You promised to keep me busy and I'm holding you to your contract. I need the money."

"Mike," said I, "it's none of my business, but I don't see where your money goes. Of course, you didn't make such a lot out that Nogales fight, but it should have been enough to tide you over awhile; for you're at no expense at all here in the camp. You haven't bought any clothes since I began managing you— fact is, you ought to, if I may say so. You look rather seedy. Then, you don't make any whoopee. You're never seen with a girl; you don't drink—you don't gamble—"

"Have I ever tried to borrow money?" he broke in, white about the lips. "Have I ever grouched about being broke? Then what business is it of yours—"

"None at all," I hastened to assure him. "You're a model lad as far as training and abstinence go, and I've no kick about anything. Don't get sore; I beg your pardon and I won't intrude on your private affairs again."

The glare faded from his cold eyes.

"I apologize too, Steve," he said abruptly. "I should have known you weren't trying to pry into my business. But I do want another fight, as soon as you can arrange it."

"Alright," I gave in. "Understand, I don't believe you're ready to go in with a first-string man. But since money is the object— Monk Barota is on the coast now, padding his k.o. record. He'll be looking for setups and I believe I can match you up with him for a ten rounder at the Hopi A.C. where you fought Nogales. It's your best chance. If you can even hold him even, you'll get plenty of offers. But I expect you to more than hold him even. I expect you to whip him, Mike."

"I do, too," grinned Brennon.

I hoped that he was more sincere in his belief than I was. I really felt in my heart that he was not ready for a first-rater, and I had intended building him up more gradually. But there was a fierce, driving intensity about him when he spoke of the money he needed and the matches he wanted, which broke down my resolve. Brennon was, in some ways, a character of terrific magnetic force. Like Sullivan, he dominated all about him, trainers, handlers and managers. Had he been inclined to shirk his training he would have been ungovernable, for no one could force him into doing anything he did not wish to do. But only in the matter of money-making matches was he unreasonable, and this quirk in his nature amounted to an obsession.

The match maker at the Hopi A.C. greeted my proposal with delight, remembering my man's sensational k.o. of Joe Nogales.

"Sure, I'll get in negotiations with Barota's manager right away. The fans remember Brennon. He stole the show that night from the main event. Several times I've had people ask me why I didn't match him with somebody else. The boys like a puncher. Where have you been keeping him all this time?"

There is little use in stretching the tale out. Barota and Brennon were matched for a ten rounder, and at ringside Barota was a two to one favorite with few takers, even among those fans who had seen Brennon flatten Nogales. The tale of Mike's punching powers had gotten about and the people packed the arena, expecting to see a short but terrific battle, with the unknown slugger succumbing to the superior skill of the Eastern favorite.

My last instructions to Mike were: "Remember! This lad can hit! Don't tear into him wide open. Remember the crouch and weave Ganlon taught you. If you don't use some defense, he'll ruin you!"

The lights went out except those over the ring. The gong sounded. The crowd fell silent—that breathless, momentary silence that marks the beginning of the fight.

The men slid out of their corners and—

"Oh, Hades!" wailed Ganlon at my side. "He's doin' things backwards again!"

Mike wore the uncertain manner which had marked him during the first round of his last fight. He crouched too far over and held his hands awkwardly. Barota led a fast left and Brennon swayed the wrong way and took it squarely in the eye. Again Barota led and again he landed. And again. That flicking left was hard for any man to avoid but Mike was always ducking into it. Ganlon was cursing at my side. "After all these months of work, he forgets! Just a plain bonehead when it comes to boxin'. You better throw in the sponge now! Look there!"

Barota had attacked, suddenly and fiercely, straightening Brennon with a hard right uppercut and battering his head with a venomous left hook that had Mike's head bobbing on his shoulders.

Mike, stung, tried a left hook of his own. Its force was apparent but Barota ducked it with ease.

"At least," Ganlon said, "we drilled that into him so he remembers to hook instead of swing. But little good it'll do him; he can't even hook without lettin' the whole house know what he's goin' to do. Same as writin' the other bird a letter tellin' him about it."

Barota was taking his time. In spite of the fact that his foe seemed to have nothing but a scowl, no man could look into Mike Brennon's face and take him lightly at the first glance. But a round of clumsy floundering for footwork and ineffectual punching lulled the fear Barota might have entertained and he abandoned his dancing, jabbing tactics.

Ganlon was nearly weeping with rage beside me, as if his pupil's inaptness somehow reflected on him.

"All I know, I taught him, and there's that wop makin' a monkey outa him. Go on in, you ham! Let him knock you out and let's get this over with!"

At this moment, with the round about thirty seconds to go, Barota tore in with one of his famous attacks. Mike abandoned all attempts at science and began swinging wildly and fiercely—and futilely. Barota worked between his flailing arms and the Italian's hands, shooting in an out like pistons beat an incessant barrage against Mike's head and body. The gong stopped the punishment and

Barota ran lightly to his corner, raising one finger as an indication that he would finish his man in one more round.

Mike's face was somewhat cut but he was fresh and showed no signs of having just gone through a severe beating.

He broke in on Ganlon's impassioned soliloquy to remark: "This fellow can't hit."

"Can't hit!" Ganlon nearly dropped the sponge. "Why, that boy's got a k.o. record as long as a subway! Ain't he just pounded you all over the ring?"

"I didn't feel his punches, anyway," answered Mike and at that moment the gong sounded.

Barota came out fast; he was in a mood to bring this fight to a sudden termination. He was proud of his skill; preferred to show his wares against a worthy foeman; was rather irritated that he had been pitted against this clumsy, aimless slugger.

But Mike was not clumsy, nor was he slow. He only seemed so from his wild and erratic way of battling. Still, he seemed like a sacrifice for the sneering Italian who jabbed his head back cruelly, bringing a flow of blood from his cut lips. Barota launched a sudden attack and began hammering at Mike's body with the left-handed assault which had softened so many of his opponents for a k.o. The crowd went wild as he avoided Mike's returns, but suddenly I felt Ganlon's fingers sink into my arm.

"Bat Nelson true to life!" he whispered, his voice vibrating with excitement. "Look! The crowd thinks, and Barota thinks, that them left hooks is hurtin' Mike! But he ain't weakenin'; he ain't even feelin' 'em! That boy's solid iron. Watch now! Mike's got one chance—when Barota shoots the right—"

At this moment Barota evidently decided that Brennon was "softened" for the kill. He stepped back, feinted swiftly, and then shot his right. Barota was proud of the bone-crushing quality of that right; prouder of it than of all his skill. A clear opening he had and every ounce of his weight went into it. The leather guarded knuckles backed by the sparlike arm and heavy shoulder crashed flush against Mike's jaw. The blow was plainly heard in every part of the house. A gasp went up and nails sank deep into clenching palms. Mike swayed drunkenly but he did not fall. And he returned to the attack on the rebound.

Barota had stopped short for a flashing second. The realization that he had struck his man flush with everything he had, and had even failed to knock him off his feet, stunned him—froze him for a split second. And in that instant Mike swung a wild left and landed for the first time. It was a glancing blow, high on the cheek bone but even so, Barota went down. The crowd rose screaming.

Dazed, the Italian rose without a count and Mike tore into him with the ferocity of a tiger that scents the kill. Barota, blinded and dizzy from that sudden and fearful blow was in no condition to defend himself, yet Mike in his eagerness missed with both hands, until a minesweeping right-hander caught the Italian flush on the temple and he dropped—not merely out but senseless.

The crowd was screaming, but Ganlon said to me: "He's an iron man, don't you see? A natural born freak like Grim and Nelson. He'll never learn anything. Not if he trains a hundred years."

Chapter .3.
"It's Your Brain—A Cog Missin'—"

It was the day after Mike Brennon startled the sports world by his knockout of Monk Barota. Mike, Ganlon and I sat at the breakfast table, and despite the fact of victory, we were a far from merry gang.

"Listen," Ganlon read a morning paper: "The foremost fistic upset of the year occurred last night in San Diego, at the Hopi A.C. when an unknown named Mike Brennon stopped Monk Barota in the second round. This is Barota's first defeat and he wept like a child in his dressing room after he came to, at the thought of losing to a novice. This Brennon, it seems, has been pushing over second-raters on the coast for some time. He is under the management of Steve Amber, known to the sport world as having guided the destinies of two champions. It would seem he has a third titleholder in the making."

Ganlon flung the paper down. "Here's what a local scribe wrote: 'Fans at the Hopi A.C. last night were treated to the surprize of their lives when a local boy, Mike Brennon, stopped the highly touted Monk Barota in two rounds. This boy Brennon looks like the real class. He took Barota's best offerings without wincing and in uncorking his own punch, showed a power that Dempsey need not be ashamed of. Fans who saw Brennon flatten Joe Nogales a few months ago will remember the circumstances of that knockout, and will note a startling similarity in the two fights. In each case Brennon shambled and shuffled through the first round, making himself look the veriest palooka. Then in the next, having lulled his opponent into a feeling of security, he suddenly uncorked the k.o.

'That shows class. C-l-a-s-s, with a capital C! Any fighter who can outthink Monk Barota is going some. Old timers are comparing Brennon to Bob Fitzsimmons who used the same tricks. This boy is the next champion or I miss my guess.'"

"Carried away by his enthusiasm," snorted Ganlon. "Here's a sportswriter who comes from Los Angeles to see the fight. This boy's got an eye for the game. Listen: 'San Diego fans are very much worked up over a new wonder which has apparently risen in their midst. I of course refer to Mike Brennon who put the skids under Monk Barota in the second heat of a scheduled ten frame go at the Hopi A.C. last night.

'This was indeed a jolt to the sporting fraternity and I make so bold as to say that it had all the signs of a fluke to me. If I am not mistaken, Brennon is the dub who lost a ten rounder to Sailor Slade last year, in which he got a terrific beating and looked like a deckhand. Slade was not as good then as he is now, and he lost his last fight on points to that same Barota who fell before Brennon's haymakers. They say Brennon was shamming in the first round. If so, he ought to be on the stage for I never saw a more realistic imitation of a terrible dub. In the second Barota made the mistake of thinking he could drop Brennon with one smash. His failure threw him off his guard. That is a mistake many a man has made. When Brennon failed to go down from that terrific slam, Barota stopped to think what might be holding him up. It is my opinion that the clout which put Barota down for the first time was landed by mere chance—one of those lucky blows which have had such a large part in the annals of the sport. It is significant to note that after Barota rose, stunned, Brennon missed a couple of haymakers before he finally landed.

'I do not seek to detract from Brennon's victory. He showed plenty of courage and a ruggedness I never saw excelled. But it is my honest opinion that he is simply a tough, strong second-rater who beat a better man by chance.'"

"A trifle caustic," said Ganlon. "But he just repeats what I been sayin'. As a fighter, Mike, I take pain to say it, but you're a false alarm. It ain't your fault. If it was, I wouldn't be urgin' you to step outa the ring. It's your brain; a cog missin' somewhere. Somethin' left out. You got the body and the heart but you ain't got no more natural talent than a ribbon clerk and you can't learn. You got the fighting instinct, but not the fighter's instinct—and they's a flock uh difference!

"You're just a heavyweight Joe Grim. An iron man. Never was a iron man except Jeffries who could learn anything. Every man's got his faults. And each man's got a fault he can't overcome if he fights a hundred years. Look at Johnny Dundee; as brainy, classy a fighter as ever lived but he never learned to hit. Look at Firpo; a natural puncher with a kick like a government mule, but he never could learn to box or use his left. Look at Maher; a game, fast man with a terrible swat, but he had a weak chin. Look at Grim; as tough a man as ever lived but he never learned nothing.

"No, Mike, you're a iron man and as such I'm advisin' you to quit the ring. Your kind don't come to no good end. Specially in the heavies. It's the padded cell and the paper dolls for 'em. Too many punches about the head. They get permanently punch drunk. You don't have to go around countin' your fingers. You got brains enough to succeed somewhere else.

"You got three courses to follow: first, you can go around fightin' setups at the small clubs. You can make a livin' that way, and last a long time, 'cause you can beat anybody you can hit. Or, second, you can take advantage of knockin' out Barota and sign up with some of the offers you're bound to get. As a iron man fightin' clever first-raters, you won't win many fights, if any, but you'll be an attraction just like Joe Grim was, and you'll pull down some real money. But you won't last no time. Last, and best, you can take the money you've got and step out. If you need any more to start in business, why, me and Steve will gladly lend it to you, eh Steve?"

I nodded. Mike shook his head and spread his iron fingers out on the table in front of him. As usual he dominated the scene—a great sombre figure of unknown potentialities.

"You're right, Spike, in everything you've said. I could have told you some of that before. I've always known that there was a deficiency somewhere in my mentality—a lack of coordination or something. No man could be as impervious to punishment as I am and have a perfectly normal brain. It's not alone in boxing; I've failed at other jobs; I grasped the ideas but it was hard for me to put the theories into effect. Bad coordination somewhere.

"As for boxing, the crowd dazes me for one thing. I can't think straight. When I try to remember instructions I get rattled and forget everything. And when I start slugging naturally, as you say, I have none of the true slugger's instinct for the game.

"Nature gave me an unusual constitution and physique but at the cost of my reflexes. Mind and muscle won't act together and all the drilling in the world won't teach me. But—! *I can take it!* That's my only hope! That's why I'm not quitting the game. You admit that iron men are drawing cards. I'm an iron man. I've been cut to pieces in the ring but the only man who ever hurt me or knocked me down was Sailor Slade last year in Los Angeles—and he couldn't stop me.

"I've never been knocked out, and I don't believe there's a man in the world who can flatten me for the count. I don't feel the blows. I'm like Battling Nelson—not human when it comes to taking punishment. Eventually, after years of battering, someone will knock me out. When that happens I'll quit the game but before that time, I'll accumulate a fortune, if I'm handled right. I'm going to cash in on my ruggedness! Capitalize on the fact that no man can keep me down for the count!"

"Great heavens, man!" I exclaimed. "Do you realize what that means? The frightful punishment, the batterings, the mutilations? You won't be fighting dubs now; you'll be fighting men as fast and strong as you, men who carry terrific punches and who are so clever you won't be able to touch them. They'll hammer you to a red pulp! You have no defense, and you can't learn!"

"My defense is a granite jaw and iron ribs," he answered. "I'll take on everybody who will meet me, and wear them down."

"Maybe you will and maybe not," I said. "A man can wear himself down punching a granite boulder, as I've seen men do with Tom Sharkey and Joe Goddard but what about the boulder! You've been lucky. Nogales was careless and Barota was astonished and forgot himself. The next man you meet will be watching his step. If he's a boxer, he'll outstep and outpoint you. If he's a slugger, he'll still outstep you and pound you to pieces."

"They can't hurt me. I can beat any man I hit. Win or lose, I'll be a drawing card and that will mean large purses. That's what I'm after. Do you think I'd go through this Purgatory for glory, or if the need wasn't great?"

"If it's poverty—" I began.

"What do you know of poverty?" he cried out in a strange passion. "Were you left in a basket on the steps of Saint Joseph's boy home? Did you spend your childhood mixed in with five hundred others, where the need of all was so great that no one of you got more than the barest necessities of life? Did you pass your early boyhood as a tramp and a hobo worker, riding the rods and starving? Or your early youth as a dish washer, factory hand and preliminary boy? I did!

"Poverty! I've felt its sting in the soul of me, and its pinch in the brain of me. But that's neither here nor there; nor it isn't my own personal poverty so much that drove me back in the ring—but let it pass. I'm fighting until somebody knocks me out. That will finish me as a drawing card.

"Now then, as my manager, I want you to get busy. Match me with a fellow I can hit. I've been lucky in these last two starts. If I can win another fight it will increase my prestige and draw the fans—with their money. I don't expect to win many. Later, I'll pack them in just as Joe Grim did—to see if I can be knocked out. Until the fans find out that I'm an iron man, I'll have to go on my merits. Barota wants a return match. I don't want him now, or any other clever man who'll outpoint me and make me look like a worse dub than I am, even. Get me a mankiller—a puncher who'll come in and try to murder me. Get me Jack Maloney! I want the fans to see me stand up under the blows of a hitter—I want them to see me bloody and staggering, and still carrying on! That's what draws the crowd and the money!"

"It's suicide!" I cried, horrified. "Maloney's a slugger but at that I doubt if you can hit him. And he'll kill you! I won't have anything to do with it!"

"Then, by heaven!" Brennon roared, heaving erect and crashing his fist down shatteringly on the table, "I'll get me another manager! I'm in this for the money and if you fail me, our ways part here! But I'd rather have you piloting me than anyone else. You know the ballyhoo. You could help me if you were willing."

"If you're determined," I said huskily, my mind almost numbed by the driving force of his willpower, "I'll do all I can. But I warn you, you'll leave this game with a clouded brain."

He gripped my hand with a nervous grasp which nearly crushed my fingers and said shortly: "I knew you'd stand by me. Never mind my brain; it's cased in solid iron."

As he strode out, Ganlon, slightly pale, turned to me and said in a low voice: "A twist in his head, sure. Money—money! I never saw an Irishman before who was so crazy about money. This mornin' I says to him, I says: 'Mike, you better get you some new shoes with some of the money you got last night.' He says, 'I can wear these I got for a month yet.' Lord knows I'm no dude but he dresses like a wharf hand. What's he do with his money? He ain't supportin' no aged mother, it's a cinch. You heard him say he was left on a doorstep when he was a baby."

I shook my head. Brennon was an enigma beyond my comprehension.

Chapter .4.
The Rise of the Iron Tiger

The rise of Iron Mike Brennon is now ring history and of all the vivid pages in the annals of this heart-stirring game, I hold that the story of this greatest of all iron men makes the most lurid, fantastic and pulse-quickening chapter of all.

Iron Mike Brennon! Look at him, as he was in the year of 19- when his exploits swept the country. Six feet one from his long narrow feet to the black tousled shock of his hair; one hundred and ninety pounds of steel-spring whalebone and iron muscle. With his terrible eyes glaring from under the heavy black brows, his thin blood-smeared lips writhing in snarl of battle fury—still in my memory, when I dream of the super-fighter, there rises the picture of Mike Brennon—a dream charged with bitterness. Mike Brennon, with his wonderful body and his terrible punch—and the instincts and style of a docks brawler.

Take a man with an incredible stamina; give him a punch that will fell an ox; take from him the ability to even remember one iota of science when in actual combat, and leave out of his make up the instinct of the natural fighter and you have Iron Mike Brennon. A man who would have been the greatest champion of all time, could he have learned a tenth of what I tried to teach him.

His first fight, after that memorable conversation at the breakfast table, was with Jack Maloney, at San Francisco. Jack Maloney—one hundred and ninety-five pounds of white hot fighting fury, with a right hand that was like a caulking mallet.

I had offers from various promoters, all anxious for the service of the man who had flattened the Italian wonder, Barota—from Chicago came an offer to meet Sailor Slade; from New York, a bid for Johnny Varella. But Mike wanted Maloney. I set the old ballyhoo to working, with the aid of Spike Ganlon and the various sportswriters who knew me as a friend. The papers were full of the deeds of Mike Brennon. They pointed out that he had over twenty knockouts to his credit, ignoring the fact that these victims were all unknown dubs with the exception of the last two. They glossed over the fact that he had been several times outpointed by second-raters, and twice beaten—once by Sailor Slade and once by Johnny Varella. They stressed the fact that Brennon had taken everything Barota could hand out, and angrily refuted the repeated charges made by the old-timers, that the k.o. was a fluke.

The stadium was packed when Mike Brennon met Jack Maloney. The crowd paid their money and they got the worth of it. In his corner before the bell, I was whispering a few instructions which I knew would be useless, when Mike cut in with a sort of fierce eagerness:

"What a sell out! What a purse! Look at that crowd! And if I can win tonight it'll mean more sellouts! Heavier purses! Oh, God, I've got to win!"

His eyes gleamed with ferocious avidity—the gong sounded— two giants crashed from their corners.

Maloney came in like the great slugger he was, body crouched to protect his solar plexus, chin tucked beneath his shoulder, hands high. Brennon, forgetting everything before the blast of the crowd and his own fighting fury, rushed like a longshoreman, head lifted, both hands clinched at his hips, straight up and wide open—as iron men have fought since time immemorial—with only one thought, that to get to the foe and crush him.

Maloney landed first, a terrific left hook to the body which brought the crowd to its feet roaring; a short right cut Brennon's lips and spattered him with blood and I heard a note of relief in the shouts of Maloney's manager. This bird was not going to be so hard after all! As for Maloney, like most sluggers when they find a man they can hit easily, he had gone fighting crazy. Left, right, left, right he battered Brennon about the ring without a return while the crowd went roaring wild. He was hitting so hard and fast that Brennon had no time to get set; the few swings he did try, swished harmlessly over the bobbing Maloney's head.

"He's slowin' down," muttered Ganlon to me, as the first round drew to a close. "The old iron man game! Maloney's punchin' hisself out!"

True, Jack's blows were coming, not weaker, but more slowly. No man could keep up the pace he was setting. Brennon seemed strong as ever and just before the gong he staggered Maloney with a sweeping left to the body—the first blow he had landed.

Back in his corner, Ganlon wiped the blood from Mike's battered face and grinned savagely.

"Joe Goddard had nothin' on you. I'm beginnin' to believe you'll actually beat him. You've took terrible punishment but you're fresher than he is. He'll come out strong for this round but each round he'll get weaker and give out quicker."

"I'll beat him," Mike answered grimly. "I can beat any man I can hit; and I can hit him occasionally."

The crowd thundered his acclaim as Jack Maloney rushed out for the second round. But he had sensed something they had not. He had hit this man with everything he had, and had failed to even floor him. Something wrong here! So he tore in like a wild man and again drove Brennon about the ring before a torrent of left and right hooks that sounded like the kicks of a mule and doubtless felt worse. Brennon was badly battered now, his eyes were almost closed, his lips pulped, his nose broken but he showed absolutely no sign of distress, until the latter part of the round when Maloney landed four times to the jaw with his maul-like right. Then Brennon's knees trembled momentarily, but he straightened and opened a cut on his foe's cheek bone with a glancing right.

Now at the gong, the crowd began to sense something. They had been shouting the praises of Maloney, and jeering Brennon for a pushover, but now they realized that Maloney had hit his man again and again with all his power, and yet Brennon's shoulders had not yet touched the canvas. The timbre of their shouts changed slightly. Fans began to inquire at the top of their voices if Maloney was losing his famed punch, or if Brennon was made of solid iron.

Ganlon, wiping Brennon's gory features and giving him the smelling salts to sniff, said swiftly: "His legs trembled as he went back to his corner; he looked back over his shoulder at you like he couldn't believe it, when he saw you walk to your corner straight up without a quiver. He knows he ain't lost his smack! He knows you're the first man that's ever stood up to him, wide open thata way. He knows you been through Hell and high water, the last two rounds, and still you ain't even saggin'. You got him buffaloed. Now get him!"

"I'll get him!" muttered Mike almost deliriously. "More fights—more money—"

The gong sounded and Jack Maloney came in like a whirlwind to redeem his slipping fame as a knocker-out. His blows were like a rain of sledgehammers—left-right—left-right! And before the mallet-like right which crashed again and again against his body and head, Mike Brennon reeled and went down.

The referee began counting. Maloney reeled back against the ropes, his breath coming in great gasps, his legs trembling— completely fought out, finely trained athlete though he was.

"He'll get up." said Ganlon calmly.

Brennon was half-crouching on his knees, supporting himself with one arm. He shook his head, looked up at the referee. He was dazed, not hurt. I saw his lips move, and though I could not hear what he said of course, I read the motion— "More fights—more money—"

At "Nine!" he bounded erect. Maloney's whole body sagged; he seemed on the point of collapse. The fact that Brennon was able to arise before the count after the beating he had taken, took more morale out of Maloney than any sort of a blow would have done. He lurched forward half-heartedly and Brennon, sensing his mental condition and physical weariness, tore in like a tiger. Left, right he missed, shaking off Maloney's weakening blows as if they had been slaps from a girl. At last he landed—a wide left hook to the head. Maloney tottered, a wild over hand right crashed under his cheek bone and he went to his knees. At "Nine" he staggered up, but another right, a sweeping haymaker that a blind man in good condition could have ducked, dropped him again. The referee hesitated, then beckoning to Maloney's seconds, lifted Brennon's right hand in token of victory.

As Maloney, aided by his handlers, reeled to his corner on buckling legs, I noted the ironical fact; the winner was a battered and gory wreck as to outward appearance, while the loser had only a single cut on his cheek bone. I thought of the old fights in which the iron men of another day had figured: how Joe Goddard, the old Barrier Champion had outfought the great Joe Choynski, and had finished each of their terrible battles a bloody travesty of a man— but winner. I thought of Tom Sharkey dropping Kid McCoy after a cruel battering—and Battling Nelson outlasting Gans—Young Corbett—Herrerra. And I sighed. What a champion Mike Brennon would make if he had any defense at all. But he, like all these other great iron men would eventually crack under the strain and fall, possibly before some second-rater. For of all the men who ever relied on their ruggedness to carry them through, Brennon was the wildest, the most wide open, the most erratic hitter.

As I sponged his cuts in the dressing room, I could not forbear to say: "You see how it is to meet a first-string hitter— you won't be able to answer the gong for a month."

"A month!" he mumbled through battered lips. "You'll sign me up with Johnny Varella for a bout in New York next week!"

Thus was born, figuratively speaking, Iron Mike Brennon. After his fight with Maloney, fans and scribes realized what he was—a fighter with a granite jaw—and as such his fame grew. He became a drawing card just as he had said—one of the greatest of his day. And his inordinate lust for money seemed to grow with his power as an attraction. He haggled over prices with promoters, held out for every cent he could get, but rather than pass a fight up, would always lower his price if he had to. His price, I say, because as a manager I was only a figure-head, for the first and only time in my life. Mike Brennon was the real power behind the curtain.

And he insisted on fighting at least once a month. In vain I argued with him—told him that he should take time to recover fully from one beating before going into another.

"This way," I said, "you'll crack three times as quick. Otherwise you might last for years."

"But why stretch it out?" he asked. "I'm in this game to make all the money I can, as quick as I can. If I can make the money in a few months, fighting every week, that I'd make in that many years, fighting every few months, what's the odds?"

"But consider the strain on you!" I cried.

"I'm not considering anything about myself," he answered roughly. "Get me a match."

The matches came readily. He fought them all—ferocious, rushing sluggers, clever, dancing boxers, crafty, dangerous fighters who combined the qualities of the slugger and boxer. When first- rate opponents were not forthcoming soon enough, he went out into the outlying districts and knocked over second-raters in the small fight clubs. As long as he was fighting and making money, no matter how much or how little, he was satisfied and it mattered not to him whether his opponent were a near champion or a setup dub. What he did with the money thus acquired I did not know. He never made any attempt to swindle me or any of his training staff; he always shot square with his just obligations. But beyond that he was a miser. He stayed at the training camps or at the cheapest hotels in spite of my protests; he bought cheap clothes, and allowed himself no luxuries whatever. I could not understand it, but I asked no questions.

At first, he won consistently. The luck of the iron men seemed to be with him, and his style of fighting was new to these modern boxers. His speed, his aggressiveness, his toughness, more than all the strange desperate intensity of his attack brought him many a victory. He was always dangerous because no matter how badly he was outpointed, he always carried T.N.T. in those wild sweeping haymakers, which though easy to avoid, yet meant destruction if they landed. Many a man sampled this fact on the very crest of victory. Some of his foes, after testing their knuckles on his adamantine skull, retired into their shell and refused to fight. Some punched themselves out on him and went down to defeat.

Two weeks after he fought Maloney, Brennon met Johnny Varella in New York. Mike carried into the ring with him the signs of his battle with Maloney, and before the ferocious appearance he presented, Varella showed his nervousness. He had outpointed this man before but it was easy to see that he was not sure of himself.

Still, he put up a great battle, and made Brennon look bad for eight rounds. Then in the ninth, getting panicky because of his failure to hurt the iron man, the Italian went into a wild frenzy of slugging and broke both his rather brittle hands on Mike's skull. He refused to come up for the tenth, and the referee awarded the fight to Brennon on a technical knockout—yet Mike had scarcely laid a glove on the speedy Italian!

Managers were wary about throwing their men in with Mike. He could make any of them look punchless and he was likely to beat anybody—just as likely to be beaten by the veriest dub. But there was always a crowd out to see him perform and packed houses meant heavy purses. More, the clever boys considered it a cinch to outpoint Brennon and each of the heavy hitters had a secret desire to be the man that should finally drop the iron man for the long count, so we found it easy to get matches.

As I say, Brennon was dangerous to any man in the early part of his career. Coupled with his abnormal endurance was a mental state—a sort of driving savage determination which dragged him off the canvas time and again. This was above and behind his natural fighting fury, and he had somehow acquired it between the time he had first retired and the time I next met him.

Following the Varella fight, he met and knocked out a second-rater whose name I forget, in New York, the next week, then he travelled to Chicago where he met Young Hansen. The powerful Norwegian gave him a terrible hammering but finding himself unable to even floor Brennon, he blew up in the thirteenth round and went all to pieces, going out in the next round from a volley of swings he was too weary and muddled to duck.

The next start was in Los Angeles where Barota outpointed Mike in a return engagement. Barota, taking no chances, boxed cleverly and won the decision with a serpent-like left jab and an occasional very wary right cross; I doubt if Mike landed two solid blows the whole fifteen rounds, but his fame was impaired not at all. His drawing power now rested solidly on his ability to absorb punishment and no mere decision rendered against him could detract from this fact. The average fan likes blood, action and courage. They saw plenty in the fights in which Mike Brennon figured, and if he sometimes provoked his admirers by his senseless style and lack of skill, he made up for it by an unflinching gameness that kept him walking stolidly into terrific punishment. Then, there was always the chance that he might land one of his crushers and waft his opponent into dreamland. At the time he was in his prime, there was a wealth of material in the heavyweight ranks. Not to be compared, perhaps, to the fighters of the Golden Era, that period when Jeffries ruled the greatest assortment of heavyweights the ring has ever seen at one time, Brennon's contemporaries were still good men. Fast, crafty boxers, hard hitters, tough sluggers—good game men all. And Brennon loomed among them as the one man none of them could knock out. That fact alone caused him to stand out; put him on an equal footing with men in every other way his superiors.

Following his second fight with Monk Barota, the public began to clamor for a match between my iron man and Yon Van Heeren, the Durable Dutchman, who up to that time had been considered the toughest heavyweight in the world, and who, like Brennon, had never been knocked out. Like Brennon, his only claim to fame was his durability, and this was proven in a most gorily ghastly manner, was inferior to that of Brennon. Matchmakers hesitated, the Commission went into doubtful session, but the public prevailed as it always does, and the match was made. The result aroused a wave of indignation among lovers of boxing science, and a renewal of activities among the foes of the game—the reformers. Even the hard-boiled fans who saw the slaughter were almost nauseated, but one thing is certain—none who saw that horrible affair will ever forget it.

Before they went into the ring, the principals made the referee promise that he would not stop the fight, no matter how badly either or both of them were punished. A rather unusual proceeding, but easily understandable considering that the fame of both rested on their ruggedness, and each considered it a soul- killing humiliation to be forced to quit while still able to stand.

A certain famous sportswriter, referring to this fight as a "brawl between two barroom thugs" said, "This unfortunate affair has set the game back for twenty years. No sensitive person, seeing this slaughter for his or her first fight, could ever be tempted to see another. A few more matches like this will turn public sentiment against the whole game, as people who do not know the game, are likely to judge the whole boxing fraternity by the two gorillas, who utterly devoid of science, turned the ring into the shambles."

Very true. It was a strange experience to Mike Brennon; most of the punishment was on the other side. Van Heeren, a hulking, burly fellow, six feet two and two hundred and ten pounds in weight, was a terrific hitter but lacked Brennon's dynamic speed. He did not fight quite as wide open as did Mike, but his slowness counterbalanced this advantage. Oh, he hit Mike; hit him hard, time and again. A blind man could hit Mike Brennon. He floored Mike twice, and cut him up, but really hurt him far less than either Maloney or Hansen had done. The fans thought Mike was undergoing terrible punishment before those wide clumsy wings, but those blows lacked the sharp explosive kick of a real hitter. When they landed solidly, they knocked Mike down or hurled him across the ring by their pure force, but there was no great punishment in them for a man like Brennon.

As for Mike, for the only time in his life he had found a man he could hit at will and he sailed in to make a quick job of it. But Van Heeren too was an iron man, and not to be knocked out without a hideous beating. And Mike delivered it. Those sweeping haymakers which had missed so many other men, crashed blindingly against the Dutchman's head, or sank agonizingly into his body. At the end of the first round, Van Heeren's face was a gory wreck. At the end of the second, his features had lost all human semblance, and his body was a battered mass of bruised and reddened flesh. Oh, Mike was taking punishment too—punishment that would have wrecked many men, but nothing like the beating Van Heeren was taking. They stood toe to toe, round after round, neither taking a back step, neither making any attempt at defense. They swung and they missed from pure clumsiness, or they landed and spattered each other's blood about the ring. It was evident from the first exchange that Brennon was the harder hitter and the tougher man. But it took time for even a puncher like him to wear the Dutchman down.

The third, fourth, fifth, sixth and seventh rounds were nightmares in which Mike kissed the canvas twice and Van Heeren went down four times. The end of the eighth found Van Heeren on his knees with the referee counting over him, while Mike held on to the ropes, dizzy and nearly punched out for the only time in his life. All over the stadium, women were fainting or being helped out by their escorts. Fans were shrieking for the referee to stop the fight.

At the beginning of the ninth, Mike launched another desperate attack and dropped the Dutchman with a volley of left and right swings to the head. Van Heeren lurched up, a hideous and inhuman sight and tried to fight back, but the sting had gone from his weakening punches. A blood and sweat-soaked glove crashed against his jaw and he dropped face down on the red stained canvas and lay motionless, four ribs broken and his features permanently ruined. He was still writhing blindly, drunkenly trying to rise when the referee tolled off the "Ten!" that marked his finish as a fighting man.

Mike Brennon stood above his victim, acknowledged king of all iron men. Aye—that fight finished Van Heeren and nearly finished boxing in that state, but it added to Brennon's fame, and his real pity for the broken Dutchman was mingled with a fierce exultation at the knowledge that no one now questioned his strange superiority of ruggedness. More packed houses—more money! To me his greed seemed the one flaw in his nature.

Chapter .5.
The Trail of the Iron Men

Mike Brennon, the world's greatest iron man! They wrote that after his name, the sportswriters.

Men who fought him called him the toughest piece of human architecture that ever lived, and the fans for whose edification he allowed himself regularly to be butchered proved their appreciation by packing the stadiums in which he appeared.

In the three years he fought under my management, he met them all; all except the champion of his division. He lost about as many as he won, but the only thing that could impair his drawing power was a knockout—and this seemed postponed indefinitely. He won more of his fights against punchers than against light tappers. Sluggers hurt him more, but he preferred to fight them. They battered him to a red ruin but they could not stop him, and many a hard hitter, after bouncing the iron man repeatedly off the canvas, only to see him rise, and after hitting him with everything except the ring posts, lost heart and fell before his aimless but merciless attack. He broke the knuckles and he broke the hearts of the men who tried to stop him.

The light hitters who knew that they could not dent him, took no chances and easily outboxed him. They jabbed him and cut him up, but did not hurt him. Barota outpointed him, and Tommy Feltz, Jackie Finnegan, Undelo Boriotta, Frankie Grogan, Johnny Thomas and Flash Sullivan, the clever light-heavy champion. But none of these men was able to put him on the canvas, even for an instant, and he was dangerous even to them, as Flash Sullivan found when one of Mike's wild swings dropped him for the count of nine in the last round of their bout.

With the hard hitters, he found the going rougher and he finished most of his bouts in a dazed condition, terribly battered—but still on his feet. Soldier Handler dropped him five times in four rounds, then got careless and stopped a right-hander that knocked him clean out of the ring and into fistic oblivion. Jose Gonzales, the great hitter from South America punched himself out on the Iron Tiger and went down and out more from pure weariness than from Brennon's swings.

Gunboat Sloan battered his way to a red decision over him, but was unable to stop him; and still believing that he could achieve the impossible, went in to trade punches with him, wide open, in a return engagement, and lasted less than a round, thereby proving again Brennon's assertion that he could flatten any man he could hit.

He finished Ricardo Diaz, the Spanish Giant, in a couple of rounds, and pounded down Snake Culberson in eleven, after his ruggedness had broken the Brown Phantom's heart. He won on a foul from Ace Brannigan and lost on a foul to Tom Flynn, on a low blow accidentally delivered, when with both eyes closed tight shut he could not see his man and did not know where his swings were going. He won a decision from Jacques Descampo when the flashy foreigner, after sampling the power of Mike's right, made a foot race out of their ten round fight and refused to lead all the way through.

He met Whitey Broad and Kid Allison in no decision bouts, and he fought a terrible fifteen round draw with Sailor Steve Costigan, a tough game man who, though never rated better than a second-class man, yet gave some first-raters terrific battles. He was almost as tough as Brennon and knew only a little more about the game, but Brennon always said that Costigan was the hardest hitter he met in his entire ring life.

The wonder was that Mike could stand up as long as he did, fighting so often. To you readers who are not versed in the game, who do not believe that flesh and blood can endure what Mike Brennon endured, I beg of you to look at the records of the ring's iron men. When they cracked, they cracked suddenly, but until that time, they fought often, and in each fight took punishment that would kill an ordinary man.

I point to your attention Tom Sharkey plunging round after round, headlong into the terrible piledrivers that were the fists of Jeffries; of that same Sharkey shooting over the ropes from the blows of Joe Choynsky, headfirst onto the concrete outside the ring—twice!—and yet finishing the fight a winner. I call your attention to Mike Boden, whose only blow was a roundhouse right, and who had no more defense than Brennon had, staying the limit with Choynsky, taking without wincing every blow of that really wonderful puncher—the puncher who knocked out Jack Johnson and once put Bob Fitzsimmons on the canvas—yet Boden was on his feet at the last gong. And consider Joe Grim taking the punches of that master of all punchers, Bob Fitzsimmons—was it fourteen or fifteen times that Fitzsimmons knocked him down? But Grim was still fighting back when the round ended. No; no man can understand the iron men of the ring. Theirs is a long, hard bloody trail with oftentimes nothing but poverty and a clouded mind at the end, but the red chapter their clan has written across the chronicles of the game will never be effaced.

And so Mike Brennon fought on, taking all his cruel punishment, hoarding his money, saying little—as much a mystery to me as ever. The sportswriters discovered his passion for money and raked him in their papers. They accused him of being miserly and refusing aid to his less fortunate fellows—of refusing to aid the battered tramps who occasionally will strike up a successful fighter for a handout. This was partly true. Brennon did occasionally give money to men who needed it badly, but rarely.

Then Brennon began to crack. Ganlon, his continual companion first sensed it. Crouching beside me behind Mike's corner, the night Brennon fought his no-decision bout with Kid Allison, Spike whispered to me out of the corner of his mouth.

"He's slippin', Steve! Look—he's slowin' down. And punches that once wouldn't have shook him, stop him in his tracks. It's the beginnin' of the end."

Brennon finished that fight in a blaze of glory for the rough and rushing Kid grew winded toward the last, and the iron man floored him twice in the last two minutes of the bout.

That night Spike spoke plainly to his friend.

"Mike, you're about through. It's time to step down and out. You're slippin', no use to deny it. It's just barely perceptible now—

but you're slower than you was and the punches jar you worse than they used to. You knew you couldn't last at this pace. I'm surprized you've lasted this long. I expected to see you punched cuckoo within a few months. You've lasted three years of terrible hard goin'. You've got plenty of money—or ought to have."

"I said I'd quit when I got knocked out." Mike said stubbornly. "I haven't taken the count yet."

"But man," cried Ganlon sharply, "when a man like you takes the count, it's somethin' terrible! It means he's a punch-drunk wreck! When the blows begin to hurt you, it means the shock of them is reaching the brain and hurtin' it. Remember Van Heeren, the Dutchman you finished! He's wanderin' around, doin' road work, says he's trainin' to fight Fitzsimmons, that's been dead for years. Clean batty! And so'll you be, too, if you don't stop."

A shadow crossed Mike's dark face at the mention of the Dutchman's name. The batterings he had taken had disfigured him, and given him a peculiarly sinister look, which however did not rob his face of that strange dominating quality.

"I'm good for a few more fights," he answered. "I need more money—"

"Money!" I exclaimed. "Always money! You must have half a million dollars, at least. You've saved every cent above expenses—at least I suppose you have. You never spend any. I'm beginning to believe what the sportswriters say—that you are a miser! Why risk your future for more money, when you have enough to set you up in business now?"

"Steve," said Ganlon suddenly, "I found out that cuckoo Van Heeren was around here yesterday."

"What of it?"

"Mike," said Ganlon almost accusingly, "give him a thousand dollars."

I gaped in astonishment.

"What if I did?" cried Brennon in one of his rare, inexplicable passions. "The fellow was broke—and he's in no condition to hold any kind of a job. I finished him in the ring— why shouldn't I help him a little? Whose business is it?"

"Nobody's," I answered. "But it only shows that you're not what I said—a miser. And it deepens the mystery about you. Won't you tell me why you feel that you must have more money?"

He made a quick impatient gesture.

"There's no need. There's no point to the question. You get the matches, I do the fighting, we split the money and that's all there is to it."

"But, Mike," I said as kindly as I could, "there is more to it. I like you. I feel your interest more at heart than just as a manager. You've made me more money than either of the champions I've managed, and if I didn't sincerely wish for your own good, I'd urge you to stay in the ring. Yes, you have a few fights left in you. You can take a few more beatings before you go under. You don't seem to have slipped much. But men like you crack quick and sudden and the first signs of slipping are danger signals.

"You're on the borderline. Quit now and you'll be alright. You can even get your features fixed up so you won't look quite so terrible—plastic face building is a wonderful art. Fight one more time, even, and you may spend the rest of your days in a padded cell."

"I'm still tougher than you think," he answered. "I don't feel the blows, even if you do say I flinch. I'm as good as I ever was, and I can still prove it. Anyway—the press has been raving for a match with Sailor Slade. Sign him on; it'll pack any stadium in the country. I've always ducked him since that first time I met him—you know, before you started managing me. He's the one man I've always figured might have a chance to knock me out. He's got everything, including my goat. He's tough and fast, can hit nearly as hard as Steve Costigan and is ten times as clever as Costigan.

"Get him for me. I'll beat him."

"If he beat you once, how do you figure to stop him now? You're no better than you were then—worse, if anything, and Slade has improved."

"When I met him before, I didn't have the incentive to win that I have now." he answered.

I nodded. What this incentive was, I did not know, but I had seen him rise again and again, from what looked like certain defeat—had seen him, writhing on the canvas, turn white, seen his eyes blaze with sudden terror, as he dragged his bruised and battered form upright, with a determination that overcame the flesh. Terror? Of losing! A terror that kept him going despite himself, when even his iron body was tottering on the verge of collapse, and when the old fighting frenzy had ceased to function in the numbed brain. What prompted this dread? I could no more fathom the reason than I could fathom his strange money-lust.

"You'll get me Slade." he was saying. "I'll beat him, or stay the limit. If I can beat him, my next fight ought to be the greatest sellout yet. It ought to pack the fans in solid. You'll sign me for four fights—with Sailor Slade, Young Hansen, Jack Slattery and Mike Costigan."

"Mike Costigan!" I exclaimed sharply. "Mike, you're out of your mind! It's suicide, I tell you! You've picked the four toughest battlers in the world!"

"Sign me up," he answered. "I know you can. Hansen will be easy. I beat him once and I can do it again. Slattery, I don't know. I want to fight him last. He looks like the greatest battler we've had since Dempsey's time. First I've got to hurdle Slade, though. And after him, I'll take on Costigan. He's the least scientific of the four, though the hardest hitter. If I'm slipping like you say, I want to get him before I've gone too far along the line."

I was sweating profusely and Ganlon's eyes were gleaming. "It's suicide, I tell you," I cried. "If you've got to fight, pass these sluggers up and take on a few setups. Even if Slade don't knock you out, he'll soften you up so that Costigan will punch you right into the nut-house. That fellow's a murderer! They call him Iron Mike, too. He's nearly as tough as you are and he can hit as hard—almost. He's a better man than his brother Steve, who held you to a draw when you were better than you are now."

"I'll pack them in," he answered heedlessly. "Slade's nearly the drawing card I am, and as for Costigan—the fans always turn out to see two iron men matched. There's no use talking; you do as I say."

As usual, there was no answer to be made.

Chapter .6.
"For a $100,000 Purse And—"

It was a few nights before the date of the Brennon-Slade match. I had wandered into Mike's room at the training quarters, and my eye chanced to fall on a partially completed letter on his writing table. Idly and without any intention of violating any rule of manners, my eyes wandered down the written page, noting that it was addressed to a girl named Marjory Walshire, at a very fashionable girls' school in New York state.

I had never known Mike to go with any girl at all. I knew he sometimes received letters addressed in a feminine hand, but I had never asked him, and he had never volunteered any information about it. I wondered what a girl in a society school like that would be doing writing to a prizefighter. I noted that a letter from this girl lay beside the one Mike had been writing. I admit it was not a sporting thing to do, but I took up the partially completed letter and glanced idly over it. A few phrases caught my eye and the next moment I was reading the letter with a fierce intensity, all scruples forgotten. Having finished it, I took up the other—the letter the girl had written Mike—and ruthlessly tore it open.

I had scarcely completed reading it when Mike entered, with Spike Ganlon. His eyes blazed with fury when he saw the letter in my hand, his mighty fists clenched but before he could say a word, I launched an offensive of my own. For one of the few times in my whole life, I was wild with anger.

"You born fool," I snarled. "So this is why you've been forcing me to get you matches that I knew were ruining you! This is why you've stinted yourself at every turn! This is why you're a battered wreck, ready for the junk heap today! And why you insist on going on, like a fool, until your brain crumbles! Maybe it seems noble to you, but as far as I'm concerned, you're a born fool!"

"What do you mean by getting into my private correspondence?" his voice was husky with fury.

I sneered. "I'm not going to enter into a discussion of manner and etiquette. You can beat me up afterwards, if you want to, but just now I'm going to have my say!

"You've been keeping some frail in a ritzy finishing school back East. Finishing school! It's nearly finished you! What kind of a dame is she, to let you go through Hell for her, that way? I'd like for her to see you now, with your battered map! While she's been lolling at her ease in the most expensive school she could find, you've been flattening out the resin with your shoulders and soaking it down with your blood! Why she—"

"Shut up!" Brennon roared, white and shaking. "Shut up! Or before God, I'll kill you!"

He leaned back against the table, trembling, gripping the table edge so hard that his knuckles whitened—fighting for control. At last he spoke more calmly.

"Yes, that's the incentive that's kept me going—that will keep me going to the end. That girl is—the only girl—I ever loved. The only thing I ever had to love.

"Listen, do you know how lonely a kid is when he has absolutely nobody in the world to love? The priests in Saint Joseph's home were kind to me, but there were too many children there for any one to get any real affection. I got the beginnings of a good education—that's all.

"Out in the world it was worse. I hobo'd around, working, fighting, starving. I fought for everything I ever got. I have a better education than most, you say. I worked my way through high school, and read all the books, in my spare time, that I could beg, steal or borrow. Many a time I went hungry to buy a book.

"I drifted into the ring gradually—from fighting in carnivals and the athletic shows small town fight clubs put on. You know—I never got anywhere. I told you the night I whipped Battling Mulcahy that I was through. I started drifting again. Then in a little one-horse town out on the Arizona desert, I met Marjory Walshire.

"Poverty? She knew poverty! Supporting herself by working her fingers to the bone in a cafe. Good blood in her too—just as there is in me, somewhere. She should have been born to the satins and velvet—instead she was born to the greasy dishes and dirty tables of a second-class cafe.

"I loved her, and she loved me. She told me her dreams, dreams that she never believed would come true—of education— culture— nice clothes—refined companions—everything that any girl wants.

"I swore I'd take her out of the cafe, at least. But where was I to turn? There was nothing I could do; I could only get a job—and introduce her to the household drudgery of a working man's wife. I remembered what you had told me. I looked you up and went back into the ring. You know what happened.

"As soon as I could, I sent her to school. I've been sending her money enough to live in as much style as any girl there, and I've managed to save some too, so when she gets out of school, and when I have to quit the game, we can be married and start in some kind of business—some business that won't mean drudgery and poverty for us.

"Poverty! It didn't strike home to me what a terrible thing it is, until I saw Marjory working in that infernal cafe. But poverty is the cause of more crimes and cruelty, more hatred and suffering than anything else. Poverty kept me from having a home and people like other kids. You know how it is in the slums of the cities—parents toiling for a living, babies coming too fast; they can't support all of them. Mine left me on the doorstep of Saint Joseph's with a note: "He's honest born. We love him but we can't keep him. Call him Michael Brennon and be kind to him."

"Aye—poverty! And poverty can be as cruel in a small town as in a city. There was Marjory, who'd never been out of the town in which she was born—with her soul pinched and starved for the beautiful and good things of life, and her little white hands already reddened and calloused from overwork.

"It's thinking of her, that's kept me going. It's the thought of her that's kept on my feet when the whole world was red and blind and the fists of my opponent were like hammers beating on my shattering brain—that's dragged me off the canvas when the body of me was without feeling and my arms hung like lead to my shoulders. And it's the love of her that's sent me crashing through the cruel blows, blind and bloody, to strike down the man I could no longer see.

"And as long as the thought of her waiting for me at the end of the long trail upholds me, there's no man on earth can make me take the count!"

His voice crashed through the room like a clarion peal of victory, that somehow thrilled me to the bone. But my old doubts returned.

"But how can she love you so much," I exclaimed, "when she's willing for you to go through all this for her?"

"What does she know of fighting? She never saw a fight in her life, and besides me, she never saw a fighter. Before I sent her away—or rather before I went away to meet you, I made her promise she'd never see a fight I figured in, or any other fight. I made her promise she'd never listen to an account of my fights over the radio, never go to a movie that showed them, or even read about them in the papers! Oh, I knew what I was in for—and she's kept her word. She's never opened a newspaper that carried an account of my battles.

"I made her believe that boxing was more or less a dancing, tapping affair; she'd heard of Corbett, Tunney, those clever fellows who could go through a twenty-round battle without a mark, and she vaguely supposed I was like them. She hasn't seen me for four years—not since I left the town in which she worked. I sent her the money to go to New York on, and arranged things with the school by letter. I've put her off when she's asked to come to see me, or for me to come to see her. When she does see my banged-up face it'll be a terrible shock, but I was never very handsome anyhow—"

"Do you mean to tell me," I broke in, "that she'll never tune in on one of your fights, or even read an account of them, when the papers are full of how you look after a fight, how much punishment you've taken, and all that?"

"Sure, I do. Anyway, if she should happen on to my picture in the papers I doubt if she'd recognize it—what with my disfigurations and the faults of these newspaper pictures. And another thing—she don't know me by my real name. After I quit the game the first time, everywhere I went, some two-by-four promoter that I'd fought for was writing me, or coming to see me, to get me to fight for him again. When I blew into this town, I was going under the name of Mike Flynn—trying to duck these fellows. The first time I saw Marjory, I began to dally with going back into the ring, and I never told her any different. The money I've sent her has been in cashier's checks. To her, I'm simply Mike Flynn—a name she never sees in the papers, in case she does sneak a look."

"But her letters are addressed to Mike Brennon—" I began.

"No—you didn't notice closely. They are addressed to Michael Flynn, care of Mike Brennon, this camp. She don't know Mike Flynn and Mike Brennon are the same—she thinks Brennon is merely a friend of mine and owner of the training camps.

"No—she's been my only guiding star and will be as long as I live. It's for her I've been stinting myself, acting the part of the miser—refusing to hand out money to every fellow that came along, Steve. Van Heeren—that's different. I'm responsible, largely for his condition. I had to help him.

"These four fights now, one of them may be my last. Maybe I'm slipping. But I'll get by Slade and I may get by Costigan. I've got money, yes. But I want more. I intend that Marjory shall never want again for long as she lives. I'm to get $100,000 for this bout with Slade. My third purse of that size, as you know. I've been lucky. Since I knocked out Barota I've gotten heavy purses—have made more than many champions. Luck, good management, thanks to you, and my own attraction. Don't mention quitting to me until I'm counted out, and don't mention this matter of my girl, to anyone— not even to me, unless I bring the subject up myself."

Chapter .7.
The Border Line

I haven't the heart to tell of the Brennon-Slade fight, round by round. Mike had slipped even more than we had thought. The steel spring legs which had carried him through so many whirlwind battles unweakened, had slowed down. They trembled and faltered. His sweeping haymakers crashed over with their old power, but they did not continually wing through the air without a cessation as of old. After the first few rounds he slowed up badly. He hit less often. Blows that should not have jarred him, staggered and seemed to daze him. The squat Sailor with his abnormally long arms and broad shoulders sensed this weakness and wild with the thought of scoring a knockout, threw caution to the winds and went to kill or be killed. He hammered the reeling slugger about the ring, broken and bleeding before a perfect red torrent of smashing blows, each of which carried the kick of a mule. He floored Brennon again and again—how many times I never dared try to remember.

But Mike Brennon was still Iron Mike, the man with the granite jaw. Blind, bloody and reeling he carried on. Again and again he rose, barely beating the final count. Four times in as many rounds the gong saved him, and we had to carry him back to the corner, but we dared not throw in the sponge and the referee dared not stop the slaughter.

Toward the last Slade began to weaken. With Brennon helpless before him, he could not keep him down, and his morale began to go to pieces, as many a man had done. More, he had been fighting more or less wide open, and the body blows Mike had landed from time to time were sapping even the Sailor's iron strength. All these factors, couple with Slade's terrific exertions eventually caused him to blow up. And blow up at last he did, when he had punched himself out.

But the fight went fourteen hideous rounds before Slade went to pieces and the iron tiger whom he had punched into a red smear tore him to shreds. Somehow Mike found his foe in the red mist that surrounded him, and blindly blasted him into unconsciousness.

Brennon collapsed in his corner after Slade was counted out, and both men were carried senseless from the ring; and the punishment Mike took that night nauseates me and takes the stiffening from my knees today when I think of it.

I sat by his side that night while he lay in a semi-conscious state, occasionally muttering brokenly as his bruised brain conjured up red visions. He lay, both eyes closed fast, his oft-broken nose a crushed ruin, cut and gashed all about the head and face, now and then stirring uneasily as the pain of two broken ribs stabbed him.

Now for the first time he spoke the name of the girl he loved, whimpering over and over. "Marjory! Marjory!"—groping out his hands like a lost child. Again he fought over his fearful battles and his mighty fists clenched until the knuckles showed white, and low bestial snarls tore through his battered lips.

Once in his delirium he muttered a sportswriter's parody of Chesterton's lines, which had once taken his fancy:

"I call the muster of iron men
From ship and ghetto and Barbary den,
To break, and be broken God knows when
And only God knows why."

Then raising himself painfully on one elbow, his burning unseeing eyes gleaming like slits of flame between the battered lids, he spoke in a low voice as if answering and listening to the murmur of ghosts:

"Joe Grim! Battling Nelson! Mike Boden! Joe Goddard! Iron Mike Brennon."

I sat listening and my flesh crawled with a sort of ghostly horror. I cannot impart to you the uncanniness of hearing the muster of those iron men of days gone by, muttered in the stillness of night through the pulped and delirious lips of the grimmest of them all.

At last he fell silent and seemed to fall into a natural slumber. I rose stealthily and noiselessly left the room. And as I went into the other room, two figures entered. One was Spike Ganlon, his savage eyes blazing with a kind of fierce triumph. The other was a girl—the darling of high society, she seemed, with her costly garments and air of culture, but she was perturbed now and her eyes and actions showed it. She exhibited an elemental anxiety such as no pampered and sophisticated debutante would have done. Four years of culture and polish, but now the real woman showed through the veneer. For even before Ganlon spoke, I knew this girl was Marjory Walshire.

"Oh, where is he—where is Mike?" she cried, a kind of desperation in her tone. "Is he badly hurt? You've got to let me see him!"

"He's asleep now," I said shortly, and then added in my cruel bitterness, "leave him alone. You've done enough to him already. He wouldn't want you to see him like he is now."

She cringed as from a blow, but with the thought of all the agony Mike had gone through on her account I could not find it in my heart to pity her. For I still believed in my inmost soul that she had known all the time and was merely callous.

"Oh, let me just look in the door!" she begged twining her white fingers together—and I thought how often Mike's hands had been bathed in blood so that those white fingers should remain white and unstained by work—"I won't awake him! Oh, you've *got* to let me see him!"

I hesitated, and her eyes flamed like a cat's in the night; her whole body tensed. Now she was the primal woman.

"You'll let me see him or I'll kill you!" she cried sharply, and before I could stop her, she rushed past me and opened the door. She stopped short on the threshold. Mike muttered restlessly in his sleep and turned his blind face toward the sound of the door opening, but he did not waken. As her eyes fell on that frightfully disfigured face, I saw her sway drunkenly as though from a death blow. Her hands went to her temples and a low whimper like an animal in pain escaped her. Then, her face corpse-white and her eyes set in a deathly stare, she stole to the bedside. A moment she hung above the battered form on the bed and then with a heart-rending sob she sank to her knees, cradling that bruised head in her arms, weeping with great shaking silent gasps that seemed tearing her heart out, while her tears fell in a burning rain on her lover's face.

Mike murmured, but still he did not waken and at last I drew her gently away and led her into the next room, closing the door behind us. She made no resistance, walking like one asleep or in a trance.

But out of hearing of the sleeping man, she burst into a torrent of weeping that did her good.

"I didn't know!" she kept sobbing over and over. "I didn't know! I didn't know that fighting was like that! I obeyed him—he told me never to go to a fight or listen to one over the radio, and never to read about one, and I didn't. Sometimes I heard men talking about Iron Mike Brennon but I didn't know it was my Mike! I didn't know—until I got Mr. Ganlon's letter.

"Why, how could I know—" she suddenly thrust at me a crumpled letter. "This is one of the few letters in which he even mentioned his fights. I've kept them all—"

The date was nearly four years ago. I read an extract:

"It looks like I'm getting into the real money now, Marjory darling. Last night I stopped Jack Maloney, a foremost contender, in three rounds. He scarcely laid a glove on me, and I came out of the bout without a scratch. Don't worry about me; this game is a cinch. None of them can hit me."

I laughed bitterly, remembering the wreck Maloney had made of Mike's features before he went out.

"I've been doing you an injustice," I said shortly to hide my emotions. "I've been hating you because I thought you were merely a heartless woman—I see now that you're the true blue. I didn't think a man could keep a girl in such ignorance but I guess it's true. Now that you're here, maybe you can persuade Mike to give up the game—none of the rest of us can do anything with him."

"Surely he can't think of fighting again, if he lives?" she cried.

I laughed. "He isn't going to die. He'll be laid up awhile but I don't think he'll have any lasting injury if he don't fight again. It's up to you to persuade him. Now, I'll take you to a hotel—"

"I'm going to stay right here close to Mike," she answered passionately. "I'm never going to let him out of my sight again. Oh, I could kill myself when I think of the easy life I've been leading, the luxury and all—while Mike was going through this agony, all for me. Tomorrow I'm going to marry him and take him away."

There was a spare room in the training quarters. After she was safely ensconced there, I turned to Spike.

"I suppose you're responsible for this," I said angrily. "You might have waited until Mike was out of bed. That was a terrible shock to her."

"I intended it should be," he snarled. "I wrote and told her did she know her boy Mike Flynn that was supportin' her in such style was really Iron Mike Brennon which was swiftly bein' punched into the booby-hatch? I give her some graphic account of his battles, and I told her what I thought of a dame that would let a boy go through such for her.

"I wrote her in time for her to get here for the fight—I wanted her to see the bout herself. But she missed a train, she says. I believe she's lyin'."

I gave an exclamation of protest.

"You're buffaloed," he flamed. "She's made a monkey outa you with her sob stuff. I didn't fall for that! She don't care! All she wants outa Mike is his money."

"I don't believe that—now. If you say she was acting, you're a fool."

"Who cares what you believe—or say? Anyway, now, if she's got a spark uh real womanhood in her, she'll make Mike quit the ring. I wanted her to see him in all his glory—the marks of his money-makin'."

"I imagine," I said slowly, "I've got an idea that Mike will kill you when he finds out about this."

"Let him," Spike snarled shortly. "Mike Costigan will kill him—if they fight. I know. I've seen these iron men crack before. I was in Tom Berg's corner the night Jose Gonzales knocked him out. It was Berg's first k.o.—and I helped carry his corpse out of the ring.

He died while the referee was countin' him out. Some men you got to kill to stop—Mike Brennon's one of 'em. If he lives, he's got to quit the game—*Now.*"

Morning found the battered iron man conscious and clear of mind, his wonderful recuperative powers already asserting themselves. I brought Marjory to his bedside, and before he could recover from his astonishment enough to speak, I left them alone.

Later she came to me, her eyes red with weeping.

"I've argued and begged," she cried desperately. "And he still says he's going to fight again. Oh, what can I do?

All of us went to Mike's room and surrounded his bedside.

"Mike," I said caustically, "you're a fool. This punching's gone to your head worse than I thought. You can't mean you'll fight again!"

"I've never been knocked out," he answered. "Of course, Slade beat me up badly but no worse than I thought he would. I'm good for some more hundred thousand dollars purses yet."

Marjory cried out as if he had stabbed her.

"Mike, for heaven's sake, for *my* sake—! We have more money now than we'll ever use! Do you think I care for money? If I'd known what you were going through with, do you think I'd have stayed where I was a minute? I'd have rather gone in rags and worked my fingers to the bone in the lowest kind of work imaginable. You haven't been fair to me, Mike."

His face lighted with one of his rare smiles—a wonderful smile in spite of the copious bridge work it revealed. He reached out a hand amazingly gentle considering its strength and touched the girl's soft hand and the sleeve above it.

"White little hands," he murmured, "soft as God meant them to be, and clad in silks too, as is right and proper. Why, just looking at you now and thinking that you've been living as you should live, repays me a thousand times for all I've gone through. And what have I gone through? A few beatings! And think of the old-timers who took worse beatings and got little or nothing. But we're wealthy."

"And there's no reason for your crucifying yourself—and me—any longer."

He shook his head with that strange abnormal stubbornness which was the worst defect in his character.

"I said I'd never quit till I was counted out of the game. Then I won't be a drawing card any longer and there'll be no reason for me staying in it. But as long as I can draw down a hundred thousand dollars a fight, I'd be a fool to quit.

"Then I hope you'll be counted out in your next fight!" the girl cried in passionate intensity.

Ganlon laughed like a jackal snarling, all the bitterness engendered by his friendship and worry for Mike sounding in his voice.

"Yes! He'll be counted out when he meets Iron Mike Costigan! And the referee that counts him out will be the Man with the Hood! And after that they won't be no worryin' about a hundred thousand dollars purse, or beatin's or anything! They'll just be another slugger knockin' at the Golden Gates!"

Marjory blanched and wrung her hands, and Brennon scowled.

"Spike, I'm overlooking the fact that you wrote that letter to Marjory, after the way she begged for you, but you needn't go frightening her. What's the matter with you and Steve? You act like I was ready for the cleaners right now."

"You are," I rapped out, bluntly. "If you take one more beating, it'll either kill you or make an imbecile out of you."

"Nonsense," he answered imperturbably. "I'm tougher than even you fellows think. A hundred thousand dollars!" his eyes gleamed with the old light. "The packed stadium! The crowd roaring! And Iron Mike Brennon taking everything they can hand out, and finishing on his feet! No! No! I'll quit when I'm counted out. Not before."

"Mike!" the girl cried piercingly. "If you fight again, I'll swear I'll give you back your ring and go away! I'll never see you again."

His eyes sought hers and held them. His gaze beat her down and her head sank on her breast from the intensity of his magnetic eyes. I never saw the human—except one—who could stand the stare of Mike Brennon's eyes.

"Marjory," his deep powerful voice vibrated with confidence, "you're bluffing."

"No—no!" she cried desperately. "I mean it."

"You don't! You're mine! You're just trying to force me into doing what you want! If you go away, you'll come back. But you won't go away! You won't desert me no matter what I do! You're mine and you always will be! You don't mean what you're saying—you couldn't, after all I've endured."

"No, no," she whimpered weakly, hiding her tear-blinded face in her hands. "I don't mean it. There's no use trying to bluff you."

"No use in the world," he answered tenderly stroking her bowed head. I moved restlessly. A failure in the ring, perhaps, but Mike Brennon had a power over those with whom he came in contact outside, a power that none seemed able to overcome. There was something almost brutal in the way he had beaten down the girl's weak pretense—though he himself did not realize it.

"Mike!" snarled Spike Ganlon, speaking harshly and bitterly to hide his emotion; for a second the hard-faced middleweight with his hard-lived life and two hundred savage ring battles behind him, dominated the scene:

"Mike, you're crazy! Here you've got everything a man could want—things that lots uh men work their whole lives out for and never get! You got money—a fine girl—fame—and you're still young. You're right on the borderline, slippin' on the other side, fistically speakin'. You can't win another fight. Even a second-rater'd knock you stiff. And this Costigan ain't no second-rater! He's as tough as you ever was, and as hard a hitter. He shoots his punches straight, and he's never been floored. He's whipped men that's outpointed you.

"If I thought he'd flatten you in a punch or two, I'd say, go in once more. But he won't. He can't. He'll knock you out, but it'll be after a long hard batterin' that'll ruin you for life. You'll keep gettin' up after your brain's pounded numb. You'll die or you'll spend your life in a cuckoo house. And what good will your money do then? And what about Marjory here—you want to kill her?"

Mike took his time about replying, and again his strange influence was felt like a cloud over the group.

"Costigan's overrated." he answered. "I'll show the dub up. He never saw the day he could take as much as I can, right now. As for hitting, if I can hit him, I'll knock him out. And I can hit him."

Spike let fall his hands in a sort of helpless manner and turned away with one parting shot: "Yes, you can hit him; but you can't keep him down, and what will he be doin' to you?"

Later he said to the girl and me: "No use arguin' with Mike. It's more than money, now. He thinks it's the kale, but it ain't. The game's in his blood. And again he's jealous of Mike Costigan. He don't realize it, but he is. Remember how Van Heeren fought? These iron men is terrible proud of their toughness and terrible jealous of each other. Mike thinks he can take more than Costigan and hit harder and he's goin' to try to prove it, in spite of all we can do. And all we can do, is humor him along, help him train, and hope Costigan flattens him with the first punch, which ain't possible."

"Doesn't Mike have a chance to win?" Marjory asked tremulously.

"A bird like Mike always has a chance to win—but always, it's just a chance. And win or lose, ten rounds with Costigan means Mike Brennon's finish. Each is too tough for the other to finish quick. Whichever way it goes, it'll be a long hard fight, with both terribly battered. It don't matter whether Brennon wins or loses, as to that. He'll end that fight punched nutty, or dead. It may finish Costigan too, but it'll sure finish Brennon. Costigan's younger; he ain't been fighting as long as Mike has, and he ain't met the men Mike's met—ain't took the punishment. At his best, Brennon would likely have wore him down and knocked him out like he did Van Heeren. But Mike's slippin' and Costigan ain't begun to crack. He's at his prime—which in a iron man is the same as sayin' that you couldn't hurt him with a piledriver."

Chapter .8.
The Fall of a King

Mike Brennon, always a conscientious worker in his training, trained for the Costigan battle as he had never trained before. Which meant, mainly that he endured just much more punishment from his sparring partners, until I called a halt and discharged all of them. I realized that so far back had Mike slipped, that even the blows he received in sparring would take just that much away from his endurance and ability to absorb punishment. The last few weeks I had him punch the light bag for speed, and do a great deal of road work in a vain effort to recover some of the former steel spring quality of his weakening legs. But I knew it was vain. It was not a matter of conditioning with Mike—his trouble lay behind him, in the thousands of cruel blows that his frame had absorbed. A clever boxer may get out of condition, lose a number of fights, get knocked out, and still train up and come back; when an iron man slips he is through and there is no comeback.

In the four months which preceded Mike's fight with Costigan, an air of gloom surrounded the camp which affected all but Brennon himself. The girl, after days of passionate pleading, threatening, weeping and cajoling, gave it up and sank into a sort of apathy—the same helpless resignation which has been womankind's last refuge down all the ages. Mike was as impervious to pleading as he was to punishment in the ring. To all her pleas and tears he had one answer: that he was better than we thought, that he was still too tough to be hurt, that we underrated him and overrated his opponent, and that as long as he was a drawing card he would be a fool and a coward to step out of the game.

That he was being bitterly cruel to the girl who loved him, never occurred to Mike and we could not make him see it. He laughed at her fears and spent hours in pointing out elaborately why he was in no danger—weaving sophistry that none believed but himself. He could not realize his own stubbornness but was rather provoked at what he called our perverseness—insisting that he quit the game when he was practically at his prime—as he said. He scoffed at the results of his fight with Slade—hadn't the Sailor suffered almost as much as had he? As for that fight showing that he had slipped—far from it! It only proved what he had said—that Slade was the best man in the ring, barring only Mike Brennon! As for Costigan—forget him! A crude slugger, Brennon's own counterpart, but slower and less rugged. A few rounds of ferocious slugging and the upstart would crumple and go down and out. Who was this newcomer in the ranks of the iron men to oppose the greatest of them all?

This may seem monstrously and offensively conceited, but to hear Mike Brennon talk in that cool self-confident way of his, was not offensive or blatant. Mike was aware of his own fistic faults. He frankly admitted that any second-rater who could avoid his blows could outpoint him but—! He sincerely believed that he was superior in ruggedness to any man who ever lived, and that he could beat any man whom he could hit. Nor did he believe that any man could hit hard enough to knock him out. Deep in his heart, I doubt if Mike Brennon really believed he would ever be knocked out.

And so he prepared for his battle. One thing he insisted on: that Marjory should not see the fight.

"It would unnerve me to know that you were watching. I'd know that you'd think I was being terribly hurt. I'll be cut up a good deal, as usual, likely as not, and I'll cut the other fellow up worse. We'll be bloody and battered, and while I won't be feeling the blows, you'll think I'm being killed."

"But I want to see it," protested Marjory, "and I'm going to—"

"You're not," said Mike grimly, "for the simple reason that if you insist, I'll lock you into your room before the fight starts. I'm not going to go into that fight knowing that you're watching me. Oh, I know I'll win, but I also know that this fellow Costigan will give me a tough tussle. And I don't want you there. If it was a light-hitting boxer, it would be different. But you're too gentle and soft-hearted to stand the sight of blood and punishment and I don't want you there."

"Alright," she sighed and I pitied her from the depths of my heart. She was thinking, just as I was, of the battered wreck that would probably be carried out of the ring at the conclusion of the fight.

"Mike!" she cried out desperately, "For the last time, I beg you, don't do this! Don't go through with this insane thing!"

"No use to start all that," he answered calmly. "Think Marjory! My fourth one-hundred-thousand dollars purse! That's a record that few champions have set! $100,000 with Flash Sullivan—and with Jose Gonzales—and Sailor Slade—now with Mike Costigan! A sellout! Thousands of tickets already sold in advance! No, no! Don't ask me! I've got to go on, now, anyhow. And I'm a cinch to win."

This confidence he carried with him into the ring. As if it were yesterday I visualize the scene; the ring bathed in the white glow of the lights above it, Costigan scowling in his corner, Brennon climbing through the ropes; while the great crowd that filled the huge outside bowl, swept away into darkness on each side. A circle of white faces looked up from the nearest ringside seats. Further out only a twinkling army of glowing cigarette ends evidenced the multitude, though the impression was given of a great shadowy throng. This throng was breathlessly silent while the announcer was talking—only a vast rippling undertone of whispers and rustlings came from the soft darkness.

"Iron Mike Brennon, in this corner, 190 pounds; in this corner, Iron Mike Costigan, 195. These boys have come here to decide the question once and for all as to which is the tougher man—"

Mike sat in his corner his head bowed, a contrast to the nervous, feline-like picture he had offered in his dressing room, when he paced the floor, afire with a white-hot fighting fury, trembling to get at his opponent. I wondered if he was still seeing the tear-stained face of Marjory, and still her sobs as she kissed him in the dressing room before he came into the ring.

The men were called to the center of the ring for instructions. Costigan came with alacrity. Brennon, to my surprize, seemed apathetic. He walked with dragging feet and slow movements. However, in front of his foe, he came awake with fierce energy and I doubt if the two rivals heeded what the referee was saying, so savagely intent upon each other they were. Iron Mike Costigan was dark, also, with tousled black hair and heavy brows. Five feet eleven inches in height and heavier than Brennon, he lacked something of Brennon's fierce ranginess of appearance, but he made up for that in power. He gave the impression of oak and iron massiveness, with his mighty arms and shoulders and his barrel chest. The eyes of the two men burned into each other with savage intensity—volcanic blue for Costigan; steel grey for Brennon. Their sun-browned faces were set in unconscious snarls that writhed their thin lines into an appearance of black hatred, but this was involuntary. Neither was aware of the fact that he was scowling; to each of them, the other was merely a symbol of his own fighting fury, a rival to his own peculiar vanity and though they were ready to tear each other to pieces, they felt no real hatred toward one another.

But as they stood facing each other, Brennon's stare of concentrated cold ferocity waved and fell momentarily before Costigan's savage blue eyes. I realized that this was the first time a man had looked Mike down and I thought of Corbett staring down Sullivan—of McGovern's eyes falling before the glare of Young Corbett.

Then the men were back in their corners again and the seconds and handlers were climbing through the ropes.

"Remember!" I hissed as a parting word to Mike, "I throw the sponge in if the going gets too rough."

He did not reply. He seemed to have sunk into that strange apathy again. The gong sounded. Costigan hurtled from his corner, a compact bulk of fighting fury, vibrant with energy. Brennon came out more slowly.

At my side Ganlon hissed: "What's the matter with Mike? He acts like he was drunk!"

The two Iron Mikes had met in the center of the ring. Costigan might have been slightly awed by the fame of the man he faced; at any rate, he did not tear in as he usually did. Brennon walked toward his foe, but his legs dragged and he moved with an effort.

Then Costigan suddenly launched an attack and shot a straight left to Brennon's face. As if the blow had suddenly aroused him to his full tigerish fury, Mike went into terrific action. *Crash! Crash!* The old sweeping haymakers began to thunder with all their ancient power and speed. Costigan had, of course, no defense. A sweeping left crashed under his heart with a sound like a caulking maul striking a ship's side; a blasting right that whistled as it shot through the air cannonballed against his jaw. Iron Mike Costigan went down as though struck by a thunderbolt.

Then even as the crowd rose, thundering, even as the referee sprang forward to count over him, Costigan reeled to his feet again. An iron man never stays on the canvas a second if he can help it. But I was watching Brennon. It seemed as though that sudden burst of action had taken all the strength out of him. He sagged against the ropes, limp, cloudy-eyed. Now sensing that his foe was again on his feet, his fighting instinct dragged him forward with halting and uncertain motions, like a man drunk or walking in his sleep.

Costigan, still dizzy from that terrific knock down, was conscious of only one thought—get to his foe and smash him! The old instinct of the iron man—walk into punishment and keep hitting till somebody fell! Now he crashed through Brennon's groping arms and shot a right hook to the chin. Brennon swayed and fell, just as a drunken man falls when a prop against which he has been leaning has been removed.

Over his motionless form the referee was counting— "Eight— Nine—*Ten!*" And the ring career of Iron Mike Brennon was at an end. A silence reigned, as if the throng were stunned and Mike Costigan, new king of all iron men, leaned dazedly against the ropes with parted lips and staring eyes, unable to believe his own senses. *Mike Brennon had been knocked out!*

About the ring the typewriters of the reporters were ticking out the fall of a king: "Evidently Mike Brennon's famous iron jaw has at last turned to crockery. Tonight Mike Costigan, his nearest rival in the way of ruggedness, stopped him in less than a round, after being floored himself, for the first time in his life. The only miracle is that Brennon had lasted as long as he has, considering the terrific punishment to which he has been subjected for the last four years. Any jaw will lose its hardness under such punching and—"

We carried Mike to his dressing room, still senseless. Ganlon was muttering under his breath and as soon as we had Mike safely ensconced on a cot, with a physician looking to him, the middleweight vanished. Marjory had been waiting for us, and now she said nothing, standing close by the cot where her lover lay, with white lips and clasped hands.

At last Mike opened his eyes and looked about him. Then he bounded to his feet and starting throwing punches, while the rest of us scurried for cover. No use trying to seize and hold him and all of us had visions of stopping one of his terrible swings. Then he halted, swayed slightly and drew his hand across his eyes.

"Sit down, Mike!" Marjory was at his side and gently forced him back on the cot.

"What happened? Did I win?"

"You were knocked out in the first round, Mike." I answered, feeling it better to answer him directly. Amazement flared in his eyes.

"I? Knocked out? Impossible!"

"Yes, you were, Mike." I assured him, expecting him to do any of the things I have seen fighters do on learning of their first knockout—burst into a torrent of savage weeping, faint, rave and curse, or rush out looking for the man who beat him.

But being Mike Brennon, and a never-to-solved enigma, he did none of these things. He rubbed his chin and laughed cynically, but resignedly.

"Guess I'd gone further back than I thought, and underrated Costigan. I don't remember the punch that put me out. Unusual thing—I've come through my last fight without a mark."

"And now you'll quit!" cried Marjory. "This is the best thing that could have happened! Costigan knocked you out with one punch and you weren't punished any. You promised you'd quit when you were knocked out, Mike, you promised!" Her voice was painful in its intensity.

"You'll have to quit now, Mike." I said. "You're no longer a drawing card."

At that moment a knock sounded on the door and the face of Costigan hesitantly appeared. His ferocious features were clouded by both an air of uncertainty and of anxiety.

"Are you after bein' alright, Brennon?" he asked.

"Sure, Costigan, come in."

Still the other hesitated.

"You ain't aimin' to be hittin' me with a chair like Young Hansen did after I knocked him out?"

Brennon laughed. "Come in. I want to shake hands with you."

With an apparent sigh of relief Costigan entered, his face relaxing into a broad Irish grin. He shook hands with sincerity and said:

"Be the saint, Brennon, but that was a slam you gimme! What a polthogue you're after packin' in each mauler. I ain't mesilf yet. The firrst toime I iver hit the canvas, and this toime I thought I'd be goin' on through to the basement. It's the real regret that's on me, if this k.o. is ruinin' you as a drawing card."

"That's all right, Costigan," Brennon answered. "I'm quitting the game. And I guess I'm lucky. And Costigan, I'm telling you this, quit it yourself when you feel you're slipping."

Costigan grinned. "There, Brennon, you know yoursilf we never quit till they count 'ten' over us! A great battle that was, and a fine man ye are."

After his conqueror left, Brennon sighed, ruefully, "There goes the new 'greatest of all iron men.' I wonder who'll level him, finally!"

At that moment Ganlon burst in, panting with suppressed excitement. His eyes blazed.

"Mike," he fairly snarled. "Steve! Don't you two bone-heads see there's something wrong here? Mike, when did you begin feeling drowsy?"

Brennon started. "That's right. I'd forgotten. As I climbed into the ring I began feeling queer, now that I remember. Costigan's punches seemed to have knocked all recollection of it out of my mind. As I sat in the corner, I got dizzy and things floated in front of my eyes. I felt like a drunken man. Then I sort of woke up and we were in the center of the ring with the referee talking. It all comes back now, but how strange and vague it seems! For a moment I was perfectly normal, and I remember how Costigan's eyes blazed, then when I turned to go to my corner, I got dizzy and drunken again. But I swear I hadn't had anything to drink. Steve said something to me as he climbed out of the ring but I could scarcely hear his voice. It seemed a way off. Then I faintly heard the gong and felt myself moving out in the ring as if my limbs were working independently of my mind.

"Then I saw Costigan through a fog and he hit me a punch under the cheek bone. It was a hummer and it woke me up. I seemed to come to myself with a start; I started swinging and saw Costigan go down. That's the last I remember and it's why I couldn't believe it when they said he knocked me out."

Ganlon laughed bitterly. "Sure. I noticed how you walked and acted. That last burst of fighting was all you had in you, and you wouldn'ta had that much if you wasn't a human tiger. You was out on your feet before Costigan hit you. That right hook was plenty hard but you've kept your feet lotsa times before blows a sight harder. A girl coulda pushed you over and that's all Costigan done!"

"But what—" began Brennon.

"Doped!" I exclaimed.

"Sure, doped! And you oughta kick yourself, Steve, for not seein' it right off the bat. And you with thirty years uh boxin' experience behind you! Great cats, these managers!"

"Costigan's crowd! Or the gambling ring—"

"Naw! You been crossed by a person you wouldn't believe capable of it! I been doin' some detective work. Mike, just before you left your dressin' room, you drunk a small cup uh tea, didn't you? Kinda unusual preparation for a hard fight, eh? But you drunk it to please somebody—"

Marjory was cowering in the corner, white faced. Mike looked at her, puzzled and troubled.

"But Spike, Marjory made that tea herself—"

"Yeah, and she doped it herself, she framed you to lose!"

Our eyes turned on the shrinking girl; surprize in mine, I suppose, anger and accusation in Spike's, a deep and puzzled hurt in Mike's.

"She framed you! She slipped you the dope!" snarled Spike. "And—"

"Marjory, why did you do that?" asked Mike in bewilderment. "Why did you want me to lose? I might have won—"

"Yes, you might have won!" she cried in a sudden desperate gust of defiant fury; she was as one who has been pushed past human endurance and who no longer cares what happens. "You might have won—after Costigan had battered you into a red ruin! After your brain had been pounded numb and you had been knocked just another step along the road that leads to the padded cell!

"Yes, I drugged the tea! It's my fault you got knocked out! And you can't go back for you won't draw the crowds! I've saved you in spite of your mad vanity—you're safe now—you're out of the game for good with a sound brain. I've gone through Hell since I saw you lying on that cot after you fought Slade. Now that's over at least. I've saved you in spite of yourself! I've saved you, I tell you—from your avarice and your mad cruel pride! And it doesn't matter what you do to me now. You can beat me or kill me—I don't care!"

She stood panting before us, her small fists clenched, her eyes blazing. Then as no one spoke, all the fire went out of her. She visibly wilted and moved forlornly toward the door, her slight shoulders dropping. Her wrap which had enveloped her slender form, slid to the floor, revealing her in a cheap gingham dress. As she fumbled at the door Mike seemed to awake from a deep trance. He started forward: "Marjory! What are you doing in that rig?"

"It's the dress I was wearing when you found me," she answered listlessly. "I wrote and got my old job back at the cafe—"

"Why, in God's name?" he exclaimed, crossing the room with one stride; he caught her slim shoulder and whirled her about to face him, with unconsciously brutal force. "What's the meaning of all this?"

She collapsed suddenly into a storm of weeping. "Don't you hate me for drugging you?" she sobbed. "I didn't think you'd ever want to see me again!"

He crushed her to him hungrily. "Girl, I swear I didn't realize how it all was hurting you. I've been a blind fool. I couldn't realize how you suffered. I'm like a mad man coming back to sanity. I see things in a different light now—thank God you doped me! I must have been insane! You're right—it was pride—vanity. My eyes were blinded to my best interests—and your happiness. And darling, that's all that matters now! We've got our life and love before us, and if it rests with me, you're going to be happy all the rest of your life."

Ganlon beckoned me and I followed him out. For the only time since I had known him, the fierce middleweight's hard face was softened. The sentiment that lies at the base of the Irish nature, however deeply hidden sometimes, made his steely eyes almost tender.

"I had her down all wrong," he said softly. "I take back everything I said about her. She's a regular—and Mike—well, he's the only Iron Man I ever knew that got the right breaks at last."

Appendix 2:
Articles

Dula Due to be Champion

Arthur "Kid" Dula is due to be the middleweight champion of the world, in the opinion of Robert E. Howard of Cross Plains, who witnessed the Dula-Tramel battle in Fort Worth last week. Howard is a close student of the boxing game, and is thoroughly posted on current boxing as well as on the history of the fight game. Writing to the Bulletin today from his home in Cross Plains, Howard says:

"Last Friday night a boy went through his baptism of blood and fire and emerged victorious. The decision went against him but the moral victory was his.

"Arthur Dula of Brownwood, in his slashing, desperate battle against Duke Tramel proved that he was of the stuff of which champions are built. I have seen challengers, champions and near champions perform but that moment in the fourth round, when Dula, his back against the ropes, pinned there by Tramel's murderous attack, and dazed from a terrific right to the temple—made a desperate rally and outslugged the most dangerous slugger the South has ever produced. Outslugged, outfought and battered him back across the ring.

Again in the eighth, when dizzy and bloody the Kid reeled about the ring, out on his feet but with superhuman courage refusing to go down—again in the last desperate round when the Kid weakened by cruel punishment and low blows charged recklessly across the ring; met Tramel in his own corner. And fighting like an uncaged tiger, smashed the weakening slugger from one side of the ring to the other.

Next Champion

"All this leads to the main point; that which came into my mind as I watched that bloody eighth round. Kid Dula is the next Middleweight Champion of the World.

"The Kid has much to learn of the finer points of boxing; but he is a natural hitter, a clever boxer, tough and courageous. More he is aggressive to an extent reminiscent of Dempsey. And like all real great sluggers, like Sullivan, Ketchel, Terry McGovern, Bob Fitzsimmons and Jack Dempsey, Dula never loses his punch and is most dangerous when apparently out. This quality alone is the greatest gift a fighter can have and one which has sustained Duke Tramel also, through many grim battles and made him for a time, champion of the Southwest. And Dula besides this has other qualities which Tramel lacks, mainly boxing skill and speed. His main handicap is lack of sufficient experience.

"The fight Friday night, boiled down, comes to this: a desperate battle between two iron men, the experience and sledgehammer power of one being offset by the speed and aggressiveness of the other. A draw would have been fair to both. One of the greatest fights the South has ever seen.

"And Dula is the next middleweight champion. All he needs is proper handling. He has everything else."

Tunney Can't Win

A letter to the editor of *The Fort Worth Star Telegram*, written ca. July 13 to July 19, 1928[1]

Tunney can't win. After the fight, Tom Heeney is going to be heavyweight champion of the world, not through any special virtue of his, but simply because there's a jinx on Tunney that Gene can't whip.

Now get this: Back in 1892 James J. Corbett, a skillful boxer, whipped John L. Sullivan, a superslugger, and then knocked out Charley Mitchell, the only man who'd ever given John L. much of an argument.

Now: Some years later, in 1926, James J. Tunney, like Corbett, an Irishman, whipped Jack Dempsey, a superslugger, after having knocked out Tom Gibbons, the only man who'd been able to stay with Jack—the only difference being that Tunney knocked out Gibbons before he won the title and not after.

Now, that lines Corbett and Tunney up together enough, I guess. Both Irish, both boxers, both named James J., both winning their titles from dark-browed, furious sluggers of Irish blood.

All right: Corbett in 1897 met an ex-blacksmith from New Zealand—Irish and a rugged fighter, named Robert Fitzsimmons. Result: A new champion.

Now in 1928 Tunney meets an ex-blacksmith from New Zealand—Irish and a rugged fighter, named Tom Heeney. Result—? A new champion, I say. Heeney isn't Tunney's equal in speed, punch or cleverness, but then Corbett had it all over Fitzsimmons in the way of speed and skill.

So, just as I predicted Dempsey's defeat by Tunney when I heard Gene's real name was James J., so I now predict defeat for

---

1   REH commenting on the upcoming Heeney-Tunney fight.
    Tunney won by TKO on July 26, 1928. Published on July 20, 1928

Tunney because of the New Zealand jinx, a factor to be reckoned with. I hope Tunney wins; I like Heeney, but I like Tunney better. Still, I predict his defeat.

The Punch

Not long ago some friends were discussing that all-potent factor so much employed by the knights of the square circle, known as the "punch," the "swat," the "slam" and other equally vigorous cognomens; and were arguing as to the efficiency of the respective punch of Messrs. Dempsey and Maher.

All of which brings to mind the fact that, popular opinion to the contrary, that there is a vast difference in the blows of men of even equal weight and strength.

The ordinary punch is merely a heavy shove or push. Not one man in a thousand have the real snap to their punches that means a knockout. A heavy shove or swing often knocks a man out but it must land precisely. A real k.o. punch is one in which the whole body coordinates. Muscles of arm, shoulder and leg coil and release suddenly like one mighty spring and the result is a "snap" that drops the recipient, nine times out of ten. The distance the punch travels has little to do with the power of such a punch.

I can, at this moment, call to mind only three heavyweights who possessed this power to any marked degree; Bob Fitzsimmons, Peter Maher and Jack Dempsey. Fitzsimmons was the greatest exponent of the punch. To my mind he was the greatest hitter the world has ever known. What a build he was! Big flat feet, spindling legs and hips, topped with a pair of shoulders that were simply colossal. A fairly good boxer, only rather slow as to footwork, he placed his full confidence in his hitting ability. Nor did it ever fail him until his hands would no longer support the full power of his shoulders. No hands could remain intact from those terrific blows.

I would place him at the top of all hitters, for his knockout of Sharkey if for no other act. Anyone who ever saw the sailor in action could never doubt that his conqueror must indeed be a man of almost superhuman ability. Short and massively built was Sharkey, with great muscular legs and arms, head set solidly between gigantic shoulders, a 50-inch chest and altogether the most rugged build for his inches that the world has ever seen.

The greatest near champion of them all, he defeated all of the great ones of his day except Jeffries. And Big Jeff himself, the strongest pugilist that ever stepped into a ring, towering over the sailor by nearly half a foot and outweighing him forty pounds, failed to knock him out in two long, savagely contested battles. Yet Fitzsimmons dropped Sharkey with one punch in the second round of their second fight. Sharkey had won on a foul in their first battle but there is much to be believed in the theory that the fight was framed so Fitz could not win. Whether the fighters were parties to the "frame" if such there was, is doubtful.

Certainly both did their best. But to get back to the subject of the punch.

Peter Maher possessed about as much knock out snap to his punches as Fitzsimmons, in addition to being a much stronger man. If he had had anything to go with his hitting ability, there is little doubt but that he would have been ranked as one of the greatest of all times. But he never learned more than the veriest rudiments of boxing and was frequently half-drunk when he climbed into the ring. Then too, he was slow and possessed not half of Fitzsimmons' ability to take punishment. Yet, for all that, he knocked out Joe Choynsky with a single punch which was something no one else ever accomplished. Choynsky was often knocked out, but it took a perfect whirlwind of punches to do it. He was a tough bird and no mistake. Corbett knocked him out and so did McCoy, Walcott and Sharkey, but they did it only after a terrific battle and after they had worn down the Battling Hebrew with incredible punishment. In draws with Jeffries and Fitzsimmons, Choynsky proved his durability. Jeff was unable to jolt him and although Fitz floored him seven times, he failed to knock him out. Maher hit Choynsky just once.

And now, the modern Dempsey. In spite of what the old-timers say, Jack has a real punch. He first demonstrated its full power when he dropped Carl Morris, the Oklahoma Giant, with one punch. Morris is a little fellow standing something over six feet and three inches in his socks and scaling upwards of a hundred and forty pounds, and was a tough baby.

After having stowed away Fulton, Gunboat Smith and a horde of others, Dempsey again illustrated the efficiency of his punch on Jess Willard. It has been said that Willard averred that he does not remember anything of the fight, except Dempsey coming at him from his corner. That first terrific punch, a smashing left hook to the jaw, really won the fight for Jack. About all Willard did after that was to get up and keep getting up for which fact he should receive due commendation, for it was only the fighter's instinct, (of which Jess is reported to possess a little) that kept him climbing to his feet.

While we are on the subject, it might be well to glance at Jeffries. There was certainly no k.o. snap to his punch. It was merely a smash, such as no ordinary man could give, driven by giant muscles, and it simply shattered what it hit. It was such a punch as the old London Prize Ring Rule fighters sought to perfect.

Then there is the whiplash blow, which cuts a man and wears him down. Jim Corbett and Jack Dempsey, the Nonpareil were the greatest exponents of that punch but it was also the property of Jack O'Brien, Kid McCoy and Charlie Mitchell.

Men of Iron

(unfinished, originally untitled)

What freak of nature makes an iron man? We know that the human skull is well built to withstand violence, and that the body muscles may be developed into a steel-like toughness but this alone will not explain that strange incredible mortal known to the ring and its followers as an Iron Man.

We know that often an ordinary man is killed by a comparatively slight blow on the head and even a skilled boxer is often knocked senseless by a blow which, landing on the right place, need not be over-hard. Compare these facts, then, with the deeds of the iron men! I will mention five here explicitly: Joe Grim, Battling Nelson, Tom Sharkey, Mike Boden and Joe Goddard.

In passing, let me speak of Jim Jeffries, one of the two iron men who achieved a title. Undoubtedly he was the greatest of them all, but unlike the rest, he combined real skill and cleverness with his toughness. Just now I am speaking of men whose main, or only, asset was durability.

Joe Grim was an Italian, a native of Philadelphia. If he ever won a fight, it is not on record. He was neither a boxer or a fighter in the true sense of the word. He was wide open—a blind man could hit him—yet Bob Fitzsimmons, Joe Gans, Sam McVey and Jack Johnson failed to knock him out. Grim never weighed over 165 pounds. Consider then the fact of stacking him up against men who weighed over 200 pounds! Stanley Ketchel was accounted as tough a man as ever lived, yet Jack Johnson, rising from a knockdown, knocked Ketchel out with one blow, breaking off all his front teeth, which remained stuck in the glove. This same Johnson at his very best, weighing 210 pounds, battered Joe Grim, 165, until he was arm-weary, and failed to score a knockout. Sam McVey was a harder hitter than Johnson and much more aggressive. He had two tries at Grim and failed to stop the India-rubber Man.

Bob Fitzsimmons, without a doubt the most effective hitter in the history of the game, was matched with Grim for six rounds. Consider Fitzsimmons' record if you feel he was at fault. He was the man who knocked out the great Corbett; who knocked out Tom Sharkey, the giant Ruhlin, Ed Donkhorst, the Human Freight Car, 320 pounds, whom Bob finished with one punch. Fitzsimmons gave Jeffries the Boilermaker's most vicious battle. One boxer died from the effects of his triphammer smashes.

Now then, look! For six rounds Fitzsimmons hammered the wide-open Italian with every blow and series of blows known to the game. His deadly body blows, which had proved so effective against Corbett and Sharkey and Ruhlin, did not even jar Grim. Fitzsimmons switched to the Italian's head and knocked him down sixteen times—an average of ten times to the round. At the final gong Fitzsimmons was arm-weary; Grim landed the last blow of that fight and, reeling over to the ropes, spit out a mouthful of teeth and, grinning, made his usual speech: "I am Joe Grim! I fear no man! I challenge that bigga Jeem Jeff' fora da title!"

Scientists examined Grim and found his skull to be of extraordinary thickness, his brain cell so small that the nerves were dulled. When Joe said he did not feel the blows, he spoke the truth. A blow which would have agonized or crippled the average man only produced a dull jar and slight discomfort to him.

But that scarcely explains his body which was of such chilled steel hardness that he once allowed a man to shatter a baseball bat across his stomach. He was knocked down but unhurt.

Joe Gans came nearer knocking out this marvel in his prime than anyone else. Though a much smaller man than Grim, weighing only 138 pounds, the Old Master gave Grim a hideous battering. He worked in close, found Grim had only one style, a continuous roundhouse swinging of his arms. Gans kept in close, ducking these swings, and each time he came up again and hooked right or left to Grim's jaw. For round after round this kept up until Grim's jaws swelled. In the thirteenth round they burst and the chief of police, in horror, stopped the fight. Gans himself was willing for he was sickened at the havoc he had made, but Grim was furious, insisted he was not hurt and wished to go on!

The many batterings took their toll at last, however, and Grim was knocked out by Sailor Burke, a hard-hitting second-rater who stepped off a ship to turn the trick. His heart was broken.

One would think that falling four feet headfirst onto a concrete floor would at least render a man senseless. In his first fight with Joe Choynsky, Tom Sharkey had that experience. He not only was not hurt; he got up and won the fight. Choynsky was a venomous hitter. Though weighing only 170 pounds, Corbett said he was one of the hardest hitters that ever lived. The giant Jeffries always said Choynsky hit him his hardest blows. In their drawn battle of twenty or twenty-five rounds, Choynsky smashed a straight right into Jeffries' mouth which crushed the lip back and wedged it between the two front teeth in such a way that one of Jeffries' seconds was forced to cut it loose with a knife.

Sharkey was a raw novice; Choynsky a trained veteran. Choynsky smashed Sharkey over the ropes and out of the ring. The sailor landed on his head on the concrete with all the heft of his 190 pounds. That would have caved in most skulls like an eggshell. Sharkey climbed back into the ring and knocked Choynsky out.

Choynsky, hitter par excellence, met another tough nut in Chicago in the person of Mike Boden. This man was as wild and wide open as Grim—and about as tough. In the six rounds they fought, he landed not one solid blow while Choynsky almost broke his heart trying to put him to sleep—and failed.

In Australia, Choynsky was twice outfought by one Joe Goddard, a man who claimed that no human being could be struck hard enough to be rendered senseless. The [. . .]

Appendix 3:
Odds and Ends

"The round started slow . . ."

(incomplete, untitled)

The round started slow, both of us sparring cautiously and faking left leads. He was short with a left and then I landed a left jab to the face; we traded straight rights to the body and straight lefts to the face; I crouched and came in fast jabbing my left for the body; I missed a right for the head as I straightened and he jabbed a right to the face and a left to the body. I crouched and tore in, slamming both hands to the body; he missed a right uppercut but sent me back with a left to the head. We traded half a dozen lefts to the ribs and he landed a good right to my solar plexus. He was short with a left jab as I stepped back; he missed three more jabs and a right as I boxed on the defensive; I sent three left jabs to the face without a return, then he landed a straight right to the body. I walked in with my hands down, feinted him into leading with a straight left, side stepped it and crossed my right to his head; this was a light punch however. We traded jabs at long range and then right hooks to the chin. He feinted but I sent a long left to the face, being short with a wild right. He landed three jabs without a return and knocked me backward with a right hook to the chin. I missed a left swing for the head and we traded rights to the body.

The second round he refused to mix it, boxing at long range; we traded several left jabs and I missed a left swing; I missed two more left swings and he was short with a right. He momentarily knocked the breath out of me with a left to the body, and I blocked his next few punches. For the next few minutes we both failed to land, each of us blocking, ducking, and sidestepping, then we traded left to the body and he brought around a right to the head. I was getting warmed up now but he was too clever for me to make a slugging match out of it. He again shook me up with lefts to the body and followed with rights and lefts to the head; I made no attempt to duck or block, taking all he handed out, while I deliberately set myself for a left to the jaw which should have ended the bout; however, he back stepped just at the right instant and when I did start my punch I missed by two feet.

Then after some light sparring, I rushed him across the room, but failed to land as he blocked cleverly and countered with rights and lefts to body and face. He came in and I stood still, taking his punches while I set myself for a right hand smash; however, he stepped back, blocking it with his arm. I charged after him swinging with both hands. He backed away boxing cleverly. I was as wild as a whole zoo and missed seven roundhouse lefts and rights in succession, though not getting many punches either, on account of my weaving tactics. I was bringing my swings off the floor, from the knees, hips, and waistline. He landed several lefts and rights to the body.

The next round I missed a haymaking left for the head and took a jarring right to the jaw. He jabbed three lefts all of which I blocked in a masterly manner with my face. Frenzied at my failure to land I tore in wide open and we stood toe to toe trading straight arm smashes to the mouth; he being the first to back away; I rushed him across the room hammering my left to his body and then smashed a straight right to his jaw; he later said this was the hardest blow he ever took, but though rocked considerably, he spit some blood and came back working both arms. He had the best of a mix up at close quarters; we clinched and I missed a left on the breakaway. He mashed my lips with a straight right and I tore in crouching, starting his nose to bleeding with an overhand left swing to the face. I rushed him across the ring with a series of left hooks to the body, then rocked him with a left hook to the jaw as I straightened out of my crouch. He crowded me back across the room and shook me up with a couple of rights to the jaw. Another right to the body made my legs wobble and I smashed a left to his face. We both started a rush and met in the center of the room, I weaved around his left jab and swung a roundhouse left to his body, which sent him backward and made his mouth fly open. He backed up, blocking my punches; I came in fast, crouched under his guard, hooked my left three times to his body and nearly floored him with a right to the jaw as I straightened. In a wild mix-up he blinded me with a right to the eye and I backed away, blocking. He crowded me, shaking me up with lefts and rights to head and body though I blocked most of them. I stepped back and stopped with a long straight left to the face. Then after some dancing and sparring, I landed a left jab; we feinted and then traded jabs to the body.

The next round I missed a left jab as did he; we then traded jabs to the body and he knocked me seven or eight steps backward with a right to the jaw. He crowded me fast and in a fierce mixup landed three hard rights to the body without a return; I ducked into punches twice purposely, then feinted a duck and shot my right to his face as he lowered his hand for a punch. I feinted him into leading a straight left, slipped it and crossed a light right to the head; we hammered each other about the body in a clinch; he crowded me at a fast pace and in a fast mixup at close quarters landed a number of rights to the body as I hooked three lefts to the head. We traded jabs and suddenly I remembered I had a right and used it in a straight smash to the face that drove his head back. He knocked me backward with a left to the body that shook my breath, and was short with several jabs as I danced away. He crowded me across the room and nearly knocked me out with a right to the jaw; I crouched then, and tore into him, hooking both hands to the head; I took three or four solid smashes in the face without feeling them or slowing up any and smashed a straight right to the body; he stopped short and his mouth flew open and I rushed him across the room with two left hooks and a straight right to the face, a straight left to the body and three right hooks to the head, without a return; he clinched and I missed a left on the breakaway, completely fought out from the pace I had been travelling; he was as near out as he ever was but I was in no condition to finish him, even supposing I could have, which is not likely; my legs were ready to buckle from fatigue and he boxed cleverly, ducking my wild swings. He was better at long range but I did my best hitting close in. We sparred lightly, nearly exhausted, though this did not affect our punch any. He jabbed and I ducked, hooking my right to the body; we traded rights and he shook me with a right to the jaw; I ducked a left jab but missed a right swing. I ducked another left and landed a glancing right swing to the jaw which I brought from the floor. Light sparring followed then we traded left jabs to the face.

Jeffries Versus Dempsey

(orginally untitled, imaginary Dempsey-Jeffries fight)

John L. Sullivan knocked out Ryan with a right hook to the jaw; James Corbett knocked out Sullivan with continuous lefts and rights to face, jaw and body, followed up by a right hook, left hook and right hook to the jaw; Bob Fitzsimmons knocked Corbett out with a left hook to the solar plexus; James J. Jeffries knocked out Fitzsimmons with a right hook to the body, and a left hook to the jaw.

Jack Johnson knocked out Jeffries with continuous lefts and rights to body and jaw, especially right uppercuts to the jaw followed up by a right hook to the body and a left hook to the jaw, then several right hooks to the jaw.

Jess Willard knocked out Johnson with a straight left to the body and a straight right to the jaw; Jack Dempsey knocked out Willard with a right hook to the jaw; James J. Jeffries knocked out Bob Fitzsimmons with a right hook to the body and a left hook to the jaw; James. J. Corbett with a left hook to the jaw; Gus Ruhlin with a left hook to the solar plexus; Bob Fitzsimmons with a left hook to the jaw; James J. Corbett with a left hook to the body and a right hook to the jaw.

Round 1: Jeffries strode from his corner and assumed a half crouch in the middle of the ring; Dempsey bounded from his corner and charged headlong at his opponent, hooking a wicked left for the body. Jeffries failed to block the punch and it staggered him, but he instantly countered with a straight left to the face which stopped Jack squarely in his tracks. Before Jeffries could follow up, however, Dempsey struck out savagely with left and right, Jeffries blocking the right and countering with a left to the body, which failed to slow Jack. Jeffries blocked Jack's right, but missed with a terrific left hook for the jaw, and instantly Jack landed with a left hook to the jaw which could be heard all over the stadium. Jeffries backed away, guarding carefully. Dempsey's round by a slight margin.

Round 2: Jeffries feinted with his left but Dempsey ducked under the extended arm and landed a terrific right hook to the body, following instantly with his left. Jeffries, stung, swung a savage left for Jack's jaw, but missed and was paid with another left to the body. Jeffries was retreating and Jack had difficulty in getting through his guard. Jeffries thrust his huge left arm straight out to stave Jack off, but instantly Dempsey ducked and slammed a left hook to the body, but his right to the jaw was blocked by Jeffries left shoulder. Dempsey came in.

Jeffries caught Jack by coming in with a straight left that sent Dempsey back on his heels, following instantly with his right for the body, at the same instant Jack sent a hard straight left to the face. Jeffries missed a straight left but as Jack hooked his right to the body, he landed a short right hook to the jaw. Jeffries blocked Jack's right and left but was short with a right for the body. Dempsey was much faster, ducking, slipping, but Jeffries presented a perfect blocking defense. Round even.

Round 3: Jeffries stepped back, blocking Jack's punches warily, Jack was wild with his right and was paid by a short left jab to the face that had force behind it, Jack rushed, hooking lefts and right for the body at close range and Jeffries had difficulty in blocking his punches, Jeffries seemed solving Jack's attack, but Dempsey's left to the body was too fast for him; Dempsey slammed a powerful left to the body, which staggered Jeffries and cause him to involuntarily lower his guard; as he did so, Dempsey swung a terrific right to his jaw, which resounded all over the stadium, Jeffries staggered, then as Dempsey rushed in, set himself and sent a piledriver right to the body; that punch, with very ounce of Jeffries strength behind it, stopped Jack full in his tracks, and instantly Jeffries hooked a terrific left to his jaw. Jack was knocked halfway across the ring, but came back with a rush, wide open, swinging for the jaw with each hand.

The speed of the attack threw Jeffries off his guard; he started a hurried retreat, but took a couple of vicious rights to the face.

Dempsey was battering Jeffries all over the ring at the gong. Round even.

Round 4: Jeffries failed to land a straight left and Jack swung a hard left to his face. Dempsey landed a right to the body, a left to the jaw and a right to the body. Jeffries was staggered and missing with each hand. Dempsey swung his left for the body and instantly Jeffries hooked a short right to Jack's jaw. An instant later he took a hard left to the face and slammed a short straight right to Dempsey's body. Jack was short with a right hook for the body and Jeffries floored him with a pile driving left hook to the jaw. Jack bounded erect at the count of four and charging in wide open landed square to Jeffries jaw with a terrific right hook; Jeffries went to the mat, regaining his feet at the count of eight; Dempsey charged in to finish him and was met by a terrific left to the face; Jack swung a right to Jeffries jaw which staggered him, but failed to floor him, and Jeffries landed a left, then a right to Jack's jaw; Dempsey went down, staggered up at the count of seven, was met with a terrific left to the body and a right to the jaw, went down again, caught the ring-ropes and pulled himself erect at the count of eight, and weaved out into the ring; Jeffries stepped close and hooked his left for the jaw, Jack reeled but did not fall, and suddenly swung his right for Jeffries jaw, as Jeffries started his; both landed at the same time and dropped to the mat simultaneously; Jeffries was on his feet at the count of four, Dempsey weaved up at the count of eight. Jeffries set himself and floored Jack again with a left to the jaw, and Dempsey was counted out, though he almost beat the count, for he staggered up, just after the referee said ten. He wished to continue the bout but Jeffries answered that he had already won.

Misto Dempsey

(orginally untitled)

1.

I was present at a bout in the course of which one of the fighters took a tremendous slam on the chin and came up at "nine," cross-eyed. He weaved around, glared at his opponent as if he didn't believe it, and then started climbing over the ropes.

"Hey," yelled his manager, "what are you quitting for—are you turning yellow?"

"No man can call me yellow," answered the punch-drunk fighter, "but when they start running *twins* in one, me, I'm through!"

2.

After his man had taken a terrific flailing for nine rounds, a certain manager threw in the sponge in the latter part of the ninth. The battered slugger was helped to his corner where he collapsed. When he was brought to he stared around wildly and yelled: "What happened?"

"I threw the sponge in," answered the manager. "What round?"
"The ninth!"
"The ninth! Say, what was you doing about seven rounds ago?"

3.

I came into a dressing room one night after a bout which had ended abruptly in the first round. The loser was untaping his hands and some fellow who had bet heavily on him was raving.

"A great fighter you are!" he yelled. "You said to me, 'One punch is all I'll hit that fellow' and what happened? You rush out, trade lefts with him and then he follows up with his right and you go out like a candle!"

"Don't romp on me," answered the boxer imperturbably. "Didn't I hit him with that left?"

"Yes, once!"

"Alright, what's your kick? I never said I'd whip him, I only said I'd hit him once and that wasn't no lie because once is all I hit him!"

4.

"How did you come out last night?"

"Not so good. I lost the decision and let me tell you—that fellow's left was the most monotonous thing I ever saw."

5.

There used to be a fighter down on the Border who slung his fists on the style of Harry Greb. He looked like a buzzsaw in action and blocking his swats was about like boxing a windmill.

He was matched up with a fellow who knew nothing about his speed or style and the buzzsaw gave him a wicked beating. Finally the other fellow, after having been floored by a perfect deluge of swings, looked up and asked dazedly: "Say, fellow, how many fists have you got, anyway?"

6.

"Hear your girl gave you the gate. How come?"

"Force of habit," answered the morose slugger.

"How come 'force of habit'?"

"Whenever she'd put her arms around me, I'd forget where I was and start infighting."

7.

A few years ago when Dempsey was at his height, a local fighter, a colored boy who considered himself good, scraped up some money and went out to the champion's training camp with the intention of applying for a job as sparring partner. However, in a few days he was back and upon being asked the reason, he answered.

"Boy, listen! When Ah arrove at Misto Dempsey's camp, he wuz sparrin' wid a fellow dat looked like a twin brudder to de Woolworth Buildin'. All at once Misto Dempsey swishes loose wid his left and dis boy hits de canvas like he gwine use it for a pummament resoht. Dey carry him out and a white man steps up to me and says: 'You look like a fightuh, was you wantin' anything special?'

"Ah says, 'Misto, does you all need uh good dishwasher?'"

The Funniest Bout

Speaking of comical scraps, a match of an amateur tournament I saw several years ago wins the prize. Two lads were matched who'd never had a glove on before, tall gangling youths, both over six feet tall. They squared off and one of them reached halfway to California with his right and brought a swing clear around the house. The other lad took it full on the jaw and went through the ropes. He climbed back with fire in his eye, rushed, missed a couple of wild haymakers and nearly knocked the referee out of the ring. Then they stood toe to toe and swung with their rights, landing and missing as regularly as mechanical toys. Then one backed away, tried to do some classy footwork, got his legs tangled up, and fell down, and the fellow fell over him. They got up and one of them tin-canned around the ring, the other chasing him and pounding him on the back. Then he turned and swung, missing his opponent, of course, but handing a k.o. to a ring post.

Before the first minute of the first round, they'd closed each other's eyes nearly, and smashed each other's noses so that they were bloody, face, arms and gloves. Both of them were so enraged they could hardly see.

At the gong they'd walk to the center of the ring, scowl at each other and grate their teeth for a minute, then both haul back their rights and let go. If one dodged a punch it was because the other was too clumsy to land, and when a punch landed it was because the boxer was too clumsy to dodge.

After they'd pounded each other for four rounds, the referee called it even.

The Right Hook

(material from REH's self-publication)

From *The Right Hook* #1 (March/April 1925)

The Great Munney Ring

A certain organization in this great country has produced a champion. So *it* says. What the new wrestling champion has to do with that organization, except to afford it a little advertizing, we do not see. Personally, if we were connected to the above-mentioned organization we would hesitate before linking our name with that of the champion. The organization cannot help it, if the champ was once a member. Strangler Lewis, who had held the title for years and had done his part in making wrestling a straight, clean game (pardon sarcasm), and his manager decided that something new in the bunko line must be pulled to draw crowds. What better, then, than a defeat and a comeback? And what kind of champ is more popular than one who clambers his way up by sheer muscular power and a sort of bravery? There are certain people, noted for their great strength, in their arms, who believe that bulk and brawn can defeat skill and science. Hence, Munn! Munn, a practically unknown wrestler throws the great Lewis out of the ring! Some of the glamour fades from this performance when we learn that the act had been rehearsed for some days. But behold! Munn develops a brain of his own. Where is the return match with Lewis! Nay, the new champion decamps with the contract to a vaudeville: $1000 a week. Yet Dempsey, who never threw a match in all his career, is criticized because he worked in shipyards during the war.

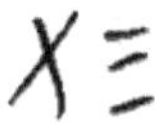

Sporting Page Lightweight Tournament

The tourney that is being held to find a worthy successor for the lightweight throne, recently vacated by the retiring Benny Leonard, is progressing. Sammy Mandell, on the virtue of his conquering Sid Terris, has assumed the title without having any real right to it. The Commission will probably demand that he prove his right to the championship by defending it against all comers. The nearest thing to a champion, to our mind, is Jack Bernstein. He defeated Johnny Dundee just before the featherweight champ retired, won a decision from the slugging Chilean, Luis Vicentino, and defeated Tommy O'Brien. He has been defeated only once lately, by Sammy Mandell, and that fight was so close that there was little to choose between them. Tommy O'Brien has leaped into prominence by his knockout of George Chaney, who has exactly 100 K.O.s to his credit. If Jack Zivic can make the weight he will be an aggressive contestant, as his recent K.O. of Lew Tendler showed. But the battler who will be the real champion, if he ever learns the science of the game, is Luis Vicentino.

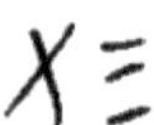

Featherweights

Louis Kaplan has been given the title vacated by Johnny Dundee, who retired some months ago, on the strength of his defeat of Danny Kramer. If Kaplan is a champion, we are a Dutchman, and it is certain that we are not. We favor Benny Bass, Mike Dundee, and Al Corbett before Kaplan. Even Eduard Mascart of France, champ of Europe by virtue of his K.O. of Danny Frush of England, stands a good chance to knock Kaplan for a row.

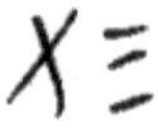

The Boxing Commission has suspended Dempsey. He cannot fight in New York. We cannot imagine Dempsey bothering his head about the Commission.

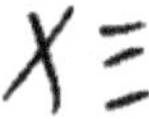

Championship Material

Bantam: Pete Sarmentio. Featherweight: Al Corbett, Benny Bass, Mike Dundee. Lightweight: Luis Vicentino, Sid Terris, Jack Bernstein. Welterweight: Jack Zivic. Middleweight: Jack Delaney. Light heavyweight: Berlenbach, Stribling, Slattery.

From *The Right Hook* #2 (April/May 1925)

MUNN! MUNN! MUNN! MUNN! MUNN!

The very Olympian gods of brawn must roar with Gargantuan mirth! Munn! Big Munn, of the six feet six inches and 280 pounds of muscle, thrown clear of the wrestling throne, which he had held only a few months. And by whom? By old Stanilaus Zbyszko, who is nearly sixty years old, who stands barely six feet and scales 230. The Pole who came to America some 25 years ago to challenge Gotch. Old Stan, who held the title years ago until it was wrested from him by the man, whom thousands of innocents believe was fairly defeated by Munn (Big, Big, Munn!), Strangler Ed Lewis; Zbyszko who will wrestle Joe Stecher; who also held the title and was defeated by Lewis. Munn, (Big, Big Munn!) showed great skill in one way: he managed to pick up fifth-raters no better than himself, whom he could defeat by sheer strength. He was looking for a set-up in old Stan! Ha! Ha! Ha! Ha! Ha! Ha! Ha! Ha! Ha!

On May 29 Mike McTigue and Paul Berlenbach fight for the light heavyweight title of the world. Next to Dempsey, Berlenbach is the most terrific hitter in the world. Out of 25 fights he has scored 21 K.O.s and has been knocked out only once, in the early part of his career, by Jack Delaney. McTigue has never been knocked out in 110 fights and has 53 knock outs to his credit. He was born in Ireland, in County Clare, and won the title from Battling Siki. He will either outpoint Berlenbach or Berlenbach will knock him out. McTigue has a chance of winning by a K.O., but Berlenbach has no chance of out boxing the champion, McTigue.[1]

From *The Right Hook* #3 (June/July 1925)

I progress slowly rather in my classification of champions. Few people are interested enough to bother. Of course, I have not yet heard from Nicky Walter, Billy Britton, and Jack O'Brien. I find that Dempsey holds the majority of votes for first place, with John L. Sullivan in a close second.

The Police Gazette Editor's Classification:
Jack Dempsey, 2. John L. Sullivan, 3. Peter Jackson.
Damon Runyon: Sportwriter
Jack Dempsey, 2. Peter Jackson, 3. James J. Jeffries.
Arthur T. Lumley: Sportwriter, one of Sullivan's managers
John L. Sullivan, 2. Peter Jackson, 3. James J. Corbett.
James J. Corbett: ex-champion and sportwriter
1. Peter Jackson and Jim Jeffries, 2. Bob Fitzsimmons, 3. John L. Sullivan.
Fred Takel: English Sport-editor *Boxing* London.
1. Bob Fitzsimmons, 2. Charley Mitchell, 3. Tom Sharkey.
Winfred Brigner: Boxing authority and athletic coach
1. Jack Dempsey, 2. James J. Jeffries, 3. Jim Corbett

---

1   Despite being knocked down, Berlenbach won the title on a decision.

A partial classification of my own. Only champs and near-champs are listed.

Skill	Hitting ability
Jim Corbett	Bob Fitzsimmons
Peter Jackson	Jack Dempsey
Kid McCoy	Jim Jeffries
Jack Johnson	PeterMaher-SulEvan-
Bob Fitzsimmons	Tom Sharkey

Toughness	*Fighting Instinct*
Jim Jeffries	Jack Dempsey
Tom Sharkey	John L. Sullivan
Jack Dempsey	Bob Fitzsimmons
Bob Fitzsimmons	Tom Sharkey
Jess Willard	Jim Corbett

Speed	*Cleverness*	*Courage*
Jim Corbet	Jim Corbet	Jack Dempsey
Peter Jackson	Kid McCoy	Jim Jeffries
Jack Dempsey	Peter Jackson	John L. Sullivan
Kid McCoy	Charlie Mitchell	Bob Fitzsimmons
	Jack Johnson	Tom Sharkey
	Jack Dempsey	

I like John L. Sullivan. I know that he was a whisky-soaked bum, but I'm a bum myself. I like him more for what he stood for than for what he was. He stood for Personal Liberty. That's my hobby: Personal Liberty. Liberty to live your own life, do as you please, so long as you don't encroach upon others. In France I see where chorus girls who take part in so-called indecent plays are to be punished publicly by the audience in a most outrageous and indecent manner. "Uphold the morals of our land!" bray the good citizens, flapping their long ears most ingenuously. Do you think old John L. would stand for anything like that? Why, I can fairly see him, pounding on a handy bar with a hammer-like fist and bellowing, "On wid the play. Back up ye scuts. Lit the gurls dance bare nakid if they want to. Phot is ut to ye? Phot, talk back, is ut. There! Take him out and trun some wather on him and he'll be comin' to presently. My name's John L. Sullivan and I kin lick any _______________ in the worruld!"

Put 'er there, old John L. If the orthodoxies are right we may get together some day, and I want, if we do, to reach over the coals and take your hard, wicked old mitt and say, "John L. you damned old sinner, you lived like a swine, you guzzled booze in every city in the world, you paraded the Bowery, the slums and the Barbary Coast, but by Satan, old boy, you're a better man than the pious that are smiling 'I-told-you-so's to see us sizzle. Put 'er there."

Yes, they're going to punish the girls. The managers, writers, producers that put such stuff on the stage will get off free. The poor little devils that have to make spectacles of themselves to make their living, they'll be the ones who'll get it in the neck. The audience will seat themselves quietly and watch the performance. Then they'll rise, march up on the stage, take the girls captive and proceed. The strong, silent, Puritanical men, who have been hugging themselves with lascivious glee at the very scenes they are condemning, the honest, decent women who are so damned jealous of the beauty of these girls that they are fairly sizzling with hate and malice. But the managers and the writers and the producers will get off all right. Sure, they've got the mazuma. If you've got the cash you can get away with anything. I guess the ladies and gentlemen I've been discussing, if they bother to regard me at all as anything other than a half-witted blasphemous imbecile, would like to put me under the same thing as the chorus girls. All right. But I warn you, I'm no chorus girl. No, though I stand a scant six feet and weigh only 150 pounds and am something of a weakling.

Take your priests and your smug pious saintly brethren, take your sects and your creeds and give me a man like old John L. For though he spoke in a harsh, belligerent voice, though he spun his talk with curses, yet his was the voice of Liberty, which is the voice of Progress, with the voice of all the Universe.

Call me an Anarchist, call me a fool, a modernist, a clod, a long-haired idealist; and I'll tell you to go to Hades. Have any opinion of me you want; that's your privilege. But let me alone. But don't try to make me believe what you believe. Don't interfere with my course.

Give me a man that grants somebody else a mind. Who don't relegate a fellow to the sizzlings of Hell simply because his beliefs differ.

Kid McCoy, doing time in San Quentin Prison, Old John L., guzzling booze in a bowery saloon, Tom Sharkey refereeing fights on the West Coast, Jack Dempsey, polishing bars and bouncing bums in a third-rate saloon and dance hall on the Barbary Coast, Jim Corbett, sitting in your mansion in Manhattan and writing articles for such fools as I, listen. You don't fool me. I know what you've been. I know what some of you are. But curse you, I admire you. Whatever else you were, you were what you were. There wasn't a particle of hypocrisy about you. Here's an extract from one of old John L.'s letters—"School of philosophy and a damn poor school it is. You and I have seen life, old pal, the good and the bad and we know! We sift the good and the bad and when we do, we find a lot of each in the either."

Yes, give me a man and I care not if he be a statesman or a prizefighter, a king of finance or a bum. Longfellow or McAulliffe.

Ringside Tales.

Marks was a giant. Nature had given him an incredibly powerful build, and his work—he worked on the cotton wharfs—had supplemented that build until he was accounted the most powerful fighter on the coast. He was surprizingly fast for a man of his weight and knew more than a little about the art of self-defense. Betting went up to three-to-one on Marks when the fighters appeared.

Sullivan entered the ring drunk, as usual. A big man himself, he seemed dwarfed by the giant he confronted. He floundered about the ring, swinging aimlessly, missing and almost falling. Marks set himself and began to swing terrific haymakers with a certain amount of science and a great amount of force. He caught John L. full on the jaw and staggered him. He reeled, straightened, then, with a bellow of rage, he rushed Marks. A weaving, blundering, drunken rush, yet one which Marks could not avoid. Ducking in under a savage swing, John L.'s right whipped up in a fierce uppercut that caught Marks under the chin and rocked his head back. Before he could regain his balance, Sullivan sent in a left hook and Marks went down. John L. stooped, lifted the half-conscious fighter and propped him against the ropes. Then, with a ferocious curse, he swung his right with all his immense strength. Marks whirled clear over the ropes and out into the orchestra, for the fight took place in a theater, and landed among the musicians, smashing the bass drum and three fiddles. Sullivan regarded the proceedings owlishly, then "Damnation! I've done him in!" he exclaimed and rushed behind the stage in a wild endeavor to conceal himself behind the scene. But Marks was far too tough to be much put out in such a trivial manner.

$$X\equiv$$

"Science will always beat brute strength," Gentleman Jim nodded. "Not always," he amended, "but usually."

"For instance?" I challenged, noting the reminiscent look in his eyes.

"Did you ever hear of Hank Griffen?" he asked, irreverently, I thought.

"Griffen? Why, it seems so. West Coast heavyweight wasn't he? Johnson beat him."

Johnson beat him when he was long past his prime. And before that he fought draws with Jack and had the best of it in a no-decision bout. A tall, lean fighting machine, standing over six three and scaling 190 or more, a coolly scientific battler, a terrific hitter, with a streak of cruelty in him, build like a bronze statue, splendid muscles rippling under sable skin, that was Hank Griffen in 1893, when he came to the Puente oilfields from the coast.

He walked into a bar and threw a handful of gold on to the bar.

"Money says Ah kin lick any man in thisyer camp," he drawled in his soft, musical voice. The workers and the loafers looked him over and nobody took any bets.

"Go git the Big Fellow," whispered the bartender to a loafer, and the man sneaked out and started off for a run.

Griffen was still talking fight when the loafer re-entered. Another man came in with him. And that fellow was big! Though he seemed stocky by Griffen, he stood over six one and he tipped the scales at 200. He had a good-natured face and seemed to have no love for the task before him. But he walked up to Griffen and shed his coat. "Get goin'," he said. No insults, no blustering.

Griffen laughed. "Yuh got me wrong, white man," he said. "Ah mean Ah can lick any man in this camp, in a regular ring, Marke uh Queensberry rules. Ah'm Hank Griffen, 'case you don' know, an' Ah've licked everybody on the coast, 'cludin' Joe Goddard, champeen uh Australia."

There wasn't a ring in the camp but the men soon built one. Griffen and his followers bet every cent on the prize fighter and the Big Fellow's friends rallied to his support. In a little while every cent in the camp was wagered one way or another.

Hank sat and grinned, looking across to where the Big Fellow, an embarrassed grin on his face, sat looking out at the crowd. Not at his ease you see, being the center of attraction. At the gong Griffen was out of his seat like a tiger, and his fists thudded against the face of the Big Fellow who came ambling out uncertainly. It was the Big Fellow's first real fight. He'd never even seen a boxing glove before. He felt hampered, uncertain. Griffen, a grin of pure savage cruelty on his face, set to work in earnest. In and out he flashed, avoiding the Big Fellow's clumsy swings with an ease that made the big white man look ridiculous, jabbing away with short, fast, straight lefts and rights. Round after round the one-sided fight went on. Round after round Griffen bounded in and out, hammering the white man's face. Round after round the Big Fellow plodded after his elusive foe, silently and savagely taking all the punishment that was handed out, for he did not even know the art of dodging; one arm, his left, held in front of him in a clumsy effort to guard, his mighty right drawn back for a terrific swing. But that swing never landed. Griffen was enjoying himself but was puzzled. The man he fought seemed to have unfathomed powers of taking punishment. Time and again those short vicious jabs should have worn him down and toppled him over, yet, though they made a savage mask of his face, they seemed to really bother him little. The white man apparently had little real fighting instinct, yet he possessed limitless courage. The courage which enables a man to keep coming up for more punishment.

At the fourteenth round the Big Fellow had not landed one punch. Griffen, tiring, decided to put a sudden stop to the fight. But he underrated his man. As the Big Fellow plodded to the center of the ring, Griffen leaped forward and lifted a swinging right clear from the floor. The Big Fellow stuck out his jaw invitingly, then stepped forward, clumsily but quickly. Griffen's right whipped about his neck and he hooked his left to Griffen's body. The negro spun halfway across the ring and went down. He was out ten minutes.

Gentleman Jim laughed and rose, stretching himself to his full, lithe height.

"But who was the Big Fellow?" I asked, not satisfied. "What did he do?"

Gentleman Jim laughed again, rubbing his jaw in a reminiscent manner. "He went into the ring. He learned some science, though he was never a McCoy. As for his name, it was James J. Jeffries."

Appendix 4

The Lord of the Ring (part 1)

(by Patrice Louinet)

There is little doubt that Robert E. Howard bought the first issue of *Fight Stories*—the first pulp magazine devoted solely to boxing fiction—on the day he saw it on the newsstands, around May 1928.

The young Texan was a lifelong admirer of the boxing world, and his early writings amply demonstrate that prizefighting fiction had been on his radar well before the advent of *Fight Stories*. In 1925, he had self-produced three issues of a mimeographed fanzine—*The Right Hook*—dealing with boxing in all its forms; in 1927, he had a short story—"Cupid vs. Pollux"—published in the student paper *The Yellow Jacket*. He had also just submitted a poem—"Kid Lavigne is Dead"—to *The Ring*, not to mention several poems, many of which were included in letters to his friend Tevis Clyde Smith, as well as short pieces that were clearly not aimed at a professional market.

On top of these amateur efforts, Howard had also begun writing boxing stories with the aim of selling them on a professional basis. The earliest of those, a short story titled "The Spirit of Brian Boru" (pg. 207), dates from around 1923 or 1924, before the Texan's first professional sale. It is an odd mix between Howard's arising interests in the boxing world and in Celtic lore. Of greater interest were two quite ambitious stories found in his papers after his death. Both were written well before *Fight Stories* was announced, which may explain why Howard didn't complete/submit them.

The first one, "A Man of Peace" (pg. 221), dating from early- to mid-1926, foreshadows many a future Howard tale and protagonist. The Texan wrote two drafts for that story, recycling most pages of the first draft into his second, at the same time expanding and completing the tale. Its protagonist, Slade O'Shane, is of Irish stock (half-Irish, we are told), of a restless nature, feels alien in his own surroundings, and is described as a "dark, silent man," who "came" to Despree Settlement when he was a boy. His parents are unmentioned. Thus a typical Howard hero in many ways, he is as much a Conan (leaving his hostile homeland) as a Bran Mak Morn (living in a region of giants, he is "five feet, six and three-fourth inches," "and he weighed one hundred and thirty pounds, stripped.") The typescript for this tale is untitled and is rather rough in spots, clear indications that this was not a final draft, and thus that the tale was apparently never submitted.

The other story, "The Atavist" (pg. 247), was never finished and probably dates from the fall of 1926. It is in that story that we encounter the prototype of Howard's future "iron men" in the character of Steve Devlin. In that story, Kelliher is the one who tries to understand what makes Devlin the kind of man he is:

> "Atavar!" exclaimed Kelliher. "That's what you are, Dev! I've been trying to think of a word to suit you! You're atavistic! A reversion to the primitive man of the Stone Age! That garb is the only one I ever saw you in that suited you!"

Howard understood the word "atavar" as the noun applied to someone imbued with atavistic features, someone who displays signs of a reversion to one or several primitive features. The word "atavar" (not to be confused with "avatar") is not a Howard coinage. It is found in some contemporary books and publications, and notably in Otto Augustus Wall's *Sex and Sex Worship*, a book Howard owned at the time of his death (and may thus have been familiar with as early as 1926), though for Wall "atavar" is merely another word for "incarnation" or "embodiment."

The appearance of *Fight Stories* in 1928 offered Howard the unique opportunity to write about a subject he loved probably as much as weird fiction. Up to that point, Howard had sold fiction to one market, and one magazine only: Farnsworth Wright's *Weird Tales*. *Fight Stories* was the brainchild of William H. Kofoed, who would later write of the birth of the magazine in a letter to Sam Moskowitz:

In 1928, I tried to sell George Delacorte on the idea of publishing a pulp called Fight Stories. He thought the market too limited, so I took it up to Jack Kelly, co-owner with Jack Glennister of Fiction House. [...] Kelly was a fight fan, so he went for my *Fight Stories* right off. I wanted part ownership, which [...] he could not grant, so he gave me a bigger salary than any of the other editors except the then managing editor, Meredith Davis. [...] I was also supposed to be cut in on the profits above a certain figure, but that didn't materialize. [...]

From '28 to the deepening depression in '31 and '32, *Fight Stories* averaged around an 80% sale and had a very loyal audience both in the United States and England. But the depression, with about 18 out of 45 million workers in the U.S. out of jobs, not only the Fiction House magazines but all magazines along with *all* other businesses were taking a clobbering. [...] Kelly [...] had been plagued with arthritis and, having his million or more salted away, consented to an exploratory operation on his gall bladder in the hope of allaying the nagging pain. He recovered from the operation but died of ether pneumonia three days later. In spite of his own illness [coowner Jack] Glennister came East and took over, but the depression finally proved too much for him, for he had no intention of sinking his money in keeping unprofitable mags alive, so, first he killed some of the titles, then all of them, intending to revive them when the depression was over... a day he didn't live to see. Under the hand of a nephew or some other relative, the firm was moved later on to Connecticut and some of the titles revived, but the golden days were over, and after a while the line died out.

Howard's tactic when tackling a new market was to mix familiar elements in his repertoire with the requirements of the new market he was trying to crash. And since his only market to date had been *Weird Tales*, his first boxing story would mix the fantastic and the ring. "The Spirit of Tom Molyneaux" was written in July or August 1928, merely a few weeks after the inaugural issue of *Fight Stories* hit the stands, and sent to the new publication which rejected it. Howard then submitted his story to *Argosy*, once again unsuccessfully, and eventually to *Ghost Stories*, which accepted it in November of that year. Howard received $95 for this story, which was published as "The Apparition in the Prize-Ring." Howard's first professional sale outside *Weird Tales* was not in the magazine he probably had in his radar. In many ways, though, "Molyneaux" was right down *Ghost Stories'* alley, with its spooky theme.

Two typescripts are extant for the tale. The first is a carbon, very probably corresponding to the final version submitted to *Fight Stories* and *Argosy*. It is written in the third person and the ghostly element is less marked. The second typescript, also a carbon, is rewritten in the first person and the supernatural angle is much more pronounced. Glenn Lord once surmised that the first person rewriting may have been the work of the *Ghost Stories* editor, but this is not the case. Howard himself did that, either before sending his typescript or in answer to a request by the editor of *Ghost Stories*. Which is not to say that there are no problems with the published text. The carbon shows some marked differences with the published version, especially in the last few pages of the story. While we may be certain that the changes introduced by the *Ghost Stories* editor were numerous, Howard was still in the habit of preparing a carbon with his first—and most of the times final—draft for a story, only to retype the last few pages to polish his tale, often without bothering with a carbon for those last few pages. So, there's no way to be certain that the last portion of the published version of the story is pure Howard or was extensively rewritten by the editors of *Ghost Stories*. Howard's final version—as taken from his carbon—appears in the main body of this book while the version as published in *Ghost Stories* appears in the appendix.

Howard apparently intended this Ace Jessel story to be the first of a new series aimed at Fight Stories, not *Ghost Stories*: the second tale in the series—"Double Cross"—was indeed written in the third person, apparently circa August or September 1928, that is to say before the sale of "Molyneaux" to *Ghost Stories*. Once again, this was rejected by *Fight Stories* and *Argosy*, and *Ghost Stories* was not in the market for recurring characters. The original to the typescript for that story was sent to Otis Adelbert Kline after Howard's death and is presumed lost. Only the carbon survives, though its condition renders it difficult to read in spots, making an accurate interpretation subject to conjecture.

Over the years, some scholars have pointed out the Jessel stories as an indicator of Howard's "progressive" ideas, but while it was certainly unusual to use an African-American as the protagonist of a tale, Ace Jessel, noble character that he is, is often portrayed just as stereotypically as Aaron Gold, the avaricious and treacherous Jew of "Double Cross." This being said, it is certainly not by chance that Jessel's best friend in that story is a Clive, precisely the name Howard gave to his best friend Tevis Clyde Smith in his *Post Oaks and Sand Roughs*, written during the same period. Howard's boxers, just like his Fantasy heroes, were outcasts, alien to their surroundings; they were the underdogs. Ace Jessel is no exception, and a case could be made that this was exactly how Howard felt, a man who was never fully accepted by his fellow townsmen.

"The Weeping Willow" and "The Right Hook" were probably written just between the two Ace Jessel stories in late summer, 1928. Once again both tales were unsuccessfully submitted to *Fight Stories* and *Argosy*, then shelved indefinitely. "The Weeping Willow" introduces a character named Monk Costigan. It was not the first Costigan of Howard's career, but it was a name which would come to become associated with Howard boxing stories in the years to come. As to *"The Right Hook,"* it doesn't sport (bad pun intended) a Costigan, but its hero is a Steve (Harmer), sailor on a merchant ship. It wouldn't take long for Howard, first to combine the names (and the profession), and second, to dissociate the comical and more tragic elements from his stories.

In the space of a few weeks, Howard had sent four stories to *Fight Stories*, all of which had been turned down. This nut was tougher to crack than the Texan thought, and since he needed "mazuma as usual," he concentrated the following weeks on writing weird fiction, selling his longest piece to date, the novella *"Skull-face,"* whose protagonist is a certain Stephen Costigan.

Howard apparently resumed writing boxing yarns a few weeks later, in February 1929. That month he would create the character of Steve Costigan, sailor and boxer, who would eventually become a regular in the pages of *Fight Stories*. Howard would write more Costigan stories than of any of his other numerous creations, so numerous in fact that they will take up two of the four volumes that comprise this collection. However, the tough slugger yarns were far from being the only prizefight stories he was working on.

The fragment beginning "I had just hung..." (pg 279), starring an "Iron Mike Costigan," reads like an aborted prototype for the Steve Costigan series, which it probably was. Howard would soon reuse that particular form of the cognomen for some of his more serious stories.

Another fragment, "The Ferocious Ape" (pg. 283), is also in the tragi-comic vein, with a hero who is apparently "an atavist; a reversion to some remote ancestor of the cave days. One look at his face would convince the average man that he is not altogether human." The tale was probably never completed and survives as an unfinished first draft with a few pages of carbon.

"The Voice of Doom," written about February 1929 and evidently submitted to *Ghost Stories*, probably at the time "The Spirit of Tom Molyneaux" was nearing publication, failed to find acceptance and was relegated to the archives.

After those many failures, Howard was ready to embark upon much more ambitious tales. He would proceed exactly as he had done a year before with the tales of Solomon Kane, which had been sent first to *Argosy*, then, after their refusal, to *Weird Tales*. This period of intense creative activity was not confined to boxing fiction, as Howard would pen in the spring of 1929 such stories as "By this Axe I Rule!" "Swords of the Purple Kingdom" and "The Blue Flame of Vengeance," ambitious stories aimed primarily at *Argosy* and *Adventure*. Two of those longer efforts would be in the prize-fighting domain: "Crowd-Horror" and the tale many Howard aficionados consider as the Texan's best boxing story: "Iron Men" (published in

Fight Stories as "The Iron Man"). But the road that led to "Iron Men" was paved on the ruins of the one that led to "Crowd-Horror"…

In March 1929, Howard wrote Tevis Clyde Smith: "Upon my return I found a returned manuscript from *Argosy* with a letter saying the story was good but too long, and if I'd reduce it to 6,000 words they'd take it. The original was 13,000 and I've worked myself into a state of nervous exhaustion and after rewriting and rewriting it's still 8,000 and if I shave it down any more it won't make sense. Therefore I guess I don't sell it." The story in question was "Crowd-Horror." After reducing his story's length to about 8,500 words (rather than 8,000) Howard sent the result to *Argosy*, and wrote to Smith in April that: "soon after returning I got a letter from *Argosy*, accepting that story that I told you about. They said it was still far too long but they'd cut it down and make the necessary changes themselves. The day after getting that letter I got a check from them for $100." The published version ran 7,250 words, so had been amputated by another 1,200 words by the editor.

The *Argosy* version of "Crowd-Horror" is a somewhat interesting tale, though not great by any means. Howard's original tale isn't a great story either, but it was certainly more ambitious than the published version. This first, uncut, version had never been published before the present edition, though readers familiar with Howard's boxing stories will undoubtedly experience a sensation of déjà vu, for the tale was, originally, much closer to what "Iron Men" would be. What Howard had done after being asked to excise his text was to recycle many of these pages into his next—and infinitely superior—tale: "Iron Men." It could even be argued that "Iron Men" became what it is because of the editorial demands of the editors of *Argosy*. Last element: since *Argosy* had asked Howard to cut pages from his tale, it was simply impossible for the Texan to reuse those same pages for another story aimed at that magazine. "Iron Men" was thus written specifically for *Fight Stories*.

Christopher Gruber's introduction to the present volume carefully and thoroughly delineates the importance of "Iron Men" in

Howard's career, so I will concentrate here on the editorial tribulations of the tale, probably the most complicated of Howard's career.

As mentioned above, several passages and themes of the original version of "Crowd-Horror" were simply reused, almost verbatim, for the first version of "Iron Men," with the name of the hero changed from "Iron Slade" Costigan to "Iron Mike" Brennon. The first four pages of the typescript, as well as several ulterior passages are identical almost word for word. Both tales feature a Gloria. The name of the managers are different in the pulp versions of the tales only, respectively Steve Amber ("Iron Men") and Steve Palmer ("Crowd-Horror"), but the latter was a name change introduced by the editors of *Argosy* over Howard's "Steve Harmer." Steve Harmer, in turn, was the name Howard had originally given to Steve Amber before changing his mind.

Howard completed his first version of "Iron Men" in March or April of 1929. That first version was sent to *Fight Stories* and apparently considered far too long by the editors who probably asked for a rewrite. That initial version (draft a) would eventually be published many years later, in *Boxing Stories* (Bison Books, 2005), with a statement that this was Howard's final version of the tale, whereas it was only the first submitted one. The analysis of subsequently discovered versions of the typescript has since shown that the tale had been rewritten a few weeks later by Howard, two successive drafts (drafts b & c) which condensed the story. It was that last version (draft c) that was eventually sent to and accepted by *Fight Stories*. However, when the tale appeared in May 1930, it had been heavily edited by Fight Stories (after they had nearly lost the typescript), and Howard wrote that he didn't recognize this published version as his own: "Fight Stories was kind enough to give me the cover design this month but they changed the title and the chapter headings and made quite a number of changes throughout the story which seemed not only needless to me, but in some places entirely distorted the original meaning. I think some of the changes must surely have been mistakes in printing." Fortunately, the carbon of that final version of the tale survives, and it is presented in this volume for the first time ever.

When restored to their original versions, we have to conclude that "Crowd-Horror," after an interesting opening and some promise, has a second part which doesn't live up to the standard of the first, the "crowd horror" element upon which the plot hinges seeming somehow anticlimactic. The psychological "kink" of the main character is interesting, but only goes so far, which is to say not very far for so long a story. Conversely, the central idea behind what would become "Iron Men" wouldn't be the "crowd horror," or even the love element of the story, but the thorough exploration of the psyche of an "iron man," an "atavar" (or "atavist"), a throwback, and it took the rejection of the first two versions of "Crowd-Horror" for Howard to be ready to write his ultimate story on the subject. Depending on your tastes, you will find the long version of "Iron Men" (found pg. 333) richer or overly verbose compared to Howard's third, (shorter and final) version (pg. 99), but most Howard scholars agree that this is probably Howard's best serious boxing story, and his best illustration of the fascination those atavistic boxers with a granite jaw held for the Texan.

Probably at about the same time, Howard wrote "Men of Iron", an essay on the subject of those "iron men" (pg. 405), providing a non-fictional counterpart to his story.

The unfinished, incomplete (and originally untitled) fragment "Night Encounter" (pg. 301) is primarily of interest to Howard scholars because it seems to be yet another link in the chain that led from "The Isle of the Eons" to "The Gods of BalSagoth," with its World War One and friend/foe theme (See my essay in *The Dark Man*, vol 3, #1, completed before I obtained a copy of this fragment.)

"The Ghost Behind the Gloves" (pg 295) seems to be an attempt at yet another "ghostly boxing" story and was probably written in the first half of 1929. We do not know whether Howard left the tale unfinished or if it was completed and subsequently almost entirely lost. It was obviously aimed at *Ghost Stories*, but of course we do not know if it was submitted, while we know "The Mark of a Bloody

Hand" (pg. 137) to have been submitted to—and rejected by—that magazine later that year.

It would prove difficult for Howard to top or even equal the heights he had just reached, but it was only to be expected that he would do his best to achieve that, at least up to his probable realization that editors would be far more demanding on his serious boxing stories than for the easy sells that were most of the early Steve Costigans.

One of those interesting efforts was to remain unfinished and untitled. "The Folly of Conceit" (pg. 315), is an aborted attempt that was probably written in the fall of 1929, at the same time as "Iron Men," and perhaps abandoned when Howard was encountering difficulties to sell that latter story. The tale was clearly an ambitious one, with yet again an Irish boxer / Harmer manager combo, but this time the woman of the tale was a Lilith, not an Eve (or, to put it into Celtic Howardian perspective, the Gaelic hero is threatened by a Cromwell lady.) Still, the first few pages are particularly noteworthy for being an almost autobiographical account of Howard's own lineage (or rather, the lineage he wished himself to have had), in terms that are remarkably close to similar accounts found in Howard's correspondence. It is also one of the very rare Howard tales in which the hero mentions his mother.

"They Always Come Back," which also dates from the fall of 1929 is obviously another attempt by Howard to follow on "Iron Men." Maloney's defeat at the hands of Brennon was an episode of that latter story, and Howard tried to write a tale around that peripheral character. "They Always Come Back" is a tale of disgrace and redemption, but the story is far less convincing than its august predecessor, with several episodes stretching the boundaries of verisimilitude a bit too far. The original typescript for this was sent to Otis A. Kline after Howard's death and is now presumed lost. The tale survives as a carbon.

The 1929 cutoff date of this volume places "The Trail of the Snake" in the ultimate position. Featuring Steve Costigan as a guest star in a story that is not part of the regular Steve Costigan series,

Howard fans had long wondered why the tale had never seen the light of day until it was published in The Last of the Trunk. Featuring a Howard in his worst stereotypical efforts, the tale is particularly painful to read for a modern audience. Written in December 1929, probably as Howard was about to come back to Cross Plains after living several months in Brownwood, the tale was submitted to— and rejected by— *Fight Stories*, though the racial element probably didn't play any factor in the rejection. It was apparently submitted to another market in early 1930, again without success. While Howard was successful at using racial stereotypes to great comic effect in the regular Steve Costigan stories, "The Trail of the Snake" is an embarrassing read at best, and a repulsive one on the whole.

In a little more than a year, Howard had carved his small niche in the pages of Fight Stories, but the one ambitious boxing story that he had managed to sell the magazine had to be reduced in length, then was butchered by the editors. The slapstick comedy of the Steve Costigan yarns was proving infinitely easier to sell. Howard decided to concentrate on that particular brand of boxing stories for the months to come…

ROBERT ERVIN HOWARD (1906-1936) grew up in the boomtowns of early twentieth-century Texas, eventually settling in Cross Plains where he lived for the remainder of his short life. Deciding early on a literary career, he spent the bulk of his time crafting stories and poems for the burgeoning pulp fiction markets: *Weird Tales, Action Stories, Fight Stories, Argosy*, etc. Howard's literary reputation was assured with the publication of "The Shadow Kingdom" in 1929, which featured a unique blend of Fantasy and Adventure which has since been termed Heroic Fantasy. The creation of Conan the Cimmerian in the pages of *Weird Tales* has earned him lasting recognition.

DR. PATRICE LOUINET, from Limoges, France, is a renowned scholar in Robert E. Howard studies. His passion for Howard's work was ignited in 1983 upon discovering the Conan stories. He completed his Ph.D. at La Sorbonne, Paris, focusing on Howard in 2020. Patrice has edited the definitive three-volume Conan series for Del Rey Books and authored *Le Guide Howard*, published in France. His editorial and scholarly contributions extend across numerous publications in Europe related to Howard. Honored with the Lifetime Achievement Award from the Robert E. Howard Foundation in 2014 and the Special Award at the Imaginales in France (2012), Patrice's work continues to significantly influence the understanding and appreciation of Howard's legacy.

CHRISTOPHER GRUBER has been deeply involved in Howard Studies for over a decade and serves on the review board for *The Dark Man: The Journal of Robert E. Howard Studies* since 2008. An author of numerous award-winning essays and introductions, his works appear in publications like *Boxing Stories, The Cimmerian*, and *REH: Two-Gun Raconteur*. Chris edited the Boxing Stories by Robert E. Howard for the University of Nebraska Press and co-edited the *Fists of Iron* four-volume collection by the REH Foundation Press. Residing in Eldorado at Santa Fe, New Mexico, he works for St. John's College (Annapolis/Santa Fe) and the State of New Mexico. Outside of academia, he enjoys hiking, brewing beer, and family time with his wife and three children.

MARK FINN, is an acclaimed author, essayist, playwright, and recognized scholar in Robert E. Howard studies. His notable biography, *Blood and Thunder: The Life and Art of Robert E. Howard*, was a finalist for the 2007 World Fantasy Award and the Locus Awards for Best Non-Fiction. Mark has made significant contributions to Howard scholarship, including his role as one of the editors for all four volumes of *Fists of Iron*, the boxing tales of Robert E. Howard. His articles and essays have been featured in publications for the Robert E. Howard Foundation, Dark Horse Comics, Boom! Comics, and others. Beyond Howard studies, Mark writes comics and fiction, serves as a creative consultant, and is actively involved in community theater. He has also been honored as one of Texas's top movie critics by the Texas Associated Press Managing Editors in multiple years. In 2023, Mark married Janice Schange. They reside in North Texas.

PAUL HERMAN, long-time engineer and intellectual property attorney, began publishing REH in 1999 via his own Hermanthis Press and later, Wildside Press; he has edited well over one million words. His etexts have been the starting material for a significant number of REH books published in the last 25 years. His REH bibliography, *The Neverending Hunt* became the new standard when it was first published in 2006, and is the basis for the HowardWorks website. His wife of 38 years, Denna, continues to tolerate his hobbies. Paul currently resides in Weatherford, Texas, a few miles from Robert E. Howard's birthplace.

MARK WHEATLEY holds the Eisner, Inkpot, Golden Lion, Mucker, Gem and Speakeasy Awards and nominations for the Harvey Award and the Ignatz Award. He is also an inductee to the Overstreet Hall of Fame. His work has often been included in the annual Spectrum selection of fantastic art and has appeared in private gallery shows, the Norman Rockwell Museum, Toledo Museum of Art, Huntington Art Museum, Fitchburg Art Museum, James A. Michener Art Museum and the Library of Congress, where several of his originals are in the LoC permanent collection.

STÅLE GISMERVIK has been passionate about Robert E. Howard since discovering his work in 1990. In the mid-1990s he created one of the earliest and largest websites devoted to Conan and Howard's fiction, and today manages the comprehensive Howard resource *The World of Robert E. Howard* at https://reh.world. He also administers the Robert E. Howard Foundation and REH Foundation Press websites, overseeing the design, editing, and digital production of the Foundation's eBooks. Since the summer of 2024, he has led the preparation of the Robert E. Howard Foundation Ultimate Editions, contributing to the preservation and promotion of Howard's literary legacy.